An old flame +
= compromising positions

"You had your shot at me when I was nineteen and you didn't think I was worth keeping. Once you've thrown me away, you don't get another chance," Daisy spat.

"I didn't throw you away!" Nick stared at her as if she'd just suggested he'd broken the last remaining law of decency. "I know I handled matters poorly that evening—"

"You think 'poorly' covers it? That must be one of those understatements you prep-school boys are so fond of. My God, I was a virgin—"

"I didn't know that!"

"Maybe not when we went up to the room," she conceded ungraciously, "but—"

"You gotta admit you acted as if you knew the score."

"How? By dancing with you at the reception? By *flirting*? You swept me off my feet. I thought you were so . . ." *Dazzling. Interested in me.* He'd been a god, golden and exciting, and he'd made her feel exciting too. "You were happy enough to relieve me of my virginity, but, boy, the minute you got yours, you sure couldn't wait to get out of there."

"What did you expect? That I'd say making love with you was better than anything I'd ever experienced before? That I'd suggest we rush right off to the nearest Justice of the Peace?" He made his tone deliberately mocking, because the truth was he'd been tempted to say and do exactly that. And it had scared the hell out of him.

Other Avon Books by
Susan Andersen

BABY, I'M YOURS
BE MY BABY

SUSAN ANDERSEN

Baby,
DON'T
Go

AVON BOOKS
An Imprint of HarperCollins*Publishers*

AVON BOOKS
An Imprint of HarperCollins*Publishers*
10 East 53rd Street
New York, New York 10022-5299

Copyright © 2000 by Susan Andersen
Excerpt from *Almost Home* copyright © 2000 by Barbara Freethy
Excerpt from *A Scandalous Marriage* copyright © 2000 by Catherine Maxwell
Excerpt from *Rules of Surrender* copyright © 2000 by Christina Dodd
Excerpt from *Never Love a Cowboy* copyright © 2000 by Jan Nowasky
Excerpt from *Baby, Don't Go* copyright © 2000 by Susan Andersen
Excerpt from *What the Heart Knows* copyright © 1999 by Kathleen Eagle
Inside cover author photo by Teresa Salgado
Library of Congress Catalog Card Number: 99-96449
ISBN: 0-380-80712-2
www.avonromance.com

First Avon Books paperback printing: May 2000
First Avon Books special printing: December 1999

Avon Trademark Reg. U.S. Pat. Off. and in Other Countries, Marca Registrada, Hecho en U.S.A.
HarperCollins ® is a trademark of HarperCollins Publishers Inc.

Printed in the U.S.A.

WCD   10   9   8   7   6   5   4   3   2   1

This is dedicated, with love

To Jen,
for saving my bacon just when
I thought it was fried but good

To Mom, Mimi, Toni, Aunt Thelma, Elaine,
Vernetta, Winnie, and Margaret,
for years of support and the
world's fastest sell-out booksigning

And to the Methow Valley gang,
for good food, great skiing,
and a whole lotta laughs

Life doesn't get much better than this

—Susie

PROLOGUE

nine years ago

DAISY Parker gave a sigh of pleasure as the weight of Nick Coltrane's naked body pressed her into the mattress. Sweat bonded their bodies together, while his muscular arms held her tight. She could hardly believe she'd just surrendered her virginity to him—let alone with such enthusiasm. As he pressed kisses into the side of her neck, her body hummed with little aftershocks of satisfaction. Wrapping her arms around his neck, she stretched with voluptuous delight.

To think she almost hadn't attended Mo's wedding reception—which was still in full swing ten floors below. Two years ago, she'd tried to sever all ties with the Coltranes. She'd detested Nick and Maureen's father for the cold premeditation with which he'd ended his marriage to her mother, not to mention the way he'd arranged to have Mama's name smeared all over the tabloids. She'd seen no point in staying in touch with any of them.

But Mo had refused to let the connection lapse.

She'd sent occasional notes that would have been rude to ignore, since Daisy's beef had never been with her stepsister. So Daisy had written back, and every now and then they'd gotten together for a lunch or dinner. When the invitation to Mo's nuptials had arrived, Daisy hadn't been able to resist.

The wedding at Grace Cathedral had been like something out of a fairy tale to Daisy's nineteen-year-old eyes, and Mo and her handsome groom had looked deliriously happy. But when Daisy arrived at the reception at the Mark Hopkins Hotel a few hours ago, she'd had second thoughts about the wisdom of attending.

She didn't belong with the throng of San Francisco's elite that crowded the Peacock Court—she never had. Being thrust into their company again had driven home the fact, and she'd planned to leave as soon as she paid her respects to the bride and groom.

Until Nick had swept her off her feet and blown all rational thought clear out of her mind.

She still couldn't believe he'd greeted her like a long-lost friend and ditched the reception line to squire her around. He'd always done such an excellent job of ignoring her that the sudden attention had been like grabbing hold of the business end of a live wire—hot, terrifying, and excitingly disorienting.

There'd been a look in his eyes that she hadn't been able to define: a sense of displacement maybe, an impression of recklessness, for sure. But he'd charmed her and kept her so off balance with his touch—a guiding hand in the small of her back here, long, warm fingers wrapped around her forearm or brushing her bare shoulder there—that she'd told herself it didn't matter. He was a golden-skinned god with flashing white teeth and streaky brown hair, dancing attendance on her, snapping pictures of her from the camera around his neck, leaving her breathless, exhilarated, dizzy.

And that was before the dancing began and she got a taste of being in his arms.

When the lights went low and the music turned slow and torchy, she'd been a goner. He'd held her so closely she'd felt him from chest to knees, and he'd been warm, hard, and *very* happy to see her, as the old saw went. The next thing she remembered, they were in the hotel elevator and he was kissing her; then they were in this room, on this bed, and her heart was pounding, pounding, pounding, her pulse throbbing in places she hadn't dreamed *had* a pulse; and he'd been on top of her, inside of her; and just as the slight sting of her hymen rupturing pierced her consciousness, his slow hands and urgent hips had driven her to a place of screaming release.

And all Mama's talk about love finally made sense.

She breathed in his scent as he slowly pushed up on his elbows. He looked down at her.

"Are you all right?"

"Yes." She was more than all right. She felt stupendous.

"Good." He rolled off her and climbed to his feet, and Daisy propped her head in her hand to admire the play of lamplight across his naked flesh. He was so gorgeous.

That wasn't the most masculine word in the world, she supposed, but it suited him to a T. And no one in their right mind would ever deny he was masculine. Consummately, incomparably masculine. His shoulders were wide, his biceps hard, and lean, strapping muscle defined his chest. Body hair that looked silky and soft grew in a tree-of-life pattern, a fine fan that spread over his pectorals, then dwindled into a narrow trunk that ran down rigidly defined stomach muscles to disappear into the waistband of the tuxedo slacks he'd pulled up his hard flanks.

She blinked. He was dressing? "What are you doing?"

"I've got to go."

A moment ago she'd felt supremely confident in her nudity; now she suddenly felt exposed. Looking around for her dress, she blushed to see it dangling from the bedside lampshade where it had snagged by a strap. Plucking a couple of tissues out of the box on the table, she dabbed surreptitiously at the smear of blood on her inner thighs and shot him a glance. "Why?"

She watched as Nick pulled on his shirt and his jacket but didn't bother to fasten them up. He scooped the handful of shirt studs into his palm and dropped them in his pocket. Tie dangling, hands stuffed deep in his pants pockets, he looked over at her. His blue eyes softened, the corner of his mouth crooked up, and he took a step toward the bed.

Then, just as she was sure he was going to

reach for her again, he pulled himself up short and squared his shoulders. "I've got an appointment in the morning," he said lightly. "This has been great, but a guy needs his sleep."

"But, I don't understand. What about . . . what you said?" *What about when you said you loved me?*

He stared at her and just for a moment she could have sworn his eyes reflected tenderness and longing . . . regret. Then he shrugged and the moment was gone. "You really are young, aren't you, Blondie? You know how the game is played—people'll say anything in the heat of the moment."

She *hadn't* known, hadn't even realized it *was* a game, and she could only stare at him in humiliated misery as he bent down, gave her a friendly peck on the cheek, and murmured for her to take care. Then the door swung closed behind Nick's back.

And Daisy was left all alone in a room high atop the Mark Hopkins to contemplate her passage into adulthood.

1

monday

DAISY hadn't even cleared the office door before she caught a load of grief.

Her secretary screeched and stared at her in horror. "*Please* tell me you don't actually plan on wearing that," he said.

Stopping short, Daisy glanced down at her gold wool blazer with the crest on its breast pocket, and the navy and gold plaid kilt it topped. She shut the door behind her. "What's wrong with it? You're the one who told me to wear a skirt."

Reggie rolled his eyes and smoothed his own dapper suit as if to reassure himself that one of them at least was blessed with fashion sense. "I didn't tell you to dress like Mary Catherine Parochial meets GI Jane."

"What, the boots, you mean?" She gazed down the navy-nyloned length of her legs to her lace-up boots and the bit of scrunched socks that topped them. "They're navy; they go."

"Sure, if you're bucking for the Best Dressed Combat Soldier Who Ever Rolled a Schoolgirl award. Why don't you just throw on a set of cammies and be done with it? I can probably scrounge up some green and brown eye shadow; we'll camouflage your face, too."

Daisy scowled at him. "You said put on a skirt; I stopped at home and put on a skirt. I'm sorry if it isn't up to your high standards of sartorial elegance, but I'm a security specialist, not a debutante. I don't wear heels, Reg, so you can just forget it. I'd be useless if I needed to run."

"It's my fondest hope that the only running you'll need to do is straight to the bank to deposit this new client's check." Reggie gave her outfit a final disparaging glance before he turned back to his computer, muttering, "That's if he *gives* us a check once he gets a gander at your idea of professional attire."

Knowing it made him crazy to be loomed over, Daisy slapped her hands down on his desk and leaned her weight on them. "*Maybe,* unlike most men," she said between her teeth, "he'll actually have half a brain in his head and realize this *is* professional. Granted, it's not banker pinstripes, but it's eminently suitable for a woman he'd like to guard his ass."

Reggie was clearly unimpressed, and she straightened. "For crying out loud, Reg. Who is this guy, anyway—the crown prince of England?"

"Close," said a cool voice from the doorway behind her.

No. Oh, dear God, please; no. Her heart

pounding an erratic tattoo against her ribs, Daisy slowly pivoted, hoping against hope that her ears had played a trick on her.

They hadn't. It was exactly who she'd feared it would be: Nick Coltrane. The last man in the world she wanted to see.

He was as gorgeous as ever, too, damn his blue eyes. That long, beautifully formed body looked as hard and fit as she remembered, even covered by an old pair of jeans and a V-necked sweater that was accessorized by the camera around his neck. Mo used to say that Nick looked like he was born in his tennis whites, and it was true. He had an air of casual sophistication, of *belonging*, that was as natural to him as breathing.

But then, why shouldn't he? He did belong; he always had. It was she who had been the outsider.

She watched him look around her office, and seeing it through his eyes, immediately disregarded the inviting butter-cream paint job she and Reggie had given the walls to showcase the bright posters they'd framed and hung up. She didn't see the glossy six-foot ficus tree, or Reg's gleaming genuine woodlike desk. Instead she saw only the scuffed linoleum and the two battered wooden chairs with the garage-sale table between them against the window wall.

Then she squared her shoulders. So, big deal, it wasn't upscale. At least it was all hers. Well, hers and the bank's, anyway.

Nick gave her a through perusal. "How are you, Blondie? You're looking good."

"Don't"—she took an incensed step forward before she caught herself—"call me Blondie," she finished with a mildness that burned her gullet. The nickname was a hot button, and he damn well knew it, which was undoubtedly the reason he'd pushed it. She'd been sixteen years old to his twenty-two when he'd first started calling her that, and fish that she was, she never quit rising to the bait. Feeling heat radiating in her cheeks, she drew in another deep breath and held it a moment before easing it out again, perilously close to losing her composure.

She would eat *worms* before she gave him that satisfaction. And certainly before she'd allow him to see that when he looked at her with those cool, casually amused eyes, she felt the screaming ache of rejection all over again.

Thrusting up her chin, she gazed at him without speaking. He lounged against the door, ankles crossed and hands in his jeans pockets, and looked back at her.

"I take it you two know each other," Reggie said when the silence had stretched thin.

"My father was married to her mother for a while," Nick said.

Daisy froze. *That* was what he saw as their strongest connection? It shouldn't hurt—not after all the other ways he'd managed to hurt her. Yet it did, and she badly wanted to get in his face and hurt him back, but damned if she'd let him see he still had the power to get to her.

Reg came to attention behind her, giving her a distraction to focus on. "Yeah?" he demanded. "Which marriage was that?"

"Her third," she said.

"It was my dad's fifth," Nick offered.

Reggie, bless him, ignored Nick. "That woulda been the rich guy, then, right? The one who landed your mom on the front page of all the tabloids?"

Daisy narrowed her eyes at Nick, daring him to say one word. If he knew what was good for him he'd keep his mouth shut, because it was his father's fault her mother had been hounded by those journalistic rags in the first place.

Nick merely gave her a level-eyed gaze, and determined to behave like an adult, she met it with a levelness of her own. "So, what's it been, Coltrane, six, seven years since we last saw each other?" As if she didn't know to the minute.

"Nine."

"That long? My. Time really flies when you're not being annoyed. What brings you slumming in my neck of the woods?"

"Uh, he's our two o'clock, Daise."

Slowly, she turned to look at her secretary. "He's what?"

Reggie held his palms up in surrender. "When I made the appointment I had no idea he was your step—"

"I am *not* her brother," Nick cut in peremptorily, his voice flat.

Daisy turned her attention back to him. "No," she said, "you certainly never wanted that role, did you?"

He met her angry gaze head-on. "No. I didn't. And if you haven't figured out why by now, you're not half as bright as I always thought you were."

She felt her face flame again, in remembrance and in shame. "You want to hire me?" she demanded incredulously.

"I don't *want* to be within five miles of you."

She was proud of her reasonable tone when she suggested, "Then go home. I don't have time for your rich boy games; I've got a business to run."

Nick looked around. "Yeah, I can see you've got clients stacked up like cordwood, all right. How do you ever get anything done?"

Please, God, let me hit him just once. Just one little pop and I'll never ask anything of You again. "Goodbye, Nick." Her pleated skirt flared out around her thighs as she turned on her heel and stalked to her office.

"Daisy, wait."

Reluctantly she turned back to face him, aware of Reggie's acute interest. Great. He'd be all over her the minute Nick left, and this fiasco would never be allowed to die a natural death. Face stony, she looked at Nick.

"I apologize," he said. "That was uncalled for. I do want to talk to you about hiring your services."

Damn. The gesture she made toward her door was jerky with nerves, and she blew out a frustrated breath. "Come into my office. Reg, hold my calls." The phone hadn't exactly been ringing off the hook lately, but Nick didn't have to know that.

The walls seemed to close in on her the moment he stepped through the doorway. She'd forgotten how tall he was until she found herself at eye level with his collarbone as he moved past her. His camera brushed her breast, and her gaze flashed up to lock with his. Jerking it away, she waved at the visitor's chair facing her desk. "Have a seat."

She scooted around the desk and flopped into her own chair, angry that she was still so aware of him after all these years. Crossing her arms beneath her breasts, she gave him an impassive look across the desk. Without Reggie as an audience, she didn't feel compelled to mind her manners. "What the hell are you doing here, Coltrane?"

Excellent question. It was one Nick had been asking himself since the moment he'd walked through the door and seen Daisy leaning over her secretary's desk. He could have gone to any number of security firms, and if he were smart, he wouldn't be within miles of big-eyed Daisy Parker and her wise-ass attitude. There was just something about her that never failed to access feelings he was better off not feeling.

But when he'd started calling around, her name kept popping up as one of the best in the business. At the same time, he'd heard from more than one source that her fledgling company was barely staying afloat. So why not kill two birds with one stone and throw his business her way? It would help her, and he'd get the protection he needed at a price he could afford.

What the hell, that night at the Mark Hopkins

was years ago. They were both adult enough to put it behind them.

"I find myself in need of your services," he said coolly.

"What's the matter, Coltrane—fast living finally catch up with you?"

He'd debated all the way here how much to tell her. Up until this moment, he'd actually considered the whole truth, but it didn't take a genius to see that wouldn't fly. It'd hit too many of Daisy's hot buttons.

The mess had all started because he hadn't given his usual one hundred and fifty percent on Saturday. He had a reputation for one-of-a-kind, can't-find-them-anywhere-else photos. People said they spoke intimately to the moment, and the truth was, he wasn't particularly modest when it came to his ability with a camera: he did have a sixth sense or an inner eye or something that simply *knew* when the shot was there. So he was exceptionally good at capturing the essence of his subjects. And since he was pretty much wedded to his Nikon, people tended to forget it was even there.

The result was that he sometimes caught moments on film that had the potential to damage or outright destroy a reputation. The tabloids routinely offered him a small fortune for any embarrassing photos he might care to pass along, but he always destroyed the negatives. Having grown up a part of the society that kept him employed, he knew very well that a significant part of his success was due to his discretion.

But Saturday afternoon he'd been worried

about the phone call from his sister just before he'd left to drive up to the Pembroke estate in the wine country, and he hadn't given the big society wedding his trademark single-minded concentration.

Who would've thought, though, that practical, levelheaded Maureen would do something so criminally un-Mo-like as to juggle funds between the escrow accounts in her real estate business? He didn't doubt for a moment that she'd done it for a good cause, given her propensity for smoothing over everyone's problems, but it was still idiotic. It was also guaranteed to land her in serious trouble, since the commission she'd counted on to pay back the account had vanished when her sale of a Nob Hill apartment building fell through.

Wracking his brain for a way to help her, he'd photographed Bitsy Pembroke's wedding on autopilot. Which no doubt accounted for why he'd missed what was going on in the background.

When he'd left the Pembroke estate, he'd driven straight down to Monterey for a Sunday shoot. His concentration had been better on that job, but he'd still been chewing over Mo's dilemma when he'd climbed out of his car last night and found two muscle-bound bruisers tearing up his garage darkroom. They'd pounced on him, demanding his film.

They hadn't specified from which shoot, and he hadn't volunteered that all his film from the past two days was in his duffel bag, which was behind the driver's seat. Instead, upon seeing all the contact sheets from other shoots that they'd ruined, he'd told them to eat him—a suggestion to which they'd taken exception.

His Nikon had been around his neck as usual, and they'd offered him one last chance to do things the easy way by handing it over. He'd declined, and before the wail of cop sirens had broken up the party, they'd dislocated his shoulder trying to get it.

He'd told the cop who'd shown up everything he knew, but that was damn little. It wasn't until he'd gotten back from the ER that he'd been able to develop the film the goons had been so hot to get their mitts on. And at first he hadn't seen a thing worth being roughed up over. He'd blown up frame after frame before he'd spotted what the goons had tried to prevent him from discovering.

And he was stunned.

Bitsy had insisted at the last minute that he shoot her and her groom in the gazebo. In the background was a beautifully restored gatekeeper's cottage. And inside the cottage were a man and a woman having sex. They could be seen through a window, if one knew enough to search it out.

The surprise wasn't that a couple was screwing their brains out. People sometimes knocked back more champagne at these functions than was wise, and ended up celebrating in ways they'd never intended and had years and years to regret. God knew he was a walking testament to that.

The shocker was the man's identity.

J. Fitzgerald Douglass was an icon, the grand

old man of San Francisco society. At the age of sixty, he was the stuff of legends. He'd inherited a declining family business and turned it into a multimillion-dollar enterprise. He had then turned to philanthropy, using much of his profits to endow libraries and churches.

His moral rectitude was the stuff of legends, and the media had been all abuzz recently about his probable appointment as an American ambassador to a small but strategic Middle Eastern country. Everyone considered him a shoe-in—it only needed the stamp of approval from a very conservative Congress at this point. And since no one was more conservative than Douglass, that appeared to be a mere formality.

So what the hell was this living monument to morality doing with his very married hands all over a woman young enough to be his granddaughter?

Considering Douglass' goons had left Nick with a messed-up arm, a trashed darkroom, and an unhappy insurance agent, his attitude toward the older man was seriously unsympathetic. But he now knew how he was going to raise the money for Mo. He was breaking his own iron-clad rule and selling the damn pictures to the tabloids.

He didn't think he'd share his solution with Daisy, however. Although the screaming pain of his dislocated shoulder had dissipated as soon as the ER crew had put it back in place, he'd been left with deep-tissue bruising from shoulder to elbow. The arm was usable but weak, and would be of no use at all if Douglass' men came back. Which he knew they'd continue to do until they finally got their hands on the film they sought.

He needed a bodyguard. Blondie needed the work. So what was the sense in telling her that his plans included the one thing she'd never tolerate?

Fingers snapped in his face. "Are you zoning on me?"

He snagged her hand and moved it away from his nose. "No. I'm thinking." Shaking off the sudden awareness that touching her brought on, he released her.

"Then perhaps you can tell me why you want to hire my services." Rubbing her hand against her kilt, she scrutinized him speculatively. "Why wouldn't a ritzy guy like Nicholas Sloan Coltrane call one of the uptown outfits?"

"Who says I didn't? But uptown firms demand uptown retainers, Blondie." Which was true, even if he hadn't really considered one of them.

"What does that make me, then, the K mart of security specialists?" She surged to her feet and pointed a slender finger at the door. "Get out of here, Nick. I knew this was a mistake the minute I saw your lying face."

He looked at her standing there, all long legs, big flashing eyes, and hot-cheeked indignation, and said, "I'm telling the truth, Daisy. You're what I can afford, all right?"

She blew out a disgruntled breath, but resumed her seat. Looking pointedly at the Rolex on his wrist and his cashmere sweater, she said, "You honestly expect me to believe you're on a budget?"

"Hell, yes, I'm on a budget! The family fortune is long gone and I live on what I earn. Dad had six wives, and they didn't come cheap, doll face—especially when it came time to say goodbye." His father had been a spendthrift in far worse ways as well, but that was none of her damn business.

"Oh, please. Your father didn't fork over a dime when he kicked Mom and me out of that great white hotel you Coltranes called home. I bet he *made* a bundle when he manufactured that horseshit about my mother and sold it to the tabloids." She gave him a look of disgust. "She and I, on the other hand, had the clothes on our backs when we returned to the 'burbs. And we were damn lucky to have that much."

"You want me to admit my dad screwed over your mom? I freely admit it. But *he* did that, Daisy—not me."

"Guess it's an inherited trait then, isn't it?"

Too fast and overpowering to defend against, visions of the night of Mo's wedding exploded across Nick's mind. Daisy, hot and responsive, moving beneath him, tendrils of her blond hair stuck to her damp face, chocolate brown eyes heavy-lidded and out of focus, sassy mouth for once in her life following his lead without a single argument.

Ruthlessly stomping the memories down, he forced himself to meet her gaze calmly. "Yes, I suppose I behaved badly, too."

"But, hey, boys will be boys, right? You were just a chip off the old block."

It was a direct hit, since he'd spent his entire life trying to be the exact opposite of his father. "It was a long time ago," he said stiffly.

"Yes, it was," she agreed. "How many years did you say it was again? Seven?"

"*Nine.*" And he'd never forgotten it, no matter how hard he'd tried. The fact that she didn't seem equally burdened by unwelcome memories bugged the hell out of him. Rash words sang a siren song in the back of his throat, but he swallowed them unsaid.

With deliberate aloofness, he said, "The fact remains that my budget is extremely limited, and that's why I'm here."

"And just what makes you think you can afford me?" One of her eyebrows rose superciliously, disappearing into the shaggy tendrils over her forehead, and he got sidetracked by her haircut. Short petals of white-blond hair exploded from her head like the flower for which she'd been named . . . or a dandelion gone to seed. Uneven wisps clung to her cheeks and her nape. Had she actually *paid* someone to do that to her?

Shaking off the thought, he stated flatly, "Your secretary said a four-thousand-dollar retainer would get you started." He saw her swallow hard and pressed his advantage. "So are you interested or not?"

He had to hand it to her, she recovered quickly. Meeting his gaze squarely, she picked up a pen and held it poised above the legal pad on her desk. "That depends," she said briskly. "Why do you need my help?"

Because he'd set a bidding war in motion between the journalistic bottom feeders otherwise known as the tabloids. For the first time in his life, he planned to sell a compromising picture for publication.

His decision would undoubtedly come back to haunt him by destroying his credibility with the very society that kept him employed. Had J. Fitzgerald simply trusted in his reputation and left him the hell alone, it never would have occurred to Nick to cash in on the man's indiscretion.

But Douglass hadn't left him alone, and when Nick weighed the interests of a hypocrite with political aspirations against those of his sister, there was simply no contest.

Of course if he told Daisy the truth, she'd probably toss him out on his ass. She hated the tabloids. It was hard to fault her for it when they had publically branded her mother a slut, but he had a bad feeling he needed someone to watch his back until Friday night, when the highest bidder would be determined in this dangerous game he played.

He summoned his most charming smile and lied without compunction. "I took some . . . compromising . . . pictures of a lady. Her almost-ex-husband is a bit irate."

It never occurred to Daisy to doubt his story. Nick had charisma to burn and probably went out with a different debutante every night of the week. That he had sunk so low as to mess with a married woman made her long to denounce him as a pig and toss him out on his ear, but the thought of a four-thousand-dollar retainer stopped her. "How irate?"

"A couple of his goons dislocated my arm and trashed my darkroom."

He looked hale enough to her. "Which arm?"

"The left."

"What's its condition now?"

"It's weak, but no permanent damage was done. I'm on anti-inflammatories for a week or so."

She stood up and came around the desk. "Let me take a look at it."

He stared at her for a moment, then struggled out of the left side of his sweater. She could tell by his awkwardness that the arm was still tender.

She saw why the moment it emerged from his sleeve. The arm was bruised dark purple from his elbow to where the short sleeve of a white T-shirt stretched over his hard biceps. She sank to her heels at his side and gently pushed the sleeve up as far as she could. She studied the discoloration, probed it gently with her fingertips, then glanced up at his face. "Looks painful."

"It's not so bad; I just don't have a lot of strength in it. But the doc said it would get stronger every day."

"Hmmph." She eased the sleeve back into place, then pinned him in place with a stern look. "This is what you get for messing around with a married woman."

A sharp crack of laughter escaped Nick's throat. "Beautiful. Is that the kind of sensitivity training they're teaching bodyguards these days?"

"Security specialist!"

He shrugged, then winced. "Whatever. Don't they teach you folks that the customer is always right? Whatever happened to TLC?"

She glared at him as she returned to her desk. "If I take this job, Coltrane—and that's a pretty big if—tender loving care will not be part of the package. Deal with it or go home." She picked up a pencil and tapped it irritably against the desktop. "Did the goons use a weapon?"

"They used their great hurkin' fists, sweetheart. I assume they also wore guns, but the cops arrived before they got around to using them."

"Who called the police?"

"My neighbor. She saw them break in before I got home. I walked in to catch 'em in the act."

"Why don't you simply give the guy his wife's photos, Nick? It was tacky to take them in the first place. It seems kinda low to hang on to them."

Something crossed his expression, but she was unable to pin it down before he said, "I don't have them to give—I gave the negatives to her. What she does with them is her business."

"Then what's the problem? Tell him that and get him off your back."

"The *problem*, Blondie, is that I refuse to sic him on her. I don't know what this guy will do. I mean, do you really find it rational to send a couple of hired guns after me just for taking a few nudie shots of his estranged wife?" He held up a big hand to forestall her answer. "Never mind, don't answer that—you probably do. But I don't. They've been separated for a long time, and until she tells him about the negatives herself, I'm gonna have a couple of muscle-bound, pistol-packing morons tracking my every move and doing their best to beat the information out of me in order to locate them."

She pulled over a legal pad. "I'll need Hubby's name."

Nick stilled. "I don't want you getting him all riled up."

"I don't have the authority to question him, Nick." She kept her voice noncommittal. "But neither can I keep you safe from the world at large. So give me a starting place."

He hesitated, then said, "John Johnson."

"John Johnson." Hard-to-verify aliases tended to make her suspicious. "Not Smith? That ought to narrow it down considerably."

"Okay, that's it—I tried." He pushed his chair back and stood. "If you're going to doubt every word that comes out of my mouth, this isn't going to work."

Something about his wording caught her. "What do you mean, you tried?"

He ignored the question, looking at her though narrowed eyes. "Coming here was a dumb idea that's clearly destined to fail. Sorry I wasted your time." He headed for the door.

Daisy wanted to let him walk away. Desperately, she wanted that. But four thousand dollars . . .

Her firm was only six months old and she was operating on a shoestring. She had rent to pay, both here and on her apartment, plus Reggie's salary. And she had this sneaking fondness for eating on a semi-regular basis. So she stood and said to the tense set of his shoulders, "Nick, wait."

He halted and turned to face her, his blue eyes free of expression.

"Please. Have a seat. I apologize." She pulled a contract from her desk drawer and slapped it on the desktop. Punching down the intercom button, she said, "Reggie, would you come in here, please?" As Nick resumed his seat, she looked across the desk at him.

Then, hoping she wasn't making the biggest mistake of her life, she separated the fee schedule from the contract, pushed it across the desk to him, and said, "Let me explain how your retainer will be allocated."

2

⌒∞⌒

LATE that afternoon, Daisy boarded a bus for Nick's. Staring out the window, she gazed blindly at the passing scenery and allowed the gentle rocking, the monotonous stops and starts, to lull her into a drowsy, near-hypnotic state. Unbidden, her mind began to wander.

If there was one thing she had learned in her twenty-eight years, it was that men don't stick around. Growing up, it had mostly just been her and Mama. The men who'd come and gone in their modest house in the suburbs had seemed more like visitors than anything resembling family. She supposed her father qualified as family, but he had traveled almost constantly, and besides, he'd taken a hike when she was nine years old.

Mama had often touted herself as a woman who needed a man to feel complete. "You'll understand, baby, when you're a little older," she used to say. But Daisy never did quite grasp the concept. From everything she'd observed, it simply meant that a woman set herself up to

25

spend the majority of her life feeling incomplete. For instance, her mother had married again when Daisy was eleven, but Papa Ray had already been gone by the time she turned twelve.

The summer following her sixteenth birthday, her mother was romanced right off her feet by Nick's father, Dale Coltrane. And their life got swept up into something entirely different.

At first Daisy truly believed that her lifelong yearning for a stable family with a father who stayed and siblings she could call her own had come true. She was still a cockeyed optimist then.

She and Mama didn't belong in the Coltranes' world, though, and boy, did those who did ever rush to point it out. She'd never realized there were so many ways in which they could fail to measure up. The criticism was constant, but always handled with an exquisite politeness and subtleness that was difficult to defend against. That never stopped Daisy from trying, of course, which was simply another mark against her. While she railed against the snobbery, Mama desperately tried to fit in.

The sibling aspect didn't work out quite the way Daisy had hoped, either. Mo was kind and friendly and willing to take Daisy under her wing. But she was five years older and had her own interests and friends. And Nick was mostly a muscular back that Daisy saw leaving whatever room she entered. On the rare occasions they were thrown together, he treated her like an amusing pest from a foreign country. And before Daisy had the chance to turn him into the brother she'd always wanted, their parents' marriage had ended in unspeakable ugliness.

At first it wasn't anything Daisy hadn't heard before: bitter voices behind closed doors, cold silences, half-stifled weeping. But then Dale, with deliberate cruelty, took it to a depth she didn't understand to this day: he vilified her mother in the press and destroyed her reputation. It paid to be rich and have even richer friends, she supposed, for how else could he have sold the tabloids such a patently untrue story about Mama's alleged lurid sexual practices with the heir of the Campman Winery, who was supposed to be his good friend?

Campman's strident denials and solicitous comforting of Mama, which had been captured by tabloid photographers, just lent credence to the stories which Dale's testimony alone might have lacked.

By the time the marriage was over, Daisy had come to realize she was never going to be part of a Cosby-type family. She had no control over that, but she did vow that she would never repeat her mother's mistakes. She believed that somewhere out there was a man she could depend upon one hundred percent to love her until death did them part, and at the age of seventeen, she swore to save herself for him.

So what the hell had ever possessed her to sign a contract with the very man who'd sweet-talked her into breaking that vow a mere two years after she'd made it?

The bus rattled over a set of trolley tracks and she frowned at the overcast day. Money wasn't exactly a negligible reason when one had as little of it as she did, of course. But she had her emotional welfare to consider, too—and hard experience had taught her that Nick Coltrane was *not* good for her in that respect.

The bus was almost at her stop, though, and she reached up to pull the cord. She'd just have to set aside her doubts. A deal was a deal, and it was too late to back out now.

She wrestled her luggage and assorted paraphernalia off the bus, cursing her ingrained frugality. A cab ride wouldn't have blown the budget, and it would have made a much better impression than showing up on Nick's doorstep like the poor little match girl. She seemed to adopt that role much too easily whenever she got within breathing range of the man. Just once it would be nice to act from a position of strength. Well—next time.

Daisy looked up the almost vertical hill, adjusted everything as best she could one last time, took a deep breath, and started walking.

Several blocks later, she stopped outside a wall surrounding an enormous brick mansion. Pulling a scrap of paper from her hip pocket, she checked the scrawled numbers against the brass script on the driveway gatepost. This was the place.

Looking at its sheer size and opulence, she didn't know whether to roll her eyes at Nick's skewed idea of "poor" or to congratulate herself. This was exactly the sort of barn-sized dwelling she'd envisioned when she'd agreed to move in to guard his sorry butt. The gated wall was a tad ostentatious, but would make it easier to set up parameters for keeping Nick safe. Heck, if they stocked up with enough provisions they wouldn't even have to leave the joint, which would cut down dramatically on the number of situations that would put him in danger. She rang the bell set into the post.

The speaker crackled a moment later. "Who is it?" demanded a woman's voice.

"My name is Daisy Parker—"

"Oh! You're Nicholas' bodyguard!"

"His security specialist, yes, ma'am."

"You don't look big enough to be a body-guard."

Daisy frowned at the camera at the top of the post. If she had a buck for every time she'd heard that, she'd be rich enough to tell Nick to find somebody else to guard his treacherous hide. And she wasn't even particularly little; that's what really got to her. She was almost five-seven, but that was immaterial.

The real issue was that she wasn't a man.

The woman seemed to be waiting for a reply, so Daisy said, "I'm taller in person." Silence greeted her remark and she added, "I assure you I'm very good at my job, ma'am." Still the woman didn't respond, and Daisy finally lost patience. "Listen, lady, I can't *do* my job if you won't let me in."

"Nicholas warned me you'd be abrupt." The driveway gate hummed as both sides slowly swept open, revealing a drive that curved to the right. "He's in the carriage house."

" '*Nicholas warned me you'd be abrupt.*' " Daisy

mimicked sourly. Great. Five minutes in his world and already she'd been found wanting.

She repositioned her bags and stepped through the gate. And what was this about a carriage house? Sizable lots and places to park were both at such a premium in San Francisco that it seemed the height of luxury to own one's very own on-site, multicar garage. Nick had one helluva nerve talking about budgets.

The original doors of the carriage house had been replaced with automatic garage doors, and two of them stood open, rolled up into the ceiling. Gratefully setting her gear down, Daisy peered into the dim garage. A classic Daimler was parked in one pristine bay and an older Porsche in another. The third bay stood empty, except for a chest freezer tucked in the corner. No one was around and she called out Nick's name.

"That you, Blondie?"

The voice came from overhead, but when Daisy peered up, there was nothing to see but rafters. Then a racket sounded from outside and she walked back out onto the apron. Following the clatter of footsteps, she rounded the corner in time to see Nick hit the bottom step of an exterior wooden stairway.

He swooped down on her. "Where's your stuff?"

Her heart lodged itself so firmly in her throat that she could only wave a hand at the heap just inside the garage. Once again, she questioned her intelligence in accepting this job. Coming face-to-face with a client didn't usually make her heart thunder like a junior high school girl confronted with her first big crush.

Daisy straightened her spine. Dammit, she would not feel this way. She wasn't thirteen; she was a grown woman. She was a professional—she'd been a cop, for cripes' sake. She snatched her custom-fitted weapons case out of Nick's hand. "I'll take that. You can get the rest." Remembering his bad shoulder, she guiltily swept up her suitcase also, and left him with the lightweight plastic grocery sacks she'd stuffed full of odds and ends.

Looking around, she saw that a narrow path wound through a small, beautifully planted yard to the back door of the mansion. "Where do we go?" The back door would be her guess, but since she was on her party behavior for now, she refrained from simply barging ahead on her own.

"Up here." His hands full, Nick used his chin to indicate the stairs that climbed the side of the carriage house. One of the bags slipped and he adjusted his grip. "Jesus, Daisy, what is all this stuff?"

Daisy looked up the stairs. Clearly there was an apartment up there that he'd been readying for her. Equally clearly, he didn't grasp the basics of security. "I can't protect you, Coltrane," she growled in disgust, "if you're in one place and I'm in another."

Nick gave her a baffled look. "If I'm in . . ." A startled laugh escaped him. "You think I live in the main house? Man, you just won't listen when I tell you I'm not rich, will you? I rent the carriage house from the owner of the place. C'mon."

Daisy warily followed him up the stairs, and she knew she was in big, big trouble the moment she walked through the door. Instead of the massive space all decked out in cold chrome and leather that she'd expected, the place was a dollhouse. A compact, cozy, inviting little dollhouse. Her stomach took a dive right down to her toes as she peered down the short hallway into the main room.

This was awful.

The ceilings were high, the floors were gleaming hardwood, and the walls were brick. Mullioned windows overlooked the drive and the tiny yard, and compelling black and white photographs she figured for Nick's work graced the walls. A breakfast bar defined the kitchen space at the far end of the room, and midroom, a plush maroon velvet couch and two overstuffed tapestry chairs faced a fireplace and entertainment center. Nick looked at her over his shoulder, and Daisy realized she'd stopped dead at the end of the hallway, by the only plaster wall. There were two closed doors in it that she assumed led to the bedrooms. Or perhaps to a bedroom and a bathroom.

"Where's your, ah, darkroom?" she asked as she edged past. What she really wanted to know was where he expected her to sleep, but her nerve failed her at the last minute. That would never do. She had to start off on more dominant footing if she didn't want to lose control of the entire situation.

"Down in the garage," Nick said as he

watched her set her suitcase on the floor and the smaller case on the antique trunk that served as a coffee table. "I just finished putting it back together after yesterday's rampage." She'd changed into jeans and a burnt-orange chenille sweater, and he watched her long-legged stride as she prowled around the apartment, checking this and peering into that. She stopped at the humpbacked trunk under the windows and squatted down in front of it. His eyebrows rose along with the lid she raised. "You looking for something in particular there, Blondie?"

"I just like to know what's around me." She scowled at him over her shoulder. "And I've told you before, Coltrane, don't call me Blondie."

"Fine, then—Daisy. Get out of my stuff. Your mother raised you better than to go poking through people's closets."

"She tried, but as you can see, it didn't take. If something's there, I'm gonna look." She surged to her feet. "Where do you want me to sleep?"

His muscles went tight at the answer that leapt to mind, but he forced himself to relax as he turned and headed for the bedroom. He opened the door and looked back to find her right on his heels. "In here."

She brushed past him and walked around his room, giving it the same close scrutiny she'd given everything else. She picked up his odds and ends and then set them down again. She eased open a nightstand drawer, peered inside, and then slid it shut. After giving the professional-quality punching bag that hung in one corner a left-right-left series of jabs, she sat on the side of the bed and bounced a couple of times. "Nice." Then she looked over at him. "This is your room? And the only bedroom, I take it?"

He nodded.

"Then where do you plan to sleep, if you turn it over to me?"

"On the couch."

She eyed the length of his legs and laughed skeptically. "Yeah, right." She rose to her feet. "Keep your room. I'll sleep on the couch."

Every chivalric lesson ever drummed into his head protested the idea. "That's not necessary."

"Actually, it's mandatory. For one thing, I'll fit the couch a lot better than you. More importantly, my services aren't going to do you a fat lot of good if hubby's goons manage to get in here and beat the bejesus out of you while I'm sawing Z's in the bedroom. The whole idea is for the bad guys to have to go through me in order to get to you." She breezed past him. "C'mon, let's go see what kinda stuff you keep in your medicine cabinet."

Her cocky posturing rubbed him the wrong way and impulsively he reached out and grabbed her arm to tell her to can the attitude. But when her momentum swung her around and she stopped dead in front of him, he caught her scent and forgot what he'd planned to say. She smelled of laundry soap and shampoo and a faint, musky, underlying hint of woman, and he had an insane impulse to back her up against the nearest wall and sniff out the origin of each and every fragrance.

Then he got a look at her face, which was coldly furious. Hand fisted and arm cocked back from the elbow, she strained stiffly against his hold, staring first at his fingers, then at his face. "Get your hand off of me."

He knew that was exactly what he should do, but something inside him refused to obey. "Or what?"

She reached down and brushed her fingers in warning against the fly of his jeans. "Or I'll rip your pride and joy clean off and feed it to the first dog I see."

It was an ego bruiser, how fast he took his hand off her, and he snarled, "Still the low-rent little street fighter we all knew and deplored, I see. I must have been crazy to think this would work."

Daisy's face went blank. Then she turned and without a word began gathering up her motley collection of bags.

"What are you doing?" As if any idiot couldn't plainly see, but he had to ask anyway. He really wished he hadn't, though, when she turned to look at him. The contempt in her eyes seared him right down to the bone.

"Getting my stuff and going home. I'll return your retainer in the morning."

Maybe she was right. Given their turbulent history and the close quarters, he didn't know if he could handle having her stay here with him. Yet he liked the alternative even less. All this flip-flopping from Hiring-Her-Is-a-Sound-Plan to

This-Is-the-Worst-Idea-I've-Ever-Had put him on edge, and a fire began to smolder deep and low in Nick's gut. He raked a hand through his hair. "Is that it, then? You're just gonna leave me staked out here like a sacrificial goat?"

Her bags hit the floor with a thud, and she faced him with her chin thrust forward and her hands fisted on her hips. "What do you want from me, Coltrane? Do you want me to stay, or do you want me to go?"

"I don't know, dammit! Hiring you was an impulse—probably because Mo mentioned a while ago what you do for a living."

"Well, if you kept your busy little hands out of married women's pants, you wouldn't *need* anyone's services," she said hotly.

He thrust his face down close to hers and warned, "Don't even go there." Pleased as punch when her mouth snapped closed, he took a large step back and straightened. For some reason it bugged the hell out of him that she believed he'd fool around with a married woman—even if he had told her so himself.

"It's not up to you to judge me," he said coolly. "Not if you're willing to take my money. And as your employer, I want some information I should have asked for earlier. Your little offer of a demonstration aside, Blondie, I don't actually know squat about your qualifications." Her fine-boned, slender build and that stubborn little chin that barely cleared the middle of his chest gave him serious reservations. "Face it, you don't exactly look like anyone's idea of a bodyguard."

She made a sound of disgust deep in her

throat, but her expression was neutral when she said, "Believe it or not, Coltrane, that actually works to your benefit, since people constantly underestimate me. I am nevertheless fully qualified."

"How's that? You go to the ITT Peterson school of Bodyguarding or something?"

Her chin rachetted another notch higher. "Oh, very cute. Insulting and inaccurate, but terribly cute. You rich boys certainly have this repartee thing down to a fine art, don'tcha?"

He raised his camera and looked at her through the viewfinder. "Your qualifications, Daisy?"

"I graduated third in my class from the police academy."

"You were a *cop*?" It caught him by surprise and he lowered the camera. She and Mo had kept in loose touch, so over the years he'd heard things about her. But never once had Mo mentioned Daisy joining the police force. He lowered the camera and gave her a skeptical once-over. "Get outta here."

"You get out of here. It's true."

"Where?" He'd guess Mayberry, Middle America.

"I was with the Oakland PD for four years."

Okay, not Small Town, USA. He eyed her with interest, trying to imagine her patrolling some of the meaner streets of Oakland. "So why did you leave?"

"There're a lot of politics involved in that sort of bureaucracy." She hesitated and then admitted, "I wasn't very good at playing the game."

That tugged up a corner of his mouth. "No, I don't imagine you were. Diplomacy never was your strong suit."

She shrugged, acknowledging it. "And honesty isn't always the best policy in civil service." Then her eyes narrowed on him. "Is a background in law enforcement qualification enough to suit your royal highness?"

What could he say? If she'd been an Oakland cop for four years, she was qualified, mouthy little brat or not. He nodded.

"Fine. Then do you want me to stay or to go? Make up your mind, because I'm not playing this game again."

"Stay." Shit. He regretted the choice the instant it left his mouth, but he needed someone, she was here, and she was qualified. He'd just have to live with it.

But damned if the concessions would all be one-sided. "Provided you can act like a woman who's been trained by the academy, and not some loose cannon commando queen."

Her jaw tightened, but she said, "I can do that." She stooped to gather up two plastic grocery bags, then walked to the kitchen. After opening the refrigerator, she started emptying the bags.

"You brought your own groceries?" He walked over to see.

"I didn't know how long I'd be here and I hate going home to spoiled food." She set a half gallon of milk on the shelf next to the quart of orange juice she'd already put there, and reached in her bag for two oranges, a container of fresh pineapple, and a container of cubed cantaloupe.

"Wouldn't it have been easier to just toss it out?"

"I don't waste perfectly good food, rich boy."

He blew out a frustrated breath. Maybe if he changed the subject it would take his mind off how good it would feel to wring that long, slender neck. "There's space in the garage if you want to move your car in. I'm surprised you managed to find parking out on the street."

"I didn't." Daisy shut the fridge door and turned to face him. "I came by Muni."

"By *bus*? You don't have a car?" He couldn't conceive of life without wheels.

Her expression was hostile. "We can't all be born with a silver spoon in our mouths."

"Dammit, Daisy, would you give that a rest?" Ten lousy minutes in her company and all his emotions were seething. "I'm not rich, okay? Hell, compared to my friends I'm dead broke."

"If you can write me a check for four thousand dollars, trust me, you're not dead broke. I know about broke. Until Reggie deposited your check I had exactly one hundred thirty-eight dollars and forty-one cents in my account."

"Yeah? In that case, I'd think you'd be a whole lot nicer to me."

She made a rude sound. "Oh, please, do me a favor. Hold your breath waiting for that to happen."

"Sounds to me like I'm single-handedly keeping the wolf from your door, cupcake."

She looked him dead in the eye and said, "Then isn't it funny how, every time I look at you, all I can think is, *What very big teeth you have, Grandma*?" She rubbed her arms as if chilled. "And I moved in with you anyway."

Nick watched her come out from behind the breakfast bar and said, "Listen, Daisy, maybe we oughtta clear the air."

She walked over to the couch and sat, leaning forward to snap open the clasps on the case she'd set on the trunk earlier. Thumbs poised on the lid, she looked over at him. "Clear the air of what?" She raised the lid and reached inside.

Nick looked away, then back at her profile. "We've got to talk about the night of Mo's wedding." An apology from him was long overdue.

Daisy couldn't think of anything she wanted to do less. Rising to her feet, she faced him, her face stonily unencouraging and the pistol she'd picked out of the case held down at her side. "You can't be terribly smart," she said flatly, "or you'd never mention that night when I have a gun in my hand." Especially when that hand trembled with the overwhelming desire to point it straight at his lying heart. She turned and carefully placed the weapon back in its slot in the box. "Luckily for you, I'm a professional."

"Listen, all I wanted to say—"

"I don't give a rip what you want to say, all right? Just drop it."

"Dammit, Daisy, I—"

Deliberately tuning him out, she headed for the bathroom. She needed a few minutes with a door that locked and water she could run to drown out his voice. He seemed determined to keep pushing, and she was terrified it might goad her into committing an irrevocably stupid act. Nothing punched her buttons the way that night with Nick did, and the smart thing would be to remove herself from the situation until she could shake the desire to respond on a personal level. She needed to gather her professionalism around her like a bulletproof vest.

When her arm was suddenly grabbed in a steely grip, whirling her around, she didn't stop to think—she simply reacted. Spinning in to press her back against his front, she gripped his arm, twisted, and bent forward with a snap.

Nick flipped over her shoulder and sailed several feet, landing flat on his back on the floor.

3

〰️

"HOLY shit, Daisy!" Nick pushed up on an elbow and sucked in a careful breath. "All I wanted to do was apologize."

"Save it for someone who cares."

"I'd say you must care a whole hell of a lot, or you wouldn't be trying to slam the breath out of me."

She laughed without humor. "Don't flatter yourself. I cared once, but I don't anymore."

She did lean down and offer him a hand, however, hauling him to his feet when he reached out and gripped it. It was ludicrous to miss the warmth of her hand when she dropped his an instant later, yet he did.

"The only way this arrangement has a snowball's chance of working is if we keep things between us purely professional," she said coolly. "And, okay, I admit maybe this wasn't exactly the way to start us off." Her shrug didn't strike Nick as particularly repentant, and her chin was elevated as she added, "Leave it alone, Nick. You got what you wanted when you copped my cherry, then walked out on me." She turned away.

God, that was almost funny, considering. He hadn't walked out; he'd *run*, and it had been an act of pure self-defense.

All his life he'd watched his father go through wives like a kid through a Pez dispenser, and had seen the havoc it had wreaked. It had made him decide at a young age that he would never marry, and he'd given up even bothering to get to know his various stepsiblings, since they were never around long enough to make the effort worthwhile. Mo had been the only person he could count on to be there for him through the good times and the bad.

Then, the year he graduated from college, Daisy had come into their lives.

Right from the start she'd proved different from the stepsiblings who had come and gone before her. She hadn't even been in the Coltrane mansion an hour before she'd begun to make her presence felt. At sixteen, she'd already been outspoken and full of attitude. She'd run through the corridors, flopped on the furniture, and hadn't thought twice about putting her size-nine feet on a couch or a coffee table. She'd done all the things he and Mo had rarely dared to do. There had just been something about her, a warm quality that drew anyone who got close to her, and she'd been eager as a puppy to be his and Mo's sister.

Her sloppy, rampant emotions had tugged at something in him, perhaps because he was always so careful to keep his own strictly under control. He'd been drawn not only to her unin-hibited laughter but to her stormy rages, and her sheer lack of restraint had made him itch to get close to her. But his feelings had never been the least bit brotherly, and that—he hadn't doubted for an instant—was a dangerous thing. So he'd watched her from a distance whenever he was home, but carefully rebuffed every overture she'd made.

It had turned out to be the right decision, too, for their parents' marriage had started to go sour a few weeks shy of its first anniversary. And thanks to Dad's decision not to be stuck with yet another alimony payment and his subsequent machinations, Daisy and her mother had been packed and gone before that date ever rolled around.

Nick watched Daisy now as she sat on the couch and picked up another pistol, efficiently breaking it open and searching for God-only-knew-what inside. He sat down on the love seat at right angles to the couch and raised his cam-era up to his eyes, looking at her through the viewfinder. He clicked off a few frames, and she looked up.

"Don't take my picture."

"Why not? I've always liked your face."

She scowled at him and he clicked off a shot of that, too. She must have decided it wasn't worth fighting over, for she went back to the gun, loading it and placing it back in its slot, then reaching for another weapon.

He *had* always liked her face, from the very first time he'd seen it. It was expressive and full of character. She had big Hershey's-Kisses-colored eyes and high cheekbones. Her eyebrows, several shades darker than her hair, tilted up at the outside corners, her nose was prominent, and she had a soft mouth that was offset by the stubbornness of her chin. Daisy's thoughts were generally right there for the world to read on her face, although she'd clearly become adept at hiding them when she wanted to. He clicked off another shot.

"Would you put that stupid camera down!" Daisy leapt to her feet, tucking the gun into an inside holster in the front of her jeans and covering the butt of its handle with the hem of her sweater.

"This stupid camera is what gave me four thousand dollars to turn over to you," Nick replied mildly as he lowered the camera.

She moved restlessly. "I'd like to get out of here for a while. Let's go walk the grounds. The wall around this place looks pretty substantial, so I'd like to see how Hubby's goons were able to get in here yesterday."

"Yeah, okay." He climbed to his feet, happy to forsake his little stroll down memory lane. Daisy was right: they needed to keep their relationship on a purely professional footing.

So the last thing he should do was revisit that evening nine years ago in a hotel room with Blondie, ten floors above his sister's waning wedding reception.

Reid Cavanaugh tracked his wife to the study. He walked straight up to the desk where Mo sat tallying figures and slapped the paper in his hand down on the polished surface in front of her. "You want to tell me what this is?"

She marked her place on the column of numbers with her fingertip and looked first at his face, then at the legal document in front of her. Then she looked back up at him again, and Reid's gut knotted. God, she was so incredibly cool these days. "It's notice of a paid loan."

"Paid by you."

"Yes."

"Is your name anywhere on the original loan papers, Maureen?"

"No, but—"

"No, period. Mine is. I cosigned for the fuc . . . for the loan." Hands braced on the desktop, he leaned forward to level a look into her clear blue eyes. "Not you. Me."

"That's all very well, Reid, but I notice you didn't loan Pettigrew the money through Cavanaugh Bank."

"That's right. He didn't have the proper collateral to satisfy the loan committee."

"Yet you *personally* cosigned?"

"He needed the money, Mo."

"They always need money, Reid! God, you're such a soft touch! And every deadbeat ex-school-chum knows it. What earthshaking emergency did Pettigrew have, a sudden need for a new polo pony?"

"Are you really interested in knowing, or would you rather sit there on your moral high ground, tossing off sarcastic remarks?"

"You lent our money to someone you'd never consider in a professional capacity!"

"Oh, so today it's our money, huh? Don't you think that's a touch hypocritical, considering any reference you've made to our finances in the past several years has been strictly in terms of your money or mine? Besides, he'll pay it back."

"I heard you telling someone on the phone the other day that Pettigrew defaulted and left you holding the bag."

"And if you'd eavesdropped a few minutes longer, or bothered to talk to me when I got off the phone, you would have heard me say that I know he'll be good for it in the end."

She simply gave him that pitying look she was so good at, and he knew she thought he was dreaming. Again. Her continued lack of faith in his judgment flicked him on the raw. "It was *my* problem, Mo! I've been working on a contingency plan until Pettigrew comes through, but could you trust me to handle it myself? Hell, no. Who do I have to thank for that, I wonder? My guess would be Big Daddy, if you and your brother are anything to go by. The two of you sure put the fun back in dysfunctional."

Cheeks reddening, she surged to her feet. "That's low. And unfair." The space that separated them was suddenly much narrower than it had been a moment ago, and it crackled with emotion.

He leaned forward, bringing them closer yet. "Maybe so, but it's also dead-on accurate. We've tiptoed around the mess our marriage has become way too long. Your dad was an emotional screw-up, so Nick takes a hike whenever a relationship even hints at growing serious. And you"—he laughed without humor—"well, you're pretty well determined to stick with me to the bitter end no matter what, aren't you, Mo? We sure wouldn't want you to be accused of being anything like your father."

Her cheeks went from red to white. "Is that what this is really about? Do you want a divorce?"

"What I *want* is for you to believe in me for just one lousy minute. I want to be treated like a contributing member of this family, not some incompetent teenager who needs his mom to get him out of a jam." What he wanted was his old Mo back—but she'd been gone a long time now, and for all he knew, she was gone forever. Somewhere along the line, their marriage, which had started out so happy and full of love and hope, had grown stagnant and stale. They used to spend every moment they could steal away from their obligations together. Now they rarely saw each other at all. And the thing she'd once loved best about him, his optimistic willingness to lend a hand to a friend in need, was the very issue that had driven a wedge between them. Which was ironic when you considered the way *she* was forever jumping in to solve everyone's problems for them.

"I don't understand you," he said in frustration. "I've never risked the roof over your head or the food on your table. You had no business butting in—you should have left it the hell alone."

She hesitated and then gave him a tight smile. "Believe me, you don't know how much I wish I'd done exactly that. Now, if you'll excuse me, I have quite a bit of work to do." Without another word, she resumed her seat and went back to tallying the column of figures as if he'd ceased to exist.

4

∽∘∾

tuesday

DAISY awoke to find Nick squatting next to the couch, his face less than a foot from hers. Mumbling an oath, she scrambled upright, her hand reaching beneath the pillow for her gun, her gaze scanning the apartment. "What? What is it? Is someone trying to get in?"

He didn't immediately answer. Following his gaze, she saw that her blanket had slipped, revealing glimpses of the tank top and panties she'd slept in. Although neither was exceptionally revealing, she pushed upright against the end of the couch and pulled the errant cover up around her neck, a heightened awareness snapping along her nerve endings. "What do you want, Nick?"

"Sorry, I didn't mean to startle you."

The morning light, pouring through the mullioned windows, picked out the subtle streaks of gold, russet, and mahogany in his thick brown hair. Overlong and ruler-straight, it had the rich luxuriousness of an animal pelt.

He snapped his fingers in her face. "Earth calling Blondie." She blinked, and he said, "I said we've got to leave in forty-five minutes. If you want a shower, you'd better grab it now. I know how long it takes you women to get ready to go anywhere."

She rubbed the sleep out of her eyes. Giving his stupid crack the zero attention it deserved, she locked on to the one pertinent word in the conversation. "Leave? Leave for where?" A huge yawn cracked her jaw and she shook her head in disgust. "Sorry. I don't function very well before my first cup of coffee."

"I'll make you one. You go take your shower." He headed for the kitchen.

Wrapping the blanket around her shoulders, she clutched it closed with one hand and pulled her gun out with the other. Then she padded after him. "Wait a minute. What did you mean when you said we had to leave in forty-five minutes?"

Nick looked at his Rolex. "Forty, now."

"The number's not the point, Coltrane. I don't recommend you go anywhere. We need to establish some parameters to assure your safety."

"You'll just have to do that on the move, cupcake. I've got commitments to honor."

"Like what? Got a hot date?" *Oh, not good, Daisy. Remember your professionalism.*

"No," he replied evenly. "I've got back-to-back photo shoots scheduled."

She drew in a deep breath and slowly eased it out. "I strongly advise you to curtail those appointments wherever possible. I'm very good at what I do, Nick, but I'm only one person, and the risk factor goes up exponentially whenever you appear in public."

"Just do your best, Daisy. I committed to these photo shoots months ago, and except for one or two, they're all for date-specific events and can't be postponed."

"Send them to another photographer."

He poured the beans he'd just ground into a filtered drip cone, fit the cone over a glass pot, and held it under an Insta Hot tap. Steam drifted up as he glanced over at her. "They want the best."

She snorted. "And—what?—Annie Leibovitz wasn't available?"

"Ouch." A grin split his face, and he slapped one hand over his heart as if mortally wounded. He slid a coffee mug onto the counter in front of her and reached for the pot. When her cup was full he looked up at her, and the smile had disappeared from his face. "I gave them my word."

She sighed. Giving one's word was a concept she understood. She was just surprised that he did. Rearranging the blanket to allow her hand through, she set the gun on the counter and scooped up the mug.

Nick raised his gaze to hers. "Is it really necessary to drag that to the breakfast table?"

She shrugged. "Probably not. But wouldn't *I* feel stupid if Hubby's thugs broke in here and I'd left it over by the couch." She considered how to carry both the pistol and mug, and still keep her blanket on. She set the mug back on the counter and turned her back on Nick to wind the blanket around her torso, tucking the corner in beneath her left armpit. Then she turned back for both the weapon and coffee. "I'll go get ready." Sipping at her coffee, she headed for the bathroom.

"You've got thirty-three minutes."

Without looking back, she made a small circling motion with the barrel of the gun to indicate she'd heard.

"I mean it, Daisy. You're not gonna make me late."

"Yeah, yeah, yeah."

She was out in fifteen minutes, dressed, teeth brushed, and her wet hair sporting fresh comb tracks where she'd slicked it back from her face. She didn't know why women got such a bad rap. Reggie and the rest of the guys she hung out with took much longer to get ready than she did. Of course, to be fair, most of them were woman wannabes.

She'd taken note of Nick's silk-blend T-shirt, flannel slacks, and unstructured linen jacket, and she carried her gold wool blazer to dress up her own jeans, boots, and white T-shirt. Before donning it, she strapped a knife on her forearm and tucked her gun into its inside holster.

"You're a regular walking arsenal, aren't you?"

"I like to be prepared, just on the off chance that telling the bad guys to quit being such big ole meanies doesn't do the trick." Then she added sincerely, "It really would be better if you didn't go out. Are you positive your appointments can't be postponed?"

"Most of them. But I did start rescheduling the few that can be, while you were showering." He picked up his keys. "Are you ready to go?"

"Are we taking your car?" At his nod, she said, "Then let me grab one more thing."

"Let me guess—you forgot your bazooka."

"You're such a comic, Coltrane." She ran to the bedroom and dug something out of one of her bags. Returning to the living room, she removed a velcro strap from around the tool's two parts and screwed them together, leaving her with a long pole with an angled mirror on one end. As Nick hefted a large duffel bag, she raced to squeeze ahead of him, brushing up against him when he didn't immediately give way. She tried to ignore the fact that for someone who led such a soft life, he felt awfully hard beneath his nice clothing. "Let me go ahead of you."

"Hey, by all means, doll face, ladies first."

"It's not the gender aspect we have to consider here, Coltrane; it's the professional." Hand on her gun, she stepped out onto the stair's tiny landing and scanned the yard and the drive, paying particular attention to the shadows. "Okay. It's all clear."

Nick came out, hauling his bag. "I feel like an idiot."

"Well, don't. How's your arm today?"

He clenched and unclenched his left hand. "It feels stronger."

"Yeah?" She started down the steps. "Wanna arm wrestle?"

"I'm not even going to dignify that with an answer."

"Afraid I'll pin it to the table, huh?"

"You're really an obnoxious little twit, you know that, Blondie?" He practically tromped on her heels as they entered the garage.

She stopped short and shot out her arm to keep him from barreling past her as she peered into the shadows. His diaphragm felt muscular and warm, and she was glad to drop her arm a moment later. "Okay, which car is yours?"

"The Porsche."

"Figures. Let me check it out and then we can go." She swept the mirrored end of her pole beneath the car from stem to stern.

"You're looking for a *bomb*?"

"Yes." She pulled the mirrored section out from beneath the vehicle and broke down the tool, tying the parts back together with its velcro strap. "Pop the hood."

He did as requested, and she went over the engine compartment, then climbed in the car and leaned to look beneath the dash. Finally she straightened up in her seat. "Okay, it's clean."

"Holy shit," he muttered as he fit the key in the ignition.

She had to grin at his disgusted expression. "You know, there's one sure way to avoid this sort of thing in the future, Coltrane."

He gave her a wary look. "I'm terrified to ask." Several seconds of silence ticked by. "Okay, what the hell. How do I avoid this sort of thing in the future?"

"The next time you find a married woman who thinks you're just cuter than a bug's ear? Keep your pants zipped."

*   *   *

Mo waved goodbye to her clients, locked the key box on the Pacific Heights mansion she'd just shown them, and walked down to her car. She opened the door, then simply stood for a moment with her hand on the car's roof, staring down the hill at the planetarium and the fog-enshrouded bay beyond.

You had no business butting in, she heard Reid's voice for what seemed like the hundredth time. *You should have left it the hell alone.*

God, how she wished she had. But, no, she'd had to jump right in and solve Reid's problem for him—never mind that the manner in which she'd done so was criminal and he would certainly not thank her for it if he knew. And that, of course, was another problem entirely. Perhaps even the biggest problem.

She should have told him what she'd done. She'd meant to tell him, but then her pride had reared its ugly head and she'd let him walk out of the study without trying to make him understand. No, she'd done worse than that. She'd *driven* him out.

I want to be treated like a contributing member of this family, not some incompetent teenager who needs his mom to get him out of a jam.

"Oh, shut up, Reid," she muttered, and climbed into the car and shut the door. She didn't do that. Did she?

It was true she worried about money. Dad had kept them on the bare edge of solvency when she was growing up, despite the opulent lifestyle of the circles they moved in. And that was a worry Reid, with the weight of the Cavanaugh banking fortune behind him, simply did not comprehend. Perhaps she *had* nagged him, but he'd been so damn cavalier about tossing his trust fund away on anyone with a sad story to tell. That was the reason she'd started up Cavanaugh Realty, and she would not apologize for needing the security.

If he'd truly cared about her, he wouldn't have put her in that position in the first place. But his response, anytime her fear had caused her to nag him about fiscal responsibility, had been to withdraw into his own pursuits. It had left her with no choice but to hone her own skills to the highest level she could attain. Only then could she be certain of never again having to worry about keeping a scant step ahead of the creditors.

Mo laughed without humor. That was pretty ironic, considering. Because just look where her much-lauded efficiency had gotten her now.

She reached for the ignition key but then sat back in the driver's seat without turning on the car. Looking out through the passenger window, she watched as the fog over the bay began to burn off and weak spring sunshine broke through.

She and Reid had drifted so far apart that the strength of her desire to settle his debt had caught her by surprise. The truth was, though, she couldn't stand the thought of anything bad ever happening to him.

She made a rude sound deep in her throat. Somehow she doubted he would consider having his name dragged through the mud a good thing. She really did have to tell him what she had done to pay off the debt, *before* the warrant for her arrest was delivered to their door.

But not just yet.

The couple to whom she'd just shown the mansion had been very enthusiastic about it. She would hang on a couple of days longer, and maybe, if she was very lucky indeed, the need to tell Reid how badly she'd messed up would become immaterial. *Please, God, let it be immaterial. Let me never have to tell him how foolish I've been.* Just two or three days more—that wasn't so much to ask.

Then, if she couldn't come up with the money, she'd tell him everything.

J. Fitzgerald Douglass admired his reflection in the mirror. His steel-gray hair was barbered to perfection and his cheeks shone with the closeness of his shave. He tweaked the silk handkerchief in his breast pocket until it was arranged just so, then gave his matching tie a minute adjustment. Not until he was completely satisfied did he close the cupboard door that housed the mirror and turn to greet the two men awaiting his attention. Their presence displeased him.

"The agreement when I hired you was the same as always: that you would contact me by phone," he said. "Don't come here again. If it's necessary to meet, we can always make arrangements to do so elsewhere." His glance traveled beyond them. "However, as long as you are here, where's Jacobsen?"

"We left him keepin' an eye on Coltrane's crib."

"Excellent. What do you have to report?"

The bigger of the two, who was built along the lines of a Sherman tank, offered, "Some blond babe entered the estate yesterday. She came on foot and doesn't look like the type to be visitin' the main house. We think she moved in with Coltrane."

"I don't care about his sex life, Autry. Where's my film?"

"We came up empty on the darkroom, Mr. Douglass. And someone called the cops before we could make Coltrane talk. He went to the hospital, though."

J. Fitzgerald took a seat behind his desk. He did not invite his employees to do likewise. "Is he still there?"

"No, sir. He's back home. We haven't been able to get a bead on him this morning, though, 'cuz it's become impossible to hang around his place. The people at the main house seem to be on the lookout for outsiders loitering around the joint."

J. Fitzgerald looked from one thick-necked man to the other. "And it never occurred to either of you, I suppose, to set up surveillance at the cross streets on either end of the block."

"Huh?"

He suppressed a sigh. There was no percentage in getting angry. It wasn't as if he'd hired them for their brains.

They had damn well better do the job he'd assigned them, however, and do it soon. He wasn't about to let the fruits of what he'd labored a lifetime to achieve be spoiled by one impoverished blue-blooded photographer.

He'd found out some things about Coltrane since he'd hired these two Sunday afternoon. The most important thing he'd discovered was that he may have been a bit precipitous in bringing out the dogs. That was unfortunate, but it was too late to do anything about it now.

The die was cast. Coltrane might have destroyed the negatives Sunday night if he'd been left alone, but he wouldn't do so now. "All right, here's what you do." He outlined a circumspect method in which his hired guns could keep tabs on Coltrane without being observed. "Do whatever it takes," he said as he dismissed them. "I want those photos."

5

AN accident and men working on a gas main tangled the traffic between Pacific Heights and Nob Hill, so what would normally be a five- or ten minute drive turned into nearly thirty. They arrived at Nick's first appointment fifteen minutes late.

Daisy could tell Nick was tense about it, but although she was normally a fool for punctuality herself, she wasn't particularly stressed. Of course, it was his client and not her own, and that made all the difference in the world. She grinned. In any case, the horn-happy drivers had been left behind, no one appeared to be tailing them, and she decided with mellow optimism that a fifteen minute delay was hardly likely to make or break anybody's day.

She was wrong.

Nick had mentioned while they sat in traffic that the Morrisons were scheduled for a reshoot. And the second thing Mrs. Morrison let them know, after her maid had ushered them into the morning room, was that she wasn't happy about it. Her first complaint was for their tardiness.

"You're late," she said before Nick and Daisy had even cleared the door. Dressed with yacht-crew sportiness, her breezy look was belied by the scowl marring her elegant brow. "I cannot abide tardiness; I find it utterly unconscionable." She gave Nick's faultlessly turned out appearance a displeased up-and-down. "Perhaps if you spent a little less time blow-drying your hair and fussing with your wardrobe, Mr. Coltrane, you might actually arrive for your appointments at the time you specified."

Daisy felt her jaw drop. Though she had her own bones to pick with Nick, not even she would suggest vanity was one of his shortcomings. He did have gorgeous hair and a sense of style that was his alone, but she had never seen him spend an excess moment in front of the mirror.

"I hired you in the first place, sir, because Maria Beauchamp said you're not only the best, but the most professional photographer in San Francisco County." The look Mrs. Morrison gave him was too well-bred to be called a sneer, but it conveyed her displeasure equally well. "Professional is the last attribute I would ascribe to you. We were forced to rearrange three busy lives in order to reschedule something we had taken the time to do once already—and now you've kept us waiting on top of it." She turned a disapproving eye on Daisy. "And who is this? The last time you came by yourself."

Nick paused in the act of pulling his equipment from his duffel. "This is Daisy Parker," he said with easy pleasantness. "She agreed to give me a hand today to help expedite your sitting. Daisy, this is Mrs. Helena Morrison, her husband Herbert, and their son Donald."

Mama, Papa, and Baby bear. Except Donald wasn't really a baby. He was probably thirteen or fourteen years old—old enough to look mortified by his mother's snotty behavior. Daisy gave him points, however, for not commenting on it. Most boys that age would have been sitting there whining, "Maaawm," in counterpoint to every embarrassing sentence out of their mother's mouth.

Nick explained about the traffic, but Mrs. Morrison clearly wasn't interested in his excuses. Daisy half expected to hear him tell her to kiss off, but instead he just kept blathering on and on.

Helena Morrison suddenly turned her fish-eye on Daisy, her gaze lingering on her hair—tendrils of which Daisy could feel springing erect as they dried. "And is *she* exempt from dressing professionally for some reason?"

Unlike Nick, Daisy didn't feel like sitting back and taking it. She stepped forward. "You might consider being a little more consistent, ma'am. It's difficult to track your logic when with one breath you accuse Nick of vanity because he dresses nicely, then—"

"Say he's a fool for having a friend who won't take a minute on her own appearance?" the older woman finished coolly.

"Precisely." She glanced down at her T-shirt, jeans, and blazer, then met Mrs. M's disapproving glare head-on. "I'm clean and I'm decently covered. What gripe, exactly, do you have with that?"

"Daisy, don't." Nick's sudden grip on her forearm was firm, and he held her back as he stepped forward.

Her first inclination was to yank free of his hold. She refused to give Mrs. Morrison the satisfaction of seeing her shake him off, though, and besides, there was something in his eyes when he looked at her, some sort of sadness, as he put himself between the two women, that managed to defeat her ire. She stood quietly within his grasp.

Without releasing her, Nick turned to Helena. "I am sorry about the necessity of making you repeat the sitting, Mrs. Morrison," he said gently. "But as I mentioned on the phone, my darkroom was broken into Sunday night, and all the work that was still in progress from last week was ruined."

"And why would anyone want to destroy anything as insignificant as a family portrait?"

"There's nothing insignificant about a Nicholas Coltrane photograph," he said with quiet arrogance. "All I can tell you is that it was an act of vandalism. I doubt the vandals even looked at what they were destroying."

"Hmph," was all she had to say, but it was loaded with skepticism and Daisy marveled at Nick's forbearance. She wouldn't have been nearly so polite if their positions had been reversed. The woman was a battleax. Not only did she insult his work, but it was ludicrous to think the trashing of his darkroom was something over which Nick had the least control. Beyond perhaps staying away from married women in the first place. But that, as she'd been reminded often enough, was not up to her to judge.

"Having to redo an entire week's worth of work for free isn't exactly the best use of his time, either, ma'am," she heard herself say. Nick's hand had slid down to her wrist and he squeezed it in warning, but she added, "This truly is an unfortunate imposition on everyone involved." Then she gently extricated her arm from his hold.

Helena pinned her in place with cool blue eyes. "As you say, young woman. But this sort of thing doesn't happen in my neighborhood, I can tell you."

Daisy laughed; she couldn't help it. "Pacific Heights is hardly the slums, Mrs. Morrison. And as someone who spent four years as a police officer, please believe me when I tell you that crime happens in every neighborhood. I have yet to see one that's exempt."

The woman looked pointedly at her watch. "May we begin sometime before the sun sets?" she demanded. "I have a twelve forty-five appointment."

Well, hell, Daisy thought in disgust. *What a shame if you had to skip a fitting for your newest gown.* She wondered why the woman didn't simply reschedule, if an extra fifteen minutes was such a hassle.

She wondered, too, how Nick would get anything remotely usable when one of his subjects was so obviously hacked off.

She seriously underestimated him, however. He talked quietly to the Morrisons and used an understated sort of charm to relax them. The males loosened up first. Then, when Nick started talking about the way he could touch up certain portions of today's photographs that would make them just as good as what he'd taken last week, Helena, too, relaxed.

Daisy noticed, with the woman's first real smile, that she was actually very attractive— quite lovely, even, when she forgot to be a bitch. Her short brown hair exhibited signs of what looked to be the early stages of female pattern baldness, but it was faultlessly arranged. And her skin was porcelain smooth, her figure svelte, and her features strikingly proportionate.

The whole family was comely, when it came right down to it. Mr. Morrison was tall and distinguished-looking, his dark hair just beginning to go gray at the temples. Donald was still a little unfinished around the edges, but he showed promise of someday attaining his father's height and his mother's good looks.

And they seemed close. Daisy watched them exchange touches and soft words of encouragement as they began to relax, and she didn't get it. Mrs. M appeared to have it all: money, beauty, a family who obviously doted on her. So what made her such a malcontent?

Nick managed to wrap up the sitting in record time and immediately set about packing up his bag. Daisy went to collect the light umbrellas. As she turned to carry them back to Nick's duffel, Helena reached out to touch her arm. Daisy regarded the older woman warily—even more so when she saw Helena's nose tilted up to a snooty angle.

So it caught her flat-footed when Mrs. Morrison took a deep breath and said, "I just want you to know that I admire the way you stand up for yourself and defend your friends. Particularly the latter. I find loyalty the most important attribute a person can possess." She thrust out her hand, which held a business card. "Here. I thought you might want to give my salon a try. They can probably do something with your hair." Her chin went up, as if awaiting a dig about her own thinning tresses.

Daisy merely blinked at her, still trying to assimilate what she was pretty sure was an actual compliment. She slid the light umbrella she held under her arm and took the card. "Thanks . . . I think." She slipped the card into her blazer pocket and met the other woman's eyes. "I hope you make your appointment on time."

Helena glanced at her watch. "You know, I think I probably shall."

A few moments later, seated in the passenger seat of Nick's car, Daisy turned to face him. "Okay. I'm confused. Just when you think you've got someone pegged as a total bitch . . . Mrs. Morrison *complimented* me. Can you believe that? She said she liked the way I stood up for myself and—get this—defended you. Oh, and look." She dug around in her pocket. "She gave me her stylist's card. What is it about my hair that bugs people so much, anyway?"

Nick took his gaze off the road to glance over at her. "Aside from the fact that you're a natural blonde? Probably that it looks as if you cut it yourself with a pair of nail scissors."

She felt heat crawl up her cheeks. "Yeah? So, what's your point?"

"Holy shit." Nick laughed. "You do, don't you?"

"Well, who has time for all that salon stuff?" What could she say? Somehow she'd been born minus the girlie gene. She'd just never seen the point in fussing around with hair or makeup. In a blatant bid to change the subject, she demanded, "So what's the deal with Mrs. Morrison? I know drag queens she could give lessons to, and until today I would have sworn they're as bitchy as it gets. And yet, I kind of liked her there at the end." She'd recognized a kindred soul in the way Helena had thrust out her chin even though she'd clearly expected to have it punched in.

"She has cancer."

Shock slammed through her. "What?" Her voice emerged a whisper, and she turned in her seat to stare at Nick.

"The reason she acted out was because she wanted their portrait taken while she still has all her hair." He glanced over at her. "And while she's still here."

"My God. What kind of cancer does she have?"

"Ovarian. They caught it early and chances are she'll be just fine at the end of her treatment. But you know how it goes. She might not be."

"And the appointment she thought you were going to make her late for this afternoon?"

"Chemo."

"Ah, damn. Which is the reason her hair is thinning, I take it."

"Yeah. She had more last week."

"Of course. It makes sense now, the way she finally relaxed when you said you could touch up today's photo to be as good as the ones you'd taken last week." She studied him for several silent moments. "And her condition is the reason you didn't tell her to get bent when she was going off on you."

"I don't tell any of my clients to get bent, Blondie. Not as long as they're paying my fees. I just let it roll off my back and give them the best photo I can produce." He pulled up to a light and looked over at her, pinning her in place with the fierceness of his blue gaze. "I expect you to keep this information under your belt."

Daisy snorted. "Who am I going to tell, Coltrane—Reggie and the boys? I'm sure they'd give a great big rip."

J. Fitzgerald's hired muscle were on their way back to the Pacific Heights estate that housed Nick's carriage house when the car phone rang. Autry reached for it and punched the receive button. "Yeah."

"Hey, Autry, it's Jacobsen. Coltrane and the blonde we saw yesterday are on the move. I lost them in a traffic jam earlier, but I caught up with them again on Nob Hill just a few minutes ago."

"No shit?" Autry sat straighter. "Good work, Jake. Where are you?"

"On Broadway, just coming up on the tunnel."

"Okay, we're headin' that way. Stick with 'em, and we'll do our best to connect up with you. Oh, and Jacobsen?"

"Yeah?"

"Douglass said for us to do whatever we have to do, to make sure those photos don't surface."

The cell connection started fading in and out. But Autry heard Jacobsen say, "Gotcha," just before the connection was severed.

6
❧

THEY stopped for lunch, then drove to Nick's final appointment of the day. The Trevors were an elderly couple who lived in a plush Telegraph Hill condo with a spectacular view of the bay and Golden Gate Bridge. Eudora Trevor had the spare-boned look of a martinet, possessing the sort of ramrod posture, severe clothing, and a naturally downturned mouth that immediately put Daisy on guard. It just went to show how deceptive appearances could be, however—not to mention the way her day had gone so far—for after Nick's introduction, the elderly woman greeted her with a smile that was singularly warm and sweet.

"Aren't you lovely! Stanley, just look at the way Nicholas' young woman carries herself. Like a young warrior queen." She patted Daisy's hand. "I do so enjoy seeing proper posture." She turned to Nick, who was squatting in front of his duffel bag, unzipping its flaps. "Now, don't unpack, dear. Stanley and I want you to take our photos at Golden Gate Park."

Daisy's heart sank. "Oh, but—"

Her instinctive protest was cut short when Eudora turned back to her and said, "I know we should have arranged to meet you there and saved you the drive, but I wasn't at all certain the weather would cooperate. But it's turned quite lovely this afternoon, hasn't it, Stanley?" Without allowing Stanley the chance to reply, she smiled sweetly and explained, "We're having Nicholas take our photo to commemorate our fiftieth wedding anniversary, you see. And Golden Gate Park is very special to us: it's where we had our very first date."

Knowing that Nick would bend over backward to accommodate his clients' wishes, Daisy simply excused herself to use the phone. Stepping out onto the Trevors' terrace for privacy, she pulled her cell phone from the pocket of her blazer and punched in the office number.

"Parker Security."

"Reggie, find out if any of the boys are available. Nick has a photo shoot scheduled in Golden Gate Park."

Reggie emitted a rude noise.

"Yeah. My sentiments exactly. We're going to need enough guys for a relay surveillance. See who's available and call me right back."

She tapped her foot, looked out at the bay and the bridge, and then turned and leaned against the sun-warmed railing to peer inside the condo at Nick and the Trevors. She glanced at her watch and blew out an impatient breath. Then she pushed off the railing to open the French doors and stick her head inside. "Nick, could I speak to you for a moment?" She gave Eudora and Stanley a forced smile that probably fooled no one.

He stepped outside, regarding her warily. "Blondie, if the Trevors want their photos taken at the park, I have no choice but to honor their wishes."

"I know."

His jaw dropped a bit. "You do?"

"Yes. But given the size of the park, I'm going to need help for the surveillance. I have to know which area to put my guys in."

"Oh. And here I thought you were going to jump down my throat with your dainty blue combat boots." His eyes warmed and he closed the distance between them, putting his hands down on the terrace railing on either side of her hips. The sun picked out the russet and amber highlights in his rich brown hair and turned his eyes bluer than a Caribbean sea, and Daisy's heart stumbled.

"You know," Nick said softly, "Eudora thinks you're my girl. That's a pretty good cover. Maybe we oughtta—" He quit talking abruptly when her hands stole up to cup the back of his warm, strong neck.

"Take a look at the drop off of this balcony," she invited in a low voice, and pulled his head over her shoulder in order to see. From inside the condo, it probably looked as if they were getting mighty chummy. She fingered his ear for good measure.

"It's a steep one." But he didn't seem particularly concerned. He turned his head and Daisy felt first his warm breath, then his warmer mouth as he softly pressed it to the side of her throat.

Hot shivers raced up her spine, and she closed her eyes for a second. Then she snapped them back open and growled warningly, "You don't wanna make me demonstrate my body-throwing abilities, Coltrane."

"No, that's right up there at the top of things I'd just as soon not experience," he agreed. "Second only to having my gonads ripped off and fed to the dogs." Yet rather than backing off, he bent his knees, which enabled him to kiss a spot a little lower on her neck. His hair brushed hot and silky against her chin and along the side of her throat.

Daisy's heart thundered, and it terrified her, how much she liked the way he made her feel. She was reaching for her knife to force him to back off, when the phone in her pocket rang—which was lucky, she decided, since threatening someone she was supposed to be protecting was probably not the best way to promote her professional image.

Sliding her hands to Nick's wide shoulders, she gave him a shove, and he stepped back. She pulled out the phone and punched down the button. "Yeah!" Her breath coming fast and shallow, she lowered her head so she wouldn't have to look at Nick.

"Daise, I got hold of John, Jere, and Benny," Reggie said. "I gotta warn you, though, Benny's in his slut-on-the-skids getup."

"I don't care how he dresses, as long as he's

available." Then she shook her head, even though Reggie couldn't see. "Well, that's not quite true—I'd actually prefer him to be a little less conspicuous, but I can't afford to be fussy." She took a calming breath and expelled it. "I never dreamed we'd end up in this situation, Reg, so I don't have the ear induction system with me. I want you to give each of the guys a set, though, and have them keep in contact with each other. Send along an extra set for someone to slip me if the circumstances allow. They know the drill."

"Who should they be on the lookout for?"

"Beefy bruiser types. Hang on." She looked up at Nick. "Describe your attackers for me."

He did and she relayed the information to Reggie. "Give the boys a description of Nick as the target. Tell them he's wearing off-white slacks, a T-shirt I'd call light brown but you'd probably call something fancier, and—"

"Ecru, maybe?" Reggie suggested. "Mocha?"

"Yeah, whatever. He's also got on an oatmeal colored jacket you'd kill for. Oh, and a camera—don't forget the camera. Hang on a sec." She covered the mouthpiece and looked over at Nick. "Give me a clue where we'll be in the park."

Nick pulled his gaze off the pulse thumping in Daisy's throat and smoothed out his scowl. "The path to the side of the Academy of Sciences." He rammed his hands in his pockets. What the *hell* had he been thinking?

Okay, the truth was he hadn't been thinking at all. He'd seen Daisy standing in the sunlight, not mad at him for once, and had thought Eudora was right: she did hold herself like a young warrior queen. He'd taken in the fragile length of her neck and her fine-boned wrists, and had suddenly wondered what he was doing with a medium-sized blonde with delicate skin and a bad haircut for a bodyguard. She looked eminently more suited to the role of playmate— someone to wrestle around with in bed. It undoubtedly took juvenile behavior to a brand-new depth, given their history and the fact that he'd offered her the job in the first place, but his ego had felt a sharp zing knowing that she saw him strictly as a client.

He'd needed to assure himself that he could fluster her, that she wasn't completely indifferent to him—that was all. So when she'd yanked him over to threaten him with the dropoff, he'd just gone with the flow. It had felt natural and right to nuzzle her neck, and at least he now knew she *wasn't* indifferent. And that felt good. Really good.

The thought made him stiffen, because it was *not* good. The last thing he needed was to dredge up memories of that night for either of them.

Daisy closed the cell phone with a click, which snapped him out of his reverie. He watched her chin come up as she met his eyes.

"Well, there goes my profit margin," she said sulkily. "This is some complicated scheme to see that I don't benefit from the retainer you gave me, isn't it?"

His eyebrows rose. "Uh, a retainer is just an advance against the final charges, doll face."

She huffed out a long-suffering sigh. "I know

that, Coltrane. But I still bet if I dug deep enough, I'd unearth some nefarious motive behind your pretext for hiring me."

Against all logic, her suspiciousness served to cheer him right up. Flashing her a grin, he reached out to tug down the sleeve of her blazer until it once again concealed the exposed hilt of her knife. "There's no pretext about it, Daisy Mae."

She bristled, "My name is not—"

"Yeah, yeah, yeah. Come on." He reached for the door handle and extended his other hand to usher her ahead of him. "The Trevors are all set to go smile pretty for the birdie."

He and Stanley both wanted to take their own cars, so they agreed to meet in front of the California Academy of Sciences. Traffic was fairly light and a short while later Nick squeezed into a parking spot off Fulton. He and Daisy crossed the street and entered the park at Eighth.

"This is insane," she muttered as they dodged cars to cross John F. Kennedy Drive just inside the park.

The last time Nick had been here the street had been closed for in-line skaters, bikers, and pedestrians. But that had been on a Sunday. He watched Daisy as she kept one eye on the cars whizzing past and the other peeled for possible trouble, which, when he looked around, he saw could come from any of a dozen directions. The flat-eyed stare she gave him when their gazes collided was full of disgust.

"You do know, don't you, that you're just begging for trouble when you expose yourself to a place as indefensible as this?"

In truth, watching her try to keep an eagle eye on everything at once did leave Nick feeling pretty exposed, but he shrugged carelessly for her benefit. "Just do the best you can, Daise."

"I always do, Nicky."

He gritted his teeth, but made a mental note not to call her that again. Apparently she reserved the nickname strictly for good buddies like her secretary. "So," he was appalled to hear himself ask, "are you and Reggie an item?"

Her head snapped around. "What?"

"I asked if you and your secretary—"

"I heard what you said. I just can't believe you would think it's any of your business."

He shrugged without apology. "That doesn't stop me from being curious."

Daisy studied their surroundings, then gave him a probing glance before she went back to screening the bushes and trees that lined the avenue. "Whatever's become of the much-vaunted Coltrane manners?"

"I'm standing on them with both feet. Answer the damn question."

"No."

"No, you don't date Reggie, or no, you won't answer the question?" *Take a wild guess here, fool.*

"No, I don't date Reggie." She sounded shocked at the very idea. "He's my best friend."

The men she did or didn't date shouldn't make the least bit of difference to Nick, but his mood lightened anyway. Hoping for a flat denial, he said, "Still, maybe one day it'll ripen into something deeper."

A short, sharp laugh escaped Daisy's throat. "Not likely, Coltrane. Reggie's gay."

Excellent. "Ah," he said with a show of indifference. "Probably not, then." His rabid interest in her love life disturbed him, however. *What's the story here, Ace? You're sure not gonna claim her for yourself—but nobody else gets to have her, either?* It wasn't like him to be such a dog in the manger. He picked up his pace down a gently graded bank, past fat palm trees and bronze statuary.

After entering the music concourse that was ringed by the De Young, Asian, and Academy of Sciences museums and headed by the huge and ornate amphitheater, they circled the fountain and cut through a grove of gnarled trees just beginning to sprout greenery. They were headed for the set of shallow stairs leading to their destination when the transvestite approached them.

For a moment Nick mistook him for a twenty-dollar working girl. It was the shoes that snagged his attention. Never having seen anything quite like them before, his gaze rose no higher than the wearer's ankles.

They had probably been an innocuous pair of black, spike-heeled pumps when they were new. Now the backs had been squashed flat beneath the wearer's mesh-stocking-clad heels, turning pumps into mules. It amazed Nick that anyone could navigate in them, for the spiked heels angled down to the ground at a forty-five degree angle. Fascinated, he raised the Nikon and shot off a couple frames.

It was through the lens that his attention branched out to the entire person. He noticed the wealth of black hair and expert makeup, the exotic sloe eyes and pretty face. He also noted the hooker's hips were nonexistent beneath a tight black miniskirt, and that the slighty bowed legs were too muscular, and the bare shoulders rising above a screaming pink tube top were too wide to belong to a woman.

It was a man dressed in drag, and he was reaching for something in his purse as he headed straight for them.

Daisy's hip brushed Nick's as she stepped in front of him, and he expected to see her draw her gun. Instead, as she and the drag queen drew abreast, a fistful of black gadgetry unobtrusively changed hands. "Thanks, Benny," she murmured and kept walking.

"My pleasure, Daise. I can use the paycheck." The transvestite's gaze rested on Nick for a moment, then he flashed a cheeky smile. "Ooh." He reached out to trail hot pink fingernails down the sleeve of Nick's jacket as he passed by, and his voice floated back on the breeze. "Reggie didn't *nearly* do that face justice. I'd sure hate to see it get messed up just because he's too dumb to stay out of the park."

Daisy snorted and fell back into step with Nick, moving aside her jacket to clip what looked like a small Walkman to her jeans where her waist curved into her hip. She pinned a microphone to the underside of her blazer's lapel and screwed an earpiece into her ear. Nick watched her hand slide into her jacket to press a button on the gadget just as they began to climb the stairs to the Academy of Sciences. "Okay, guys," she said in a low voice, "everybody check in and tell me where you are."

"Walkie-talkie?" Nick guessed.

Daisy glanced up at him, then beyond, her gaze constantly on the move as it swept the area. "It's called a wireless ear induction system. But, yeah, it's a radio."

"Kind of like what the Secret Servicemen use, huh?"

"Okay, gotcha," Daisy murmured to her backup crew and then nodded in response to Nick's question. "Exactly." She looked beyond him and reached out to give him a poke with her finger. "Here come the Trevors."

They went back down the stairs to meet the elderly couple. Eudora flashed them her sweet smile as she approached. "I just saw the most interesting person! I wish I had the words to describe her shoes to you."

"I wish I had the words to describe why she had an Adam's apple," Stanley murmured dryly, but he gave Eudora a gentle smile and her hand a loving pat when she looked at him askance. "Don't mind me, sweetheart. I'm just rambling." He winked at Daisy.

Nick led them to a path next to the museum, and Daisy relaxed marginally once they'd left the open spaces of the concourse and its unlimited potential for ambush. Securing the garden paths was a much more manageable proposition.

Nick stopped when they came to a fallen log off the side of the path. "Let's start here. Eudora,

Stanley, take a seat on the log. No, down just a little. There, perfect. The greenery will make a great backdrop." He set down his bag and started pulling out equipment.

Daisy moved off to where the path intersected with another. Pushing down the transmitter button on her radio, she said, "Benny, keep an eye on the entrance to the path we entered. John, Jere, come past us and take up positions at the next two intersections. Report your situation when you're in place."

A moment later John and Jere strolled past. Fifteen minutes after that Nick moved the Trevors to a different spot within the network of intertwining paths, which necessitated moving her men. But then it grew quiet. Listening to her three helpers through the earpiece as they rhapsodized over Nick, she kept an eye on her paths and watched Nick charm smiles out of the Trevors. And she secretly hankered for a little less quiet. Professionally, inactivity was a desirable objective. But personally, it gave Daisy too much time to reflect on what a fool she'd been to take this job.

Had she really thought that enough time had passed, that because she'd learned well from Nick not to trust, it had somehow nullified her ability to ever be hurt by him again? To be *attracted* to him again?

Yes. She had. Such self-deception spelled only one thing in her mind, and that was *simpleton*. In huge, bold, uppercase letters.

She had tried so hard not to think of Nick since the night he'd left her in that hotel room all alone. And when she *had* thought of him, all she'd remembered was the bad stuff. Like having him say he loved her—only to immediately turn around and virtually tell her to grow up, that she couldn't believe what was said in the throes of sex, before he'd turned his back and walked out on her. She had somehow believed that remembering the utter pain of that would save her from ever falling back under his spell. It had slipped her mind how charismatic he could be. She'd forgotten the abundance of his charm, the lure of his humor.

He used both qualities to hold people at arm's length, and it said something about the force of his personality that no one ever seemed to realize what he was doing. She'd never seen his charm slip with anyone but herself. That should have been her first clue, but idiot that she was, she'd even romanticized that, convincing herself she was the one person with whom Nick could be himself.

What a chump she was.

She took a deep breath and blew it out. Okay. So she still felt a smidge attracted to him—big deal. Acknowledging it was half the battle. She could handle it. She'd start by keeping him well out of neck-kissing range.

But where the hell was all the action she'd counted on to keep her mind focused? It would help if she had some bad guys to fight—the bursts of adrenaline that came from physical confrontations were an excellent antidote to sexual frustration. It was beginning to look as if Nick had overestimated Johnson's determination to retrieve his adulterous wife's pictures.

Still, she instructed her team to institute a relay surveillance when she saw the photo shoot begin to wind down. Jere moved up to Benny's spot at the path entrance, while Benny moved to the grassy bank that formed the Kennedy Drive border of the concourse, and John followed behind. She was proud of their synchronization as she and Nick bade the Trevors farewell and made their way back to the car. The guys passed and repassed each other, one taking up where the other left off, so there was always someone front and back, keeping an eye out. And it was handled with such subtleness that Nick appeared not to notice. If Hubby's henchmen were anywhere about, which was looking more and more unlikely, Daisy doubted they'd notice either.

"And that's a wrap," she murmured into the mike as they reached Nick's car. "Nice job, guys. I'll call Reg and instruct him to cut y'all a check."

Nick had unlocked her side of the car and gone around to his own. She heard him swear beneath his breath and start pawing through his equipment bag.

"What's the matter?"

"I used a filter at the first location," he replied without looking up. "I remember setting the thing on the log when I took it off, but I don't remember picking it up again." He pawed through the bag some more, then wrenched open the car door and stuffed the bag in the small space behind the seat, his frustration evident in the way he manhandled it into place. Straightening, he stared at her over the top of the car. "Dammit to hell. I'd better go get it." He slammed the door and headed back across Fulton.

"Nick, wait." She squeezed between the parked cars. Down the street she heard an engine roar to life and an intuition she never argued with made the tiny hairs on the back of her neck stand up. She broke into a run. "Coltrane, move your ass out of the street!"

Daisy's voice broke into the haze of Nick's frustration, and he looked back to see her running at him hell for leather, her hand reaching into her waistband for her gun. He swung his head around to follow the direction of her gaze, expecting to see one of the men who had broken into his place the other day.

Instead he saw a black car with dark windows. It peeled away from the curb and accelerated with a roar, going from zero to sixty in under ten seconds—headed straight for him.

7

❧

HE froze for an instant in sheer surprise and the car bore down on him, a quarter ton of gleaming black steel, snarling horsepower, and lethal speed that grew larger and louder by the second. It was only a few feet shy of mowing him down where he stood when Daisy hit him with a flying tackle and knocked him out of its path. The car missed them by mere inches and Nick felt a heated whoosh of air as it screamed past.

A second later, he and Daisy hit the parking strip. His breath exploded out of his lungs as his recovering shoulder slammed into the ground; then Daisy belly-flopped over his hip and jarred his shoulder all over again. Her hands scrambled against the grass in an attempt to break her fall with something other than her nose, which was heading toward the ground at warp speed. He rolled onto his back to remove the fulcrum from her stomach, and she collapsed cattywampus atop his torso.

She lay draped across him for a moment, wheezing to regain her breath. Then she pushed back onto her knees and swung around, her gun out and her gaze intent as she stared in the direction the car had disappeared. A moment later she lowered the gun and Nick watched her shoulders relax as she turned back to him.

"I don't think they're coming back." She tucked the gun into its inside holster and looked at him. "Are you okay?"

"Yeah."

"How about your shoulder?" She reached out to touch it. "You smacked it pretty hard."

"One more bruise at this point hardly matters one way or the other." He rose up onto his knees. Adrenaline pumped through his veins and all he could think of was, "You saved my life."

Daisy shrugged. "Just doing my—"

"*Jesus*, Daise, they were going to freakin' run me down. Can you believe that? They tried to *kill* me. You saved my life!" He hooked his hand around the back of her neck and hauled her against him.

She looked as wild-eyed as he felt, and he dipped his head and kissed her, hard and deep, his hunger nearly outstripping his control. For one brief instant he was aware that her mouth was hot and her body was firm where they pressed together from knee to chest. Then his cognitive processes shut down, and he dove into the feelings headfirst.

Daisy would've stopped him in a red-hot minute if she'd had a second to prepare for it. But he caught her flat-footed, and Nick was a dynamite kisser. His mouth was insistent, his tongue commanding, and flames licked through her veins with every urgent sound that rumbled low in his throat. It was exactly the way it had been nine years ago: he touched her and she was lost. Wrapping her arms around his neck, she kissed him back.

He groaned and tightened his arms around her, nearly cutting off her breath. One of his hands speared through her hair and gripped her head; the other wrapped around her hip. Everywhere he touched, heat radiated. She felt his mouth gentling and he raised his head just long enough to change the angle of the kiss. His eyes burned with a blue flame as he stared down at her, and she couldn't prevent the little yearning sound that slipped up her throat.

"*Yes,*" he muttered roughly. Then he came at her again, his mouth hot and uncivilized in its demand.

She felt feverish and out of control as she parried the cocksure slide of his tongue with her own. She clung to him, dimly aware of the pulsing of her heartbeat in her wrists, in her throat, between her legs. Plunging her hands into the thickness of Nick's hair, she curled her fingers to hold him fiercely in place.

Then a voice demanded, "My God, are you two all right?"

It shattered the haze of frenzied passion that had her in its grip, and as footsteps pounded up the sidewalk, awareness exploded into Daisy's consciousness like fireworks in a Chinatown parade. Her eyelids snapped open.

Nick seemed oblivious and she pulled frantically at the hair wrapped around her fingers. He resisted the pressure and kissed her harder, and to her eternal shame she was desperately tempted to sink back into the sensations. Which was *not* the way to keep her emotional distance from a man who had already demonstrated his ability to rip her heart right out of her breast and then step over it and walk away as if it didn't lie bleeding at his feet. She fisted her hands and yanked.

Nick lifted his head and blinked unfocused eyes at her. Their breath sawed in and out of their lungs as they stared at each other. Then Daisy let his hair slip through her fingers and brought her hands down to his shoulders, shoving back. She jumped to her feet.

Dear God, what had she been thinking? They'd been going at it like a couple of cats in heat right in the middle of a public parking strip! Heart thumping much too fast, she pressed the backs of her fingers to her lips and winced at their tender, swollen state. How on earth had this come to pass? The rush of adrenaline from their near miss with the car must have short-circuited her brain.

The inconvenient portion of her mind that always insisted on self-honesty feared there was much more to it than that. But for the moment, that was her story and she was sticking to it.

"Daisy . . ." Nick climbed to his feet and reached for her arm, but she snapped it out of his reach as if his fingers were made of fire.

It seemed like a millennium since the car had tried to run Nick down, but in reality only a few moments had passed. The man whose voice had interrupted their kiss skidded to a stop in front of them and leaned over to brace his hands on his knees as he sucked air into his lungs. His stomach sagged over the belt of his polyester slacks.

"You saw the incident, sir?" Daisy addressed the spreading bald spot at the crown of his head, desperate to gather a cloak of professionalism back around herself. She watched as his insta-matic camera swayed back and forth where it dangled in the triangle formed by his back, arms, and thighs.

Still braced, he raised his head. "Yeah," he panted. "That was some fast footwork, lady." Cocking his head, he looked at Nick. "You nearly bought the farm, boy. I can see why you were kissin' the little lady here—you must be some grateful, and sometimes a guy's just gotta reaf-firm he's still alive and kickin'." He looked from one to the other. "So, you two okay, then?"

There was a beat of silence. "Yes," Nick re-plied, and Daisy nodded, knowing that if the heat throbbing in her cheeks was anything to go by, they must be candy-apple red.

"I couldn't believe my eyes when I saw that car heading right at ya." The man straightened and shook his head. "Guy musta been drunker 'n a skunk."

Or very determined. Daisy kept the thought to herself. "Did you get his license plate number by any chance?"

"No, sorry. Me 'n Mama were up there about a block away." He pointed across the street behind them, and Daisy blessed the fact that his position had prevented him from seeing her pull her gun. Civilians tended to freak when they saw people aiming pistols on a public street. "It happened so fast," the tourist added, "and I was too far away."

"Nick?" Daisy forced herself to look at him. "Did you get a look at the plates?" Her hands had left his hair all rumpled, and a shiny hank fell over his eyes, which were heavy-lidded as he stared at her without blinking. He looked unnervingly predatory and sexual.

"No." His eyes lost their sleepy look and blazed with intensity. "Listen, Daisy, we should talk—"

"Neither did I. Damn. We're not going to have much to tell the police."

The stranger looked alarmed. "You don't need me for that, do you?" He glanced over his shoulder. "I gotta get back to the wife. We only have today and tomorrow left of our vacation, and I'd just as soon not spend the rest of the afternoon in a police station, if it's all the same to you."

"I think you can safely forgo that pleasure," Daisy agreed. She was conscious of Nick watching her and found it difficult to concentrate. "I don't anticipate that they'll have any questions for you, since you didn't see anything that Nick or I didn't see as well. Still, I'd like your name and the hotel where you're staying, if you don't mind. That way, if they do have an inquiry for you they can get in touch."

He gave her the information, and she wrote it down in the little spiral notebook she always carried on the job. When he left she turned back to Nick, tilting her chin to a belligerent angle to discourage a discussion of the much-regretted kiss.

Since talking about it was the last thing Nick wanted to do, either, he escorted her back to the car in silence. For a rash moment or two, with the taste of her still lingering on his tongue, he'd been tempted to try to define with her just what this relationship of theirs was supposed to be. Happily, that flash of insanity had quickly passed. They didn't *have* a relationship. The word alone was enough to give him chills, since it was a term designed for starry-eyed dreamers.

But that was hardly his biggest problem at the moment. The crisis *de jour* was what J. Fitzgerald had set in motion.

The man had tried to have him *killed*. Sweet Jesus. Never in his wildest imaginings had he envisioned anything like this. But if the car had succeeded in running him down, it would have been murder, pure and simple. That wasn't an everyday occurrence in the crowd he ran with.

And the kicker was, Nick had absolutely no way to prove it. Shock began to give way to pure, cold rage.

"We should go to the Richmond station," Daisy said, "since this is their territory."

He scowled at her. "You realize we've got bupkus to offer for evidence, don't you?"

"Yeah."

"So what the hell is the point of filing a report?"

She slicked a hand through her hair and Nick watched it spring back up again in the wake of her fingers' passage. "The violence is escalating, Nick. At the very least this attempt should be on record. It will help establish a pattern when we do come up with a provable claim."

Odds were, even if he could shake Daisy long enough to share with the police his suspicions that Douglass was behind this, he wouldn't be given much credence. Even if he showed them the prints, all those actually proved was that J. Fitzgerald was an adulterous lech.

It was enough to turn a grown man into a snarling maniac.

He slammed through the Porsche's gears, and the car bottomed out when he took a hill too fast. Spearing a glance at Daisy, he expected to be told to slow down, but she didn't say a word. He slowed down anyhow. The police station was only a few blocks away.

The photos should provide enough incentive for the cops to at least question J. Fitzgerald. That would be a start. After today, Nick wanted nothing more than to see the hypocritical old prick fry—but realistically, he knew that, warming as the thought might be, it was unlikely to happen.

But wouldn't it be a cushy little irony if it did? If by some miracle the cops actually found the evidence to arrest Douglass, Nick's photos would be even more valuable to the tabloids than they were now, and the bids would go up accordingly. Not only would that keep his sister out of jail, but he would also be off the hook for going public.

The odds were heavily against him, but it had an infinitesimal chance of working. Only, however, if he made sure Daisy was nowhere around when he talked to the cops.

He pulled into the lot adjacent to the station house. Killing the engine and pulling on the hand brake, he looked over at her. "You wanna wait for me here?"

Daisy snorted and climbed out of the car.

Okay, you didn't actually expect her to go for it. While it was hard to imagine an idiot ballsy enough to try something right outside a police station, he knew she'd never let him walk unprotected from the lot. He climbed out of the car.

The Richmond station was an attractive old brick building with cathedral windows. Stubby wings protruded on either end of the building, and angled white brick defined the arch around the wing windows and the entrance door. Nick smiled crookedly at the long-suffering look Daisy gave him when he beat her to the door and held it open for her; then he followed her inside.

As he was mulling over how to shake her long enough to make his report, an incredulous female voice called out, *"Parker?"* And he thought there must be a God in heaven after all.

A dark-haired woman in street clothes walked rapidly down the hall toward them, smiling warmly. "I don't believe my eyes," she said. "Is that really you?"

"Gellahty?" Daisy laughed, and it struck Nick that she hardly ever did that anymore. He remembered her laughing a lot when she was a kid. "What are you doing here?" She strode forward to meet the woman.

"A position opened up and I transferred from Oakland a couple of months ago," Gellahty replied.

"You made detective?" Daisy laughed again as she gave the woman a spontaneous hug. "Congratulations, Sheila!"

"You know who else is here? McGee. Hang on a sec." The detective whirled and strode midway back down the hall. She stuck her head in a doorway. "Hey, Maggie. Come see what the cat dragged in."

A tall black woman came out and looked askance down the corridor. Then her dark face split into a brilliant white smile. "Daisy Parker, as I live and breathe!"

"Ach, and how is my little Irish colleen?" Daisy's laughter was deep-throated and contagious. The women met halfway and exchanged enthusiastic hugs.

Nick smiled as he walked over to the officer manning the front desk and asked to see a detective. There was something about seeing Daisy so open and happy that got to him. It certainly wasn't a side he brought out in her; the only smiles she ever bestowed on him were edged in cynicism.

The desk officer advised him to take a seat while he hunted down the appropriate officer. Nick leaned against the nearest wall instead and braced the sole of one foot against it. Raising his camera, he snapped off several frames of the women while they exchanged friendly insults and station house gossip.

"How about you, Daisy?" the dark-haired

women asked. "What have you been up to since you left the PD?"

"I opened a security firm. It's barely more than a fledgling at this point, but I'm hoping to get it off the ground." She glanced over her shoulder at Nick, then turned back to her friends. "Which brings me to why I'm here."

Shit! His smile fell apart and he dropped his foot from the wall and pushed upright. "Uh, Daisy? Could I talk to—"

A plainclothes detective walked out at that moment and said, "Mr. Coltrane?" just as Daisy turned back to her cohorts and said, "Someone just tried to run my client down with a car. He took nude photos of a married woman a while back, and the husband hired some muscle to get his hands on them. They already dislocated his shoulder and we're here to file a report of the latest incident." She turned back to Nick. "Shall I bring them up to speed, or do you prefer to do it yourself?"

All three women regarded him with expectant expressions, and even the male detective gave him his full attention, although he appeared a bit confused.

Well, fuck. If that didn't just blow everything to hell and gone. Nick barely resisted the temptation to bang his head against the wall behind him.

What was he supposed to do now? If he told the truth in the wake of Daisy's little setup, he'd discredit her in the eyes of her ex-coworkers. She'd look like a fool and be humiliated. Yet he could hardly file a false report featuring some fictitious husband/wife team. He refused to dig this pit any deeper for himself than he already had.

It left him only one choice, really. In order to spare Blondie's pride, he'd have to decline to cooperate. The decision had nothing to do with the fact that his life wouldn't be worth a plug nickel if she found out he'd been lying to her. The sacrifice was strictly for her.

"I've changed my mind," he said. "I don't want to file a report."

"What?" Daisy whispered. She couldn't have felt more incredulous if Nick had suggested something obscene about her mother. Feeling as if her professional expertise were under fire, she looked over at Sheila and Maggie. They'd adopted cop faces—that noncommittal bland look police everywhere wore when they were assessing a situation. She snuck a glance at the detective who had just shown up. He shrugged and patted his chest pocket, where a pack of cigarettes formed a distinctive bulge. With a look of longing at the entrance door, he leaned against the wall. Daisy looked back at Judas Coltrane. "Why?"

He drew himself up and demanded, "Is this the way the police conducts its business—in the middle of a hallway?"

He was right, and she wanted to smack him. In her excitement over seeing old friends, she had bypassed the usual protocol.

He didn't appear interested in a response, however. Shoving his hands in his jacket pockets, he said with the cool prep school diction he could sometimes affect, "What Ms. Parker failed to mention is that we didn't get a license plate number, which means we haven't any proof."

Everyone turned to look at her. *Oh, God, it just keeps getting better and better. I should've let the damn car run him down.*

Gathering the remnants of her authority around her, she opened her mouth to calmly explain why she'd urged him to file a report without proof.

Nick redeemed himself, if only a smidgen, by adding, "She did say filing a report would show a pattern in the event we get a provable claim, and I agreed because it made sense to me."

It was probably immature to let it matter so much, but Daisy nevertheless felt much better when the detectives nodded approvingly.

But Nick obviously didn't know when to shut up. "I had time to consider the big picture, though, while I waited for the detective here," he said, nodding at the man against the wall. "And I concluded that the risk outweighs the benefit."

"What risk?" Daisy demanded. "You simply have to give a statement."

"And will that statement then be shuffled to the bottom of the stack or perhaps buried completely?"

"Certainly not," Detective Gellahty said with a look of reproval. "A detective will be assigned to talk to the husband."

"Exactly. And that's where I start to have a problem. My, uh, friend is separated from her husband. He's not happy about it, and having the police question him is not a risk I'm prepared to take at this time. It could very well set him off." He gave them all a look. "Let's face it, trying to have me killed today was not exactly the act of a rational man. What if having the police involved just pushes him over the edge entirely and he decides to turn his ire on his estranged wife? It would be my fault."

Daisy itched to say that it was his fault anyway for getting involved with a married woman in the first place. But the male detective nodded, and McGee said, "It's a viable dilemma." Not wanting to appear any more unprofessional than she already had in front of her former coworkers, Daisy turned to them and said, "Since we don't know who's responsible, we can leave that part blank. But I still recommend filing a report of the attempt."

"She's right." The detective pushed away from the wall. "The reasons she gave you still hold true, Mr. Coltrane, so why don't you both come with me and we'll get today's incident on record." He opened a door and stood back for them to precede him.

Nick looked at Daisy and shrugged. Keeping her expression carefully neutral, she extended her palm toward the opening. "Mr. Coltrane," she said stiffly. "After you."

8

&c&c

"YOU did *what*? Hang on a minute." J. Fitzgerald
cupped his hand over the phone's mouthpiece
and said to his driver, "Close the window,
please." The divider rolled silently up to the ceiling and he removed his palm from the phone.
"Who's bright idea was that?"

"You said to do whatever it takes, sir," Autry
said. "So when Jacobsen saw an opportunity to
remove Coltrane, he took it."

"I never said to *kill* the man!" Not that it might
not be necessary somewhere down the road, but
right now there was no percentage in having
Coltrane dead. "I said to do whatever it takes to
retrieve the film. Killing Coltrane serves no purpose if the damn photos surface anyhow."

"Oh. You're right, of course. Sorry, Mr. Douglass."

He ground his teeth against the rage that
burned beneath his breastbone. But it wasn't for
nothing that he was this close to an ambassadorship. His voice was smooth and empathetic
when he said, "It wasn't your fault. But I'm

counting on you to get the word out to the others. I don't want any more screwups."

"Yes, sir."

"Thank you, Autry. I know that I can count on you." J. Fitzgerald disconnected the cell phone and slipped it into the inside breast pocket of his tux. Fucking morons. What did a man have to do to get decent help these days?

The limo crested California Street and glided silently past Grace Cathedral. A few moments later it purred to a stop in front of the Fairmont Hotel. J. Fitzgerald blew out a deep breath and shelved his frustration. He straightened his bow tie and smoothed a hand over his hair. By the time the door was opened for him and he stepped out to meet his public, his trademark benevolent smile was firmly in place.

Nick took the phone into his bedroom and shut the door. He dialed the first number on his list and listened to it ring three times before it was picked up.

"Yeah! *National Inquisitor*."

"Hank Berentinni, please." Nick heard the ebb and flow of conversation, the ringing of telephones, and the discordant squawk of fax machines in the background.

"Hang on a sec." The receiver was banged down on a hard surface. "Berentinni! Somebody wants ya, man."

He listened to the soft clack of hunt-and-peck tapping on computer keys until another line was picked up.

"Yeah. This is Berentinni."

"This is Nicholas Coltrane."

"Hang on." Berentinni's voice, muffled most likely by a hand over the mouthpiece, called, "Jackson! Hang up your phone." There was a click and the background noise lowered several decibels. Berentinni's voice was clear when he said jovially, "I'm all yours, buddy. What can I do for ya?"

"That's up to you. You can either play the whatever-does-he-want game, or you can tell me you've given serious consideration to my one-time-only proposition and you're ready to make me an offer I can't refuse."

"I tell ya what, Nick—can I call you Nick?"

"No."

"I'll tell ya what, Mr. Coltrane. I talked to my editor, and he's leery about buying pics sight unseen."

"Uh-huh. And you told him that Nick Coltrane said he's got photos that're gonna send your readership right through the roof."

"Yeah, that's exactly what I said. But you won't even disclose who you took the photos of—"

Of course he hadn't. The tabloids would send their own stringers out in a New York minute if they had the first idea what they were looking for. They'd rather line their own pockets than a middleman's. The fact that they would never in a million years trip to what he'd stumbled across with Douglass didn't enter into the calculations. Profit was the name of the game.

But this was one game he knew how to play. "Well, hey," he said. "If you're not interested, you're not interested. Sorry to have wasted your time." He laid back on the bed and stared up at the ceiling.

"Wait a second!" Berentinni yelped. "I didn't say we weren't interested. I just said we're leery about buying a pig in a poke."

You just wanna see how low you can drive the price, you mean. "How long has your rag been trying to buy my photographs, Berentinni?"

"I don't know. A long time."

"Right. A very long time. So don't fuck with me. You know damn well my sudden willingness to sell means I need the dough."

"Yeah. You'd think you'd be grateful we're willing to make you an offer."

Nick got a quick flash of how Daisy must have felt when he'd said something similar to her. "Well, let me clue you in on a little secret, Hank," he said easily. "I've always had this Things-Happen-If-They're-Meant-to-Be philosophy. So if I don't get the offer I'm looking for, then obviously it wasn't meant to be." His voice hardened. "What's it gonna be for you? Is the *Inquisitor* in, or is it out?"

"We're in. But it's gonna take a couple of days for the money men to come to a decision."

"You've got until six p.m Friday. Mail or have your bid couriered to this address." He rattled off the post office box number he used for work. "My decision will be determined strictly by the highest bid, so you might want to keep that in mind. I guess I'll either hear from you Friday or I won't. See ya."

"Wait! Give me a number where you can be

reached in case any questions come up."

"Forget it. And I'll tell you the same thing I'm telling everyone else: you call my home number or leave a message on my machine, and you're automatically disqualified. No second chances." He hit the disconnect button, then dialed the next number on his list.

Forty-five minutes later he hung up on the final call. Tossing the phone on the bed, he plunged his fingers through his hair and scraped it back from his face. He pressed his temples between the heels of his hands in an attempt to ease the headache thumping there.

He should feel great. Hell, he should be breaking out the champagne. It looked as if he were going to get the money he needed to help his sister. All he had to do now was stay alive until Friday night.

It wasn't fear of Douglass' goons that had his gut tied up in knots, however. Selling to the tabloids was a slap in the face of every damn thing he believed in. If Mo's situation wasn't so serious—if she didn't need way more money than she and Reid could raise on their own on short notice—there was no way in hell the yellow journalists would get within fifty miles of his photos. But her situation was dead serious, and if he had to whore his talent in order to get her out of it, then that was what he'd do.

He ground the heels of his hands in harder. Christ, what a day. In the space of a few hours, he'd damn near been run down by a car, kissed Daisy, lied to her and the police, and pledged to prostitute his art to every pimp in town who had a bankroll large enough to make it worth his while.

Yes, sir. A regular red-letter day.

When the going got tough, Nick believed in punching it out. So he stripped down to his boxers, tied on some gloves, and feinted and jabbed at the punching bag hanging in the corner of his bedroom until sweat flowed from every pore. Then he tossed back some aspirin, splashed cold water on his face, and pulled on a T-shirt and a pair of jeans. He headed for the kitchen to throw together something to eat.

Only to find that he still felt too misused for the exercise to have its usual soothing effect. He kept looking up from the pile of vegetables he'd assembled on the chopping block to where Daisy sat fiddling with her weaponry in an overstuffed chair across the room. She hadn't spoken a word to him since they'd left the police station, and while he'd appreciated the silence at first, now it began to grate.

It didn't help that she'd changed into a tank top; the way she looked in it just contributed to an already bad case of unrelieved tension. He didn't give a damn that it had warmed up steadily throughout the afternoon or that his second-floor apartment was stuffy. If she were the professional she said she was, she would have kept on her long-sleeved T-shirt. He'd bet his last dime she'd stripped down simply to aggravate him—probably her nonverbal way of saying, *Take a good look at what you can't have, buddy*.

One thing was for damn sure: he shouldn't

have kissed her this afternoon. Maybe if he
hadn't, he wouldn't be in such a lather now over
what she wore.

Or it was entirely possible that the circumstances were just getting to him. The tourist
probably had the right idea: following his close
shave, Nick undoubtedly would have kissed the
first person he'd seen just to reassure himself
that he was still in one piece. It was a blatant
case of survivor syndrome. Anyone at all would
have done.

The problem was he hadn't kissed just anyone;
he'd kissed Daisy. And he'd known perfectly
well how good it would be. Daisy kissed like she
did everything else in life: with a full-steam-
ahead, damn-the-torpedoes kind of passion. It
wasn't the sort of thing a guy forgot in a hurry—
no matter how many years had gone by—and
Nick could kick himself for reopening all the old
cravings and regrets he'd thought long buried.

He reached for a chef's knife and sliced the
ends off two celery stalks. Dammit, he *had* buried
those things once before, and he could do it
again. His control was stronger than any random
sexual urge.

He struggled with Daisy's silence and his own
thoughts for another minute or two, determined
to hold his peace. But in the end he folded. "You
going to sulk all night, Blondie?"

She spared him a cool glance before going
back to her knives and guns. "I don't sulk, Coltrane."

As much as he hated to admit it, she rarely
did. She neither pouted nor complained. She

simply grew very quiet and looked straight through him.

Damned if he'd concede the point aloud, however. It bugged the bejesus out of him just how much her withdrawal was getting to him. Stoic was overrated, if you asked him, and considering how edgy he felt, he longed to see a reaction from her. He didn't even care if it was a negative one, as long as it was a response. "What do you call the silent treatment you've been giving me, then?"

"Keeping my own counsel."

"Yeah, right." He cleaved a red pepper in two and cleaned out the seeds. "Like I said, cupcake—sulking."

Daisy shrugged. "Call it whatever you want. I have nothing to say that you'd care to hear."

He gave up. She'd talk again when she was good and ready, and not a moment before. And what the hell, chances were he wouldn't have to wait that long, anyhow. He hadn't met the woman yet who could stand to keep her mouth shut for more than an hour, and Daisy was already well over the limit. "Whatever. You play with your little war toys, then, and I'll cook dinner. You hungry?"

She didn't bother to look up again. "I could eat."

He fantasized shaking her until her teeth rattled. But when his fantasies immediately hared off in another direction, he just as quickly roped them in and applied his knife aggressively to the veggies on the cutting board. Five minutes later, he scraped the vegetables into the wok on the stove. They hissed as they hit the splash of hot olive oil and rice vinegar in the bottom.

He called her to dinner a few moments later and they sat down to the places he'd set at the breakfast bar. If he'd hoped that the mundane act of eating would cool his raging emotions, however, he was doomed to disappointment. Every time Daisy reached for her milk glass, the scooped neckline of her tank top gaped. He couldn't see more than a hint of the goods within, but that sure as hell didn't prevent him from giving himself eye strain trying. The portion of rounded flesh that he did catch a glimpse of was enough to convince him she wasn't wearing a bra, and the turmoil in his gut increased. By the time dinner was finished and she politely offered to clean up, he was ready to climb the walls. He watched her jeans pull tightly over the curve of her butt when she bent to load the dishwasher; his gaze tracked the dusting of freckles atop her shoulders and the smooth slide of muscle in her arms when she wiped down the counters. Shoving back abruptly from the bar, he said, "I'm going down to the darkroom for a while. I've got negatives to develop."

Daisy gritted her teeth. Great. It had been one damn thing after another all day long, and her emotions were dangerously close to overload. This was *just* what she needed to cap off her day—to be cooped up in a tiny room with Nick Coltrane.

She bit back a sigh and tossed the sponge into the sink. Her personal wishes weren't the issue; it was her job to protect him. "Give me a second to throw on a T-shirt." The garage was likely to be cooler than it was up here.

Nick, who had grabbed his duffel bag and strode down the short hallway, stopped dead with his free hand on the doorknob. He scowled back at her. "What for? You aren't coming with me."

Daisy was in no mood to argue. "Of course I am. It's the reason I'm here."

"I'm only going down to the damn darkroom."

"Well, correct me if I'm wrong here, Coltrane, but isn't that the same place Johnson's thugs trashed the other night, right before they dislocated your shoulder?"

He shrugged. "So I'll lock the door."

The look on his face made her feel like the importunate social climber the people in his world had always considered her. She was accustomed to that from others, but not from him, and she stared at him in silence for a moment. Then she turned on her heel and walked back into the living room.

She fully expected to hear him slam out of the apartment, and for a moment she didn't care if he did. She was furious and felt unaccountably betrayed for the second time in too-few hours. Instead of the door opening, however, she heard his bag drop and his shoes slap against the hardwood floor as he came after her. Flopping down on the couch, she picked up a magazine and feigned an interest in pages that might as well have been blank. Her entire focus was on Nick as he skidded to a halt and loomed over her. She immediately locked on his agitation.

Good. She didn't like feeling tense all by herself.

"I can't breathe, dammit!"

He couldn't breathe? Oh, God, that was rich. She hadn't taken a deep breath since the moment he'd strolled back into her life. She'd done her utmost to keep him from seeing how deeply he affected her, but she felt as if she'd been living on the ragged edge of her emotions *forever*, and this was the last straw. Tossing aside the magazine, she surged to her feet. "Go, then! By all means, put yourself in danger. It's no skin off my teeth, bud—I've got my retainer either way."

He towered over her. "And that's all you really give a damn about, isn't it, Daisy? Your money."

"As a matter of fact, I give a great big damn about my reputation—something you made eminently clear this afternoon you have no respect for. So, fine." It wasn't until she thrust her chin up at him that she realized just how close they were, and she took a giant step back. Reaching for some composure, she offered flatly, "I've given you my professional opinion about going down to the darkroom alone, but I can't force you to abide by it. So go do whatever the hell you want." She turned away.

His hand clamped down on her wrist, whirling her back. Off balance, she slammed up against his solid chest, and his other hand reached out to grip her upper arm, steadying her. "Just because I declined to file a report doesn't mean I don't respect the job you've done," he snapped. Letting go of her arm but retaining his hold on her wrist, he headed for the door, forcing her to trot along in his wake or be jerked off her feet.

Daisy saw red. Damn him to hell! He was the only person in the *universe* who could routinely force her to lose her cool without even half trying. Breathing rapidly, reaching deep for control, she patted her gun and fantasized how satisfying it would be to shoot him right where he lived— in his big ego.

Nick must have caught a glimpse from the corner of his eye, for he snarled, "You pull your weapon on me, you better be prepared to use it." Glancing over his shoulder as he bent to retrieve his bag, he added, "And don't even think about tossing me in another one of your fancy martial arts maneuvers, Blondie, because I'll sue your pants off. If you're such a freakin' professional, then act like one." He loped down the stairs and she had the choice of keeping up or being bounced willy-nilly behind him like a pull-toy on a string.

White-hot rage rose up her throat. "I do act like one! Maybe if you'd quit sabotaging my efforts—"

"Oh, grow up. If you hadn't blurted out my business in the middle of the police station lobby, I would've been more than happy to tell you in private that I'd changed my mind. I would've even given you my reasons why."

Since she already harbored a huge load of

guilt over that, the accusation effectively shut her up.

They entered the garage, which was several degrees cooler than the apartment upstairs. Goosebumps cropped up on Daisy's arms as Nick dragged her to the back, where his darkroom was located. Pulling her inside, he shut the door and snapped on a light.

She jerked her arm free. "Happy now, Tarzan?"

"I'll be happy the day I get that homicidal maniac off my back and my life under control again." He frowned as she briskly rubbed her pebbled arms. His gaze glanced off her chest, and the next thing she knew, he was yanking his T-shirt over his head. "Here," he said, tossing it to her. "Put that on. I didn't give you a chance to grab your own."

All the moisture in Daisy's mouth dried up as the small room seemed to constrict in front of her eyes into a single wall of bare skin. She hurriedly pulled the shirt over her head, grateful for the excuse to block Nick from view. But his bare chest was right there to taunt her again the moment her head popped through the neck opening. The new crop of goosebumps that raced down her arms had an entirely different origin than the ones that had prompted him to give her the shirt off his back.

"This really isn't necessary," she said, but hugged the shirt around her to absorb its retained body heat. Her gaze stubbornly refused to look away from his body.

Oh, God, this was awful. How on earth had

she ever forgotten how gorgeous he was without his clothing? Taking a deep breath, she forced herself to concede that she hadn't actually forgotten, so much as blocked the memory out of her mind.

And, oh, Lord. For a very good reason.

Between Nick's height, his loose-limbed way of moving, and the relaxed-fit clothing he favored, it was easy to underestimate the power of his build. Stripped to the waist, however, that power was impossible to ignore.

His shoulders and chest were broader than she remembered, but still defined by lean layers of muscle. Soft veins snaked beneath the skin on his forearms, and dark hair spread a virile fan across his chest before dwindling into a silky stripe down his diaphragm and stomach, to disappear beneath the waistband of his jeans. And he was golden-skinned all over.

That was one of her most persistent memories of him: that he always seemed so golden. She'd never been able to figure out quite why that was, since he was not a man to lie around in the sun. Yet she remembered him glowing in his tennis whites on the club court when she was sixteen. And she remembered his tawny skin glistening with a fine sheen of sweat as he'd propped himself over her on a cold November evening.

Oh, shit, oh, shit. She would not remember that. It had hurt so much and had taken *forever* before she'd been able to block it out, and she was damned if she'd allow it to get a toehold on her emotions now.

Trying to find a spot where she'd be out of the

way in the tiny room, she observed the play of muscles in Nick's back as he pulled bottles off the overhead shelf, and sternly assured herself that the tension coiling inside of her had nothing to do with the sight of a little skin. And even if it did . . . *Focus,* she urged herself. *All you have to do is focus on something else.*

"Hit the lights, Daisy."

She started. "What?" She was desperately grateful when he pulled on a ratty, once-white lab coat and began buttoning it up.

"The lights. Turn 'em off, will you? The switch is on the wall behind you."

She flipped the switch and drew in a deep breath of relief as the room plunged into absolute blackness.

9

NICK welcomed the sudden darkness. He was so visual that he could still picture her, even without the light. But at least the sights and textures that had bombarded him were given a chance to pull back from the edge of meltdown.

He felt along the countertop in front of him for a roll of exposed film, popped the top off its tiny plastic canister, and tipped it out into his palm. He wound the film onto a stainless steel reel. Placing the reel on a spindle, he felt for another roll of film and continued the process until all five reels were safely in the light-tight canister. "Okay. You can turn the lights back on."

Narrowing his eyes against the sudden glare, he reached for the brown plastic jug of developer and measured it into the tank with the can of reels. He set the timer and stood over the tank, gently agitating the canister in a steady side-to-side movement, using care not to cause bubbles, which would increase the graininess of his negatives.

"It's pretty labor-intensive, huh?"

Daisy's voice jerked him out of the semi-trance of concentration he always fell into when he developed negatives. *Now* she wanted to talk? Murphy's Law was clearly alive and well. For a few brief moments he'd been able to forget that he shared a very small room with a woman who kissed like something out of his hottest wet dream. He'd managed to forget the sight of her nipples poking at the thin material of her tank top, and the sexual tension that had tied him in knots since walking into her office yesterday had momentarily melted away.

It came roaring back. "Yes," he replied tersely.

"How come you don't use one of those red lights?"

"Because I'm developing film, not paper. When I make my prints, I'll use the red light."

The timer went off and he drained the developer, added stop bath, then went back to agitating, glad that she'd fallen silent again. A short while later he drained the tank again and reached for the fixer, but it wasn't there. Douglass' goons had emptied it all over the floor. Swearing softly, he remembered he'd meant to pull a new jug out of the storage cabinet, and he turned to get it.

Daisy stood in front of the cabinet door, and without thinking he grasped her by the hips and moved her aside. He felt her stiffen beneath his hands.

"Hey!"

"Sorry. But I need this now." Although time was of the essence, he really wished he hadn't touched her. Even though his hands had cupped her hips only fleetingly, it'd been long enough to register that she was warm and firm. The tension in the little room ratcheted several degrees higher.

Cracking open the new jug, he turned back to the workbench and then added the fixer to the tank.

He was grateful for the work that required his attention during the next several minutes. He agitated the container occasionally, then checked his negatives and returned them to the fixer, repeating the process until the films were clear. Once he put them in the wash, however, he ran out of excuses to ignore Daisy.

He heard a rustle behind him, and could picture her shifting her weight from one foot to the other. He knew without looking how the tilt of her hip would ease in, and how a second later she'd cock the opposite hip. He located busywork to occupy his hands, capping and putting away jugs of chemicals, wiping up spills with a brown-stained rag—anything to promote the pretense that the room wasn't steadily shrinking around him. And all the while, he was aware of every breath she drew, every move she made.

Finally he tossed the rag aside and turned to face her. "Listen, the negatives need to stay in the wash for at least half an hour. We might as well go back upstairs." *Where there's room to move without tripping all over each other.* He stripped off his lab coat, tossed it on a hook, then turned to herd her toward the door.

His intention was to decrease this wracking awareness and put some space between them, but it went up in flames the moment they both reached for the doorknob at the same time.

His bare arm slid along hers, and her skin was warm and soft and smooth, and the cool control in which he took such pride evaporated like mist before a blowtorch. An animalistic growl sounded low in his throat, and he whirled her around and crowded her up against the door, leaning into her, reveling in the soft feel of her breasts as they flattened beneath the press of his chest. He bent his head and kissed her—a hot, undisciplined kiss that was all dominance. His fingers gripped her head to hold her still as he plundered her mouth, but even in the face of his aggression, Daisy kissed him back for several scorching, breathless minutes.

Freeing a hand, he yanked up her borrowed T-shirt and slid a hand onto her tank-top-covered breast. It was a soft, round, giving weight beneath the press of his hand, and her nipple drilled like a diamond bit into his palm. He curled his fingers, shaping and tugging, molding the sweet form to his will.

He felt her hands work between their bodies, and he groaned at the feel of skin against hot skin when her fingers splayed against his chest. Then she gave a shove and he stumbled backward. His back hit the counter and he grabbed for the edge with his elbows. Blinking at Daisy through the hank of hair that fell over his eyes, he watched the rapid rise and fall of her breasts beneath his too-big T-shirt, and felt sluggish and stupid as he struggled to comprehend the abrupt shift in gears.

"What . . . ?"

Daisy looked back at him, and with her pulse hammering in places that only seemed to have a pulse with him, it felt as if she were viewing him through the narrow end of a long, red, pulsating corridor. She saw him with crystal clarity, however. Even wearing a befuddled expression and slumped with his elbows hooked over the counter behind him, there was something magnetic about him.

And if that wasn't a poisonous trap poised to spring, she didn't know what was. She watched him straighten up. "You keep your distance, Coltrane," she ordered in a raspy voice when he took a step toward her. Suddenly, containing the bitterness that she'd tucked away for nine long years was like trying to hold water in a colander: it leaked messily everywhere she turned. She watched him roughly finger-comb his hair out of his eyes and refused to be sucked in by the perfection of his face or the symmetry of his hard torso. "You had your shot at me when I was nineteen—and you didn't think I was worth keeping. Well, that was your only chance, you son of a bitch. Once you've thrown me away, you don't get another."

He stared at her as if she'd just suggested he'd broken the last remaining law of decency. "I didn't throw you away! I know I handled things poorly that evening—"

Daisy pulled her gaze away from his chest and laughed bitterly. "You think 'poorly' handles it? That must be one of those understatements you prep-school boys are so fond of. I thought you were a *prince,* but it turned out you were nothing but a frog. My, God, I was a virgin—"

"I didn't know that!"

"Maybe not when we went up to the room," she conceded ungraciously. "But—"

"I didn't. You wore that slinky little dress—"

She felt her jaw sag. "Are you saying that I was *asking* to get laid?"

"No. Yes. *No,* dammit. But you gotta admit you acted as if you knew the score."

"How? By dancing with you at the reception? By *flirting*? My God, Nick. You swept me off my feet. I thought you were so . . ." *Dazzling. Interested in me.* Until that night, he had acted as if she were just a pesky little kid, and she could still remember the thrill of having him treat her like a woman. Yes, she had flirted, but how could she have possibly done otherwise? He'd been a god, golden and exciting, and he'd made her feel exciting, too.

She refused to admit anything of the kind now, though. She'd sound like an infatuated dork. Giving her head an impatient shake, she searched determinedly for the conversational thread she'd dropped. "Besides, if you didn't know I was inexperienced going in, you sure as hell knew it by the time the deed was done."

God, yes. Nick was forced to acknowledge that he'd had no excuse. His finger had discovered proof of her virginity during an intense moment of foreplay. He could have, *should* have, stopped it right there.

But he hadn't. After fighting his basic instincts for what had felt like a millennium, he'd been consumed by the powerful chemistry that had drawn him to Daisy since the first moment he'd clapped eyes on her.

For years she'd been the featured player in some of his hottest, sweatiest fantasies, but until that moment he'd convinced himself that he would never give in to a lust he had no business feeling in the first place. He was stronger than that, he'd assured himself; more honorable by leagues. Hadn't he kept himself at a safe distance when they'd lived in the same house? And once their parents had broken up, hadn't he put her firmly out of his mind? Hell, yes. He'd pursued women his own age, made friends with his fist. He'd taken a lifetime's worth of cold showers.

But Mo had gotten married that night. And while he'd been happy for his sister, he'd also felt cut adrift as he'd watched his one constant ally forsaking all others to cleave unto her new husband.

And there Daisy had been, with her laughter and her warmth, and her flirty little dress and big, admiring eyes. He had fought the good fight, dammit; had fought it for a very long time. It had simply been beyond him to continue the fight when he'd had her naked and aroused in his arms. Somebody was going to relieve her of her virginity, he'd figured; it might as well be him. At least he could make it good for her.

As if she'd read his mind, Daisy said fiercely, "You were happy enough to relieve me of my virginity, but, boy, the minute you got yours, you couldn't wait to get out of there."

All Nick's defenses slammed into place. "What

did you expect, Blondie? That I'd say making love with you was better than anything I'd ever experienced before? That I'd suggest we rush right off to the nearest justice of the peace?" He made his tone deliberately mocking, because the truth was he'd been tempted to say and do exactly that. And it had scared the shit out of him.

Daisy's laugh was caustic. "No, I certainly knew better than that. But you said you loved me while you were screwing me, so neither did I expect you to roll right off me and head for the door." She hugged herself, and he noticed with surprise that she was shaking. "Call me a starry-eyed optimist, Coltrane, but I'd just given you something that I'd vowed to hang on to for my husband. I don't think an 'atta girl' would have been out of place."

To Nick's utter horror, Daisy's voice cracked on the last word and tears pooled in her large eyes, making them look enormous. Smart-mouthed, indomitable Daisy . . . crying? Before he could react, she spun on her heel and fumbled for the doorknob. He reached out for her, but the minute his hand touched her shoulder, Daisy jabbed back with her elbow, catching him in the gut.

"Back off!" She pulled the door open. "I'll stand guard out here."

The door slammed shut behind her and, rubbing his abdomen, Nick turned to lean against it. Then he slid bonelessly down its surface until he sat on the cool concrete floor. Propping his elbows on his knees, he ground the heels of his palms into his eye sockets. He felt as if he'd just been hit between the eyes with a sledgehammer. God, he was an idiot. A *blind* idiot.

How else could he have convinced himself that she'd forgotten that night? God Almighty, she'd been a flaming virgin—of course she remembered. That wasn't the sort of thing a woman just blew off. He'd been her first lover and had left her high and dry shortly after introducing her to something pretty damn momentous. It hadn't been as bad as she'd made it out to be, but the truth was, he'd protected himself at her expense. How could he have been so obtuse as to believe she'd actually forgotten about it?

His hands dropped away and his head thunked back against the door. Okay. It was not one of his brighter conclusions, obviously. Daisy wasn't exactly the sort of woman to simply forgive and forget. But until two minutes ago, he'd been convinced that night had impacted him alone, and for that he had to give the little lady a cigar. She was one cool customer. The Daisy he knew had always been brutally honest, so when she'd looked at him as if he were an egotist for thinking she might recall the way they'd burned up the sheets together, he'd fallen for it hook, line, and sinker.

Not that she'd flat-out lied. She hadn't come out and actually said she didn't remember. But she had looked right through him, and she'd pretended she didn't recall how long it had been since they'd seen each other, and he'd made the precise assumption she'd wanted him to make.

He pushed to his feet. So now he knew better.

The real question was, where the hell did they go from here?

"Absolutely nowhere—that's where we go." Back in the apartment, Daisy stared at him as if he'd sprouted an additional head. "You think just because you've come to some nine-years-belated revelation that this is a brand-new situation?" She looked down her nose at him—quite a feat, Nick thought sourly, for someone who was a good eight inches shorter than he was. "Think again, Coltrane."

What he thought was that if he were the least bit intelligent, he would have given her more than a lousy hour to cool down. Daisy's eyes were narrowed and her lips pressed together until all hint of softness was eradicated. "I don't suppose you'd accept my apologies at this late date, either?"

"You've got that right, bud. You can take your lame apologies and stuff 'em. There was a time when I would have loved to hear them. I don't care anymore."

It rankled, but damned if he'd let it show. "Good for you. Then you can just sit here and pout." The insulted tilt of her not-so-dainty nose warmed the cockles of his heart. "I'm going to call my sister."

"Yeah, well . . . tell her hello for me," Daisy muttered and stomped away.

Reid was just contemplating how quiet an empty house could be when the phone rang. He snatched it up before it had a chance to ring a second time. "Cavanaugh residence."

"Reid? It's Nick. Is Mo around?"

"No. She's showing a place tonight."

"Oh." The line was silent for a moment, then Nick blew out a soft breath and said, "It's not as if I really have anything to report, anyway. Just tell her I haven't come up with the money yet to get her out of her jam, but I do have a pretty good bidding war going with a few of the tabloids, and I'll hear something definitive by Friday night. How about you; have you come up with anything?"

An icy knot gathered in Reid's gut. Nick hated the tabloids—only something extremely serious would compel him to sell one of his photos to one. But he managed to say, "I haven't had any luck yet, either." Jesus. What the hell had Mo gotten herself into? And why did Nick know about it, when he didn't?

"Did you find out what she needed the money for?" Nick asked. "She wouldn't say, but you know Mo. It had to be to bail someone out of trouble."

Oh, fuck. Fuck, fuck, fuck. "Me," Reid said, but the word was barely audible and he had to clear his throat. "She paid off a loan that I'd co-signed. I was mad at her for not trusting me to handle it myself. And now she's . . ."

"In serious shit." Nick blew out a breath. "You can't take the responsibility on yourself, though, Reid. You and I both know she has a bad habit of smoothing over other people's problems— whether they care to have them smoothed or not. And she sure as hell didn't think this one through before she jumped in with both feet." Nick was silent for a moment, then said, "Well, listen. I'll call the minute I've got something to report. You do the same, okay?"

"Yeah, okay." Reid didn't remember hanging up the phone. He sat in a stupor in his soft leather chair, hunched over with his elbows on his widespread thighs, blindly staring at his loosely clasped fingers as shadows crept across the hardwood floor.

The entire room was enveloped in post-twilight gloom by the time he heard the front door open and close. He watched his wife cross the foyer and waited for her to step out of her heels and set her briefcase on a shelf of the small table before he spoke.

"Your brother called."

Mo slapped a hand to her breast and whirled to face the archway. "My God, Reid, you scared ten years off my life!" She walked into the living room. "What are you doing sitting in the dark?" She bent to turn on a table lamp.

"Wondering where you got the money you used to pay my loan."

Mo froze. "You say you talked to Nick?"

"I did. And a funny thing, Maureen—he has information about some trouble you're in that he thought I knew about, too." His fingers tightened as he met her eyes. "We both know that isn't true. So, I ask you again: how did you pay off my loan?"

She collapsed onto the couch perpendicular to his chair. "I borrowed from one of my escrow accounts."

His knees went weak, and in a far corner of his mind he acknowledged it was a good thing he was already seated. "You did what?" She merely stared at him over her white knuckles as they mashed her lips against her teeth. "But that's . . . not legal." And the last thing Mo would ever do was something criminal. "Why would you do that?"

She brought her hands down, fingers tightly woven together, to rest in her lap. "I thought I was helping you."

She'd wanted to help him? It surprised Reid that she'd bother. She'd been so distant for so long, he'd pretty much begun to assume she'd merely stuck with him out of a stubborn refusal to give anyone the opportunity to say, *Like father, like daughter.* It shocked him to think she would risk not only her reputation but her very freedom for him.

For the first time in months he looked at her closely. Not just at her elegant features or shiny brown pageboy, but at all of her. Mo was a big woman, tall and well rounded. He'd always liked holding her; she'd felt substantial in his arms. Today, she appeared smaller.

Somehow that made his hopes rise, which no doubt said something unflattering about his character. But she was always so relentlessly efficient that he'd long felt superfluous to their marriage. When she'd finally accepted that nagging wouldn't halt his habit of making high-risk personal loans, she'd gone out and started her own realty firm without so much as an iota of input from him. That had hurt, and his response

had been to focus on his own interests while ignoring hers, which had caused her to distance
herself further yet. Maybe now, though, he could
finally do something for her. He unlinked his
hands and leaned forward. "What made you
think that putting yourself at risk would help
me?"

"It was only supposed to be for a day or two,"
she said. "I'd sold an apartment building on Nob
Hill, and my commission would have more than
covered what I borrowed. I should have been
able to replace the money without anyone being
the wiser. Except . . ."

When she just sat there staring at the pale
tangle her fingers made against her coca silk
skirt, he prompted, "Except?"

She didn't look up. "Except the inspection
turned up substandard wiring, and the seller
doesn't think it should be his responsibility to
bring it up to code, and the buyer is talking
about backing out. And until they get it straightened out"—her plump shoulders sketched a
brief shrug—"no commission." She raised her
gaze to meet his eyes and he was shocked to see
tears standing in her eyes. Crying was not something he associated with Mo.

"I'm such an idiot, Reid. A *criminal* idiot." The
tears trickled over her lower lids and slid silently
down her cheeks.

"No, you simply took a gamble that you
thought had good odds, and the odds turned on
you. But the good news is"—he reached out to
gently wipe away her tears with his fingertips—
"you're talking to the King of Bad Odds. I know

all about turning bad ones into decent ones. So dry your eyes, honey, because I'm going to make it my number one priority to turn this mess around for you."

10
❦

wednesday

DAISY awoke slowly. She rolled onto her back, draping her arm over her eyes against the annoying light that filtered through her eyelids. She yawned hugely. She stretched. Then slowly, reluctantly, she lowered her arm and opened her eyes.

Wearing nothing but a pair of khakis, Nick squatted next to the couch, and the shocked breath she sucked in at finding him there resulted in a girlish "eek". Her hand slapped to her chest in a reflexive bid to contain the sudden kick of her heart...and encountered the warmth of skin.

She scrambled upright, aware of her bare arms and legs as she reached to the foot of the couch where she'd kicked the sheet. The apartment still retained a hint of last night's stuffiness and sunshine streamed through the windows. All indications pointed to a hotter day than yesterday. "What?" she snarled as she pulled up the sheet and tucked it under her armpits. She retrieved her gun from under her pillow. "What now?"

"Here." Nick thrust a steaming mug into her hands, and her eyes closed in ecstasy as she inhaled the aroma of freshly brewed coffee. Cracking one eye open, she gave him a wary once-over as she sipped from the mug. She sure wished he'd put on a shirt. All that skin and muscle was distracting.

He rose to sit on the trunk that served as a coffee table. Reaching back, he pushed the corner of her weapons case from under his rump; then he straightened and regarded her without favor. "You sleep like the dead."

"Well, excuse me. You'll be happy to know I don't charge for my sleeping time."

"Great. I'll take immense comfort in the knowledge when the goons goose-step past you to blow me away in my bed."

She lowered the mug. "What do you suggest, Nick, that I sleep with one eye open? Or perhaps you'd prefer that I didn't sleep at all."

"I didn't say that!"

"No, you only implied my sleep patterns make me incompetent." She eyed him over the rim of her cup. "On the other hand—and much as I hate to give you credit for anything—you do have a point. Maybe you should think about hiring someone else for the night shift." *Then I could go home and regroup—and maybe have a better handle on this crazy situation during the days.*

"Oh, yeah, I'll give that some real thought . . . the minute I earn enough money for another retainer." He stood and shoved his hands in his pockets. "Speaking of which, get dressed. We've gotta leave in half an hour."

"Dammit, Coltrane!" Daisy erupted from the couch, coffee sloshing, sheet slipping. She set the mug aside and rose to glower at him. "What will it take to keep you off the streets? Didn't yesterday teach you *anything*?"

"Sure it did. From now on, I look both ways before I cross the street." He shrugged his bare shoulders. "I have bills to meet, Blondie—obligations to my clients."

"You have a death wish, is what you have."

He ran a chemical-roughened fingertip down her forearm to the hand holding the gun at her side. "You're the one who keeps telling me how good you are."

Her flesh rose in the wake of his touch, and she slapped his hand away. "I am good. But if you refuse to exercise any precautions there's only so much I can do to ensure your safety." Despite his flippant attitude, she sensed an underlying anger in him that she didn't understand. But she saw by the closed, stubborn set of his face that she was wasting her breath arguing, so she pushed past him. "Fine. I'll go get ready." Her arm inadvertently brushed the warm skin of his side and the awareness that immediately stood every nerve on end maddened her.

Standing beneath the pounding spray of the shower a minute later, she wondered why on earth she still clung to a job that had disaster written all over it in foot-high, flaming letters.

Yes, she needed Nick's retainer. And certainly she wanted her business to succeed. But this was insanity—Nick pushed all her buttons, brought out her worst personality traits. Every minute spent in his company wound her tighter than a cheap watch, and at the rate she was going she was bound to blow sky high before too long. Then there would be hell to pay.

Nick obviously didn't respect her expertise, and she couldn't even lay the blame for that solely at his door. Not when she kept behaving so unprofessionally. She'd failed time after time to use her head when circumstances called for it and had reacted instead with a blind impetuousness most adolescents would be embarrassed to claim. Nick was the only person she knew who could annihilate her control without breaking a sweat. He annoyed her; he infuriated her.

He excited her.

No, darn it, he did not. She stuck her face in the spray.

Then she pulled it back out again and reached for the shampoo. *Skim the edges of the truth with him if you have to, Daisy. But don't pull that ostrich number on yourself.*

Damn. This honesty-is-the-best-policy business was for the birds. It was a cliché. Hell, it was *naive*. Tact alone decreed that honesty be circumvented on a daily basis to avoid crushing people's feelings right and left. And God knew she had been known to bend the truth a time or two to suit her own purposes.

Still. She tried as much as possible to avoid putting herself in those situations. And she made it a practice to never, ever lie to herself. So, taking a deep breath, she admitted that Nick did, indeed, excite her.

He'd kissed her last night as if he owned her, and instead of being outraged right down to her soul, she'd promptly fallen in with the program. It had been her protective instincts that had hauled her back from the brink—and even then, even knowing she couldn't trust Nick as far as she could throw him, it had been much harder than it should have been to push him away. So, yeah, she supposed it was safe to say he excited her.

Daisy rinsed the shampoo out of her hair. Flattening her palm against the side of her breast where her heart beat out a too-rapid tattoo, she blew out a frazzled breath.

Okay, she lusted. Big deal; she would simply have to handle it. Having emotions didn't mean you had to act on them. She would learn to cool down when dealing with Nick, to act in the mature manner she used with everyone else in the world. Cool and calm, that was the ticket. And just to get her started . . .

She cranked the shower knob all the way over to cold.

"Let me get this straight," Daisy said between her teeth less than an hour later. "You risked life and limb to photograph a *dog*?" She peered at the glossy little creature on the red silk pillow. "That thing *is* a dog, isn't it?"

The animal's mistress picked up the tiny, pure white animal and cuddled it to her breast. "Miss Muffet is not simply a *dog*, Miss Parker. She's a purebred Maltese." Bestowing a glance of disdain on Daisy, she settled the pup back on its silken perch and straightened the little bow that clipped the animal's long bangs back from its forehead.

"Sorry. Sure didn't mean to insult any pedigrees." Daisy looked at Miss Muffet's silky Fu Manchu and at her luxuriant coat, which was so abundant as it hung in a waterfall to the floor that its weight caused the little dog's tail to curve to the side. "You gotta admit, though, that if you sprayed her with a bit of Endust, you'd have yourself a handy little table-duster."

"That's enough, Blondie," Nick snapped.

Daisy turned on him willingly. He was the one she had a problem with, anyway. "Oh, it's not nearly enough, Coltrane. I'm just getting warmed up—"

Nick held up a peremptory hand that notched Daisy's temper a few degrees hotter, then turned his charm on his hostess. His smile was a benediction that visibly smoothed the woman's ruffled feathers. "Would you and Miss Muffet excuse us for a moment, Mrs. Sawyer? I'd like a word with my assistant."

Daisy took an incensed step forward. "Dammit, Coltrane I am *not* your—"

"Certainly." Mrs. Sawyer spoke to Nick as if Daisy didn't exist. "Perhaps you'll utilize the time to teach the child a manner or two." She swept out of the room. The Maltese's round, slightly protuberant dark eyes, peering at Daisy over Mrs. Sawyer's shoulder, were the last thing she saw as the dog's mistress closed the door behind them.

She swung back to face Nick, ready and willing to rumble. Then she caught herself. *Control yourself, dammit. Just, for once in your life, stay in control with him. You know what needs to be done.*

She sucked in a deep breath and thrust out her bottom lip to exhale, causing random tendrils that had fallen over her forehead to flutter. She opened her mouth, but had to take a second and then a third breath before she could force herself to say with quiet dignity, "I'll see you safely home after you take your photos of the dust mop. Then it's time you hired a security specialist more compatible to your temperament."

Nick had already taken the step that brought him looming over her, but he froze and, staring down at her, blinked. "What?"

"I'll have Reggie tally the charges for my time so far; then Parker Security will return the balance of your retainer to you."

"You can't just walk out in the middle of a job!"

"Oh, yes. I can. You clearly have no respect for my abilities—"

"That's bullshit!"

"It's not bullshit. You've disregarded every recommendation I've made so far. Well, I'm cutting my losses, Nick, before something happens and I have to live with my failure to keep you safe."

"So that's it, then? You're just gonna run scared?" Temper surged behind narrowed lashes. "What's the matter, Blondie, afraid you can't cut it in a man's world after all?"

The temptation to lash out was sugar sweet, but she managed to swallow her fury. "Yeah," she agreed coolly, although it left a bitter taste on the back of her tongue. "That must be it."

He gave her an insolent once-over. "Wuss."

"That's charming, Nick. And it's exactly that attitude that makes it impossible for us to work together. You're gender-biased."

"*What?*" He looked down his nose at her. "That's ludicrous."

"No, that's reality. You refuse to take advice from a woman and you won't keep your hands to yourself."

"Ahhhh." The sound held a wealth of enlightenment, and he regarded her with a raised eyebrow and such a supercilious expression that she longed to claw it off his face. "*That's* what this is all about. I kissed you last night and it reminded you of old times."

"No!" Then honesty compelled her to add, "Well, yes, I suppose that's partly true."

"Partly, hell—that's it in a nutshell. Well, let's just talk about the night of Mo's wedding before you go haring off like a scared little bunny rabbit—"

"Now, wait just a damn minute!"

"No, you wait, Daisy." Hands on her shoulders, he backed her against the nearest wall, where he caged her in with his body and his arms. "You've had your say ad nauseam; now it's my turn. And my memories of that night are a little different than yours. For instance, I sure as hell don't recall knocking you loose the minute I came, the way you say I did."

"For God's sake, Nick!" Heat flooded her face. But blue-hot fury burned like a gas flame in the depths of his eyes, and her discomfort at his frankness took a back seat to the realization that *this* was what had fueled the temper she had seen in his eyes earlier. The anger hadn't gone away; it had merely been biding its time, looking for an outlet.

"What's the matter, you don't like my version of the story? Too damn bad, doll face, because I remember holding you for a long time after I got mine." He pushed back. "But feel free to stick to your interpretation if it keeps you warm at night. Either way, I've apologized for it. I truly am sorry, and if you don't want to pick up where we left off, fine. But it's been nine years, for chrissake. Get over it."

"Get *over* it?" She felt like screaming, like shooting him between the eyes, like crying. Then pride kicked in and she elevated her chin. "Fine. I'm over it. But you're still a pig."

His nostrils flared, but his voice was prep-school cool when he said, "In the past couple of days, I've been threatened, roughed up, and run down. Being a New Age sensitive guy is just a little beyond me at the moment."

She snorted. "Like you've ever been that at the best of times." She straightened the tail of her sleeveless blouse and slipped past him. "Call in Mrs. Sawyer and the dust mop, Coltrane. I'll use the time you spend taking the pup's picture to see if I can come up with a security specialist in your price range."

The tension in the Porsche was thick enough to serve up as a side dish by the time Nick wheeled the car into the carriage house and cut the engine. He was edgy and angry and felt like picking a fight, but that wasn't possible because some Blondie clone had usurped Daisy's personality. Who was this cool-eyed, distant woman who responded to every dig he produced, no matter how snide, with equanimity? Jesus, she'd even apologized to Mrs. Sawyer and made friends with the pooch; by the time they'd wrapped up the photo shoot, Mrs. S was saying how utterly *charming* she was.

It was enough to make him put his fist through the nearest wall.

She turned in her seat and looked at him with such an un-Daisy-like lack of expression that his gut churned. "I came up with two names that might work for you," she said coolly. "Mitch Jones or Dega Gonzales. Both of them charge rates comparable to mine, and they're both pretty good."

He glowered at her. "Pretty good doesn't cut it, cupcake. I want the best."

"That's unfortunate, then, because I'm no longer available." She reached for the door handle.

Her fingers had barely grazed it when the passenger door was wrenched open and a beefy hand reached into the car and hauled her out.

"What the—?" Nick leaped out of the driver's

side, only to freeze in horror as he stared at the tableau on the other side of the car. One of J. Fitzgerald's minions had Daisy by the arm—and held a gun to her temple.

"Let her go," Nick ordered hoarsely. His hands curled into fists on the roof of the car.

"Shut up, faggot." If anything, the man's grip on Daisy tightened. He was built like a refrigerator—a big, solid rectangle with no discernible neck. "I want those negatives, and I want 'em now."

"She doesn't have anything to do with that. Just let her go and—"

"Give me the negatives, hotshot, or your little girlfriend here gets a bullet in the head." The barrel of the gun pressed into Daisy's temple.

Christ. She looked so little next to the muscle-bound bruiser. So fragile. Every bit of moisture in Nick's mouth evaporated. "Yeah. Okay. Whatever you say. I'll get them—just don't hurt her." He pushed back from the car.

"Smart choice, pretty boy." The thug looked down at Daisy. "And he is a pretty one, isn't he, sweet thing? How do you stand it? I mean, the guy's hair is longer than yours, he's a sharper dresser, and he's just plain better-lookin'—not that I'd chew my arm off rather than risk waking you gettin' outta your bed." He caressed her cheekbone with the barrel of the gun and Daisy made a sound of distress. Her hand flew up protestingly to pull on his wrist, and Nick took an instinctive step toward them.

"What I'm sayin' here is you're far from coyote-ugly," the thug assured her. Then he shrugged. "Still, you're no centerfold, you know what I mean? And it's gotta be tough havin' a boyfriend who looks better than you in the morning."

"It's the bane of my existence," Daisy agreed. Suddenly she did something to the man's wrist that made his hand go slack. The gun that had been pointed at her head tumbled to the garage floor, and with a smooth, fast movement she thrust out her hip and bent forward . . . and two hundred pounds of gangster sailed over her head to land on his back with a horrendous crash on the hood of Nick's car.

Nick jumped back. "Holy shit, Daise!"

Reaching for her gun, Daisy dove after the thug. Her pistol hadn't yet cleared the holster, however, when he rolled onto his side and, with a roar, sat up and took a swing at her. She stopped in her tracks, her head jerking back, but she wasn't quick enough to avoid the punch entirely. His fist caught her on the shoulder, and the force of the blow spun her sideways and threw her against the wall. She felt something sharp prick her back as she fumbled beneath her shirttail for the butt of her Glock. Time seemed to stand still as she watched No-Neck roll off the car and come after her. Then her piece cleared her waistband, and he skidded to an abrupt halt as he found himself on the receiving end of the nine-millimeter she pointed at his chest.

"You don't wanna make any sudden moves," she advised. "I'm feeling kinda cranky."

"Uh, Daisy?"

"Just a minute, Nick." Keeping an eye on No-

Neck, she pushed away from the wall and moved over to where his gun had fallen. Stooping, she swept it up and stuck it in her waistband.

"The asshole here's got something to say that you might wanna lend your attention to, little lady," a new voice said.

Damn! Daisy turned her head. Another bruiser had his gun on Nick, who stood directly in her line of fire. The second thug was even larger than his buddy, but unlike his cohort, he had a neck. His forehead was flat, though, and his nose was even flatter. Moving so she could keep an eye on the new threat and still keep her gun trained on No-Neck, she glanced over at the flat-faced man. "I guess this is what they call a Mexican standoff, huh?"

"Looks like. Tell ya what. Right now I'd just like to get outta here with everyone's skin intact. Let's do a little horse trading, whataya say?"

It was far from ideal, but . . . "I guess I can live with that." Her eyes narrowed at Blunt Face's rough handling of Nick and she snapped, "You put one scratch on Coltrane, and all bets are off."

"He kept me from putting an end to this shit once and for all, girly, and for that I oughtta kneecap the sonzabitch."

"You do that, and I'll just have to do the same to your buddy here."

"Yeah, I know—that's why I'm being such a reasonable guy." Blunt Face maneuvered Nick around the hood of the Porsche, and he clearly knew his trade, for he kept his own exposure to a bare minimum.

She was trying to figure out the logistics of the trade when Blunt Face gave Nick a hard shove, careening him into her. They stumbled against the wall and got caught up in a tangle of arms and legs, and by the time they got themselves sorted out, the goons had disappeared from the carriage house. Swearing, she ran out of the garage and down the drive. She rounded the curve just in time to see the thugs drop from the tall gate onto the sidewalk. Halting, she braced her gun hand and took aim, but she hesitated to shoot into a residential street. A car squealed to a stop in front of the two hired guns. They piled in, and the car took off in a cloud of smoking rubber before the door had even closed.

She jerked the gun up. "*Shit!*"

Nick skidded to a halt next to her. "They got away?"

"Yes, dammit. We better go call the—"

He grabbed her by the shoulders and whirled her around. "Are you okay? Jesus, you took ten years off my life when you started wrestling with the refrigerator."

"I'm fine." She shrugged off his hands. "Listen, we better—"

"Son of a bitch!"

"What? Are they back?" She whirled to face the street, her arms once again extended in a shooting stance. She expected to see the goons bearing down on them and was almost disappointed when there was nothing to see. She had a snootful of unspent adrenaline running rampant through her system and it urged her to action, any action. She turned her scowl back on

Nick. "Don't *do* that—I could've shot an innocent bystander." He had an odd look on his face,
and she stepped closer. "What was that all about,
anyway?"

He stared down at his hand, then held it up
for her to see. "Dammit to hell, Daisy. You're
bleeding."

"WHAT?" For a moment Daisy stared blankly at the blood on Nick's hand. Then her mouth rounded in an O of comprehension, and she twisted to see over her shoulder. "I must have caught a nail; I felt something when No-Neck knocked me into the wall."

Nick tweaked back the armhole of her blouse and sure enough, there just beneath her shoulder blade was a puncture wound. It oozed blood and, grasping her wrist, he hustled her up the drive and around the corner of the carriage house. He kept seeing flashes of her flying backward when No-Neck slammed his ham-sized fist into her. He also saw a repeat of Goon Number Two turning his gun on her when her attention was on Goon Number One. Fury bubbled in his veins as he hauled her up the staircase to the apartment. "You don't have the sense God gave an amoeba."

"Excuse me?"

"What the *hell* were you trying to do, Blondie?"

"My job." She danced in place like a kid in need of a bathroom while he jammed his key into the lock. "Oh, man, I've got an overload of adrenaline. It feels like an army of ants under my skin."

"Does your freakin' job call for you to get yourself killed? Jesus, Daisy! And you said *I* have a death wish." In a distant part of his mind he knew he was overreacting, but she'd scared the shit out of him. And fear was all too willing to transmute into fury.

"For heaven's sake, Nick, it was just a little pop." She rubbed her shoulder and gave him a rueful grin. "Okay, the guy had a fist like a sledgehammer, but *killed* is sorta overstating the case. And the hole in my back was inadvertent. It doesn't even hurt, and I doubt it's all that serious. I'm up to date on my tetanus shots anyway, so lighten up." She punched him on the arm. "C'mon! I told you I was good."

He dragged her into the small bathroom, flipped down the toilet seat, and had her straddle it facing the tank. She submitted meekly enough, but as he collected supplies from the cabinet, she twisted back and forth to watch him and jitterbugged restlessly in place.

"Take off your blouse." He tipped the bottle of hydrogen peroxide over a cotton ball and scowled down at the gouge in her back when she complied. "If you're so damn good, how come the second guy almost got the drop on you?"

"Blunt Face? Get outta here!" She planted her hands on her knees and bounced her legs in a surplus of nervous energy. "He didn't get the drop on me." Nick sat on his heels to clean out the wound, and she hissed when the soaked cotton came into contact with it. Then, the pain apparently forgotten, she twisted to peer at him over her shoulder and flashed him a great big pleased-with-herself smile. "You saw for yourself; it was a draw."

"No. When he pointed his friggin' gun at *me* it was a draw. But that wasn't until after I knocked his arm away from pointing the damn thing at you." He reached for the antibiotic salve.

Daisy's smile faltered. "What?"

Her revved-up satisfaction had been like steel wool on his raw nerves, but now he wished he hadn't been quite so quick to burst her bubble. "Face front, you're gonna get a crick in your neck." She did so unquestioningly, and he looked around to see if the world as they knew it had come to a screeching halt.

Nope. He gently applied the salve and a bandage, dividing his attention between the chore and her bent head. There was something about her nape that looked so . . . vulnerable. He found his fingers reaching out to touch it.

"Come on, Coltrane, you gonna give me a few details, or what? Spit it out."

His hand fell back to his side. Checking over his handiwork, he said crisply, "You're patched up as good as it's gonna get. You can turn around now."

She spun around and he handed over her blouse. Sticking her finger through the hole in the back, she grimaced at the bloodstain surrounding it. "I not putting this back on." She lobbed it into the wastebasket and surged up off the toilet seat. "C'mon," she ordered, and it was clear she wasn't talking about following her as she charged from the room. "*Talk* to me."

"You ever consider joining the Army, Daisy? You'd be a natural as a drill instructor."

She stopped dead outside his bedroom door and whirled to confront him, her chin thrust out at a belligerent angle. "I've been patient, dammit." She didn't even blink when he snorted; she just prodded him in the chest with her finger. "Tell me about Blunt Face pointing a gun at me."

"Okay, all right." He gazed down at her, trying to ignore the way she filled out her little white bra. "It all happened pretty fast, remember. Still, I'm sorry I didn't do anything to help when you and the bruiser were duking it out."

Daisy's expression was a study in surprise. "You have no reason to apologize."

"I just stood there with my thumb up my ass while you—"

"Nick," she interrupted with surprising gentleness, "I was *trained* for this sort of thing. Believe me, I know all too well how sudden violence can paralyze a person."

He stuffed his hands in his pockets and hunched his shoulders. "Yeah, well, anyhow, I was mesmerized by the action between you and No-Neck and didn't even see Blunt Face until he was right beside me. Even then, it wasn't until I caught a glimpse of his arm raising in my peripheral vision that I realized anyone was there. Then I saw he had a gun in his hand and he was aiming it at you, so I knocked it away." And stepped between her and the weapon when Blunt Face recovered enough to correct his aim. He was damn lucky he hadn't been whacked upside the head. Blunt Face must have wanted to locate the film more than he wanted to put Daisy out of immediate commission, though—and coldcocked men not only couldn't talk, they were damn tricky to haul around. Nick rolled his shoulders uncomfortably. "You know the rest."

"You saved my life?"

"Well, that might be stretching it a bit. For all we know, he wouldn't have shot you at all." He didn't know anything of the kind, of course, but she looked sort of vulnerable again, and he sure as hell didn't know for a *fact* that Blunt Face would have shot her. Odds were decent, in fact, that the goons hadn't wanted the attention gunshots would have drawn.

"What did Blunt Face mean when he said, 'He kept me from putting an end to this once and for all'?" Much as Daisy hated to admit it, it sounded very much as if Nick had saved her bacon, and honesty compelled her to say so. "He might not have killed me, but we both know he would've wounded me in a red-hot minute. They'd lost the advantage of surprise and needed to stack the odds back in their favor. So you saved me from something a heck of a lot more serious than a nail hole." She studied him solemnly. Then, raising up on her toes, she pecked an impulsive kiss of appreciation on the corner of his mouth. "Thank you."

Nick stiffened, and Daisy, who had felt the impact of the brief touch clear down to her toes, settled back on her heels. He stood very still and a dangerous light smoldered behind his narrowed lashes. Knowing she was playing with fire, but unable to stop herself, she cupped his face in her hands, raised up on tiptoe again, and aligned her lips to his for a real kiss.

The events of the past couple of days had piled and compiled, building electricity like a gathering storm, as each episode stacked escalating emotions upon the ones preceding it. Daisy's kiss was the spark that blew it sky-high.

Nick growled deep in his throat and suddenly he was kissing her in return, kissing her *hard*, moving his lips over hers until even if she'd wanted to resist, she'd have had no choice but to open up. His tongue plunged into her mouth, and she shivered as he stamped his brand on every bit of slick territory he could reach.

Then, with his thumbs firmly on her cheeks and his hands wrapped around her nape, he jerked his head back and stared down at her. "Are you messing with me?"

Every protective instinct she possessed urged her to tell him yes. She felt his breath against her damp lips, saw the wary hunger that deepened the blue of his eyes, and warned herself to be smart, to laugh in his face. *Stop this while you can*.

Instead, she heard herself denying it. "No." She tried to raise up to feel his mouth again but he held her away. "*No*." A desperate kind of need jittered in her stomach, and the fact that she cared so much infuriated her. She did laugh then, but it was a sarcastic sound, lacking cheer. "Like you'd ever turn down the opportunity for a little hit-and-run sex even if I *were* messing with your mind. Don't be a hypocrite, Nick. Kiss me."

"I'll kiss you," he said in a hard voice, and it sounded more like a warning than a promise. And kiss her he did, in a take-no-prisoners kind of way, his mouth aggressive and a little rough.

Daisy moaned low in her throat, every nerve in her body throwing back its head to howl in satisfaction. For a few intense moments she kissed him frenziedly, gripping his hair in her fists to prevent him from pulling away again. Then, abruptly depleted of adrenaline, her kisses softened and she wrapped her arms around his neck and collapsed against his chest.

Nick picked her up and carried her into his room, kicking the door shut behind them. He lowered her to the bed and followed her down. Interlacing their fingers, he swept their arms in an arc, as if they were kids making snow angels, until he was stretched out on top of her, their arms extended overhead, their linked fingers brushing the headboard. Then he bent his head and resumed kissing her: slow, deep, soul-stirring kisses that turned Daisy's bones to butter and ignited wildfires throughout her veins. A gritty little hum sounded deep in her throat, and she kissed him back, arching beneath him, loving the weight of him pressing her into the mattress.

The weight was removed when he pushed up on one elbow. He reached between them and eased her Glock from its holster inside her waistband. Setting it aside, he settled back on top of her. He caught her lower lip in his mouth and tugged at it, raking it with his teeth. Then he pulled back to look at her. "You sporting any other weapons I oughtta know about?"

"Knife." She saw him glance at her bare arms and said, "On my thigh. Take your shirt off, Nick."

He pushed back to kneel astride her legs, and pulled his shirt off over his head. She looked up at him, her gaze avid on the muscular planes of his chest and stomach. The bruise on his shoulder had faded to a paler shade of purple that was now mottled with yellow-green. She reached up to touch it with gentle fingertips.

She stroked her hands across his shoulders, outlined his collarbone with her fingertips, then flattened her palms against his chest. She was smoothing the fine hair over his pectorals when Nick reached for the button on the little skort she wore. He laid back the flap that gave it the appearance of a skirt and pulled down the zipper of the shorts underneath. She raised her hips and he pulled the garment off, leaving her in her white bra, a tiny pair of blue lace panties, running shoes and socks, and the knife strapped to her thigh. He crouched at her feet to unlace her shoes, then glanced up at her with amused eyes. "Nice tennies. I kind of missed seeing your dainty blue combat boots today, though."

"Dainty." Daisy snorted. "Right." She lifted a newly bared size-nine foot and swiveled it. "I assume you're teasing, but on the off chance you're not, it was too warm for all that boot leather." She removed the sheathed knife on her thigh and set it on the nightstand. When Nick returned to his place astride her thighs, she hooked her fingers in the waistband of his slacks and tugged. "Speaking of warm, I'm starting to cool down. Heat me up, Nick." She rubbed slow circles against his muscular stomach with the back of her hand. "Make me really, really hot."

His face went hard as the humor fled his eyes. "Damn," he whispered. Then he sprawled out on top of her, plunged his fingers through her short hair, and slammed his mouth down on hers. Daisy's blood immediately began a rolling boil.

The finesse Nick had displayed moments ago went up in smoke. In a distant corner of his mind he was aware of the rough sounds that reverberated in his throat, but he ignored them as he pressed Daisy's soft lips wider apart and sought dominion with his mouth, his tongue, his body.

She returned his hungry kisses with a hunger of her own; she clung with hands and arms and legs, her body straining closer and closer yet. Her enthusiastic response negated his attempt to show her who was boss and drove him instead to the edge of his own control.

That rang an uneasy warning bell in his brain, for his entire adult life had been built around maintaining control. He pulled back, groping through the fog of arousal to marshal a defense.

"Oh, don't," she whispered as he lifted his head. "Please. I feel so . . ."

He stared down at her swollen mouth and her slumberous eyes, which had darkened to the color of bittersweet chocolate. Perhaps control was overrated. "What do you feel, Daisy?" He bent his head and kissed the soft skin where her neck met the curve of her jaw. Shuddering, she raised her chin to provide him freer access and he dragged openmouthed kisses down her throat. "Hot?" Insinuating his hand between their bodies, he molded it around her left breast.

Daisy sucked in a breath. "Oh. God. Yes. *Hot.*" Her legs parted restlessly beneath him and she thrust her breast up for closer attention, but he ignored both invitations to concentrate on exploring the smooth skin of her throat. "So hot." She grasped handfuls of his hair and pulled his head back until he reluctantly left off kissing the vein that pulsed in the hollow of her throat and looked at her. "Do something about it!"

It was such a typical Daisy demand, it engendered an instant knee-jerk competitiveness. "You said 'really, really hot,'" he reminded her. "We've only attained singular hot. I can do much better, sweetpea—I can make you steam." *And I'd like that.* He'd like to see her totally out of control.

"Dammit, Coltrane, I couldn't *be* any hotter."

"Oh, yeah. You could be." His fingers cupped and shaped her breast, circling her nipple without touching it. "I haven't even begun to crank up the heat."

"Will you forget *degrees*? I don't need—I don't *want*—" She moved restively beneath his marauding hands. "Nick! I'm going crazy here; I wanna move faster."

"And we will, cupcake." He slicked his tongue over her lower lip and caught the impudent thrust of her nipple between his thumb and finger. "Eventually." Lightly pinching his captured bounty, he tugged.

Her breath hissed through her teeth. But she opened heavy eyelids that had drifted shut and said, "*Now*, Coltrane."

He said dryly, "We're gonna do this on my schedule, Parker. Live with it."

"Oh, no; I don't think so." Slapping her hands to his chest, she shoved, catching him unawares, and when he toppled onto his back she immediately rolled over to straddle him. She knelt with her calves pressed against his thighs, braced her hands on his chest, and aligned the damp blue lace of her panties with the prominent ridge that tented the fly of his pants. Finding the fit she sought, she gently rocked her hips. "There," she whispered and her eyes drifted shut once again. "That's more like it."

Oh. Yeah. That was good. Nick cocked his pelvis to maintain the connection and reached up to unhook the front catch on her bra. He peeled back the cups. "Ah, man. I tried not to remember these, but they were damn hard to forget. You've still got the prettiest breasts I've ever seen."

They were cream-pale curves that rose out of the lightly tanned, freckled expanse of her chest. High and gently sloped, with lush bottom curves, Daisy's breasts weren't exceptionally large. But they were exquisitely shaped, rounded and proud, with soft, blush-pink aureoles and hard nipples that pointed straight at the headboard. Crunching his abs, Nick half sat up to capture one with his mouth.

"Ah!" Daisy froze as lightning flashed from

her breast to the tight, achy core deep between her legs. She felt his hands slide beneath the leg openings of her panties to grip her bottom, and he directed her hips in an evocative rhythm that moved her against his hard erection between her legs.

She looked down at him and saw with surprise that his blue eyes watched her in return. Holding her gaze, he hollowed his cheeks and sucked on her nipple, working his tongue against its underside. More lightning flashed and she bore down on the rigid pillar of his sex in search of relief. "Oh, God, Nick, *please*." Reaching between them, she fumbled with his fly, but her fingers felt like rubber. "You win, okay? I don't want to play games anymore. Just, please, help me put out this fire." He sucked harder on her nipple and air burst out of her lungs in an agonized, high-pitched explosion of sound. "Ohplease, ohplease, ohplease."

In a sudden flurry of motion, Nick rolled her onto her back and knelt over her. Bending to pay homage to her other breast, he unfastened the button on his waistband, unzipped his slacks, and pushed both pants and boxers down his hips. He hooked his fingers in her panties and tugged them down, then reached for the drawer in his nightstand and pulled out a box of condoms. Shaking a few out on the mattress, he tossed the box aside, then rolled to his feet to kick off the shorts and slacks tangled around his ankles. He gazed down at her as he ripped open one of the packets and rolled a condom down the length of his erection.

"Ah, God, look at this," he said hoarsely and reached to wiggle a gentle fingertip in the damp crevice of her sex. "Blondie is a genuine blonde." His finger slipped and slid languidly.

She arched beneath sensations that threatened to blow the top of her head off, but managed to choke out, "And look at you." She gave his penis a nod as it bobbed, long and thick, away from his hard belly. "Coltrane is a genuine stud." But the words had no punch, forced as they were past her heart, which was lodged firmly in her throat. She reached to wrap her fingers around his erection. "No more fooling around, Nick." She moved her hand up and down the length of him, feeling the velvet slide of flesh over forged steel. "Keep me waiting any longer and I'll have to get mean."

"Ohh, I'm scared." But he fell over her, catching himself on his palms and propping himself above her. He bowed his head to kiss her and lowered himself as if performing a push-up, to rub his chest against her breasts. "Guide me," he demanded hoarsely. "Put me in you, Daisy. Now."

Fingers around the base of his penis, she rubbed its blunt head in tiny circles against her opening, then lined it up for a direct shot home. Nick nudged forward with his hips and she sucked in a sharp breath as he sank into her a short way. "Oh, *gawd*, Nick."

"Damn, Daisy, you're so . . ." Lips pulled away from his clenched teeth, he straight-armed himself away from her and looked down to where they were joined. "Tight. You're so tight."

He pulled back a little, then pushed forward gently, pulled back and pushed forward, gaining a little ground with each move. He looked up at her. "How long has it been since you've done this, anyway?"

"A while." She wriggled her hips and they both inhaled sharply as the minute adjustment sent him sliding deep inside her.

"A *long* while, if the way you feel is anything to go by." He held himself still for a moment. "God. I feel like the ugly stepsister trying to cram my big foot into the too-small slipper." Carefully, he withdrew.

"Oh!" She liked the friction but hated the emptiness he left behind. Then he thrust back in and she felt filled and restless and itchy. "Oh, please. More." She shifted her legs, not sure what to do with them. Finally she drew her knees up and braced her feet on the mattress, lifting her hips to meet his next thrust.

"Ah, damn!" His hips picked up speed. "That's it, Daise. Yes, just like that. God, you feel good." Then he ceased his thrust and retreat and rotated his hips in small, tight oscillations.

Daisy let out a strangled cry. She was so close—dear, God, so close. "Oh, please," she whispered. "I feel so ... I want to ... Nick, *please.*"

Nick's hand crept between their bodies to the soft rise of her mound. One long finger insinuated itself into the slick cleft and slipped up and down, up and down. Then, just as his hips resumed a hard, fast thrust and retreat, he located the slippery pearl of her clitoris with his fingertip.

Sensation gathered beneath his stroking finger, and at the apex of each thrust when he filled her, stretched her, bumped and retreated from a spot she'd never known existed. She began to pant, to plead, to demand. When she managed to focus unfocused eyes on Nick's face, it was to find him watching her with an unholy light in his eyes.

He gave her a crooked smile. "You want satisfaction, Blondie?"

"*Yes*. Yes, yes, yes!"

He sank into her, swiveled his hips once, and pulled back. "And what'll you give me if I see to it that you get some?"

"Anything. Well, not money—oh, God, Nick!" Daisy felt her eyes cross as he touched that place inside her again and then withdrew. "My firstborn son. The clothes off my back. Name it."

He bent his head and whispered a suggestion in her ear that caused her to clench tightly around him. He hissed air in through his teeth.

"I've never, um, performed that particular act," Daisy admitted. Moving restively, seeking the pinnacle that was just out of her reach, she looked up into his face. He looked like a fallen angel, one who held the key to whether or not she achieved satisfaction anytime in this millennium. "I could probably do it, though. Can't promise I'd do it *well*, but I bet I wouldn't be too terrible at it."

"Ah, Jesus." He hooked the inside bend of his elbows behind her knees and planted his hands flat on the bed on either side of her shoulders, lifting her hips off the mattress and canting her knees back toward her armpits. "You are something else, Daisy Parker. You are something so freakin' special I don't even have the words." He began to move his hips like a pile driver, and the new position drove him deep.

"Nick?" She locked her hands behind his neck and wrapped her legs around his back. The head of his penis hit the mark with every inward thrust, nudging that spot high inside her, and she strained against him. "Oh, please, oh, please, Nick? Uhh! I'm so—it's so—oh . . . my . . . gawwwwwd!" The relentless friction suddenly ignited, raced up a short fuse, then exploded like Hollywood special effects. Her interior muscles went berserk, grabbing and milking the source of all that pleasure as shock waves of pure, unadulterated ecstasy rocked her body. She was vaguely aware of Nick slamming deep into her one last time, and of his deep, attenuated groan in counterpart to her own breathy oh-oh-ohs. Mostly, though, she was fiercely focused on her own orgasm as it went on.

And on.

And on.

Nick suddenly collapsed on her, and she wrapped her arms around his neck and welcomed his heat and weight as she fought to catch her breath. She felt limp and languid, as if she were a helium balloon that might float into the stratosphere. She had never felt so relaxed in her life.

Until her brain started to function again. Then

unease began to creep in. God, what was she, a glutton for punishment? She felt his breath on her neck, the brush of his hair beneath her chin, and just went mushy all over. She wanted to hold him this way in her arms forever.

Yet she'd been in this exact same position before. And experience told her not to plan for tomorrow, let alone start picking out china patterns. The harder you tried to hang on to men, the quicker they were to hit the road. And Nick was probably the most commitment-shy of them all.

Lord, what had she done? She'd known darn well when she'd signed on for this gig that the chances were great he'd break her heart in two. Damn, damn, dammit. What on earth had she gotten herself into this time?

12

⁓⧟⁓

NICK lay sprawled on top of Daisy, telling himself he really ought to be a little more concerned about what he'd just gotten himself into.

Then he grinned against her neck. He knew exactly what he'd gotten himself into—Daisy. He was deep inside her, right where he wanted to be, and he liked it. A snicker escaped him at his juvenile enjoyment of the play on words, but he quickly muffled it against her throat.

"What?" she murmured.

"Nothing. I just feel good." Now, *there* was an understatement. He felt stupendous. His entire body hummed from the most satisfying sex he'd ever had.

He knew damn well that attractions came and went, and that great sex was nothing to base a relationship on. Chemistry, no matter how red-hot it started out to be, burned itself out in the end. It was the gospel according to Coltrane.

And yet . . .

That was what he'd told himself nine years ago, when he'd climbed out of Daisy's arms and

162

left her in that room at the Mark Hopkins. He'd assured himself that it wasn't really pain he felt as he forced himself to walk away; had told himself that he'd forget her in no time at all. It was merely that the sex had been so exceptional for a virgin's first time.

And no two ways about it, the sex *had* been good. But he hadn't let it sucker him into doing something foolish, and God knew, temptation had been thick on the ground that night. He'd been overwhelmed by a barrage of cravings, any of which would have spelled disaster had he allowed himself to be enticed by them. Instead, he'd done the smart thing and gotten the hell out of Dodge before he could give in to the urge to follow in the old man's footsteps.

But he hadn't forgotten that night. Nor had walking away stopped the ache. *That* had lasted for a long, long time.

His fascination with Daisy clearly hadn't burned itself out. Maybe he'd been a little too quick to nip it in the bud. Or maybe what he felt for her was different than, stronger than, he'd thought.

Maybe he ought to take a chance and see where it took him.

It would be a giant leap of faith on his part, but a relationship between them might actually have a slim chance of working—odder things had happened. And, hell, it wasn't as if he were talking marriage or anything. Just a monogamous arrangement that they could take one day at a time. Sort of a twelve-step romance.

He inhaled the scent of her and felt good. He'd

have to be careful how he presented it to her, of course. He didn't want her attaching too much importance to it, but he did want her to know that she mattered to him.

It would be a first for him. He wasn't accustomed to going out on the relationship limb to expose his feelings for a woman's exploration. But while he planned to take matters cautiously, he also thought that he and Blondie had an actual shot of seeing this thing progress.

Someday.

As long as she didn't expect too much too soon.

He'd hurt her once, and he planned to do everything in his power to avoid hurting her again. But he also planned to take this at his own pace.

Daisy stretched beneath him and murmured, "I'm glad you feel so good. Does this mean you want me to stay on the job after all?"

"Hell, yeah. It wasn't my idea for you to leave in the first place." He pushed up on his elbows and looked down at her. Her eyes were heavy-lidded and her lips looked full and well kissed, and he couldn't think of a single reason for them to get out of bed for the next several hours. "What about you; how do you feel?"

She stretched again. "Oh, I feel very, very good, too."

"Yeah?" Well, never let it be said that Nicholas Coltrane wasn't willing to help a partner recapture that "very, very good" feeling. Before he could lower his head to kiss her, however, Daisy gently pushed him back. He pulled out of her and rolled onto his side, propping his head in his hand as he watched her climb to her feet. He loved looking at her. She was lithe and fit, and just contemplating some of the possibilities for putting all that fitness to work made his heart beat faster.

"We should have done this much sooner," Daisy said casually as she located her panties and stepped into them. "It would have saved us both a ton of tension . . . not to mention all that tap-dancing we've been doing around each other." She found her bra and hooked it, looking over at him as she shimmied into the cups. "Now that we've finally gotten it out of the way, maybe we can settle down to the business at hand." She straightened the straps on her shoulders.

"What?" Unable to believe she could possibly mean what it sounded as if she meant, Nick sat up.

"We finally scratched the itch. Now we can move on."

His gut started to knot up. "And you don't expect to get the itch again?"

"I don't know—I'm not the most sexual person in the world."

"Oh, yeah, I could tell that by the quiet way you just laid there waiting for me to finish having my wicked way with you."

Her cheeks turned pink. "Okay, so this was different—you made me feel much more sexual than I usually do."

His gut seized up at her confession, but before he could pursue it, could find out how many men she'd been with and why they'd left her thinking of herself as an asexual being when any idiot could see she was about as sexual as it got, she rushed on. "What I'm trying to say is, if I do get the itch again, I imagine we could scratch that, too." She quit dressing for a moment to give him her full attention. "You don't have to worry, though, Nick. I'm not going to go all needy on you; I know the rules this time. No strings."

He thought he saw something in her eyes that belied her breezy tone, but she bent over to pull on her socks before he could be sure. Carefully, he said, "What if *I* want strings?"

She laughed. "Yeah, right. I'm gonna hold my breath waiting for that to happen."

For some odd reason, that pissed him off. He caught himself before he could lash out, though, surprised at the need to do so. He was generally much more contained than this. "Stranger things have happened, cupcake. What if I'm the one to get the itch?"

She paused in the midst of lacing her shoe to look up at him. "Then I guess you'll just have to persuade me to help you scratch it, won't you?" She finished with her shoe and stood up. "Look, we're both adults. If we want to conduct a purely sexual relationship, then that's what we'll do, right?"

Damn. Nick didn't know what to think. He should be ecstatic; she offered the perfect solution. Usually women got all huffy when he made it clear he wasn't interested in a long term-relationship.

But he'd been willing to offer Daisy more than

his usual thank-you-I'm-outta-here lovemaking.
He'd had it all figured out, but her total lack of
interest sure hadn't been part of the equation.

Shrugging, he reached for his boxers. This was
what happened when you stepped out of your
comfort zone to do something nice for someone.
He'd been willing to crawl out on a limb for her,
only to have her reach for the saw to hack the
branch off beneath his feet.

Well, the hell with it; there was no sense in
getting his nose out of joint. And no point in
bringing up his thoughts on the twelve-step relationship thing, either. She'd made her position
clear.

Which was . . . fine. Great, in fact. Hell, now
that he'd had a moment to think about it, it was
actually the best of both worlds. He got to have
sex with Daisy, without all the clinging and the
talk of the future. Really, it was perfect.

So he wondered why it felt as if all the blood
in his veins had suddenly been replaced by ice
water.

"When's that damn cop going to get here?"
Nick stopped pacing to look out the mullioned
windows for the fourth time in twenty minutes.

Daisy, who had been watching him stalk from
window, to kitchenette, to fireplace, to hall, and
back to the windows, summoned the patience to
reply—again—that she really couldn't say.
"We're in no imminent danger, so we're not
likely to be a high priority." He started prowling
again, and her patience slipped its leash. "For

heaven's sake, will you sit down? You're going to wear a path in the floor."

He plunked himself down on the edge of the black tapestry chair facing her. He drummed his fingers on his knees; he tapped his foot. Finally, meeting her gaze, he stilled. "Listen, when the cops get here, I'd like to talk to them by myself."

"What?" She snapped upright. "Oh, that's perfect, Coltrane—just shove an ice pick through my heart, why don't you? Or is this your unsubtle way of telling me you'd like a new security specialist after all?"

"For chrissake, Daisy, will you get your needle out of that groove? You're the one who was gonna quit in a huff."

"It was not a huff! It was a reasonable option, given your refusal to take professional advice."

"Whatever. It's still not what I'm saying here."

"Well, you might as well be, since you obviously don't trust me worth a damn." Thank God she'd put an arm's length between them after they'd made love. He'd stomp her feelings right into the ground if she ever went all soft on him.

Nick raked his hair back. "Dammit, this has nothing to do with trust or the lack of it! I'm just not comfortable talking about a former lover in front of you, all right?"

She made a rude noise, and he scowled at her.

"Listen, Blondie, you've made your feelings about this painfully clear on more than one occasion. So if it's all the same to you, I'd just as soon make my statement about the goons' motive without you breathing down my neck."

She crossed her arms over her breasts and glared at him. "Fine."

A growl of exasperation escaped him. "Dammit, don't do that. Don't treat me like I'm intelligence-impaired. You don't mean 'fine' at all. You mean screw you, jerk-off, only you're not honest enough to just come out and say it."

"Screw you, jerk-off."

Nick hunched his shoulders, shoved his hands in his pocket, and flopped back in the chair. He looked her in the eye. "Fine."

The atmosphere was thicker than summer fog by the time the patrolman finally arrived. Daisy answered the door and, wondering when the academy had started graduating fourteen-year-olds, ushered the young man into the living room. Nick offered him a seat.

They took turns explaining the attack and Daisy's role as Nick's security specialist. The cop looked at Nick. "Why do you need a body-guard?"

"I'd like to go over that with you in private when we're through here, if you don't mind."

"All right." The patrolman shrugged. "You said the attack occurred at approximately eleven a.m.?"

"Around then, yes."

"Yet it says in my report that you didn't call in the incident until eleven fifty-five."

Daisy's mind abruptly went blank of everything except what they'd been doing during those missing fifty-five minutes, and she looked at Nick.

He said coolly, "Ms. Parker sustained an injury when the first thug knocked her into the wall. She was bleeding, and we had to patch her up."

Daisy felt the officer's eyes on her and knew what he saw, because it was the same thing she'd seen in the mirror a while ago. Her lips were swollen from Nick's kisses, there was beard burn around it, and his mouth had left a faint mark just beneath her jaw.

A knowing smile tugged up the cop's mouth. "Emergency patch job," he murmured and caught Daisy's eye. "Gotcha."

She silently cursed the blush that rose up her throat.

Nick had been ticked at Daisy ever since she'd blown off their time in bed together, but that didn't mean he liked seeing her embarrassed. If there was any embarrassing to be done around here, it would be done by him, not some kiddie cop having too much fun letting Daisy know that he knew what they'd been doing. "Look," he said, pulling the patrolman's attention away from her. "Have you got any questions that are actually pertinent to the attack itself? If not, perhaps Ms. Parker can excuse us for a few moments while we go over what I consider to be the motive for the goon patrol descending on us."

Clearly not pleased with Nick's attitude, the cop asked them to clear up a few inconsequential details, then let Daisy go. He turned to Nick as soon as the bedroom door closed behind her. "Okay, let's have it."

"Last Saturday I inadvertently took two photographs of J. Fitzgerald Douglass having sex with a young woman who is not his wife. Since that time, I've had my darkroom broken into, my property destroyed, and my shoulder dislocated. I was nearly run down by a car, and as you already know, Daisy and I were attacked in the—"

"Hold it, hold it, hold it." The patrolman held up a hand. "You're trying to tell me that *Douglass* is responsible for all this? *The* J. Fitzgerald Douglass, the guy who's up for an ambassadorship?"

"Yes. That's exactly what I'm saying."

"Get outta here. He's Mr. San Francisco himself. He spoke at my church—hell, he gave my church *money*. The man's a saint."

Great. "If you'd care to wait here a moment, I'll be happy to go fetch the photographs Douglass is so hot to suppress. I think you'll see he is far from being a saint."

"Keep your photos." Snapping his notebook shut, the patrolman rose to his feet. "Photos can be doctored. Anybody who's ever seen some of the stuff in the sleezoid press knows that." The look he gave Nick firmly established him within those ranks.

Nick stood also. "I'm sure that's true, but I don't work for the tabloids. I'm a portrait photographer, and frankly, kid, I'm every bit as reputable in my own right as Douglass. Check it out—I was the photographer at Bitsy Pembroke's wedding the afternoon I memorialized Douglass and his little kewpie doll on film."

The officer just gave him a flat-eyed stare and Nick's temper slipped. "This is serve and protect?" he demanded. "You've made up your mind that a man you admire couldn't possibly be responsible, so you just disregard everything that's happened to me since? That's professional."

The young man flushed. "Give me the dates and places of those other attacks." Nick did so, and the officer wrote them down. "I'll take Ms. Pembroke's number, too." He gave Nick a hard look. "I will be checking you out."

"Do that." Nick got up. "Since she's on her honeymoon this week, I'll give you her mother's number—you can talk to her. While you're at it, here's Senator Slater's number, too. He'll vouch for me." He slapped the piece of paper he'd listed them on in the cop's hand. Anger had him breathing fast, and he took a deep breath, making a conscious effort to get himself under control.

Slipping the paper into his notebook and putting it away, the patrolman looked at Nick and said, "I'll pay Mr. Douglass a visit and ask him about his employees."

As if the goon patrol was likely to be on Douglass' regular payroll.

Still, recognizing it for the concession it was intended to be, Nick thanked the cop for his time and ushered him out.

He badly wanted to hit something, but failing to hang on to his cool was probably what had gotten him off track with the rookie cop in the first place. He relieved his ire by slapping his palm against the closed bedroom door with enough force to rattle it. "You can come out now, Daise."

She opened the door so fast she must have been standing behind it. "Well?" she demanded. "You boys have a nice bonding moment?"

"Shit." His laugh was brief and sour. He stalked back to the living room and threw himself into a chair.

Daisy trailed in his wake. "I guess not, huh?"

"Let me put it this way, cupcake: this is the last damn time I bother calling the cops. It's a waste of time. I don't know what it is with me and the police, but they never believe a word I say."

"Must be your prep-school charm." She moved behind him to rub his tense shoulders, digging her thumbs into the knots of frustration at the base of his neck.

Nick wilted. Damn, just when he thought he had her all figured out, she went and did something sweet like this.

"I'm not used to being treated like a congenital liar," he admitted, conveniently forgetting that he hadn't been one hundred percent truthful with anyone since this whole mess had begun. He did, however, recognize just how much he took his position in life for granted. Hanging his head as Daisy's fingers worked magic on the kinks in his neck, he said on a huff of laughter, "God, I even evoked Uncle Greg's name. I can't believe I did that."

"Who's Uncle Greg?"

"Senator Gregory Slater. He's an old family friend. He and Dad went to Choate together."

"Choate." She dug her thumbs in deeper. "My. How grand."

Wincing, he reached over his shoulder and snagged one of her wrists. He guided her around the arm of the chair, then gave a tug and tumbled her into his lap. "It rhymes with goat, doll face; how grand can it be?"

She laughed, and suddenly he felt good.

"You have to understand," he explained. "I used to hate it when my classmates did that sort of thing—threw around family names to get themselves out of jams. And here I am, doing the same thing in order to convince a twelve-year-old cop I'm not a tabloid photographer."

Daisy drew her head back. "Why would he think that?"

Oh, shit. Nick's mind went blank. *Way to go, genius. What grandiose lie are you gonna tell this time?*

Fortunately, she saved him when her eyes went round and she demanded, "Just who *is* this married woman, anyhow?"

Thank you, God. I'll be worthier; I swear. "Nobody. It's not important."

She looked as if she'd like to argue, so he bent his head and kissed her. Her mouth promptly went all soft beneath his, and what started out as a defensive maneuver immediately took on a life of its own. A low moan sounded in his throat and he shifted her in his lap for better access. He kept the kiss soft and suctioning, trying to see how long he could keep his tongue to himself.

Daisy caved first. The tip of her tongue slicked over his lower lip, and he sucked in a breath. He widened his mouth over hers to encourage deeper penetration, but for several moments she teased him with no more than the very tip. He found himself holding his breath. Finally her tongue slid in, rubbing against his own.

He groaned aloud and kissed her with a force that pressed her head back against his shoulder. Ripping his mouth away moments later, he breathed raggedly as he stared down at her. "I itch real bad, Daise." He tenderly rearranged a pale spike of hair that had drooped over her forehead.

"Ummm-hmmm?" Her chocolate-brown eyes had a drowsy, willing cast to them. "And?"

"And I wondered who I have to kill to persuade you to help me scratch it."

"Nicholas, honey, you don't have to kill a soul. You just have to ask me real nice." She cupped his jaw in her palm and gently bit his lower lip.

"Ah, God, Daisy," he murmured and shuddered in surrender. "Please."

13

∽∽∾

J. FITZGERALD allowed the very young patrolman plenty of time to exit the building before he rose from his chair and left the office. "I'll be back in fifteen minutes," he said to his secretary as he passed her desk.

The afternoon sun reflected blindingly off the chrome of the cars parked outside the office building. Blinking against the glare, he pushed through the revolving door and stepped out on the sidewalk. He ignored both the sun, which was warm on his shoulders, and the alfresco art fair going strong in Union Square as he walked briskly past it on his way to a pay phone a couple of blocks away. Arriving at his destination, he dialed a number and dropped in the proper change. The phone rang twice before it was picked up.

"Yeah."

"What's going on, Autry? I just had a visit from the police regarding Coltrane."

Autry cursed beneath his breath. Then he said, "I'm sorry about that, Mr. Douglass. I tried to get hold of you earlier, but your secretary said you'd be out of the office until two."

"Obviously I got back early. What the hell is going on?"

"We ran into a slight problem."

"Tell me something I haven't already figured out for myself. What slight problem?"

"You know the blond we told you about the yesterday? The babe we saw movin' in?"

"Yes, yes, what about her?" He'd already told Autry he didn't give a damn about Coltrane's sex life.

"Turns out she's not his squeeze, like we thought. She's his hired muscle."

"What?"

"We surprised the two of them late this morning in Coltrane's garage. But it turns out the surprise was on us. Jacobsen grabbed her to use her as leverage—you know, to force Coltrane to cooperate? And she fuckin' *tosses* him clear across the hood of the dude's car! She's fast and she's good. She took a punch from Jacobsen and still got the drop on him with her gun."

The respect in Autry's voice sent a trickle of ice down J. Fitzgerald's spine. "Are you trying to tell me you won't be able to recover my photos after all?"

"No! Oh, no, sir, not at all. I'm just telling you what's what. She managed to catch us by surprise one time. But now that we know who she is and what she's capable of, it's not going to happen again. We fully plan to do what we were hired to do, Mr. D."

"Good." He nodded with satisfaction. "See

that you do. Burn Coltrane's place to the ground if you have to. I don't want those photos surfacing."

Mo heard Reid's voice coming from the study and walked over to see who he was talking to.

He was on the phone. "William, this is Reid Cavanaugh. Great message on your machine, pal. Listen, I'm in a serious financial jam, and I wondered if you could lend me a hand."

Leaning against the doorjamb, she eavesdropped with impunity. And her heart sank lower and lower with every call she heard him place. She was still standing there when Reid finished up several moments later. She watched him toss the receiver back in its cradle, saw him dig the heels of his hands into his eyes and swivel around in his chair. When his hands dropped to his lap and he saw her, he gave a start.

Then he smiled, that slow, sure smile that still had the power to make her heart stagger like a drunk. "How long have you been standing there?"

"Long enough to hear you leave three messages and talk to Biff Pendergras." She hesitated but felt compelled to add, "It wasn't exactly what I thought you had in mind when you said you'd make it your mission in life to turn around my financial woes."

The warmth went out of his smile. "What did you think I'd do, Mo, go to my family?"

"No! Oh, no, I never meant . . ." She trailed off miserably. Reid's financial philosophy differed radically from that of the rest of the Cavanaugh men. She thought it was probably their constant criticism of nearly everything he'd ever done since the day he was born that had led to his proclivity for throwing his money at lost causes. It was either a knee-jerk reaction to their lockjaw conservatism, or a deliberate attempt to drive them crazy. She'd never figured out which. The older Cavanaughs were all about the bottom line, and Reid was about people. They were all so driven, and Reid was laid back. But she knew from experience that he couldn't be pushed. God knew, she'd made the mistake of trying often enough—and look where the two of them were now. She drew in a deep breath, then eased it out. "I only meant—"

"Because I'll go to them if I have to, okay? But understand up front that they'll be a last resort."

"I know that, Reid. I don't expect you to go to them at all. Honest. It's just . . . I don't see where calling up deadbeats who've already defaulted on the loans you've made them is going to help anything."

"Dammit, Maureen, are you going to ride that merry-go-round for the rest of your life? Just once it would be nice if you'd have a little faith in me."

She opened her mouth to say that she did have faith in him, but the truth was, if this was his idea of the way to save her hide, then she wasn't sure that she actually did. And before she could find something to say that would bridge the chasm she felt cracking open at her feet, he'd already brushed past her and walked from the room.

"I've got good news and I've got bad news, doll face. Which would you like to hear first?"

Daisy looked away from a contact sheet of the Trevors that was clipped to the drying line. She watched Nick catch the corner of a another contact sheet between his wooden tongs and lift it from the fixer, or whatever the solution was that finished the developing process. "Oh, the good news, by all means."

"I don't have a single appointment the rest of the day."

"Whoa, Nellie, stop the presses!" She eyed him suspiciously. "I know I'm going to regret asking this, but what's the bad news?"

"I've got an anniversary gig this evening, and cupcake, it's gonna be huge."

"Dammit, Coltrane!"

He grinned at her. "Yeah, I knew you'd be pleased. Be ready to hit the road by seven. And Daisy, it gets even better."

She waited for him to tell her how. When he didn't, she stubbornly resolved to wait him out. She leaned forward to peer at all twelve frames of the Morrison family's contact sheet. He truly was a fabulous photographer.

Nick poked her in her side. "Come on. Ask me how it gets better."

"Okay, I'll bite." She turned to face him. "How does it get better?"

"It's formal."

Her heart sank down to her knees. "How . . .

ducky." She *hated* dressing up. She'd never been one of those girlie-girls who seemed to know through osmosis everything there was to know about clothing and makeup. Consequently she rarely had a clue about what was appropriate.

"You want me to take you shopping for something to wear?"

Even though Daisy recognized the offer as a helping hand, it was like a cattle prod to her pride. "I don't need you to take me shopping, Coltrane! I'm neither a ragamuffin nor a charity case—I've got *plenty* of stuff I can throw on."

Nick held up his hands. "Whoa, sorry. I didn't mean to squeeze your toes."

That's when she should have shut up, of course, but some mysterious alchemy kept her digging the pit deeper and deeper. "The women you hang with aren't the only ones who've got a gown or two in their closets, you know. How dressed up are we talking?"

"Black tie."

"Yeah, well, fine. No problem." *Oh, Daisy, you could burn in hell for that.* "Excuse me, will you? I'm just going to step outside for a minute."

She walked out of the darkroom, closed the door, leaned back against it, and promptly began to hyperventilate. She didn't own a stitch of clothing that came close to qualifying as black tie formal. She wasn't even sure what that was.

Luckily, she had friends who did.

Pulling herself together, she extracted her cell phone from her pocket and punched in a number. "Reggie?" she said with breathless relief the minute he picked it up. "*Help*. I've really gone and stepped in it this time."

Nick had visions of Daisy pulling some left-over bridesmaid atrocity out of her closet for the Dillons' reception. Since he wanted her to blend in, the possibilities that popped into his mind produced moments of nail-chewing tension, and he had to bite his tongue several times during the afternoon to keep from reiterating his offer to buy her something appropriate. He managed to do so only because he knew how prickly her pride was, and because—face it—even if they attired her in the ultimate gown, she'd probably insist on accessorizing it with a plethora of weaponry.

So what the hell. Hands shoved deep in his pockets, he rolled his shoulders. She was going to look like a bodyguard any way you cut it, and that was bound to generate a host of questions as to why he should need one. So if he accepted that as a given, why go out of his way to insult her by pointing out that she wasn't very fashion-smart? Particularly when it wasn't always true. He had to admit he kind of liked her kick-ass schoolgirl look.

As the hour grew closer for them to get ready, however, and she hadn't even suggested that they go to her apartment to raid her closet, he found himself growing more and more irate. What was going on here? Did she think a dress would just magically deliver itself to his door?

As it turned out, that's precisely what happened.

Just before five o'clock he heard a clatter of footsteps on the exterior staircase. Daisy pulled her gun and held it at her side as she strode down the short hallway. She waved Nick back when he followed her, then plastered herself against the wall and demanded, "Who is it?"

"It's me," said a voice he couldn't immediately place.

Blondie slid the pistol back into its inside holster and unlatched the lock. "It's about time," she said as she pulled the door open a crack.

"Yeah, well, making sure you have just the right ensemble takes a while," the voice retorted dryly.

Nick walked up behind Daisy and reached over her shoulder to pull the door fully open. Reggie stood on the other side with another man who looked vaguely familiar. Reggie held a garment bag and the memory-tickling stranger had an ancient leather train case in his hand. "Reggie." Nick gave Daisy's secretary a nod. "What's going on?"

Reggie grinned. "We've come to dress Cinderella for the ball."

"They've come to drop off a gown. I can dress myself, thank you very much." Daisy made a grab for the bag.

Reggie blocked her with his shoulder. "That's debatable," he said, eyeing her rumpled khaki skort and the Tweetybird crop top she'd grabbed to replace her nail-hole-damaged blouse. "But even giving you the benefit of the doubt and agreeing that you can at least dress yourself, what do you plan to do for makeup?"

"I've got a lipstick around here somewhere."

The other man made a rude noise. "That's why I'm here, chickie. Now get out of the way, 'cause we're coming in. And don't give us any shit, Daisy, because we went to a lot of effort to find this stuff for you. So you can either step aside or make the alterations yourself if it doesn't fit right."

Daisy rolled her eyes. "A size ten is a size ten—how far off can it be? I'm not looking for perfection; it just has to get me through one lousy evening."

"It has to fit well enough not to get in your way, Daise," Reggie said. "We brought you a choice of outfits and both heels and flats that will go with them. I assume you'll want to wear the flats, but these outfits were designed for heels and the hems may be too long."

"Will you *move*?" the other man demanded. "Reg said you had to be ready by seven."

"That's two hours away, for heaven's sake," she protested. But she fell back from the doorway as the men determinedly advanced. "It doesn't take two hours to get ready."

The makeup man shook his head sadly as Reggie closed the door behind them. "Those ovaries are positively wasted on you, hon."

"I gotta disagree," Nick said at the same time that Daisy said, "Oh, stuff it, Benny."

The missing piece of the puzzle clicked into place. "That's who you are!" Nick stared at the slender young man and saw impeccable makeup and a pair of heels no human being should be able to navigate in. "I couldn't place you, but you're the transvest—uh, the guy in the park."

"Transvestite," Benny said dryly. "You can say the word."

Daisy gave Nick a look of disgust. "Good God," she said as she tromped down the hall and made a sharp left to the bedroom. "You should see the look on your face. If this were a cartoon, you'd have a light bulb going off over your head."

"Well, hey, excuse the hell outta me. I haven't had a lot of experience with high-heel-wearin' guys dropping by my place."

"I know what you mean," Reggie said sadly. "Since AIDS, I've had a lot fewer dropping by mine, too."

By then, they were all in Nick's bedroom. Daisy turned to Reggie and gave an impatient flap of her hand. "Okay, let's see what you've got."

He hooked the bag over the top of the closet door and unzipped it. "We brought you two choices," he said, hauling them out. "Whaddaya think? The gown or the pants suit?"

"The pants suit," Daisy promptly decided, while Nick, with one look at the skimpy bronze evening gown, said "The gown." She scowled at him, but he didn't care. He wanted to see her in that dress. Propping one shoulder against the wall, he crossed his arms over his chest and settled in to watch the show.

Reggie reached out to pat Daisy's forearm comfortingly. "I want you to try them both. It's just a matter of which one first. Hopefully, either should work for you, because Benny and I picked them out not only with an eye toward the occasion, but for accessibility to your weapons. But one may work better than the other—we won't know until you give them a try."

Clearly he knew how to placate her much better than Nick had learned to do, for she said agreeably, "Okay, you're the expert." She shucked out of her shorts, then, before Nick could say anything, pulled the T-shirt off over her head.

"Lose the bra, too," Benny advised. "Both the gown and the camisole that goes with the pants suit have li'l bittie straps. So unless you've got a strapless on . . ."

She reached behind her to unhook her bra.

"Hey, wait just a damn minute," Nick protested as the garment began to slide down her arms. "You two turn around," he ordered the men.

Daisy's bra halted midslide and all three turned to look at him with identical expressions of incredulousness. "Uh, Nick?" Daisy said. "They're *gay*."

"And it's not like we haven't seen 'em before," Benny added cheerfully. "They're very nice, but frankly, sport, they're not our thing, you know?"

Heat crept up Nick's throat and onto his jaw. On a purely intellectual level, he knew damn well he was making a fool of himself. Emotionally, however, he simply saw Daisy stripping down to a miniscule pair of panties in front of two men.

Reggie saved him from embarrassing himself any further. "Benny," he said, and twirled a finger. Benny shrugged, and with wry smiles both men executed an about face.

"Oh, for heaven's sake," Daisy said in disgust as she dropped her bra to the floor and fielded the camisole that Reggie tossed over his shoulder. She pulled it on and tweaked it into place. "You can turn around now." With a trace of sarcasm coloring her tone, she said to Nick, "Is that okay with you? I mean, they could see more skin at the beach."

"Yeah, okay." He felt like an idiot.

She stepped into the raw umber-colored silk slacks that Reggie handed her. She zipped and buttoned, then accepted the matching jacket. Buttoning the tuxedo-style jacket, she checked herself out in the mirror. She unbuttoned it, and turned side to side as she rechecked. "I don't know. I think I look a little . . . mannish."

"Yeah, it's too severe," Benny agreed. "It calls for longer hair to avoid that Nazi dominatrix look. We should have thought of that sooner, Reg. Here, give me that." He held out an imperious hand for the jacket she'd removed. "Try the gown."

She stepped out of the slacks and handed them over, too. When she crossed her hands over the hem of the camisole and began easing it up her diaphragm, her friends grinned at each other and swung around to present her with their backs. She tossed them the garment once she'd pulled it off over her head. In return, Reggie flipped the bronze gown over his shoulder and dangled it from a crooked finger.

All the moisture in Nick's mouth dried up the

moment she pulled the dress into place. Made of some stretchy, shimmery microfabric, the design was simplicity itself. It was the absolute fitness of the body beneath that turned it into a show-stopper. Narrow straps held up the deeply scooped bodice, then crisscrossed her back. The fabric clung to Daisy from her breasts to her hips, faithfully adhering to her shape. Then it fell in a graceful A-line to the floor. Slit up the front from hem to midthigh, it was a plain and una-dorned garment that had no need of embellish-ments.

"Wow," Daisy said to her reflection. "And I'm supposed to hide my weapons *where*?"

"With that slit in the skirt, you can strap a knife to your thigh and still get to it," Reggie assured her. "And your Beretta is in the weapons case, isn't it?"

"Sure, but this thing might as well be spray paint." Daisy plucked the material away from her flat stomach, and it promptly snapped back to bond to her skin the instant she released it. "Where could I possibly put the Beretta where it wouldn't show?"

"I bet it'll fit in this." He held out a beaded black velvet pouch attached to a braided velvet belt. "If you buckle it loosely so it rides your hips, it'll look *tres* medieval. No one will ever guess its function."

"Hang on." Scooping up her skirt with both hands to keep it off the floor, she strode from the room. She was back a moment later with her weapons case. She strapped on the belt Reggie handed her and dropped a small pistol into the attached pouch. "This will work." She smiled brilliantly at her secretary. "Reggie, you're a genius!" She laughed and gave him an enthusiastic smooch on the lips.

He grinned at her. "Try on the shoes. Let's see what needs to be done about the length."

"Then—speaking of genius—I have *got* to get to work on your makeup," Benny said. He looked over at Nick. "You're excused, good-lookin'. Get out of here and give us girls some time to work our magic."

Nick pushed away from the wall and collected his tux from the closet. Then, with a final look at Daisy, he walked out of the room and left her to the tender mercy of her buddies.

14

"OKAY, Daisy," Reggie said the instant the door closed behind Nick's back. "Let's have it. Just when did you and Coltrane get so damn cozy? I thought the two of you were oil and water."

"I know. And we are. Except..." She didn't know how to explain, especially since she'd been so adamant about Nick's place in her life after she'd let Reggie worm their history out of her Monday afternoon. She searched for the words anyway. "He's so—oh, God, Reg, he's just so..."

"Butch," Benny supplied.

"*Yes.*"

"Oooh. And so territorial. I *love* butch men."

"Knock it off, Benny; this is serious." Reggie looked up from where he knelt to pin the hem of her dress, and it was all Daisy could do not to squirm. "Do you have any idea what you're letting yourself in for?"

"A world of heartbreak, probably," she admitted. "But, Reg, it seems to me that it's gonna hurt now, or it's gonna hurt later. And if it's going to hurt either way, why shouldn't I get what I can before he comes to his senses and realizes we're just too different?"

"He looks pretty damn bowled over to me. Maybe you'll be the one to come to your senses."

"Oh, yeah. As if a guy like Nick would ever lose his head over someone like me. No, I've got a handle on this and I plan to be very, very realistic. It's great sex and that's all. We've really got nothing else in common, so there's not a snowball's chance of it ever going anywhere." She looked down at Reggie. "And that's okay. Really. Great sex is nothing to sneeze at."

"I hear that, sister," Benny said fervently.

Reggie looked as if he'd like to argue, but he merely sighed and said, "Take off the dress. I'll hem it while Benny does your makeup."

Neither man bothered to turn around this time when she peeled off the dress, but neither did they so much as glance at her bare breasts. Reggie tossed Daisy her T-shirt, but Benny reached up and snagged it out of the air before she had a chance to grab it. "Put on something you don't have to pull over your head and I'll do your hair, too. I'll go grab us a chair to use."

She got one of Nick's shirts out of the closet and donned it, buttoning it up the front and folding back the too-long sleeves. The tails fell nearly to her knees, so she didn't bother with her skort. She looked over at Reggie, who sat cross-legged next to the bed, pointedly ignoring her. "Are you mad at me?"

He plied the needle through the hem, pulled the thread taut, then lowered the garment to his lap and looked up at her. "No. You know I'm not. But he's hurt you before, kid, and I'd hate to see you get hurt again."

She snorted. "How many relationships have you watched me go through?"

"A couple."

"Right. *Two*—in how many years?—and neither one of them worked out in the long run. In the end, relationships always hurt. I simply don't have what it takes to make men stay around. But Reg"—she sank to her heels in front of him—"I've never felt the way I do with Nick, except the last I time I was with Nick. He makes me feel—I don't know—sexy, I guess, which is a word I wouldn't in a million years have applied to me. And I like the feeling. I want to keep feeling this way until it's no longer a viable option."

"Okay. But if he does anything to make it impossible for you to *be* you anymore, I'll hunt him down like a dog and make him pay."

Warmth bloomed in her chest. "Deal." She offered her fist.

He knocked it with his own. "Deal. In the meantime"—he gave her a slow, wicked grin—"may you fornicate like wild mink."

"Precisely." She grinned back at him as she rose to her feet.

Benny returned with a stool from the breakfast bar and thumped it down in front of the mirror. "Climb aboard, chickie."

Thinking that maybe it wouldn't kill her to know how to do this herself, she watched him drag bottles, jars, and brushes out of his old train case. "Holy carumba, Ben, is all this stuff really necessary?"

"Do you wanna look good, or do you wanna look great?"

She hated to admit it, but . . . "I wanna look great."

"It's necessary, then. Trust me, girl. Am I the high priestess of cosmetics or what?"

"You are the goddess, Benny."

"Right. So close your eyes so I can do your shadow." He rummaged around in his case and pulled forth several little pots. "I'm gonna use this Mocha Surprise on your lids, a little Golden Splendor on your brow bone, and Bronze Beauty in the crease. Then we'll finish it off with an olive liner and brown mascara."

Daisy gave up on the idea of ever doing this for herself. Head back and her eyes closed, she said, "You do know, don't you, that you've just opened yourself up to doing my makeup for the rest of your life. At least for special events."

Benny snickered. "How long have I known, you, Daise—four, five years now? This is the first special event I've known you to attend." He used the edge of his little finger to brush something away from the corner of her brow bone. "Tell you what, though. You just keep inviting me to your monthly spaghetti feeds, and I'll do your makeup whenever it needs to be done."

"Sounds like a plan to me."

"It's a deal, then. So, how do you wanna do this? Would you like to see your transformation step by step, or do you want to be surprised?"

"What the heck. Surprise me."

"O-kay." He swiveled the seat of the barstool around, which left her with her back to the mirror. "You can open your eyes if you want. I'm gonna wait until we're done with the rest before I apply your mascara. The million-dollar question is: what color foundation do we use?" He stood back to study her. "The Benny eyeball test says Ivory. If that doesn't work, we'll give Light Sand a whirl." He poured some on a small sponge and tested it on her cheek in front of her ear. "Ivory it is. Damn, I'm good."

"And so modest."

He applied more foundation to the sponge and began stroking it onto her face and blending it in. "I'm here to tell ya, hon: I don't think I'm half as good as I really am."

It took nearly forty-five minutes before he stepped back for the final time and studied her from several angles. "I'm a genius, if I do say so myself. You are looking *good*."

"I ought to be looking like Cameron Diaz, considering all the time it's taken."

He gave her an unrepentant grin. "I guess that means a day-at-the-spa gift certificate wouldn't be your first choice for a Christmas present, then. Reg, you ready with that gown?"

"Yep." He tossed Daisy a package of pantyhose. "Put these on and lose the shirt." She did as ordered and then both men very carefully lifted the gown over her head. They tweaked and adjusted, then Reggie buckled on the velvet pouch and slid a pair of shoes in front of her to step into. He dug her Beretta out of the weapons case and handed it to her, then made another minute adjustment. "Okay, you ready for the un-veiling? This is gonna knock your socks off."

She twirled to face the mirror and her mouth dropped open. "Oh, my God. Is that me?" She took a step forward, staring entranced at her image. "I look . . . pretty." Like sexy, it wasn't a word she associated with herself. She smiled brilliantly at both men, then looked back at the mirror. "I do, don't I, Reg? I actually look pretty."

"Pretty doesn't say it by half, babe. You look gorgeous."

"Not to mention hot," Benny agreed. He brushed bronzed powder across her bare shoulders and along her collarbone. Then he stood back to survey her one last time and gave her a thumbs up. "Wait until Coltrane gets a load of this. I can feel the temperature jacking into the stratosphere already."

Nick felt hot under the collar every time he looked at Daisy—and he found himself looking at her way too often as the evening progressed. It was beginning to interfere with his work.

The anniversary reception in the elegant pent-house suite atop the Fairmont Hotel was in high gear, and while he hadn't neglected his respon-sibilities, he'd sure as hell spent too much time keeping an eye on his date—much too much. And she wasn't even his real date; he had to keep reminding himself of that. She was his damn bodyguard.

He'd always loved her looks, but he'd also ac-cepted that he viewed her with an artist's eye.

She was built on a beautiful framework of bones, but she wasn't pretty by conventional standards. What she was, was much more interesting—though he understood that his taste didn't always coincide with the average guy's.

Tonight, however, not only was she beautiful in a way that was uniquely Daisy, but she was drawing attention right and left. With her proud carriage and aloof eyes she looked exotic, and she stood out in the posh crowd like a cheetah in a roomful of kittens.

Benny had given her a thirties look with dramatic eye makeup, bee-stung lips, and her pale hair done in a 'do of shining, slicked-back finger waves with spit curls in front of each ear. The slinky slip dress over her magnificently athletic body added to the illusion. She looked utterly fascinating.

He wasn't the only one who thought so, either. Daisy was a complete unknown to these people, and the women discreetly checked her out while man after man attempted to engage her in conversation. Daisy ignored the former and discouraged the latter by her complete indifference . . . or at least that was how it should have played out.

She stayed near him while he worked, even though the chances of Douglass' goons crashing an event this exclusive were slim to none. The only time she moved a short distance away was when he got caught up in an interesting shot, and that was strictly to give him room to maneuver. Her thoughtfulness proved to be more distraction than help, though, because every time she left his side, some domesticated pussycat who fancied himself king of the lion pride peeled off from the pack to move in on her. Her haughtily raised chin and unsmiling mouth drew them in like the moon drew the tides.

The irony was that he knew damn well her little chin was up in the air because she felt out of her element. It hadn't escaped him that she often felt vulnerable in his world, but she wasn't a woman to cave in to insecurity. So she kept that chin elevated, and she did the job she was hired to do. But the idiots who hovered around her watched her sip sparkling water from a crystal champagne flute and saw her gaze constantly move among the crowd rather than attend to them, and they saw only an elusive woman.

Which made her a challenge.

Looking away from the most recent candidate in the Make-Daisy-Take-Notice Sweepstakes, he saw Mrs. Dillon, half of tonight's honored anniversary couple, smiling up at her husband as she held out a chocolate-dipped strawberry for him to bite. Nick raised his camera and got off a shot just as Mr. Dillon wrapped his hand around the back of his wife's hand and, looking into her eyes with a soft expression, ignored the proffered confection and leaned forward to bestow a kiss on the inside of her wrist.

Nick knew that would be the definitive photo, the one Mrs. Dillon would cherish above all the others, because it epitomized why her marriage to Jim Dillon had lasted for twenty-five years. It was the shot Nick always looked for, the one that through diligent concentration he usually found.

And he'd damn near missed it because he'd been paying more attention to what was happening around Blondie than to the business at hand.

He forced himself to shrug the concern aside. So, big deal. Conscientious attention or pure luck, either way he'd gotten the shot he'd sought. Now he could relax and enjoy himself a little.

He swooped down on Daisy, muscling aside a would-be suitor. "I think your wife is looking for you, Manwellan," he said, interrupting the other man's no doubt scintillating conversation without compunction. "Ms. Parker"—he gave her a bow—"forgive me for neglecting you. May I escort you to the buffet table?"

Daisy gave him a dry look. "That would be lovely, I'm sure." She bestowed a solemn smile on her erstwhile companion. "Excuse us, Mr. Manwellan, won't you?"

Wrapping his hand around the nape of her neck, Nick steered her toward the laden buffet. Daisy leaned forward to pick up a small china plate and his hand slid to the shallow groove of her spine, which he skimmed with a finger down to where the back of her dress began before he reluctantly dropped his hand away from her entirely.

He felt overdressed and hot under the collar again, and shifted from one foot to the other. Watching her use sliver tongs to delicately transfer hors d'oeuvres from a platter to her plate, he thought about sex. He watched the economical movement of her hips as they made their way to a spot in the back of the penthouse that hosted a single unoccupied chair, observed the way her gown dipped away from her breasts for a moment when she seated herself, and thought about sex. Big surprise. It seemed to be all he'd thought about for the past several days.

So if it was nothing new, why did he feel low-grade miffed tonight?

Maybe because he *had* been thinking about it so much. Or maybe because he'd finally made love with Daisy again and she'd blown it off.

Yet shouldn't the attraction be waning, now that they'd done the deed and the mystery was gone? That was the way it usually worked. But he watched her daintily lapping chocolate from a strawberry, and he wanted her.

Again.

Right now.

So why not? Nick tugged at his bow tie. Truly—what was to stop him? His job here was finished and she'd *said* they were two consenting adults, hadn't she?

These urges felt very adult. Maybe if he got them out of his system he could concentrate on staying free of the rent-a-goons long enough to come up with the money for his sister.

He slid his plate onto the tray of a roving waiter and held out his hand for Daisy's. "You about finished there?" His tone clearly stated he wanted the dish whether she was through with it or not.

Daisy swallowed the bite in her mouth and looked up at him. God, he looked devastating in his tux. She wished they could get the heck out of here. "Sure." She passed him her empty plate, then took a sip of water and rose to her feet, looking around for a place to set her goblet. "Do you have to get back to work?"

"Umm."

Whatever that meant. Since he was clearly distracted, however, she let it go. She didn't even object when he took her hand and headed toward the front of the room, despite the way it hindered her gun hand. If a need arose for her to use it, which seemed pretty unlikely in this posh crowd, she could break his grip easily enough.

As they made their way through the room, several people stopped them to talk about Nick's work. He introduced Daisy to women in lavish jewels and opulent gowns and to men in hand-tailored tuxedos. He was charming and polite as he handed out business cards and exchanged idle chitchat. But he always kept them moving forward, and practically before Daisy knew what was what, they were in the corridor outside the penthouse.

She immediately became more alert, for if Hubby's goons had managed to follow them this evening, she and Nick were more likely to be ambushed out here in the hall than inside the suite where a hundred of San Francisco's most influential citizens were partying down.

"Are you finished for the night?" She practically had to jog down the hallway to keep up with his long-legged stride. She tried to discreetly disengage her hand, but he refused to let go. An instant later, they stopped in front of the elevator and he punched the down button. "Where are we going?"

The elevator pinged its arrival and the arrow above the doors lit. A second later the doors swished open. They stepped into the car and Nick reached out a long finger to jab the lobby button.

"Cat got your tongue, Coltrane?" Daisy was beginning to feel a tad riled at his continued silence and jerked her wrist free as the doors swooshed closed. She suddenly found herself penned in a tuxedo-clad cage as he loomed over her.

"What?" she demanded, back stiffening as she stared up at him.

"This," he growled and, bending his head, rocked his mouth over hers.

Lust detonated low in her stomach, and she kissed him back with an explosive passion that matched his own. Curling her fingers around the lapels of his tux, she rose up on her toes to get as near to him as she could. Nick's hands slid off the wall and onto her back, warm fingers massaging her bare skin before flattening to pull her into his body. And all the while, his lips moved hungrily over hers.

Then his mouth was gone as he lifted his head to stare into her eyes, and his breath was warm and uneven against her moist lips. "Did I tell you how beautiful you look in your party dress? All I've wanted to do, ever since I first saw you in it, is get you out of it. Isn't that crazy? I've seen you naked and all but naked, but it's having you covered up that's got me climbing the walls." He bent his head to press his lips to her jaw, her cheekbone, her temple. Then his breath traveled down the whorls of her ear as he breathed, "What are you doing to me, Daisy?"

What was *she* doing? That was rich. But she didn't get the opportunity to address the irony of it, because he kissed her again, and just like every other time he'd ever laid lips on her, her mind went blank. Unlike most of the other times, though, she went with the flow and didn't fight it.

Nick's thumb was easing a narrow strap off her shoulder when the elevator glided to a stop and the door opened. Daisy failed to notice until someone cleared his throat and Nick raised his head. She blinked up at him with a lazy appreciation for the blueness of his eyes, then he pushed back and turned, wrapping an arm around her. Her face flamed at the sight of a small group of people discreetly gawking as she and Nick stepped out of the car. She thrust her chin out and strode with head high across the lobby.

Good God—the goon patrol could have mowed them down where they stood, for all the attention she'd been paying. Ignoring Nick's conversation with the woman at the front desk, she diligently checked out the lobby.

"Come on," Nick said huskily a moment later, and they walked back to the bank of elevators. The doors of an empty car opened just as they approached and Nick pressed the button for the fourth floor. The moment the door closed he turned to her, but Daisy held up a forestalling hand.

"Don't even *think* about making a move on me again."

He grinned at her. "That wasn't one of my brighter ideas, obviously. But it's not as if you were the one tenting the front of your trousers all the way across the lobby."

"Nick Coltrane!"

"Yeah, that's who was sportin' the big one, all right. Now, you, on the other hand, skated. Everyone took one look at you and thought, *She's hot.* Me, they looked at me and thought, *And she's leading that guy around by his co—*"

"*Nick!*"

"Coattails. I was gonna say coattails."

"My God, I don't believe this conversation. People don't look at men's you-knows in public. And they certainly don't have conversations like that."

"You-knows." He gave her a tender smile and reached out to trace her eyebrow with the tip of his finger. "How does someone who hangs out with drag queens ever reach the exalted age of twenty-eight with all that innocence intact?"

She pushed his hand away. "I am not innocent!"

"It's not an insult, cupcake." The elevator stopped and Nick stood back with an elegant gesture for her to precede him out of the car. "After you."

"Where are we going?"

"Down here." He took her elbow and steered her down the corridor. A moment later, he stopped in front of a door and inserted a key card.

"What is this?" It was a stupid question, but she didn't understand what they were doing here.

"A room. I didn't think you'd appreciate me following my first impulse, which was to drag you into one of the penthouse's bedrooms and ball your brains out while a hundred people celebrated the Dillons' anniversary in the next room. And I don't think I can wait until we get home." He pushed open the door, then turned and swept her up in his arms. She embarrassed herself by emitting a schoolgirl squeal.

"You don't strike me as a quickie-in-the-supply-closet kinda gal," Nick continued, as he stepped over the threshold and kicked the door closed behind them. "So I rented us a room."

15

❧

DAISY gazed around the sumptuous green and white room. "I thought you were broke. This place looks like it'd set you back a bundle."

"That's why they invented American Express, sweet thing—so guys like me don't have to worry about it until next month."

"Do you do that, too?" She gave him a brilliant smile. "That's funny, I always envisioned you peeling hundreds from a solid gold money clip." She much preferred the image of him racking up debt on a credit card, because it made him seem more of a regular Joe. She kicked off her shoes as he carried her across the room. "Thank God for plastic, though, huh? Not that I have a real grown-up limit or anything—they lowered mine to practically nothing when I left the force. Well, not the minute I left the force, I guess, but the minute they discovered that not only was I no longer a civil servant, but self-employed to boot."

"Daisy."

"Yeah?"

He landed on the bed with her in his lap. "Shut up and kiss me."

She laughed deep in her throat, because he made her feel so sexy and that was exhilarating. Her right arm was already hooked around the back of his neck, and she framed his lean cheek in her free hand and pressed her mouth to his. The way his lips immediately opened beneath hers caused a vibration to hum along her nerve endings, and she allowed her tongue free reign to explore his mouth.

"Uhhh." Without breaking the kiss, Nick tipped over onto his back, then rolled so that he was propped half over her. His kiss drove her head back into the thick floral bedspread, and his fingers curled around one of the slender straps that held up her gown, slipping it down her shoulder. The flimsy bodice sagged and Nick peeled it away from her breast. He raised his head to look down at what he'd exposed. "Ah, man."

He bent his head and pressed a soft kiss on her nipple, and it immediately went from quiescent to diamond-hard distension. Nick opened his mouth and captured it lightly between his teeth, giving a gentle tug, and lightning streaked through Daisy's body.

Then he was gone, rolling away and climbing to his feet. "Wanna get naked with me, Blondie?" He pulled off his tux jacket and tossed it on one of the nearby club chairs. He reached for the studs on his shirt.

"Wait." Daisy sat up. "Let me help. Jeez, you're always in such a hurry."

A strangled laugh got caught in Nick's throat. "That's pretty good, coming from you. The last time we did this, you all but held a gun to my head to make me hurry up."

She pursed her lips and blew out a soft *pff* of repudiation. Daintily gathering the hem of her dress high, she knee-walked over to the edge of the bed. His mouth watered at the sight of her exposed breast and the long, firm length of her thighs as they played peek-a-boo through the front slit of her gown. "You got panties on under that, Daise?"

"Of course I've got panties on!" Her chocolate-brown eyes were scandalized. "My God, what kind of women do you hang out with, anyway? They sound a lot more adventuresome than I am."

He had a feeling that wouldn't take a great deal—not if adventuresome equated with vast carnal knowledge—but he was smart enough not to say so. Watching her unfasten the studs on his shirt, he smiled. She thought she was such a tough guy, and admitting to limited experience in any field clearly wasn't part of her self-image.

She suddenly yanked his shirt off his shoulders and down to the middle of his back in one smooth movement, and his collar rasped loudly in the quiet room as it was ripped out from beneath his bow tie. Leaving the shirt tangled around his elbows, she raised both hands to his chest and splayed her fingers through the silky fan of hair that covered it. She stretched up to bite his lower lip.

He reached for her, only to discover that his

cuffs were still fastened. His abrupt movement turned them inside out, and they gripped his hands like Chinese finger puzzles that grew tighter the harder he pulled. He returned her kiss fiercely for a moment. Then, breathing roughly, he lifted his head. "You forgot to undo my cuff links."

"Mm-hmm." She leaned to kiss his sternum, then turned her cheek and rubbed it against his chest. Reaching behind him, she unfastened his cummerbund and dropped it to the floor.

"So, undo me."

"I don't think so. I've got you in my power now, and that makes you my sex slave." She sat back on her heels and reached for his waistband.

"Trust you to go for the role reversal." He wrestled with the cuffs for a few more moments, but the feel of her fingers rubbing against his stomach as she undid the button made him still. He watched as Daisy kissed his stomach, then tipped her head back to smile up at him.

"Yes," she said. "*Trust* me." She laughed low in her throat. "Or we could just skip straight to the part where I break out the restraints." She grasped the zipper tab of his fly and eased it down.

"Yeah, right," he scoffed, getting a flash of her calling his dick a "you-know." "Is this the same woman who—*ah, God*, Daise—" Her hand had dipped into the open fly of his trousers and glommed onto his cock, and he forgot what he was going to say. He'd had a point to make . . . but he couldn't for the life of him remember what it was.

"Why, Nicholas Sloan Coltrane," Daisy breathed, "*you're* the one not wearing any undies."

He looked down at her as his pants slid down his legs. Then he scowled. "Men don't wear *undies*," he informed her hoarsely.

"I can see that."

"No, Blondie. I mean, men wear *shorts*; they don't wear anything so girlie as—" She moved her hand in a way that had him sucking for breath and he shut up. What the hell. When a guy's pants were down around his ankles and his arms were trussed like a turkey getting ready to be stuffed, lecturing didn't make him look any smarter. He started wrestling in earnest with his cuff links. Attempting to undo them behind his back from inside the damn cuffs was an exercise in frustration, but by God he *would* get them free. Little Miss Parker needed to be shown who was boss.

Daisy, looking for all the world as if she were preparing to clean a pair of glasses, bent her head and *ha!'d* warm air on his erection where it emerged from her fist. Then she polished it free of her misty breath by rubbing its increasingly sensitized head against the lush inner curve of her bare breast.

"Ah, Christ." He simply stood there rigidly at attention and stared down at her, breathing raggedly.

Daisy returned his look and her brows drew together as if wondering if she'd gone too far. Then she gave him a little three-corner smile. "I owed you that for this afternoon." She blinked up at him innocently. "It *was* a buff job you told me I had to give you, wasn't it?"

Word games were beyond him at the moment. "Help me out of my shirt, Daise," he demanded hoarsely. "C'mon. I'd just as soon not rip it, but that's what I'm gonna do in about two seconds if you don't—"

"I don't think that's a real good idea, Coltrane—"

"Nick," he insisted, staring down at her. "Anyone who burnishes up the Bad Boy the way you just did oughtta be on a first-name basis with its owner."

"Well, I'll tell you what, Nick. It occurs to me that if I help disentangle you, you're gonna make me pay for having a bit of innocent fun."

"And you're a smart woman to worry." He planted his knee on the mattress and smiled when she promptly released him and scooted back. "But I don't think you've considered the big picture here."

"And what might that be?"

"For starters, the fact that I'm going to get out of this shirt one way or the other, even if I have to rip it to shreds. And it's not like you can actually *go* anywhere, Daisy, so you might as well help me out of the damn thing sooner rather than later. If you make me wreck my shirt for no good reason, I'm likely to be feeling a little testy by the time I get free. And then where will you be?"

"Headed straight for the lobby door with your pants in my hot little fist." She adjusted her dress to cover her breast and looked around for the shoes she'd kicked off.

"And leave me here undefended? You're too professional. Besides . . ." He licked his lips and moved a little closer. "You're gonna *like* the way I make you pay."

She slid her straps off her shoulders and gave a little shimmy, and the dress slithered down to her hips. "You'd better see that I do, or I'll make *you* pay in ways you don't want to contemplate." She unbuckled the velvet pouch belt and her gown slid down her thighs to pool on the mattress around her knees, leaving her in sheer black pantyhose and a minuscule pair of panties. "Turn around."

"And lose this view? I don't think so."

"You want help getting out of your shirt, or not?"

"There's more than one way to do that, doll face. Experiment. This is your chance to be more adventurous." He moved closer yet and she moved to meet him. They knelt in the middle of the bed, and her bare breasts flattened against his diaphragm as she reached around him to ease his shirt back into place. A second later his cuff links were removed and Daisy yanked the shirt off and tossed it aside. He reached for his bow tie, but she stayed his hand.

"I like you wearing nothing but a bow—it's like having my very own present." She grinned. "You can lose the socks, though."

He eyed her pantyhose. "You, too."

He finished first and knelt over Daisy, who had sat back to remove her hosiery. He reached for the waistband of her pantyhose where she had pushed them down around her thighs, and she fell back on her elbows and watched as he took over easing them down her legs and off her feet. He flung them aside and stretched out on top of her to kiss her again. Within moments, they were straining together, breathing heavily.

He moved a little lower to kiss her neck, then lower still to string kisses across her collarbone, and down her chest to the gentle rise of her breast. But although he cupped its soft fullness in his hand for a moment, he kept working his way lower. Finally he reached his goal.

He made a place for himself between Daisy's thighs, kneeling to pull the black wisp of satin from her hips. Then he sprawled on his stomach and propped himself up on his elbows to stroke his fingers over her inner thighs as he gazed upon the luxuriant little triangle of blond curls between them.

Suddenly her hand blocked his view, curving protectively over her mound.

"Ah, Daisy, don't," he whispered, reaching out to pry her fingers loose. "Don't cover it up." He looked up to see her staring back at him uncertainly. "It's so incredibly gorgeous." He turned his head to press his mouth first against her right thigh, then against her left. "So sweet and female and gorgeous." He brushed his chin back and forth against her downy curls.

Taking his time, he spread kisses across her thighs, in the crease where her thighs joined her torso, and across the soft beginning swells of her bottom. He petted and patted and lightly brushed the feminine curls of her mound.

But it wasn't until her hips instigated a soft rocking motion and her thighs spread of their own volition that he touched her with his tongue. His reward was hearing her heartfelt moan, feeling her thighs open and close around his ears, and her fingers clutch his hair to hold him close.

He drove her to within seconds of a screaming orgasm, then pulled back. Kneeling between her sprawled thighs, he donned protection.

Her dark eyes were lambent, her cheeks and chest flushed. "Hurry," she whispered, looking up at him. "God, Nick, please!"

He fell over her, catching himself on one hand, and reached between them with his free hand to thumb down his erection. Then he pressed his hips forward, inhaling sharply at the slick heat that opened for him as he sank all the way into her, then closed tightly around him. "Oh, God, you feel good."

She made a low sound of agreement and undulated her hips. He braced both hands on the mattress and contracted his hips, almost withdrawing. Then he pressed forward again.

He watched her face as the slow rocking of his hips drove her closer and closer to orgasm. Her eyes grew heavy-lidded and her teeth sank into her lower lip, while a flush spread across her cheeks. She was silent except for the ragged blast of her breathing. But her hips moved in synchronization with his, rising off the mattress for each of his downward thrusts to facilitate the deepest penetration possible, and her short fingernails began to press with increasing pressure into his back.

"Oh, please," she whispered. "That feels so—" She sucked in a quick breath and looked up at him as she once again bit into her lower lip. Then her reddened lip slid free of the white teeth gripping it, and she avowed fervently, "—*wonderful*. Oh, God, Nick, it feels so wonderful. I wish it could last forever."

But his hips had already begun to pick up speed, and she didn't hesitate to meet each thrust. He felt her tension grow and grow, and knew by the way she strained that her needs weren't being fully met. He changed his angle slightly to accommodate her, and savage satisfaction filled him as he watched her eyes go blind and felt her start to contract around him. Her nails dragged down his back with enough force to leave welts on his hide, and her thighs clamped down fiercely on his hips.

And all the while, that hot, slick passage squeezed and pulled at him, as if demanding equal commitment.

He dug into in the mattress with his toes and thrust himself deep within her, trying to hold back the moan clawing at his throat as satisfaction began to boil deep in his loins. Then everything blew, and his back arched and he roared her name as he came, and came, and came, in violent, scalding pulsations.

He finally eased down on top of her, burying his face in the curve of her neck. "Ah, God, Daisy."

Her arms tightened around him.

Before he had a moment to think it through, he heard himself saying, "Have I mentioned my idea for a twelve-step romance?" Tension immediately gathered in his stomach. Where had that come from?

She laughed deep in her throat. "What on earth is a twelve-step romance?"

What the hell—in for a nickel, in for a buck. He pushed up on his elbows to look into her face, and the knot in his gut relaxed a little at the sleepy smile she gave him, and the way she reached up to loop her arms around his neck.

"It's a romance that you and I take one day at a time . . . with the thought that we've got a possible future in front of us. Maybe. Someday." Her expression went blank, and he felt her muscles tightening beneath him. He stroked her face with his fingertips. "I realize you're probably confused, since I've never even told you that I care for you. But I do, you know."

"I know you care for sex with me."

"That goes without saying. But if you think that's all it is, Blondie—"

"You don't have to make me any promises, Nick." She unlinked her hands and slid them down to his shoulders, giving him a shove. He didn't budge, and her brows drew together. "In fact, I'd really rather you didn't. I accepted a long time ago that long-term relationships and me are an oxymoron." She looked him squarely in the eye. "I don't know how I can say it any plainer: I have zero luck in the romance department."

The vulnerability in her expression punched

him in the gut, and he said firmly, "That's because you've never had a relationship with me." It was hard to believe the *R* word was even coming out of his mouth, considering how he usually choked on it. And yet . . . "Hold on to your holster, cupcake, because your luck is about to change."

If anything, she grew stiffer. "And how do you see that happening, Nick—by conducting a romance like a couple of drunks one bottle shy of falling off the wagon? Why can't we just leave things where they are? Let's enjoy what we have together while we have it—and accept that sooner or later it's going to come to an end."

He opened his mouth to debate her assessment of . . . he wasn't sure what. Her take on the lasting qualities of a relationship? The relationship he specifically offered? Either way, he was stopped by the look on her face when she said, "Could we please change the subject? I don't want to talk about this anymore."

"Okay. Do you wanna stay here tonight?"

"After the fortune you've spent to rent the room? Of course."

"It means you'll have to walk through the lobby wearing your evening gown tomorrow morning."

That startled a deep and rollicking laugh out of her, the likes of which he hadn't heard since she was a teen. "And this is supposed to bother me *why*?"

"Damned if I know. It's just one of those things that would bug nine-tenths of the women I date."

She grinned up at him. "I don't know whether to wonder how many women you've lured into hotel rooms, or to point out the obvious."

"Which is?"

"I'm not the usual high-brow woman you date—though I have to wonder how high-brow they are if they run around without their underwear. But that's beside the point. I'm just a low-rent girl from the 'burbs who doesn't know enough to be embarrassed about being seen in her evening gown the morning after."

"You're low-maintenance, doll face—I wouldn't call you low-rent."

"Whatever, I'm not your usual type. And getting back to staying the night, at least the goons won't know where to find us, huh?"

"There is that. Before we get settled in for the night, though, we should make a trip down to the gift shop to pick up a few essentials."

"Such as?"

"Toothpaste, toothbrushes. More condoms."

She shoved at his shoulders again, and this time he rolled off her. "So what are we waiting for? We don't want the shop to close before we can get"—her gaze raked down his torso and lingered for an instant on his sex—"toothbrushes. Clean teeth are a priority, you know." She jumped out of bed and grinned at him. "Man, I hate to see you put your shirt back on. I love the look of you in just that cute little bow tie. Maybe I ought to go down by myself. I can get dressed faster than you can, anyway."

"Honey, the woman hasn't been born who can dress faster than a man."

"Haven't you learned anything from the past couple of days? Twenty bucks says I can beat you without breaking a sweat."

"You're on."

They dove for their clothing, and a moment later she was buckling on the little pouch that held her gun while he was still struggling with the many studs that fastened his shirt.

She stepped into her shoes and came over to help him. "I almost feel guilty for taking your money. That was too easy."

"You left off your pantyhose."

"Big deal. I could put them on and take 'em off three times and you'd still be struggling with all these silly little things."

"You've got a point there." Leaving his collar unbuttoned with the bow tie inside its opening, he tossed his cuff links on the dresser and rolled back his sleeves. "You ready?"

Daisy snorted. "Ten minutes ago, bud."

He admired the minimalist swivel of her hips as she preceded him from the room, and thought about what she'd said regarding her luck with relationships and leaving things the way they were. She was undoubtedly right. He'd argued the same points with himself ad nauseam. Yet he grinned as he closed the door behind him.

Because she'd never been wooed by a Coltrane. And it occurred to him that, at the very least, he owed it to her to show her what she'd been missing.

16

thursday

"DID you know there's a *phone* in the bathroom?" Briskly rubbing her hair with one towel and wearing another, Daisy walked into the bedroom. It was time to put a little professionalism back in this relationship. Somewhere in the last twenty-four hours she had let that slip away.

She looked over at Nick, who had gathered their breakfast dishes together and was setting the room service tray out in the hallway. For just an instant her attention got caught up in the way his tux slacks, the only garment he wore, pulled tautly over his very nice buns. Then she hauled her wandering attention back. What had she been saying? Oh, yes—"Why on earth would anyone want a telephone in the bathroom?"

He shut the door and turned to face her. "You got me; I suppose it's a perk that a certain element appreciates. Workaholic businessmen, maybe."

"Phoneaholic bathers," she couldn't resist contributing, but then drew herself up. Dammit, they weren't here to engage in nonsensical banter, no matter how infectious the urge might be. "But that's neither here nor there. It's time that we—"

"You look kinda hot, Daise." His voice adopted that low, sexual tone she had become so familiar with during the night, and her hair towel slid from suddenly nerveless fingers. He stepped close and pressed a finger into her flushed chest and they both watched the color flood back into it when he lifted his hand. He trailed the backs of his fingers across her shoulder and down her arm. "I think we oughtta get you out of this stuffy old towel and cool you down."

She managed to raise a brow. "Generous, the way you're always looking out for me."

"I know about these things. Just do whatever I say, and you won't go wrong."

She guffawed. "In your dreams, ace."

"All right." He lifted one shoulder as if it were her loss. "But you'll notice *I'm* not all flushed from being bundled up in yards of terry cloth." His fingers tugged at the fold where she'd tucked the plush towel between her breasts, but he seemed unfazed when she slapped his hands away. "You really should take this off. Be nice and cool, like me."

"Oh, yeah. That'd make us equal, all right. You with your bare chest, me buck naked."

He appeared to think it over. "You're right," he agreed. He unfastened his slacks and pushed them down his narrow hips, and they fell to the floor, leaving him gloriously naked. "There. Never let it be said that Nicholas Coltrane doesn't do his part to support equality." He reached for her towel again.

Staring at him, watching his body transform in front of her eyes, she realized he was correct about one thing. She definitely felt overheated. And really, half an hour one way or the other wouldn't matter.

She allowed him to untuck the towel.

He held it wide and slowly tracked every exposed curve with his gaze. He bent his head and kissed her shoulder. "Now, isn't that better?"

"Mmm. Much."

"Not to mention more befitting the occasion." He kissed the side of her neck. "We're just damn lucky you didn't decide to swaddle yourself in one of the guest robes. No telling what extreme measure of resuscitation *that* would have called for."

"Well, you know me." She managed a faint shrug even though her muscles were dissolving. "Always clueless about the appropriate thing to wear."

With a grip on either end of the towel he'd allowed to slip down to her hips, he hauled her in. "I'm always happy to guide you."

She looped her arms around his neck, appreciating the hard warmth of his chest. Swaying from side to side, she lightly rubbed her breasts against him. "This doesn't change anything, Nick. You should be aware of that."

"Shh," he said, and bent his head to kiss her. "I know."

*   *   *

Forty-five minutes later they walked off the elevator and crossed the lobby to the front desk. The clerk passed the bill across the counter for Nick to check, then said, "I have a message here that two men were asking about you last night, Mr. Coltrane."

Nick stilled, aware of Daisy doing the same. "Did they leave their names?"

"No, sir. The night clerk noted that they didn't appear to be our usual type of guest. She also said they became abusive when she refused to give them your room number, then declined to use the courtesy phone when she offered to ring your room for them."

"Hmmm." He handed over his credit card. "I can't imagine who it could have been. But thank you for the message."

Daisy didn't say anything until they paused outside the Fairmont's entrance. "Blunt Face and No-Neck, you think?"

He stared blindly at the Flood mansion across the street. "Had to have been." He was aware of her alertness to their surroundings, and decided it wouldn't hurt to pay closer attention himself to the activity going on around them as they made their way down the hill to the spot where he'd been lucky enough to find street parking.

Then he spotted his Porsche and was forced to reevaluate the luck factor. "*No!*"

Daisy took her eyes off the streets to look at him. "What? What is it?" She followed his gaze. "Oh, my God. Oh, Nick! Your beautiful car."

Someone—and it didn't take a card-packing

Mensa member to figure out who—had taken a tire iron to his Porsche. Its windows and head-lights were smashed, its top slashed to ribbons, its pristine body dented and caved in. It sat on four flat tires, and where it hadn't been bashed, obscenities had been scratched deep into the paint.

"Fuck," he whispered hoarsely. He circled the car, once, twice, three times, a frigid knot sitting heavy in his gut and red-hot rage clouding his brain. He lashed out at the driver's-side tire with his foot. "*Fuck!*" Then he whirled away, plunging all ten fingers into his hair, scraping it away from his face with a force that stretched the outer cor-ners of his eyes, the heels of his hands digging into his temples where a headache had begun to throb. He stared off into the distance, unaware of anything but the red mist of his temper for several long moments.

Then gradually Daisy's warmth, pressed against his back, began to penetrate. She'd wrapped her arms around his waist and her hands rubbed soothing circles on his stomach. "I'm sorry," she whispered and it occurred to him to wonder how many times she'd already said those words while he was oblivious to all but his anger and pain. "I'm so sorry."

"I love this car," he said hoarsely. "It was the first thing I bought when I began to earn more than just grocery and rent money. Even then, it took me three and a half years to pay the damn thing off." And he'd been proud of it, had kept the car in immaculate condition as a testimony not only to his increasing earning power, but to his independence from his father's spendthrift lifestyle.

"But big deal, huh? What the hell. It's not like my *dog* died—it's just a thing." But it had been *his* thing, dammit, earned with his own two hands. He felt stifled suddenly, overheated and hemmed in, and his voice came out harsh when he said, "Do you mind, Blondie? Your gun is goosing me."

He felt her stiffen, and her arms dropped away from his waist. A second later her warmth was removed from his back as she stepped away.

He discovered that the breath of coolness bestowed by his newfound freedom wasn't a big improvement. Without thinking, he turned and hauled her into his arms. She stood stiffly while he rubbed his hands up and down her back and pressed his chin against the crown of her head. "I'm really pissed, Daisy."

"So you thought you'd take it out on me?"

"Yeah. Something like that." He bowed his head to kiss her temple. "It was unfair," he admitted huskily. "I'm sorry."

"No, you were right." She pushed away. "I wasn't behaving at all professionally—"

"Ah, great, play the guilt card." It worked like a charm, too, which pissed him off all over again. "Dammit, Daisy, why not just rub a little salt in my wounds while you're at it?"

She had the temerity to laugh. At the same time, however, she reached out to touch conciliatory fingertips to his jaw—and looked so appealing with the sunlight shining in her eyes that he found his anger fading.

"I'm not trying to make you feel guilty, Nick," she assured him. "I really didn't act in a professional manner. Chances are the goon squad is hanging around, ready to pounce while we're distracted by the mess they made of your car. I should have been on the lookout for them instead of—"

"Offering me a sugar tit."

Her cheeks flushed with hot color. "Well, I wouldn't have put it quite that way, but . . . yeah."

The truth was, he liked the fact that she'd offered him comfort. She'd made it clear how important her professionalism was to her, so it showed he must be, too, if she'd put his feelings first.

He also knew better than to get sentimental over the fact. She'd just get all protective of her tough-guy image and end up making them both pay. "What do you suggest we do next?"

"You're not going to like this, but we have to call the police."

Every defense snapping firmly into place, he glared at her down his nose. "Forget it, Blondie."

"You have to file a police report before you can even talk to your insurance company, Nick."

Well . . . hell. She was right. "Fine. I'll file the report. But damned if I'm going to play the who-coulda-been-responsible-for-the-damage   game with them."

"Part of me would like nothing better than to debate the merits of that with you."

Oh, big surprise. He snorted. "Let me guess. Could it be the ex-cop part?"

She shrugged. "I'm sure you'll be thrilled to hear that the cops couldn't do anything even if you *were* willing to discuss it with them, because we don't have a shred of proof to offer. So we'll do it your way." She looked around. "I guess I was wrong about the goons lying in wait for us. I'll call a cab to take us back to your place, and we can call the cops from there to get you a case number for your insurance company. Is there anything you need from inside the car?"

He had his photo bag with him, which was his most immediate concern. He nevertheless looked inside the car—and immediately wished he hadn't. The interior had also been ripped to shreds: the leather seats torn, the rugs pulled up, the dash mutilated. The glove compartment door had been hammered until it sprung, and the knob was missing from the gearshift. Swearing under his breath, he straightened.

Daisy rubbed a comforting hand against the small of his back. "C'mon," she urged. "Let's get the hell out of here. I know you're furious, but I'd really like to avoid a shoot-out on a public street if the thugs are still around. Innocent people could get caught in the cross fire."

"Yeah." He drew a couple of deep breaths to get his emotions under control. "Let's go home."

Jacobsen shifted impatiently from one foot to the other as he looked over at Autry. "So, what are we waitin' for?" he demanded. "Let's go get 'em."

Autry was torn. Coltrane and the blond who'd bested Jacobsen were exactly where they'd set them up to be. He knew Jake was frothing at the mouth to pay Coltrane's hired muscle back, and she was all decked out in a dress, which could only slow her down. Conditions were about as favorable as they were going to get.

And yet . . .

Their pigeons looked pretty damn cozy. They'd clearly spent the night together in the hotel, and he had a feeling Douglass could use that in some way.

"*C'mon*," Jacobsen growled.

"We aren't gonna do it."

"*What?*" His partner swung around on him. "Are you fuckin' nuts? Why the hell not?"

"Where would it get us, Jake? We've already tossed the car—we know it's clean. Coltrane's not likely to be carrying the prints on him."

"So we'll beat the shit out of him until he *tells* us where he's hiding them."

"No. We're gonna play it smart this time. Coltrane's gotten pretty tight with his bodyguard. Let's take that information to Douglass—and see what he wants to do with it."

Mo watched Reid sit down across the dining room table. He was dressed in his conservative banker's pinstripes; only his rep tie had yet to be tightened; the knot was yanked down between the first and second buttons of his shirt. He returned her gaze across the polished mahogany, his hazel eyes level and his mouth unsmiling, and she thought he looked like a stranger.

An exciting stranger.

She shifted in her seat. Where on earth had

that come from? It was ridiculous, preposterous . . .

And *true*. The Reid she'd fallen in love with and married was an easygoing man, quick to laughter and slow to anger. Though their relationship had been strained for the past few years, that hadn't affected the inherent easiness that formed the basis of his personality. But the Reid looking at her now looked as if he'd be a harder sell entirely. He looked determined and somehow predatory. Sexual, even. As if he might sweep the china and silver from the table at any moment and have wild, uncontrolled sex with her on its surface.

Good grief. She pressed her thighs together. Clearly it had been much too long since they'd had *any* kind of sex, let alone the wild, uncontrolled variety. She resisted the urge to pick up her linen napkin and fan herself with it. Instead, she sat up straight and raised her eyebrows at him inquiringly. This was *not* the time to be indulging in ludicrous adolescent fantasies.

"I've got something for you," Reid said and reached into the inside breast pocket of his suit jacket. He pulled out a small stack of checks and tossed them down on the table. They fanned out when they hit the highly polished surface, but he planted a fingertip on the top one to anchor them, then pushed them over to her side of the table.

"What is this?" She reached to scoop up the stack, sorted through them one by one, then looked up at him again, her heart beginning to pound. "Reid? My God. This is—"

"About half of what you need. A few of my loanees came through for me."

Exactly the way he had said they would. *Just once it would be nice if you'd have a little faith in me.* She heard his voice in her head yet again. Apparently, he had followed up on the phone calls that she'd blown off as useless. Either that or his deadbeat school chums had come through for him just as he had said they would.

She looked across the table at him. "I . . . I . . . I . . ." She cleared her throat. "I don't know what to say."

"Say, 'You were right, Reid. I was wrong.' "

A laugh exploded in her throat. That sounded like the old Reid, but he still wasn't smiling. "You were right, Reid. I was wrong."

"Now take off your clothes."

"*What?*"

"Never mind. Just kidding."

"Oh." Too bad. She realized with surprise that she desperately wanted to get naked with the man across the table.

"Please pass the sausage before it gets cold."

She did so, as well as the fruit platter and the basket of toast she'd prepared. As they dished up their food, all was silent except for the sound of cutlery against china. Reid took a couple of bites and then set his fork down on his plate.

"Is my tux home from the cleaners?"

"Yes." She looked at him askance.

"Good. If you've got anything on your calendar for Friday night, clear it off. We're going to the Whitcomb gala."

She looked at him in surprise. "The one for J. Fitzgerald Douglass?" Usually Reid would rather contract the Black Plague than attend a mad-crush social event such as that promised to be.

"Yeah. I expect several of my old buddies to be in attendance. One or two that I've already left messages for, as well as several that I haven't gotten around to contacting. It's time to remind the first group I mean business and to let the second know their payment is overdue."

Mo set down her fork also. He looked so tough and competent, and longing rose up inside of her as she gazed at him across the table. "*Reid.*"

"We're going to get the rest of the money you need," he assured her coolly and picked up his fork again. "Then you and I are going to sit down and talk about our marriage."

17

～ oo ～

THEY were less than a mile from the carriage house when Nick suddenly ordered the cab driver to pull over to the curb. Thrown forward by the cabbie's prompt compliance, Daisy peeled herself off the back of the front seat and raised an eyebrow at Nick, who had climbed out of the car and turned to lean back in.

"Come on," he commanded impatiently and extended a hand to help her out of the cab.

The look on his face made it clear she shouldn't hold her breath waiting for an explanation, so she scooted across the seat and got out.

"Keep the meter running," Nick told the driver. "We won't be long."

Daisy resisted the drag on her hand that urged her to follow in his wake like a good little soldier. Instead she stood her ground, forcing him to stop. Shaking her gown back into place, she looked up at him. "You want to tell me what the heck is going on, Coltrane?"

"I'm cranked and I need a distraction to help

me work it out," he said. He pinned her in place with the intensity of his eyes. "But there's a limit to how many times I can nail you without making you sore."

"For heaven's sake, Nick." Heat flared in all those places he'd trained to expect pleasure, and she felt it throbbing fiercely in her cheeks.

He looked down at her and smiled for the first time since he'd seen the wreckage of his Porsche. "Just stating the facts, ma'am. Except I should have said 'make love.'" He ran a fingertip over the bridge of her nose. "I don't have anything scheduled this afternoon, and that means I'm going to have to pace myself with you. So that leaves . . . videos."

"Videos?" She looked at the storefronts and saw that they were, indeed, in front of a video store.

"You know—little movies you watch on your TV? Lots of cars and buildings exploding, people getting blown away in gloriously gory Technicolor?"

"My, doesn't that sound ducky." She grimaced but slipped beneath his arm as he held the door open for her. "How about a nice calming classic instead? *The Sound of Music*, maybe."

"Oh, yeah, that'll work out my aggressions. Next you'll be suggesting one of those artsy subtitled foreign films."

"Nah. I've never particularly cared for reading my movies."

The store was deserted at that hour of the morning, but the young woman behind the desk stopped in the midst of checking in a stack of returned videos to stare at them. Her jaw ceased masticating her gum midchew.

"What?" Daisy stared the girl down. "Don't all your patrons come in dressed like this?"

"Um, no, ma'am."

Daisy's head reared back. "*Ma'am?*" she whispered in horror.

Nick tugged on her arm. "Come on. The meter's running."

She strode along in his wake, but not without shooting a last, malevolent look over her shoulder. "She called me ma'am, Nick. My *mother* is a ma'am."

"It's not an insult, Blondie. The girl's just being polite. Consider it a sign of respect."

"Respect, my ass. It's a sign of age." She peered at her reflection in a piece of chrome shelving as they whizzed past. Granted, she didn't look nearly as good as when Benny had fixed her up. But she was pretty sure she didn't look any older than she had yesterday.

He stopped in front of a shelf and pulled down an empty video box. "Now, *this* is a classic."

"*The Abyss*? Ooh, it's got Ed Harris in it. I like him." She took the box from him and flipped it over to read the back copy. "Nick, it's science fiction!"

"Yeah, but you'll like it. It's got lots of female-friendly stuff in it."

She narrowed her eyes. "Define female-friendly."

"You know, love stuff." Her eyes must have grown downright dangerous because he quickly amended, "Did I say love stuff? I meant chick-empowerment stuff. Now you pick one."

"I bet I know where I can find something male-friendly." She dragged him over to the cartoon section.

"Very funny. You going to actually pick something, or are you going to leave it all up to me?"

"Fat chance. Like I want to spend the afternoon watching exploding cars or women with grossly augmented boobs." She walked over to the classics and checked out the titles. "How about *Harvey*? Or *Friendly Persuasion*, maybe."

He leaned to study her selections. "My choice is rabbits or geese?" Shrugging, he straightened. "You're right. This was a dumb idea."

"I never said that."

"Yeah, well, you're right anyway. Let's go home. I'll go back to Plan A."

"I know I'm going to regret this, but I'll bite. What's Plan A?"

"That's where I spend the afternoon ruining you for other men."

She had an awful feeling he'd already done that, and her chances of getting out of this relationship with a whole, unbruised heart were growing slimmer by the hour. That didn't stop her from angling her chin up at him. "I don't know how to break this to you, Coltrane, but your ego is immensely larger than your di—"

He clamped a hand over her mouth. But he grinned down at her and some of the shadows fled from his eyes. "Miss Parker, please. If you can't say anything nice, at least have the decency to be vague."

She pulled his hand away. "That's very cute, Nick. Did you learn that at the Thumper School of Charm?"

"No, I'm pretty sure it was at a survival training course for the ever-fragile male id." He jerked his thumb at the video shelf. "Make your selection. If we don't get a move on, our cab fare's going to rival the national debt."

Clouds had begun to roll in from the ocean by the time the taxi dropped them off, and the temperature had dropped a good fifteen degrees. Daisy went straight to the bedroom to change into a sweater and jeans. When she came out, Nick had taken off his tux jacket and was on the phone at the breakfast bar, reporting the damage to his car. She listened as he finished the conversation with the police department, then dialed his insurance company.

He was tense when he joined her on the couch a few moments later, and the shadows were back in his eyes. She tossed aside the magazine she hadn't really been reading and swiveled to face him, hugging her knees to her chest. "Are you okay?"

"No." He yanked off his bow tie and started working the studs out of his shirt. "I'm hacked off all over again. Those goons wrecked my car for no good reason, my insurance company is probably going to raise my rates, and I'm being persecuted by a man everyone else considers a—" He cut himself off and stared down at a pearlized stud that refused to slip free of its hole. "This freakin' shirt isn't helping. Who the hell invented these fasteners, anyway?" Curling his fingers around the plackets, he pulled roughly with both hands, threatening the hand-sewn buttonhole that hadn't released its stud quickly enough, as well as those still fastened below it.

"Easy," she said softly and rolled onto her knees in front of him. She brushed his hands away and eased the last few studs free. Then she rose up to push the shirt off his shoulders and down his arms.

As it fell to the couch behind him, he stared at her with eyes that burned like blue flames. "Wonderful. And to top it all off, I'm acting like an idiot."

"Don't be so hard on yourself, Nick. It's been a stressful morning. You're entitled to a little temper."

"Ah, man." He framed her face in his hands. "I love you, girl." Then he bent his head and kissed her.

Her heart smacked up against the wall of her chest, where it throbbed in hard, heavy beats even though she knew perfectly well that he didn't mean *love* her love her. It was a figure of speech. He'd hadn't meant it as if he were *in* love with her, or anything.

Which was fine; that was exactly the way it should be. Theirs was strictly a physical relationship. And a temporary physical relationship at that.

The warmth wrapping itself around her heart was simply generated by the presence of shared body heat on a chilly spring day.

She told herself that several times as he undressed her and stretched his warm, hard length out on top of her. She tried to keep it in the fore-front of her mind as he made tender, careful, slower-than-molasses love to her. She clung desperately to it as he rocked her into sweet oblivion, whispering, "I love you, Daisy. Love you, love you, love you," as he drove her over the precipice into a place that was hot and pulsating and reverberated with the shuddered sighs of satisfaction.

Satiated right down to the bone, she found it difficult to think coherently, let alone erect an armor of attitude around her. So she lay quietly in Nick's arms, and he held her for a long time before he finally sat her up and tucked her into the corner of the couch with an afghan around her. He braced his long hands against the arm and the back of the couch to cage her in and stared down at her. "Ah, man, Daise." Bending his elbows, he pressed a soft kiss to her lips. "*Thank* you. I think I might actually be able to cope now."

See there? she told herself. *It was sex talk. Nothing but sex talk.* Something in his expression, though, some tenderness or amusement as he smiled down at her, made her shift uneasily. But before she could run it to earth and interrogate it until it gave up all its secrets, he'd scooped up his discarded tux and padded naked from the living room.

He was back a few minutes later, his feet bare, wearing an old pair of jeans and pulling a faded navy sweatshirt over his head. By then she'd decided that the less said, the better. The smart money said everything would be back to normal tomorrow, so what was the point of borrowing trouble today?

Finger-combing his hair out of his eyes, Nick went straight to the kitchen. A minute later the sound and smell of popcorn popping wafted down to her. Daisy rose up on her knees and turned to watch him over the back of the couch. "What can I do to help?"

"Get the video ready. You can fast-forward through the coming attractions." He glanced over at her. "What would you like to drink?"

"A Coke, I guess."

"I've got beer, if you'd rather have that."

"Not for me, but you go ahead. Any kind of cola will be fine." She was still on the job, no matter how much he tried to confuse her into thinking this was a date.

A few minutes later, he carried over a tray and lowered it for her to pick up the icy can of pop and a glass full of ice. While she popped the pull tab and poured, he set his long-necked beer bottle down on the trunk and grabbed up a big bowl of buttered popcorn and a stack of napkins. Then he dropped down next to her. Gesturing for her to spread the afghan over both of them, he set the bowl in her lap, picked up the remote to activate the video, and settled back as the movie he'd selected began, draping his arm over her shoulders.

Daisy settled against the solid warmth of his side. She picked up her drink and tangled fingers with him when they both reached into the bowl of popcorn at the same time. But her gaze didn't leave the television; she was already drawn into the story unfolding on the screen.

She would kiss a snake before she'd admit it, but she found herself enthralled by the movie's love story. She assured herself it was strictly due to the heroine, who was unexpectedly neither a wimp who depended upon the hero to save her sorry rear or one who allowed him to walk all over her. Instead the heroine strode into the first scene in kick-butt mode and didn't seem to care if people liked her or not. Daisy strongly suspected that Nick had been jerking her chain when he'd made that crack about female empowerment, but in truth the heroine took care of business even though she had problems of her own, and Daisy liked that very much.

She also liked *this*: being with Nick, lounging around passing an afternoon watching videos. It caught her by surprise, in part because never in a trillion years would she have pegged him as the type to be content with such low-maintenance entertainment. She always thought of him in conjunction with pricey wines, stylish clothes, and sophisticated company. Someone who dined out more often than not and used his home mainly as a place to change for the next event.

She was beginning to suspect she'd been doing him an injustice. True, he was totally at home in the midst of San Francisco's society scene, and he dressed like a GQ model most of the time. But he appeared equally comfortable cooking in his kitchen, guzzling beer, and wearing old jeans. And his place was undeniably homey and obviously well lived-in.

He started messing with her before the movie ended, fingering the curve of her ear, sliding his hands beneath her sweater. Engrossed in the video, she hunched her ear to her shoulder and fended him off with an elbow.

But he managed to get her fully primed all the same, and the instant the credits started rolling across the screen, she swung around to straddle his lap. She gave him a fiercely carnal kiss, and the next thing she knew, she was lying spent and limp against his chest with a smile on her face, her jeans on the floor, and her sweater shoved up to her armpits. Nick was in an similar state, except his jeans had only made it to his knees.

He stretched hugely, and she rode the swell of his chest as his arms reached for the sky. Then he brought his hands down and rubbed them slowly up and down the bare curve of her rear. He tucked his chin into his neck and smiled down at her. "I love you, Daisy."

Her relaxed state vanished and, feeling awkward and gawky, she disengaged herself and climbed to her feet. She bent for her jeans and discovered her panties dangling from one ankle. Straightening them out, she stepped into the other side and pulled them up, then grabbed for her jeans, looking up at him. "You don't have to say that." And she really, really wished he wouldn't. The words came much too easily to him and hearing them was too painful, when he'd taught her that the next step was watching the door swing shut behind his back. "You're going to get laid either way, so please don't, okay?" She tugged down her sweater. "You hungry? Why don't I go throw together a couple of sandwiches."

He didn't say anything and she escaped to the kitchen, furiously aware that she felt like crying. She sucked air in through her nose, gritted her teeth, and stared with hot eyes into the bread drawer until the feeling passed. She pulled out a loaf of twelve-grain and turned to slap it on the counter.

Nick stood on the other side. She hadn't heard him approach, but there he was. Hoping that if she ignored him he'd let it drop, she reached for the little plastic clip holding the bread bag closed.

She should have known better. His hand flashed across the counter to clamp over hers, and she knew fighting him for possession of it would only delay the inevitable. Standing very still, she met his gaze and heaved a long-suffering sigh.

He gave her a tender smile and released her. "Look, ma, no hard-on," he said and stepped back to spread his arms wide, inviting her to make her own inspection. When she did precisely that, one corner of his mouth kicked up. He gave her a moment, then said, "You think we can both agree that I'm not looking to get lucky right this minute?"

She shrugged.

"I'll take that as a yes. Okay, then read my lips, cupcake, because this isn't my dick talking.

This is straight from here." He slapped his hands over his heart. "I love you."

She threw the loaf of bread at him. "Stop saying that!"

"I can't." He vaulted the breakfast bar and landed in front of her. He stroked his fingertips down her cheek and smiled crookedly when she slapped them away. "I love you."

A secret part of her thrilled to hear it, and she backed away from him in horror. *No*, dammit. She was not going down that road again. She had a bad, bad feeling that this time it would be even harder to recover than the last time they'd played this scene. She welcomed the hot rush of anger that suffused her from head to toe; it enabled her to face him coolly. "Wait five minutes," she advised him flatly. "I'm sure it will pass. Isn't that the way you usually operate?"

He took a step forward for every backward one she took. "You think I didn't fight this? The last thing I want is to be in love—you and I know better than most what the odds are of a relationship panning out."

"I also know better than anyone that you can say, 'I love you,' with a perfectly straight face one minute and then turn around and say, 'Just kidding,' the next."

"I never said, 'Just kidding'!"

"Close enough." Her butt hit the counter and she angled her chin up at him. "You said not to be naive, that it was just hormones talking. Then you turned around and walked right out the door."

"I was so freakin' shook," he said hoarsely. "I

felt like I'd set off an atom bomb when all I'd thought I had my hands on was a cherry bomb."

"No pun intended, I'm sure."

"I'm not kidding around, Blondie. I felt everything too keenly that night, and I tell you true, it scared the shit out of me. I *wanted* it to be just sex talk. Because if it wasn't, I was pretty damn sure I'd end up living my dad's life."

The intensity in his voice and eyes made her heart beat so furiously she half expected to see its imprint against her sweater. But she stiffened her spine and met his gaze head-on. "I have to hand it to you—you're quite the spin doctor. It takes real talent to rewrite history."

"Yeah, and talk's cheap. So I guess I'm just going to have to prove it to you over time."

"There is no 'over time,' Coltrane. Not for you and me. There's only this assignment."

"There's today, Parker. I'll start with that." He cupped her face with butterfly gentleness. Daisy grasped his wrists to tug them away, but without any seeming effort his hands remained exactly where they were. He gave her a crooked smile, then lowered his head and bestowed upon her lips the softest, tenderest kiss she had ever received. All the starch left her backbone and she wilted against the counter.

She kissed him back with unchecked ardor. But somewhere in a hazy corner of her mind she assured herself she wasn't falling for his blarney hook, line, and sinker. No, sir.

She was simply taking a tiny time-out.

18

friday

NICK slept like the dead and awakened disoriented, but strangely content. It was still dark, and for a moment he couldn't tell what day it was or even where he was. Fuzzy-minded and inert, feeling as if someone had snuck in during the night and stolen his skeletal system right out from under his skin, it took him a while to become aware of the heat that burned against his back, the arm that lay heavy over his waist. He rolled carefully onto his back and looked down on Daisy. Contentment blossomed into full-bloomed happiness.

She'd flopped half onto her face with the removal of his back's support, and even in her sleep she didn't take kindly to the treatment. Her eyebrows drew together and her soft mouth pursed in disgruntlement. She shivered as the blankets he'd displaced allowed the chill morning air to reach her bare skin, and then her hand swept across the mattress in search of him. The moment her fingers came into contact with his hip, she squirmed across the sheet until she was snuggled up against his side. Her cheek found itself a resting place in the hollow beneath his collarbone, and she cuddled closer yet, wedging a thigh between his.

Nick lifted his head and tucked in his chin to watch her, enjoying the smooth slide of her legs, the press of her breasts, as she shifted in search of the perfect position. Her hand left a trail of prickling awareness as it slid up his chest, over his collarbone, and along his neck, to finally tangle in his hair. A smile curled her lips and she made a sound of satisfaction deep in her throat. Then she went boneless and heavy as she sank back into a deeper sleep.

He wrapped an arm around her and grinned in the dark. Who would've thought that someone who could be so prickly when she was awake would turn out to be such a cuddler? Although, once he thought about it, he realized it shouldn't come as a surprise. Daisy was an extremely tactile woman. God knew she had never hesitated to lay hands on *him*—be it with friendly intentions or hostile.

But the real question was, who would've thought he'd turn out to be such a fool for love? And he *was* in love, despite the lengths he'd gone to deny it.

It had hit him like a club upside the head when they'd stood in that video store with his hand over her mouth to keep her from disparaging the size of the Big Guy. He'd felt like hell up until that moment, sick with an impotent fury that had churned his gut over the destruction of his car. Every other woman he knew would have poor-babied him until he got a handle on the situation. Although Daisy had been supportive and sympathetic when they'd first seen the car, she hadn't given him any special consideration. Then he'd embarrassed her with that ruining comment. Not one to take such things lying down, she'd angled that stubborn chin up at him, gave him her usual rash of shit, and *POW*! Just like that, he'd felt *happy*, when he had absolutely no reason to be. It was beyond rationality, and he'd known in that instant he was a goner. He simply couldn't pretend anymore that he wasn't.

His feelings for her were so powerful, they scared the bejesus out of him. But everything was sharper, clearer, *brighter* when Blondie was around—reams more vibrant and worlds more exciting. He had a perfectly acceptable life without her, but ah, God—*with* her he felt a hundred times more alive.

So, yeah, he'd be a fool not to be scared. Daisy had the power to hurt him in ways he wasn't sure he even fully comprehended. But he was through trying to delude himself. It wasn't merely lust, or affection, or friendship. The truth was, he'd probably been in love with her nine years ago. He just hadn't been ready to acknowledge it.

He was fascinated by every aspect of her, but particularly by the contradictions in her personality. The way she could be so physically fearless and yet so emotionally shy. She could take a hit from a man twice her size without a blink ... then turn around and blush like a schoolgirl at a little sex talk.

Then she could turn around yet again and participate in the act itself with all the enthusiasm—if not the practiced moves—of a courtesan trained from birth for that express purpose.

She could be tactful; she could be blunt to the point of abrasiveness. He'd seen her display phenomenal patience one moment and be downright temperamental the next. She could be brusque or charming. He never knew quite what to expect from her ... except that she would always be honest with him. Daisy didn't have a pretentious bone in her body and her bullshit quotient was pretty much nil.

He also knew that he had his work cut out for him if he hoped to have her return his love. She had given it to him freely once, and he'd thrown it back in her face. It wouldn't be a stroll down the Embarcadero to win it back.

What was needed here was some serious courting. But how was he supposed to pull that off when he and Daisy lived in each other's pocket? It wasn't as if he could show up on her doorstep with a fistful of posies, or serenade her beneath her window, or whisk her off for a night of candlelit dining and slow dancing.

Still ... it wasn't impossible. There were always things that could be done. Kissing Daisy's brow, he eased her off of him and onto the mattress. She muttered a protest, but he slid a pillow beneath her head and tucked the blankets around her, and she settled in. Then he climbed from the bed and reached for his jeans.

Time was in limited supply, and he had a lot to do.

The distinct click of the front door closing awakened Daisy, and she sat straight up in bed. Nick was not beside her, and she didn't pause to think twice. She tossed back the covers and shot out of bed, stark naked. Heart pounding, she grabbed her gun and ran for the living room, fully expecting to see Nick in the goon squad's clutches.

Instead she found him sauntering alone down the short hallway that led from the front door, his eyebrows drawn together as he studied something inside a cardboard folder in his hands. She skidded to a halt, anticlimax causing her gun hand to drop limply to her side.

The commotion of her entrance made him look up, and he stopped dead. "Whoa," he said with a crooked smile. "Am I dreaming? 'Cause this is the *embodiment* of a running fantasy of mine." He gave her that eyebrow-lifted, wry look he was so good at. "Except for the gun part. Usually the naked women in my fantasies have one of those French white baking dishes in their hands, or a sautéeing pan or something—symbols that signify they're whipping up goodies to fulfill my second greatest desire." He gave her a slow up-and-down perusal, his gaze lingering on her breasts. "You look cold, cupcake."

She *felt* cold. The shock of brisk morning air against her sleep-warmed skin had raised a fine crop of goosebumps from ankles to throat and had shrunken her nipples to achy little points. When she went to rub her hands up and down her arms to restore a bit of warmth, she was reminded of the gun in her hand, and she activated its safety catch and set the weapon down. "I heard the front door, and I thought for sure the goons had arrived."

"So you came racing out in your birthday suit to save my hide. Ah, Daisy, you are the best." He tugged his sweater off over his head and tossed it to her.

Catching it in both hands, she stared at the folder he'd clamped between his knees to free up his hands. Gesturing at it, she demanded, "What have you got there?" She pulled on his sweater, shivering in appreciation of its retained body heat. Pushing up the sleeves, she reached for the folder, which was back in his hand. "Did somebody leave that out on the landing? You shouldn't have opened the door without backup, you know." She made another grab for it when he held it out of her reach. "Coltrane, do you mind? Let me check it out."

He fended her off. "Nobody left it, Blondie, so you don't have to worry about it being a letter bomb or anything. I just got done developing it."

She stilled, one hand braced on his chest, the other halted midreach. "You what?"

"Just developed it. It's a photograph."

"You went down to the darkroom without me?"

"Yeah, I wanted to surprise—"

"*Without me?* Dammit, Nick!" She thumped him on the chest. "Are you out of your mind?

What will it take before you realize that these guys are serious? They don't *like* you."

"And I'm not wild about them, either." He grabbed the hand she'd hit him with and kissed her knuckles. "Which is why I was extra, super careful. Caution is my middle name."

"Sloan is your middle name, Coltrane. Or is that Stupid? I know it's one of those *S* words."

"You're so cute when you're worried."

That really made her see red, but he took a swift step back from her, his hands held wide. He turned in a full circle. "See? I'm all in one piece."

Fear was so much easier to deal with than rage. Taking a deep breath, though, Daisy sucked up both emotions.

Like the man said, he was still in one piece. Yelling at him for what *could* have been would be satisfying, but ultimately it would only make her look like a girlfriend or something. She raised her chin. "You hired me to keep you safe. I can't do that if you persist in running off without me."

"What 'persist,' Blondie? It was one time." He swept her up in his arms, but she held herself stiffly, refusing to be charmed. Stepping abreast of the small hall table, he dipped his knees. "Grab your gun. I know you don't like to get too far away from it."

She picked it up. "What's in that folder, anyway?" she demanded. She made a grab for it, then clutched at his neck when he spun in a fast circle. "Put me down, you fool."

"I don't think so. I like the way you feel in my arms."

Man, she wished he wouldn't say stuff like that. It made her feel way too high-school-girlish inside.

He collapsed onto the couch with her in his lap, and she was aware of the worn texture of his jeans beneath her bare legs. "So," he said. "You want to see what this is, huh?" He wiggled the folder in front of her nose.

"Yeah. I would really like to see what you consider important enough to risk your neck over."

He handed it to her without comment.

Shooting him a curious glance, she unwound the string that looped in a figure eight between two flat buttons, opened both flaps of the folder, and found herself looking at a five-by-seven black and white photograph of—"Oh!"

Her. It was a head shot of her. And not a pose that showed her all made-up and glamorous, the way she'd looked last night, but one depicting her everyday self—only better. It was a she who was all shadows and eyes, killer cheekbones and mystery, a she who looked so much more interesting than she knew was actually the case. Even her nose, which occasionally gave her fits of self-consciousness, looked just as it should be—and not too large at all.

"Oh, Nick. This is so . . ." At a loss, she lightly traced a finger over the planes and hollows of her image. It was so lifelike she found it difficult to believe the photo could possibly be only two-dimensional. Then, becoming aware of Nick's stillness beneath her, of the rigidity of his bare arm supporting her back, she met his eyes. "*Fabulous*. This is just so utterly fabulous."

"Yeah?" He let out a breath as if he'd actually worried about her reaction. "That shot was my favorite of the lot, but I never know for sure which one a subject might like and which one she'll hate."

She was touched by his uncertainty, for he had to know how special this was. "Well, I love it. Thank you." She tilted her head to bestow a kiss of appreciation upon his lips. She lingered for a moment, then pulled back. "It was a wonderful surprise," she admitted, then narrowed her eyes at him. "But don't go down to your darkroom without me again." Reopening the folder, she admired the photograph anew.

He slid his hand up her bare thigh and beneath the hem of his sweater. "Yes, ma'am."

She grabbed his wrist to put a halt to the encroachment before it touched upon some very personal territory. "For heaven's sake, Coltrane," she demanded, "don't you ever think about anything else?"

"When I've got a half-naked blond in my arms?" He made a derisive noise. "Yeah, right—let's talk mathematical theory."

He wiggled his fingers and the brush of his fingertips against the downy curls at the apex of her thighs felt so good, she found herself parting them to allow him closer access. The instant she realized what she was doing she clamped her legs together again, but that simply trapped his hand right where he wanted it—and with a murmur of approval, he oscillated his fingertips to devastating results within the limited confines allowed him. Her voice was a little desperate and a lot breathy when she demanded, "What's on the agenda for today?"

"Well, you might want to contact Benny, because we've got another gig tonight that requires dressing up." He bent his head to plant a soft kiss on the vulnerable skin behind her ear. Then he moved his lips forward a fraction and whispered, "And we have appointments to go over the contact sheets with the Trevors and the Morrisons, so they can make their selections and place their orders."

He was merely replying to her question, but he might as well have been whispering red-hot promises in her ear; the effect was the same. And that was *before* he caught her earlobe between his teeth. She was highly aware of his warm breath bathing the whorls of her ear and the goose-bumps that trailed from that point down the entire left side of her body.

He shifted her around and she felt his erection nudging insistently against her bottom while his fingers continued their frontal assault. "But that's not until this afternoon," he said huskily. "And in the meantime, Ms. Parker . . ."

What the heck. She unclenched her knees and let her legs slide apart. "In the meantime, Coltrane, you're wearing way too many clothes." Twisting around on his lap, she kissed him with fierce intent and reached for the button on his waistband.

Less than an hour later, Daisy felt physically replete but emotionally tattered. Stepping from the shower, she cleared a circle in the steamy mirror above the sink and stared at her damp reflection. What on earth was she going to do about Nick? He persisted in saying he loved her.

Daisy brushed her teeth to within an inch of their life while stewing about such unfair tactics. Every time he said it, the words *did* something to her, stirred feelings that she had long believed safely harnessed. He had to quit making love with that slow-handed tenderness that nearly brought tears to her eyes, too.

She spit foamy toothpaste into the sink and turned on the water to rinse her mouth. Darn him, anyway! She wasn't the weepy, clingy type, yet every time he'd gotten his hands on her since that first, treacherous "I love you" had slipped out of his mouth, she'd had this insane urge to cling and to beg and to make all sorts of unrealistic promises.

She ruthlessly slicked her wet hair away from her face, plying her comb until regimented tracks cut furrows from her forehead to her nape. Then she pulled on her panties, applied lotion in a slapdash manner, and climbed into her jeans. She took a deep breath and reached for her orange chenille sweater.

Okay, so he was being sweet. That didn't mean she had to react like the gawky high school jock she once was. But truthfully, that's how she felt—as if she were suddenly being rushed by the hippest, most popular guy in school.

She ought to simply enjoy the attention while she could. *Heartbreak Avoidance 101: Enjoy it, but don't get used to it.* That seemed simple enough.

Except . . .

God, she liked the feeling she got when he turned the focus of all that attention on her—she liked it way too much. She loved feeling as if she were pretty and interesting and desirable, and knowing that Nick wanted *her* when he could have any woman in San Francisco.

But she'd be a fool to grow accustomed to it. *That* could land her in some big-time trouble indeed. She studied her reflection in the mirror, searching for whatever it was that seemed to draw him. It wasn't an awful face, by any means. It was simply . . . ordinary. She sure didn't see the interesting bones and shadows that she'd seen in Nick's photograph of her. She didn't see the mystery.

And that was all right. She straightened away from the mirror. She was who she was: a down-to-earth woman who was sometimes pretty, but mostly just kind of average. She didn't apologize for it. Neither did she see the point in attempting to change it at this late date.

She drew in a deep breath. Darn it, she *would* enjoy Nick's attention while it lasted. And the next time he said he loved her, she would continue to do exactly what she was doing right now: she'd bite her tongue against the words that crowded up her throat.

She would *not* say she loved him back.

19

~∞~

DAISY jumped a foot when the doorbell rang shortly after lunch. She hadn't heard anyone come up the exterior stairs, and that wasn't good. The stairs were made of creaky wood; a person would have to work overtime to keep from making a lot of noise.

Waving Nick back, she picked up her Glock and removed the safety. Holding it in a two-handed grip pointed at the ceiling, she sidled down the hallway, stopping short of the door to plaster herself against the wall. "Who is it?"

"Florist, ma'am. I've got a delivery."

Sure he did. "Leave it on the landing."

"I can't, ma'am. I need a signature."

Great—she was a sitting duck standing here. "Hang on a second." She stealthily eased back the deadbolt, then stole silently back down the hallway and around the corner. Seeing Nick watching her from the couch, she whispered, "Get out of the line of fire."

"Uh, Daise—"

"Please, just this once, don't argue with me."

256

He shrugged and came to join her against the wall. She poked her head around the corner and raised her voice to say, "Okay, you can come in." Then she ducked back out of sight.

The door opened with enough force to hit the wall, and Daisy waited for the sound of a shotgun blasting through the solid panel. That's what a professional would likely do: assume his quarry was hiding behind the open door and remove the threat in one economical move.

But there was only silence. Then the same voice said tentatively, "Ma'am?"

She pivoted away from the wall, landing in a semi-crouch in the hallway, her weapon extended in a two-handed shooting position. In her sights was a slightly built young man in a white T-shirt and khakis, holding a box containing an arrangement of coral-hued roses and little daisies.

He took one look at the gun pointed at his chest and turned as white as his shirt. The flowers fell to the floor as his hands shot up in the air. "Christ, lady, don't shoot me!"

"You really do have flowers," she said stupidly and lowered the gun to her side. "I'm sorry. I thought . . ." Watching his gaze, bug-eyed and glazed with fear, as it locked on the gun, she shook her head. "I guess you don't give a rip what I thought. But I do apologize." Then curiosity got the better of her. "Who are the flowers for, anyway? Are they okay?"

Nick gently moved her aside. He squatted to right the box, reaching into the now-damp florist paper to resettle the vase within its folds. It was a miracle it hadn't broken. Then he rose to his feet and pulled his wallet from his hip pocket. He extracted a large bill and handed it to the delivery boy. "Major PMS," he murmured. "Which is why she's getting flowers in the first place."

Daisy grimaced, but didn't correct the outrageous falsehood. She simply watched as Nick signed the shaken young man's clipboard and ushered him out.

"Well." Shutting the door, he turned back to her with a crooked smile. "That was entertaining."

Heat scorched Daisy's cheeks. "I expected the goons. How was I supposed to know that one of your girlfriends would send you flowers?"

"They aren't for me, doll face. The card says Daisy Parker."

"What?" Her heartbeat picked up an extra throb. "Let me see that. There must be some mistake; no one sends me flowers."

He was leaning over to pick up the box, but stopped midbend to stare at her. "You're kidding. Surely someone's sent you flowers in your lifetime."

"Well, my mom sent me a real pretty spring bouquet when I graduated from the academy. And Benny and the boys brought me a fistful of tulips and daffodils once when I had them over for a spaghetti feed. But that's about it. I've never—you know—gotten flowers from a boyfriend, or anything. I'm not the type."

"Huh. You must be more the type than you think, because this definitely has your name on it." Stopping in front of her, he offered the arrangement.

Tempted to snatch the bouquet out of his hands, she forced an air of nonchalance when she reached out to accept it. That was about as far as her cool would stretch, however. The lush, rounded arrangement of plump coral roses, made lacy with clusters of miniature yellow-centered daisies, drew her like a siren song, and she carefully unseated it from its cushioning box. A moment later, she held the vase with its filmy, opalescent bow in her hand. She stared at the bouquet in awe.

"God, Nick, have you ever seen anything so pretty in your life? And they're for *me*." She buried her face in the flowers, inhaling the earthy scent of daisies and ferns, the richer, sweeter perfume of roses.

Coming up for air a few moments later, she delved within the blossoms for the little white envelope. After opening it up, she extracted the tagboard card inside. " 'To my darling Daisy,' " she read aloud, then skimmed ahead. "Oh!" Her gaze flew to Nick's face, then back to the card in her hands, and her heart began to thunder.

"Read it out loud. All of it."

Face hot, throat thick, she read, " 'I ran away from the truth once, but I'm—' " She choked into silence, unable to speak past the lump in her throat.

" 'But I'm running no longer,' " Nick continued. He gripped her shoulders and gazed down at her intently. " 'You own me, body and soul. All my love, Nick.' "

"Oh." To her acute embarrassment, scalding tears rose in her eyes.

"You do, you know," he said fiercely. "I was a chickenshit nine years ago, but I'm through running away from my feelings. I love you."

"I love your flowers," she whispered.

"You love more than my flowers."

She swallowed hard. "Yes. I love the photograph you did of me, too."

He gave her a little shake. "You love *me*."

"No." But she couldn't quite look him in the eyes. She stared at the arrangement in her hands.

"Yes, you do." Hands tightening on her shoulders, he bent to peer into her face. "You love me, Blondie. Admit it."

That brought her head up. "I admit nothing."

"You love me." And he kissed her, softly, sweetly. She was limp and dazed by the time he lifted his head again. It was so unfair, this easy ability he had to muddle her. "You love me," he insisted. "Say it."

"Maybe I love you." Her chin shot up even farther. "But don't go getting a fat head over it, Coltrane—because if I do, it's only just a little."

"Just a little." He nodded once and gave her a small, one-sided smile. "Gotcha. So, you want to put some water in that vase? Most of it wound up all over the floor."

Daisy peered at him suspiciously. "That's it? I tell you I might love you, at least a little, and you want me to water my flowers?"

"What can I say?" One big shoulder inched up toward his ear. "I have to settle for whatever you'll give me, right? Or did I misunderstand?

Do I get the option of picking what's behind door number two, instead?"

"No."

"Not much point in arguing about it, then, is there?" But Nick's eyes narrowed, and the look that glinted at her from behind his thick lashes sent her heart into hyperdrive. "But don't get too comfortable, Parker. Because it's only for now."

When Nick wasn't cuddling, teasing, or otherwise messing with Daisy that afternoon, he was gazing upon her with a great deal of satisfaction. She loved him. And not just the miserly amount she'd owned up to, either—she loved him, period. He dwelled upon it, reveled in it, thought about it almost constantly. And it warmed him right down to his bones.

He found his own fatuousness amusing, and just the tiniest bit embarrassing. Yet he was filled with the excitement of emotions he couldn't even fully identify . . . but which made him feel mighty good anyway.

He wanted to pin Blondie down and make her admit to more, to make her confess that she yearned for permanence in this cockeyed relationship . . . the same way he did.

And wasn't that a giant kick in the pants?

Suddenly, though, a relationship didn't seem so all-fired scary. And it wasn't necessarily preordained to fail. He didn't know why it had taken him so long to figure it out, but any idiot could see he wasn't his father—and didn't have to make the old man's mistakes.

He suddenly understood that he had his own

choices to make, and that he could do a much
better job of marriage than dear old Dad ever
had. Every time the thought crossed his mind, it
brought what he was sure was an imbecilic grin
to his face. Suddenly life was grand, and all he
wanted was to see this thing with Daisy last.

Till the high noon of forever.

Who would have thought it? He could feel the
dopey grin tugging at his mouth again. The very
idea ought to scare the crap out of him, but instead he felt great.

Right up until the moment the reality of his
situation started to sink in. Which, of course, it
eventually did. And once it had—once it had
sunk in good and deep—he came to an important realization.

He was screwed.

For he'd left one teeny, tiny detail out of the
idyllic future he'd been building for them in his
mind. He'd left out how fast and loose he'd been
playing with the truth up to this point. Funny,
how conveniently he'd managed to forget that.

Because Daisy was big on honesty. And he
had a feeling that she wasn't going to be nearly
as insouciant as he was about his ability to lapse
in and out of it.

Especially if the worst case scenario came to
pass, and they ran across J. Fitzgerald Douglass
tonight.

Knowing that this evening's gala was being
held to honor Douglass, Nick had thought a lot,
the last couple of days, about what he should do
about it. A bright person probably would have
begged off, considering the man was trying to

kill him. But until the other night, he had pretty much forgotten that J. Fitzpatrick was even the featured guest.

In his own defense, he hadn't had a personal connection with Douglass when he'd accepted tonight's commission. So he'd simply marked the assignment in his day planner and allowed it to drift to the back of his mind. And while the smart thing—once he had remembered—would have been to plead an illness, it was too late now to tell Mrs. Whitcomb and the committee who had worked so hard to organize the evening's event that they had to find someone else.

He did have a standard or two.

Besides, he was damned if he'd allow Douglass to send him scurrying for cover. Nick was a fan of old spaghetti westerns, and he knew what Clint Eastwood would do in this situation. He'd shift his cigar to the other side of his mouth, tuck his duster behind his six-shooter, and make his presence known. Which was pretty much what Nick planned to do tonight. He might not get in Douglass' face, but he wasn't about to hide in the shadows, either. He was the good guy in this scenario.

The drawback to doing that was its potential to screw him up with Daisy, since he hadn't set the record straight with her yet.

Watching her talk on the phone, he debated telling her now, before they made their rounds with the contact sheets. He blinked when she suddenly covered the mouthpiece with her palm and turned to him.

"Do we have time to stop by Benny's workplace so he can do my hair and makeup? It's pretty much now or never, he says. After the next hour or so, he's going to be tied up."

"Helena Morrison can't be changed because of her chemo appointment, but we're not scheduled to be there until two-thirty. Let me call the Trevors. If I can push them back to three-thirty or four, it should be fine."

"Benny," Daisy said into the receiver. "I'll call you back in five minutes." She disconnected and handed him the phone.

Ten minutes later he was backing the rental car out of the carriage house. He looked over at Daisy as they pulled up to the gate. "Where to?"

"Post Avenue. It's a place called the Motherlode."

Nick stood on the brakes and stared at her. "Are you kidding me?"

"Of course not. It's where Benny works. Why, have you heard of it?"

Hell, yes, he'd heard of it. The Motherlode was fairly notorious—the only club in San Francisco that featured not only drag queens, but transvestites and transsexuals as well. And Benny worked there? "I don't suppose he's the bartender?"

"No, he's part of the act on Friday nights. The gate's open, Nick." She flashed him a grin, reaching across the console to pat his thigh. "Relax. You've got me to protect you, remember? As long as I'm guarding your body, I'll make sure your virtue's safe as well. I won't even charge extra."

"That's exceedingly kind of you." He wasn't

homophobic, but the thought of being surrounded by the type of men who were often vocal about thinking he was just cuter 'n a bug's butt didn't exactly thrill him, either. He never knew quite how to respond to that kind of thing, and it gave him empathy for women who had to deal with unasked-for attention.

On the other hand, he supposed he'd better get used to it, since most of Daisy's buddies seemed to be more in touch with their feminine sides than she was. And if that's what blew their bubble, they could tuck and tape to their hearts' content. He didn't pretend to get it, but neither did it make him want to hunch protectively in his seat. The idea of willingly seeking castration in order to cross over to the Venus side, however—now, *that* made him long for an iron cup.

As it turned out, the Motherlode was locked when they got there, so his concerns were unfounded. Daisy watched the streets for trouble as he knocked on the bar's front door. No one answered at first, but a few moments later he heard footsteps cross the floor. Then the tumblers clicked into place and Benny opened the door.

"Sorry," he said, stepping back to hold the door wide. "Have you been out here forever? I was in the back shaving and just now heard you."

Nick looked at Benny's still-shadowed jaw and wondered what the hell he'd been shaving. He refused to even consider the possibilities.

As soon as they stepped inside Benny, relocked the doors. He saw the dress bag over

Daisy's arm and reached for it. "Well?" he demanded. "How did it work?"

"It was great, Benny. Just perfect. I thought I'd better return it in case someone needs it for this evening's performance, but if they don't, could I borrow it again tonight?"

"Actually, I've got something else I'd like you to try. Come on back."

They followed him to a dressing room that had makeup scattered across what looked like a fifties diner counter, complete with red-vinyl-padded chrome stools situated in front of a brightly lit mirror. A rack of gowns and costumes took up one corner and a double sink occupied the other.

It was to the latter that Benny crossed. "You mind?" he asked and picked up a shaving brush, stirring it inside a shaving mug to work up a lather. "I just wanna finish this up while I'm thinking about it." He spread white, foamy lather across the backs of his fingers and picked up a razor. Then, with careful concentration, he shaved between his knuckles. Looking up a moment later, he caught Nick watching and grinned. "Bet you've never given a moment's thought to the hair on your hands, huh?"

He was so cheerful Nick had to smile. "Can't say that I have."

"Luckily, I don't have much chest or arm hair, and I have my legs and pits lasered every three months or so. But my hands I'm forever having to shave. There! All done." He rinsed his hands and his shaving mug and neatly stored his supplies. Then he turned back to survey Daisy.

"Let's see if the outfit I picked out is going to look as good on you as I think it will."

He crossed the room and selected an outfit from the rack. Carrying it over to Daisy, he held the hanger high and slipped an arm beneath the bottom portion, presenting it to her like a high-priced salesperson in a house of haute couture.

Nick, who had been hoping for another slinky dress, was disappointed to see it was a pants suit, but Daisy seemed pleased. "Oh, Benny." She immediately began stripping out of her clothing. With a cheeky grin for Nick, Benny turned his back.

He clearly had an eye for fashion, because Daisy looked spectacular in his selection. The pants suit was made of heavy silk in a soft butter-cream color. Satin a shade deeper faced the lapels on the jacket and comprised the tux-edo stripes that ran down the outseams of the slacks. With a conservative blouse beneath it, it could have been worn to any well-heeled busi-ness function. The glittering gold bustier Benny had paired it with turned it into sexy party ap-parel.

"It's great, Benny. Absolutely perfect." Daisy leaned over to plant a kiss on his cheek.

"I knew it was you, chickie, the moment Chan showed it to me."

"And he doesn't mind my borrowing it?"

"Not as long as you get it back to him in time for tomorrow night's show."

"This is *drag*?" From what Nick could see, it could have belonged to any woman he knew.

"Hon, you're born naked, and everything you

put on after that is drag." Benny grinned. "Or so says RuPaul."

"Well, if RuPaul says it . . ."

"Exactly. The Queen has spoken."

Watching Benny deftly apply Daisy's makeup and style her hair, Nick went back to debating the merits of telling her about J. Fitzgerald. He looked at the pros and cons from every angle, but couldn't come to a conclusive decision. Finally he decided to shelve it for one more day. He needed to think about how to explain the situation to her in such a way that she wouldn't want to bust his balls. He was sure it could be done.

He just wasn't sure how.

20

〜〜〜

"NICE function." Sipping a Napa Valley merlot, Mo looked around the crowded ballroom.

Setting his glass on the tray of a passing waiter, Reid hooked a finger beneath his bow tie and stretched it away from his neck. "I guess. If balancing a glass of wine and a plate of hors d'oeuvres in a crowd of overdressed people is your idea of a good time."

Her wine glass paused on its way to her lips and, regarding him with faint exasperation, she said, "Attending this was your idea."

"I know. I'd just forgotten how claustrophobic these events always make me feel."

She studied him in silence with those fine blue eyes of hers and he nearly squirmed. To disguise the fact that she could make him feel like an errant twelve-year-old caught out by the headmistress, he gave her a slight twist of his lips and raised his goblet in a mocking toast. "Okay, I admit they serve a decent glass of wine. But don't these people have anything better to do than slobber praise all over a man who's already been acclaimed from here to infinity?"

"I thought you liked J. Fitzgerald."

"He's all right. But doesn't his constant need for adulation strike you as a tad self-absorbed?"

"For heaven's sake, Reid, he wants that ambassadorship. I'm sure he wants to keep his name in the papers so Congress will be reminded of his existence come appointment time."

"I'm sure you're right." He silently conceded he might be in need of an attitude adjustment. As Mo had reminded him, coming here had been his idea—and he'd had a definite agenda in mind when he proposed it. Sure, the ballroom had a damn sight too many overprivileged people milling about. But he'd known that would be the case, so it was time to get over it and get down to the business of saving his wife's shapely butt.

"Hello, old son."

Well, well. How timely, he thought as Sheldon Fitzhugh sauntered up to them.

There was something about Sheldon that always made Reid want to grin. It was more than his long-faced, large-toothed resemblance to the horses he loved. He possessed a sort of sweet goofiness that made it almost impossible to keep the muscles around Reid's mouth from quirking. He managed to bite back the impulse and summoned a disinterested gaze for his old schoolmate. He greeted him with a cool nod of his head. "Fitzhugh."

Sheldon shuffled in place and tried his smile on Mo. "Maureen," he said and bowed over the

curved-down fingers she extended to him.
"You're looking exceptionally lovely this evening."

I'll second that. Reid's gaze got tangled up on
her. Attired in a white, low-cut Hervé Léger
gown, with her dark hair swept up to show off
the diamond earrings he'd bought her for their
fifth anniversary, Maureen looked both elegant
and sexy.

She smiled distantly, however, and slid her
fingers free. "Thank you, Sheldon. You look
quite dashing yourself."

"Thanks. Would you, uh, excuse us for a moment, Maureen? I'd like a private word with
Reid."

"Certainly." With a slight smile above the
glass she'd raised to her lips, she eased away.

Reid watched her join another group a few feet
away, then turned to Fitzhugh. He waited.

"My apologies, Reid," Sheldon said, reaching
inside his tux to pull forth a slender checkbook.
"I've been remiss in my loan, and you've been
the soul of patience. Let me rectify the situation
at once."

Reid watched him scratch his signature across
a check. When Sheldon extended it to him, Reid
glanced at the amount before tucking it in his
breast pocket, and his eyebrows rose.

"I added a little interest." Sheldon lowered his
voice. "I value your friendship, Reid. I'd hate like
the dickens to see it hurt because I was so late
in paying you back."

"Hey." Reid faked a punch at Fitzhugh's im-
peccably tailored arm. "You're here for me ex-

actly when I needed you most." *Not to mention your bonus, which is a very nice touch.* "That's pretty much the definition of friends."

"Yeah? Well, that's certainly a load off." Sheldon's sudden smile displayed his considerable set of teeth. He snagged a couple of glasses off the tray of a circulating waiter and handed one to Reid. "I say, have you had a chance to see the new pony Pettigrew added to his string?" His homely face lit up.

Mo watched the byplay from several feet away. And while she sipped wine and chatted inconsequentials with longtime acquaintances, she kept coming back to a brand-new realization. It was way past time to rethink something she'd taken for granted for far too long now.

For years she'd blamed Reid for the distance that had grown between them, for the strain that had come into their marriage. She'd faulted his profligate tendency to lend his personal wealth to poor risks, condemned his reckless disregard for her feelings.

But Reid hadn't been the one to change. She had.

She'd been drawn to him in the first place because he'd had humor to spare, a rare loyalty to the people he considered his friends, and no earthly use for the silver spoon he'd been born with.

He'd spit that out without a moment's hesitation. If not for her he probably would have tried his hand at something other than the staid family bank, where his empathy for loan applicants that the rest of the board considered a

waste of time was viewed as a sign of weakness.
It took rare strength to stick with a job he dis-
liked in order to assuage his wife's insecurities.
Day after day he'd put up with having his views
denigrated by the tight-fisted, bottom-line board
of directors. For her. Then when she, too, had
turned away from him, he'd thrown all his free
time, money, and effort at causes that everyone
else wrote off as hopeless. Causes he'd called
friends.

His family hadn't understood it. God knew,
she hadn't. They'd all seen it as throwing perfectly good money after bad. But even though
the school chums she'd termed deadbeats had
taken their own sweet time repaying his loans,
when Reid had needed them the most, those for
whom he'd put his money and his faith on the
line had come through for him. Exactly the way
he'd said they would. In the past couple of days
she had seen exactly how many friends her husband had.

And it was more than she could claim.

Sheldon wandered off a few moments later,
and she rejoined Reid. Over the next half hour,
they were approached by several more of Reid's
friends. All entered the couple's orbit with
sheepish smiles that were nearly identical, but
they were a diverse group. Not all of them were
trust-fund babies who were hopeless at manag-
ing their money or at listening to the people they
paid to manage it for them. For several, attendance at expensive private schools had been at
the whim of a scholarship, and from listening to
their conversations, Mo learned that Reid had

gotten them started in their respective businesses. She began to wonder if she'd ever given him any credit at all.

Checks changed hands with varying degrees of discretion. As the total began to mount up, it started to look as though she might avoid prosecution after all. Not only would she avoid jail time, but she'd most likely emerge with her reputation intact as well. She ought to feel profoundly grateful that her bacon was being hauled so expeditiously from the fire. Instead, she started to suffer some serious pangs of anxiety.

Because none of that mattered, if in the end it meant she lost Reid. She'd undervalued him—she knew that now. She'd taken him for granted.

And it would kill her if she got what she deserved and was forced to watch him walk out of her life.

Her nerves grew tighter and tighter. When the man talking to Reid walked away and she found herself alone with him, or as alone as two people in the midst of a ballroom full of people could be, she drew a ragged breath and gathered her courage in both hands. Though confrontation was the last thing on her mind, sheer tension caused her voice to sound adversarial when she said, "Are you going to divorce me?"

Reid only heard the dreaded *D* word and her tone; the fact that she'd inquired whether *he* desired a divorce escaped him entirely. He felt as if he'd been kicked in the solar plexus—a particularly stunning sensation considering just sec-

onds ago he'd thought he was pitching his flag
on top of the world.

"Is that what you want?" he demanded. He
didn't give her a chance to reply. Blood pumping
hot and furious, he grabbed her wrist and
headed for the ballroom doors. Once out in the
lobby, where both the temperature and the de-
cibel level dropped several degrees, he hesitated
for just an instant, looking left and right.

"Reid." She tugged at her wrist.

Feeling savage and raw, he turned on her. "If
you're smart, Maureen, you won't say a word."
Tightening his grip, he strode across the lobby
to a small offshoot hallway that promised privacy. He pulled her down its carpeted length.
"I've knocked myself out, trying not only to keep
your butt out of jail, but to get back in your good
graces. Well, you know what? To hell with it. No
more Mr. Nice Guy. If you plan on leaving me
anyway, I might as well just take what I want—
and screw your wishes."

"I never said *I* was going to—"

Some of the ferocity that consumed him must
have shown in his eyes, for when he turned his
glare on her she abruptly shut up. He twisted
the handle to the ladies' room at the end of the
hall, pushed the door open, and pulled her inside.

The room was empty, and he slammed the
door behind them and twisted the lock to keep
it that way.

The room was tiny, just two stalls and a sink
with a short marble vanity counter. Swinging
Mo around, he clasped her hips and lifted her

onto the countertop. Kneeing her legs apart, he stepped between them.

She looked down her nose at him. "What *do* you think you're doing?"

"What I should have done a long time ago. Demonstrating once and for all who wears the pants in this family." Clamping her head between his hands, he slammed his mouth down on hers.

Mo's hands came up to his shoulders and he braced himself to be shoved away in outrage. Instead her fingers curled into his tux jacket to anchor herself and she kissed him back every bit as frenziedly as he kissed her.

The last of his control hit the skids, but it didn't seem to matter, for Mo was out of control too. Hearts thundering, breath soughing, they strained together in an embrace that was all raw carnality. Finesse was forgotten as the lust each had suppressed for far too long swamped them. Reid pulled her gown up around her waist, then swore at the pantyhose that guarded her as implacably as a harem eunuch.

"Take off those pants you're so damn proud of wearing," she commanded hoarsely. While he kicked them off, she rocked first onto one hip, then onto the other, until her hosiery had been wrestled down to hang from one ankle.

He immediately stepped back between her thighs, growling his approval when she widened them to accommodate him. Scooping his hands beneath her lush bottom, he jerked her forward, seating himself with one deep thrust in a humid vise that clasped him with warm welcome. He pulled back and thrust forward again. "There. Will. Be. NO. Divorce," he said in time with each pump of his hips. Burying himself deep, he stared into her eyes. "Got it?"

"Oh, God, yes," she moaned and he felt her interior muscles bear down around him as she began to come. "I've got it. Most definitely."

"You know, don't you," she asked as she leaned forward to watch him reorder his clothing, "that I never said I wanted a divorce in the first place?" She frowned at the pantyhose coiling from one foot. "Damn, this is all twisted."

"Let me help." He squatted in front of her and untangled the hosiery. "There. Put your foot in here." He looked up at her. "You did ask for a divorce. I distinctly heard you—"

"Ask if *you* wanted one."

His head reared back. "Why the hell would I want one?" Satisfied the pantyhose situation was under control, he surged to his feet and regarded her, hands on hips.

"Because I've been realizing all this week just how poorly I've upheld my end of the marriage. And you *said* we were going to sit down and talk about our marriage after we got this mess straightened out. I just assumed—"

"That I wanted out?" It was the last thing he expected to hear and he stared at her in stupefaction.

"Yes."

He rubbed his forehead. "And exactly what makes you assume you haven't been holding up your end of our marriage?"

"Everything you've accused me of lately is true. I didn't stop to think you might actually know what the hell you're doing with your own money. I've treated you more like an irresponsible adolescent than my partner. And you hate your job, don't you? I never even realized that until today."

"I don't hate it. The board of directors are a pain in the ass—but let's face it, baby love, we knew from the get-go that my relatives were a bunch of stiffs."

A strangled laugh escaped her.

"Where did you get the idea I hated it?"

"They never let you make the kind of loans you want to make, and I thought—I *still* think—that you've stuck with it primarily to alleviate some of the issues I have with financial security." She admitted, "You were right when you said I'm dysfunctional."

"Ah, Mo." He shifted uncomfortably and reached out to skim his knuckles down her cheek. "I was frustrated when I said that. I shouldn't have."

She leaned into his touch and smiled. "No, it's true. But you were wrong in thinking I've stayed with you because my father couldn't stick with any of his relationships. I'm not saying it hasn't been a factor in my determination to make our marriage work; of course it's played a part. But I never would have stuck it out if I didn't love you, Reid. My biggest mistake has been expecting you to understand why I'm so insecure about financial matters when I've never actually con-

fided some of the reasons behind it." An unhappy laugh escaped her. "God, it's pretty
ironic, when you come right down to it. Here all
these years I've thought you were the cause of
our problems . . . when all along it's been me."

Part of him reveled in hearing her say that he
wasn't a screwup; that she'd been wrong. But a
stronger part of him hated seeing her humbled.
So he gave her a cocky smile and said, "Damn
straight it's been you. And if there was just a
little more room in here, I'd do a victory dance
to hear you finally admit it."

She looked shocked. Then a tiny sound of
amusement burbled out of her throat. "You pig!"
She punched him on the arm.

"Well, please, Maureen, get a grip. You always
were a drama queen. First everything was all my
fault; now it's all yours. The truth is likely somewhere in between." He kissed her thoroughly,
then pulled back to look at her, satisfied at the
smoldering, heavy-lidded gaze she returned. He
rubbed a thumb over her mouth. "We still need to
sit down and really talk about all the crap that's
been between us. I think we've both kept too
many things to ourselves for much too long, and
it's time to get them out in the open. But that's
gonna have to wait. Because right now—"

"Are you harboring the illusion that you're
running the show now?" Her nose tilted ceiling-
ward as she slid off the counter, and he grinned
to see her back in form.

"It's no illusion, sweetheart; it's a fact. And as I
was saying before I was so rudely interrupted—"

She snorted inelegantly.

"—right now we're going to go terrorize some more money out of my buddies. I'm not about to rest until I'm a hundred percent certain that you're going to stay the hell out of jail."

21

~~~

NICK viewed the ballroom through the lens of his camera, looking for the perfect shot. He swept the room slowly from one side to the other, then front to back, but except for the two frames he'd taken of Daisy earlier, he didn't come close to anything that was remotely usable, let alone a definitive moment he could memorialize for all time.

The biggest problem was his frame of mind. They'd stopped at his post office box on the way here and he'd collected the bids from the tabloids. It was tough to dredge up the enthusiasm to search for the ultimate shot when he was about to flush his career down the toilet.

He'd thought there was at least a bright side in knowing things couldn't possibly get any bleaker. Then he saw his sister and brother-in-law walk in again. He lowered the Nikon and stared at them across the room. Great. The I'm-screwed factor had just shot up a hundredfold. It was tough enough keeping track of all the balls he'd set in motion without adding Mo to the mix.

He'd been lucky earlier: she and Reid had been tied up with a parade of people, and he'd managed to keep Daisy out of sight on the opposite side of the room fairly easily.

He didn't even want to think about Blondie's reaction if she learned that—she'd think he was ashamed of her. But he simply didn't want to face the barrage of questions from Mo if she found Daisy in his presence. Like what had brought her back into his life in the first place. That could only lead to other questions he'd just as soon not answer—not before he had a chance to explain to Daisy that things weren't exactly the way he'd told her.

So he'd thought Dame Fortune was smiling on him when he saw Reid drag Mo from the room. It looked as if they were having an argument, but he couldn't even scrape up the grace to feel concerned about it. It was every man for himself in love and war, and damn near *anything* was fine with him if it prevented his relationship with Daisy from getting all balled up. Besides, his sister was a strong woman.

And none the worse for wear, obviously, because she and Reid looked pretty darn cozy now. He must have been misread the situation when they'd left. This was the reason he generally favored honesty. Lies had a nasty way of twisting around on a guy to bite him on the butt.

So think, genius. If you want to hang on to Blondie past the next fifteen minutes, you'd better think of something good.

Or prepare to kiss your future goodbye.

*   *   *

Daisy looked around the sumptuous ballroom and wondered what the poor people were doing tonight. This was quite the do—flattering lighting, elegant, unobtrusive music, wonderful food. She'd bet her last buck the wine was excellent, too, but had to forgo the pleasure of testing the theory since she was on the job.

She wished Reggie and the boys were here. They'd get such a bang out of this—especially the quality of the tuxes and the big-deal evening gowns. Somewhat to her surprise, however, she didn't really feel out of place. The people she'd talked to tonight were pretty nice, and it made her think maybe she ought to deep-six all her old ideas about society types once and for all. Those impressions were highly colored by her teenage experiences, which, she had to admit, might not be the most reliable view in the world.

She'd have to learn to get along with these people anyhow, if she planned on hanging out with Nick.

She stilled. Did she? He'd said he loved her, but could she trust in that?

How could she admit, even to herself, that perhaps she loved him more than the tiny bit she'd owned up to? It called for a huge leap of faith to hand over her heart to a man she didn't fully trust not to smash it into a bazillion pieces.

So, the big question was: did she dare? Wishing she could see into his mind, she stared at Nick's profile as he scanned the room through the lens of his camera.

And she admitted that, yes—she dared. When it came right down to it, what other choice did she have? She could deny it until her last breath left her dying body, but it wouldn't change the truth: that she loved him with her entire being.

She needed to let go of the rest. That had been years ago and he'd grown up a lot since then. They both had. She'd guarded her heart for a long time now, but without risk there was little chance of growth. And she'd always believed that when you quit growing you died.

As if feeling her gaze, he suddenly turned his head and stared at her. Letting his camera hang from its neck strap, he crossed the few yards that separated them and stepped right up to her until his Nikon grazed her glittery bustier. Reaching out to clasp her head, he tilted her face up to his, bent his head, and slammed his mouth down on hers.

Daisy was so shocked that her hands flew away from her sides as if someone had poked a gun in her ribs and said, *Stick 'em up*. They hovered near his shoulders, undecided whether to grab him and kiss him back, or smack him silly for putting them on display. Before she could decide one way or the other, he released her and stepped back.

"I love you." His voice was low but vehement. "Don't you forget it."

"Okay." She blinked up at him. What on earth was going on here?

"I mean it," he said. He looked beyond her, and whispered something profane under his breath. "Here come my sister and Reid. Look, Daise, don't tell her that I've got trouble, okay? I don't want her to worry."

Daisy froze. She was starting to get a bad feeling here. Lifting her chin, she drew herself up to her full height. "What's going on, Coltrane?"

He shook his head. "Nothing I can talk about right this moment. I'll tell you everything later, though, I promise."

"*Daisy?*" Mo reached them. "My God, it is you. I thought it was when I saw you from across the room, but I wasn't certain." She pecked a kiss on Daisy's lips, hugged her to her generous breast, then stepped back, holding Daisy at arm's length to study her from head to toe. "You look wonderful! Very chic, very sophisticated." She looked at her brother. "What were *you* doing kissing her?"

Daisy's flush barely had a chance to spread across her cheeks before Nick shrugged as if the subject were of the greatest indifference to him. "You kissed her," he said. "Why shouldn't I?"

Her heart dropped to her stomach and she looked at him, willing him to meet her eyes. Was he going to deny their relationship?

"*I* didn't swab her throat with my tongue," Mo retorted coolly. "It's a slight but telling difference."

"Oh, nice imagery, Mo. Especially when I barely used any tongue at all. Did I, Daise?"

Okay, that did it. She opened her mouth to respond, only to shut it when she realized she didn't have any idea what to say.

"That didn't stop it from looking mighty darn carnal," Mo said sternly. "And it didn't look to me as if she were participating, Nick. Are you going around attacking young women at social events now?"

"Only Blondie here." Nick's arm slid around Daisy and pulled her against his side. "We don't consider it attacking, though, since she's living with me now."

"She's *what*?" Mo's mouth dropped open. "Since when?"

"What are you, Maureen, the Spanish Inquisition?" He turned to Reid. "Control your wife."

Reid snorted and Nick turned back to his sister with a shrug. "Fine. Since Monday, okay?"

"Tuesday," Daisy corrected. "Remember, on Monday you came—"

"Several times," he murmured and it was Daisy's turn to have her mouth drop open. Nick guided it closed with a gentle fingertip beneath her chin.

A blush scalded her from toes to hairline. She could not believe he'd said that! She'd been about to say he'd come to her office, but he'd made it sound as if . . .

Good God. He had her blushing so hard she'd probably glow in the dark if the lights went out.

"And you moved in late that afternoon, doll face, remember? Or, depending on your definition, early evening." His wide shoulders twitched impatiently. "Either way, by Tuesday morning I was making coffee to kick start your day."

"Oh. Yeah. I guess you're right."

He wiggled his little finger in his ear, then pulled it out to examine its clean tip. "Say again?"

"You're such a comic, Coltrane. You oughtta take that act on the road. I said you're right."

He rubbed the hand hugging her up and down her arm and grinned. "Now, *there's* a concession that's music to my ears."

"I'm confused," Mo said.

Her brother turned to her. "And is it absolutely mandatory that you're crystal clear on our relationship, Mo?"

"Relationship," she repeated slowly, as if sounding out a foreign word. "You have a *relationship*."

"Isn't that what I've been telling you?" Nick's arm tightened around Daisy. "This is the real deal, Maureen. I love her."

Warmth bloomed in Daisy's breast and spread until she felt incandescent right down to her toes. Nick *did* love her. He'd said so loud and clear. He'd have a hard time wriggling out of it now, because the words couldn't be recalled.

Mo stared at her brother. "This is rather sudden, isn't it?"

"For you, maybe. For me it's long overdue." Nick hugged Daisy even closer to his side. He smiled down at her, then looked back at his sister. "I've had feelings for Daisy since way back when. My mistake was in running away from them."

"So how did the two of you get together?"

"I looked her up."

Mo looked as if she'd like to interrogate them further, but to Daisy's relief a friend of Reid's came up. After a moment of pleasantries he edged Reid aside and talked to him in an urgent undertone. Then he pulled out a checkbook and started writing.

"That reminds me." Mo guided Daisy and Nick a few steps away and lowered her voice. "You know that trouble I was in?"

"My, God," Daisy blurted, "what does it do—run in the family?"

Mo raised a brow at her, Nick's hand tightened on her upper arm, and she shook her head, giving Mo an apologetic smile. "Sorry. Never mind."

Maureen looked confused but shrugged it off, turning to her brother. "Anyhow, I won't need your assistance with my problem after all, Nick. Reid straightened it out."

"Mo, that's fantastic!" Nick released Daisy and swept his sister off her feet, swinging her around despite her demands to be put down. Ignoring all the heads turned their way, he grinned as he set her back on her feet. "I can't tell you what a load off that is."

"I thought you'd like hearing it," Mo agreed. Breathless and flushed, she straightened her gown and gave him a dazzling smile as he rejoined Daisy. "And not merely for my sake. Reid told me the lengths you were prepared to go to, to bail me out. He said you were actually going to sell your photos to—*What?*"

Daisy had felt Nick stiffen next to her and looked up in time to see his finger slicing across his throat. She caught the tail end of a facial contortion that effectively cut off whatever Mo had been about to say, and it didn't take a cop's instinct to see that something was up. "Okay, let's have it, Coltrane. What's going on?" she demanded.

"We'll talk about it later." When she opened her mouth to protest, he brushed silencing fingertips across her lips. "I promise." He looked over at his sister. "Mo, will you excuse us? I've gotta get back to work—I haven't had a lot of luck so far getting the shots I'm looking for." Then he flashed a smile that lit up his face. "But I have a feeling I'll do a better job now. I'm glad you shared your good news."

She studied him for a moment, then turned to Daisy. "Let's get together real soon. We'll do lunch. Or perhaps you and Nick could join us for dinner some evening."

"I'd like that—either one."

But at the moment she had bigger fish to fry. Nick was up to something, and not having a glimmer of what that something was made her uneasy—both professionally and personally.

She watched him prowl the ballroom with his Nikon glued to his eye, and tried to pinpoint the exact moment he'd begun to behave differently. The closest she could figure was after they'd stopped off at his mail center on their way here.

He'd had a strange expression on his face as he'd sorted through the envelopes he'd pulled from his box, but when she'd asked if anything was the matter he'd stuffed them into his tux jacket, rolled his shoulders impatiently, and said no. As he'd locked the letters in the glove compartment, though, he'd seemed to lose a little of the spark that had lit him from within.

Or maybe that was her own emotions speaking. She conceded she'd been riding pretty high from hearing him say he loved her—even though she'd industriously denied it to herself. She couldn't even say with certainty that the spark had been there in the first place. Perhaps she'd simply projected the radiance that she had felt onto him.

She shrugged impatiently. She'd worry about motives later—both his and her own. Right now her time would be better spent finding out exactly what Nick was up to. She had a nasty suspicion that whatever it was could affect his safety.

Was he going all protective on her? Daisy nodded to Sue and John Smart, a couple with whom she'd had an engaging conversation earlier, and kept moving. She waylaid a waiter to request a club soda and, accepting it from him a moment later, set out after Nick again.

Without encroaching on his work space, she kept within a reasonable distance of him. Watching him snap off frames, she sipped her club soda and went back to the thought that had popped into her head, worrying it like a puppy with a knotted rag.

Was he going protective on her? Was that what this was all about—that he'd decided he was in love and had to protect the little woman?

If so, he didn't have to worry about Hubby and the goon patrol—because she'd kill him herself.

The more she thought about it, though, the less sense that made. Why would he have such an abrupt change of heart? He'd been smart

enough to come to her in the first place because
he'd known he was out of his depth. Plus he had
machismo to spare, and he'd never indicated by
word or deed that having a woman in charge of
his security threatened that. So why would telling her that he loved her suddenly change a perfectly workable arrangement?

This was ridiculous. Was she going to spend
the rest of the night trying to *guess* his reasons?
Or did she tackle Nick, right here, right now, and
find out what the heck was going on?

Ah, gee, let me think. Tough decision.

Setting her glass on an empty table, she strode
up behind Nick and tapped him on the shoulder.

Nick finally had a decent shot lined up, and
he shrugged her hand aside. "Just a second,
Daisy." He snapped off the shot, then lowered
his camera and turned to face her.

"How did you know it was me?"

He looked at her flushed cheeks and determined chin, her Hershey's Kisses' eyes that shot
sparks and challenge, and felt the corners of his
mouth quirk. "When it comes to you, cupcake,
I've got second sight."

"Yeah?" She thrust her chin out at him. "How
about precognition, Coltrane—you got that, too?
Because we've gotta talk. Now."

Oh, hell. His heart sank, for she had that I'm-
kicking-butt-and-taking-names look on her face.
Without much hope, he said, "I'm working,
Blondie."

"Me, too. The difference is you've had me
working blind all evening, and I want to know

why. I don't *like* being kept in the dark, Nicholas."

"But you disguise it so well," he muttered.

She ignored the aside. "I've asked this before, but now I'm not budging until I get a straight answer. What the hell is going on?"

Feeling hunted, he thrust back a strand of hair that had flopped forward and said, "I said I'd tell you everything later, Daisy, and I meant it. As soon as I finish here—"

"I've got news for you, bud: later has arrived. You don't hire me to keep your hide intact and then prevent me from doing my job with a 'later, baby.' Next you'll be telling me not to worry my pretty little head."

"Only if I have a sudden urge to commit suicide."

"Very funny, Nick." She thrust her nose up under his. "You'd better resign yourself to packing up your camera for a while. Because you and I are going to go out in the lobby and have a nice little talk."

"It's time you and I had a talk, Coltrane," echoed an urbane voice behind them.

Daisy didn't bother to look to see who had spoken. "Take a number," she snapped.

Nick's sentiments exactly. Everyone seemed to want a piece of him tonight.

On the other hand, if it meant he could put off telling Daisy that he'd been lying to her all along, he was grateful for the interruption. Until he turned and found himself face-to-face with J. Fitzgerald Douglass.

Then he knew he should have jumped at the chance to get everything out in the open the minute Blondie had offered him the opportunity.

22

BLOWING out a quiet breath, Nick turned to Daisy. "Could you excuse us for a few minutes?" When he saw her eyes narrow and her mouth start to form a protest, he met her gaze levelly. "This is my livelihood, Daisy, and that has to take precedence when I'm on a gig. You and I will talk, though, I promise. The minute we get home."

She snapped her mouth closed, but he knew damn well she wasn't going to budge. Then she looked at who had interrupted them, and her eyes widened.

"I do apologize," J. Fitzgerald said, flashing her his no-really-you-mustn't-canonize-me smile. "It is important that I speak to Nicholas, however."

And it was, after all, his party.

"All right." She looked at Nick. "You've got five minutes." Then, shoulders straight, she stalked away.

He waited until he was sure she was out of earshot before he turned to Douglass. "What the hell makes you think I've got anything to say to you?"

"You don't have to say a word," the older man said smoothly. "You merely have to listen."

He snorted but said, "You heard the lady: you have five minutes." He made a point of consulting his Rolex.

"I realize I misjudged you."

"Damn straight you did. And if you wanna piss away your time stating the obvious it's fine with me—but if I were you I'd tell me something I don't already know."

"My actions were unconscionable—I panicked at the thought of those photographs floating around where anyone might see them," Douglass said. "I wanted quite desperately to retrieve them."

"Then you should have just asked me for them. Either that, or you could have taken five lousy minutes to ask around, and you would have learned that I've never failed to destroy a compromising negative yet." He wanted an apology. He deserved a hell of a lot more, but he'd settle for an apology—at least for tonight. Getting into a pissing match with Douglass would only earn him a lifetime of more nasty surprises. An intelligent man would definitely hang on to his cool until he could sit down, think things through, and come up with a plan that would get his dick out of the wringer once and for all.

"You're absolutely right," Douglass agreed easily. "And I'd very much like to make up for my lack of foresight now." He reached inside his tux and pulled forth a checkbook. "Name your price."

"You think I'm a *blackmailer*?" Nick was insulted right down to his tasseled loafers. "Take your checkbook and shove it, old man."

"You're not being reasonable, Coltrane. By all accounts you're an astute businessman—"

"Reasonable?" Shoving his face close to J. Fitzgerald's, Nick sucked in a deep breath against the rage burning a hole straight through the center of his good sense, and said through gritted teeth, "I didn't give a good goddamn about your sex life until you started messing with me. But you just had to push it, didn't you? Your gorillas trashed my darkroom and dislocated my arm. They destroyed my Porsche, held a gun to Daisy's head, and tried to fucking *kill* me with their car! You think writing a check will just erase all that?" He drew himself erect and did some more deep breathing. He was teetering on the edge of doing something he knew he shouldn't—something he'd no doubt regret. And he tried to pull back; he really did. Then . . .

Fuck good sense. That had been eroded away by one hell of a rough week. "You're right about one thing," he said. "I am an astute businessman. So I'll tell you what I'm gonna do."

J. Fitzgerald straightened, ready to deal.

"I'll sell my negatives to the tabloids, highest bidder take all." He bared his teeth in a carnivorous smile. "That oughtta garner me a bundle."

Douglass looked stunned for a second, but he recovered with record speed and met Nick's gaze head-on. "You're not going to do that," he said with assurance. "You'd cut your own throat. Who do you think would ever trust you after that? You'd be washed up in this town."

"Hmm, you do have a point." Nick gave him a look of faux admiration. "There must be a way around it. But . . . maybe not. Damn. I guess I'll have to concede to your superior intelligence."

Douglass started to smile.

"And just send the suckers anonymously."

For a fleeting instant, the mask fell away and the thirst for power at any cost shone out of Douglass' eyes. Nick raised his camera and shot off a frame, but he couldn't be certain he'd captured it, for even as he depressed the shutter button the man's countenance smoothed back into its familiar benevolent lines.

His voice low and pleasant, J. Fitzgerald leaned into him and said, "I'll bury you, you little son of a bitch. You think my security team has been tough so far? You haven't seen anything yet."

"Huh. I'm shaking in my boots." *Jesus, Coltrane, what is this—the playground? Shut the fuck up before you dig a grave for yourself clear to Asia.* His temper was riled, though, and that meant testosterone was in charge of his thinking— never a good idea, but something that was damn difficult to correct once his control had slipped its leash.

Forgoing the immediate gratification of popping the old hypocrite in the mouth, he focused on the primary goal: finding a long-term solution that, just incidentally, would stick it to Douglass but good. He breathed deeply, sucking air to the bottom of his lungs and holding it in an attempt to harnass the fury running rampant through his system.

He might have succeeded, too, if J. Fitzgerald had just left Daisy out of it.

"You think that blond bodyguard you're fucking is going to save your butt?" Douglass demanded. "Think again. Hell." He lowered his voice and smiled benevolently. "She'd be even easier to arrange an accident for than you'd be, and who would miss a little nobody like her, anyhow?"

Faster than thought, Nick's hands whipped out to grip J. Fitzgerald's lapels. Hauling the older man up onto his toes, he bent until they were nose to nose. "The Oakland PD, for starters," he snarled through the mist of red rage in front of his eyes. He retained just enough sense to keep his voice low. "They tend to get damn testy when one of their own is hurt, even if she is retired from the force." He tightened his grip until Douglass was all but *en pointe*. "But understand this, asshole—if anything happens to Daisy, it won't come to the cops, and you won't have to worry about the circulation of a few lousy pictures that show you banging your brains out with a girl young enough to be your granddaughter." He drilled Douglass with his glare. "Because I'll kill you myself."

It wasn't until he abruptly released J. Fitzgerald with an insolent flick of the backs of his fingers against the magnate's lapels that he realized they had attracted an audience. A pocket of silence surrounded them as those nearest stared at him aghast. Daisy was watching him with her soft mouth slightly agape and a perplexed frown pleating her eyebrows. Reid looked faintly amused, but Mo looked downright horrified. She cocked a brow at him demandingly the moment she caught his eye, asking, *What the hell is this?*

He flashed the small crowd what he hoped was one of his most charming smiles. "Sorry, folks. I get a little passionate about my soccer team."

They weren't about to take his word for it—everyone looked to J. Fitzgerald for verification. He tugged his lapels straight and nodded. "I guess he does! You don't ever want to—what's that word the kids use these days for not showing respect?"

"Diss," Nick supplied.

"Right. You don't ever want to diss the Galaxy to this boy. Not if you know what's good for you."

"Damn straight." Nick essayed a cocky grin. But he couldn't help but suspect he'd just made a huge mistake.

One that had the potential for disaster written all over it in foot-high letters.

During the ride home, Daisy tried very hard not to jump to unwarranted conclusions. It would be the height of unfairness to go off half cocked on Nick before she'd heard so much as a drop of evidence against him. Especially when all she really had was a feeling.

Not that her instincts were to be sneezed at. She'd learned long ago never to sell them short, for they were generally right on the money.

On the other hand, she had taken a huge step tonight when she'd acknowledged her feelings for Nick—at least to herself—so she *had* to give him the benefit of the doubt. Didn't she?

She straightened infinitesimally in her seat. Yes. She did. Trust, in the end, was pretty much what love all came down to.

Why, then, did she have such a bad feeling in the pit of her stomach?

She snuck a look at Nick as they sped up Divisadero. His features sprang in and out of clarity beneath the streetlights they blew past, and he looked remote, very unNick-like. She'd already asked him more than once tonight what was going on, and he had managed to ignore his sister's grilling after the incident with Douglass. So what was the point in starting something now when his attention was definitely divided between her and the road?

They pulled into the carriage house a short while later. Remaining in her seat while he reached across her to pop open the glove compartment, she watched as he retrieved the slim stack of envelopes he'd collected earlier from his post office box. His expression didn't change as he slid them inside his tux jacket, and he barely glanced her way. Frustrated but struggling not to overreact, Daisy reached for the door handle.

"It's a funny thing," she said, meeting his gaze across the top of the car as they climbed out, "but since you and I have hooked up, I don't believe I've ever seen you tune in to a single soccer match."

He merely shrugged.

Oh, God, Nick, what are you up to? "It's way past time you and I talked, Coltrane."

"I know." He hiked up the strap of his camera bag, arranging it more securely on his shoulder. "Let's go upstairs."

He followed her into the apartment and dumped his duffel on the floor by the couch when she turned to face him. "No matter what else happens," he said, "I want you to remember one thing."

She found herself gripping the back of the chair. "And what's that?"

"I love you."

"Oh, God, Nick, what have you done?"

That elicited a faint smile. "Trust you to assume that whatever it is, it must be my fault."

She felt a thrust of hope. "It's not?"

"No. Well, I didn't start it, anyhow. I admit I've made some pretty poor choices, though."

Frustration escaped her in a sound that could give a teakettle a run for its money. "Tell me!"

He untied his bow tie and slid it out from beneath his collar. "Unarm yourself first."

She pulled her gun out of its inside holster and set it on the trunk. Yanking off her jacket, she removed the knife sheaths from her forearms and tossed them next to the gun. Then she straightened, hands on hips. "What does Mr. Douglass have to do with all this?"

He picked up the weapons and carried them over to the entertainment center, where he set them on the uppermost shelf.

As if she'd ever—

"He's the guy you've been protecting me from."

She was sure she must have heard him wrong. Then the implication hit her like a body slam. "My God. You slept with *Mrs.* Douglass? She must be sixty years old!"

His mouth dropped open, but he closed it with a snap. "Do you hear yourself, Blondie? I figured you for a feminist."

"What's that got to do with anything?"

"Douglass is sticking it to a woman young enough to be his granddaughter, but Mrs. D can't have a little fun with a younger man?"

"Frankly, I think it's equally creepy either way. I mean, I can see maybe a ten-year age difference, but twenty or thirty years? *Ick.*"

He scrubbed his hands over his face, then dropped them to his sides. "Listen, we're getting off track here—"

She kept remembering the look on his face when he'd hauled the guest of honor off his feet at tonight's shindig. "Are you in love with her?" He couldn't be. He'd said he loved her.

"Huh?"

"Mrs. Douglass. Are you in love with her?"

"I don't even know the woman!"

"Then who did you sleep with? Do they have a daughter?"

"Beats the hell outta me. Listen, let me start from the beginning, okay? I know I can make you understand—"

A chill began to trickle down her spine. "Tell me about the compromising pictures."

"Good idea; that's where it all started. See, it

has to do with two pictures I took at Bitsy Pembroke's wedding. Only I didn't know what I'd taken until later, because I was worried about a jam Mo had gotten herself into and wasn't as observant as usual. It wasn't until I walked in to find my darkroom being trashed by the goons that I realized I must have caught something in one of my frames, but I didn't know what. As soon as I was sprung from the ER Sunday night, I made prints of everything I'd taken that weekend, to see what they were so damn hot to get their mitts on." Hands shoved deep in his pockets, he faced her earnestly. "Even then, I had to blow the frames up to find anything at all. But eventually I located him through the window of a caretaker's cottage that was in the background of a shot of the bride and groom."

"Douglass?"

"Yeah. Going at it hammer and tongs with a nubile young thing who wasn't his wife."

What the hell did that have to do with Nick sleeping with someone's wife? "He brings on heavy-duty muscle over a picture you had to blow up to even find? I don't get it."

"Probably because it doesn't make sense." He shrugged. "Over the years I've caught more compromising moments on film than I can remember. I always destroy them, and that's the end of it. Everybody and his brother *knows* I destroy them, too—my discretion is a widely recognized part of my reputation."

"So what happened this time?"

"I guess he didn't trust that I'd do what I'm known for doing."

"So let me get this straight. J. Fitzgerald Douglass is the man responsible for all the attacks on you. There is not and never has been a married woman whom you took naked pictures of."

"Yeah, that's the good news—"

"The good news," she repeated flatly. "That you *lied* to me. That from the very *beginning* you've lied to me."

He gave her an earnest look full of charm. "I've got a good reason for it, though, Daise."

Years of professionalism went up in smoke, and she took a swing at his head.

She didn't even get close. He must have expected something of the sort, because he tackled her before her fist connected, and they tumbled to the floor, sending the trunk skidding. He rolled on top of her and grabbed her wrists, pinning them to the floor on either side of her head.

Nick stared down at her as he shifted his weight to secure her beneath him. He had no intention of being on the receiving end of some martial arts move that would land him on his ass.

Her cheeks were flushed, her dark eyes nearly black with rage and hurt, and she was all but bursting out of her glittery little bustier. Its boning held it rigidly in place, and their tussle and the position in which he'd locked her arms put her dangerously close to popping out the top. He watched crescent shaped slices of blush pink come and go as her heaving breasts exposed and then concealed the uppermost curves of her aureoles. Knowing that his chances were pretty damn slim of ever seeing her nipples in their entirety again—never *mind* getting within tasting range—his jaw tightened.

"Dammit, Blondie, is that your answer to everything? To pound me?"

She tried to buck him off and growled. "No," she snapped. "Sometimes I consider shooting you instead." She suddenly went limp beneath him. "You think I like acting this way? This doesn't happen with anyone but you. I was a cop for four years, dammit—it taught me to sublimate my emotions and act rationally no matter what the provocation. Then you came tramping back into my life and, in less than a week, I've become a wild-eyed reactionary."

She tested his grip on her wrists, looking him squarely in the eye when he maintained a tight hold. "Get off me, Coltrane. I don't like what you've turned me into, and I'm getting the hell out of here while there's still something left to salvage."

He rolled off her but had no intention of letting her walk out the door. She didn't mean it anyhow—she was too professional to walk away and leave him unprotected.

He watched her climb to her feet. She gripped the boning of her bustier and tugged the top up while shimmying to settle everything within. Then she walked over for her knives and began strapping them back on.

"Why the big song and dance, Nick? Why didn't you simply tell me what the story was from the very beginning?"

"Because Mo desperately needed money, and I knew that if I told you my plans to raise it for her—not to mention get even with the guy screwing up my life—you'd never agree to be my bodyguard."

She paused with one arm thrust into a jacket sleeve to stare at him. "I know I'm going to regret asking this, but . . . what were your plans?"

He hesitated but then pulled the envelopes out of his inside breast pocket and extended them to her.

She finished donning her jacket, then reached for the stack, opening the top envelope and pulling out a sheet of paper. The color leached out of her face as she read, and by the time she looked at him again her eyes were like two burn holes in a blanket, dark and hollow. "Tabloids? You planned all along to sell the photos you took to the *tabloids*?"

"*Was* going to sell them. Past tense." The agonized betrayal on her face didn't lessen and he rushed to explain, "I no longer need to, though, don't you see? And I didn't want to do it in the first place, but Mo was in a real jam, Daisy. She's always been there for me; I had to so something to help her, and I just couldn't think of any other way to raise a lot of money fast."

He found himself talking to her back and lunged to grab her arm as she headed for the door.

Snapping it free, she whirled back to face him. "*Don't* touch me. Just . . . keep your hands to yourself."

He held them wide in entreaty. "Don't go, Daisy. We can work this out—I know we can."

"No. We can't." But she turned to walk back

into the living room, and for a moment he thought she had changed her mind. She simply collected her gun off the entertainment center, however, and stuffed it in her holster, then stormed into the bedroom, where she started throwing clothes helter-skelter into a suitcase.

He could barely breathe past the knot in his chest as he stood in the doorway watching her. "I *love* you."

She froze for an instant. Then she resumed stuffing her boots into the corners of the bag. "You don't know the first damn thing about love. Or you never would have lied to me."

"I didn't *know* I loved you when I lied about Douglass! And by the time I realized that I did, I'd dug myself a pit clear up to my eyeballs."

"Yeah, well, we both know how easily you say the words, don't we, Nick? Whether you mean them or not." She clicked the locks shut on the suitcase and dragged it off the bed. Bits of apparel stuck out either side.

"When I went off on Douglass tonight, Daisy?" The words felt like razors, slicing at his throat. "That was because he threatened you. I heard that and I just went apeshit."

"Quite unnecessarily," she said coolly. "I can take care of myself."

He didn't step aside when she got to the doorway and she stopped in front of him. Her chin elevated. "Get out of my way, Coltrane."

"No. Please. You've gotta listen—"

"*Move*. If you make me set all this shit down to wrestle my way past you"—she indicated the weapon's case she'd collected on the way across the room, as well as her suitcase and little hand-bag—"I'll shoot your kneecaps off—I swear I will. Either that, or that big ole dick you're so proud of."

He stepped out of her way. His gut churning in sick despair, he watched helplessly as she grabbed the keys to the rental car off the trunk and slammed out the front door.

23

$\backsim\!\!\circ\!\!\sim$

REGGIE opened his door, took one look at Daisy, and said, "Oh, hell. What did he do?"

"He broke my heart, Reg." She allowed him to take some of her luggage, then docilely followed when he grasped her arm and guided her into his apartment. She didn't know quite how she'd gotten here. One minute she'd been throwing clothes into the suitcase and the next thing she knew she was outside Reggie's door. In between was mostly a blur of neon streaking past the windshield. "He's diabolical," she informed the back of her friend's head. "He sucked me in against my better judgment and made me fall in love with him all over again. Then he turned around and broke my heart. *Again*. And it hurts, Reggie. God, it hurts so much." Scalding tears rose in her eyes, but she blinked furiously to dispel them. Damned if Nick Coltrane would make her cry!

"That son of a bitch." Reggie seated her. She was vaguely aware of him chafing her hands between his own, then he was gone. He disappeared into the kitchen, and she stared blankly into space until he reappeared a moment later with a cup of tea that he extended to her. "Here. God bless Insta Hot. Drink up, Daise; it's a nice, soothing chamomile. And look, I've got some of those pumpkin biscotti you like."

She knew her world was every bit as shattered as she'd feared when she looked down and saw he had arranged the biscotti on a plate from the prized B40 dinnerware he'd bought at Biordi's. Usually he wouldn't let her anywhere near the set, claiming she lacked the necessary appreciation and handling skills. "*Oh*," she said in a tiny voice. She picked up the plate and carefully set it in her lap, her fingers curling around the scalloped edges. And the dam broke, sending scalding tears splashing down her cheeks.

"Heyyy." Reggie sat down next to her. Slinging an arm around her, he plucked the plate away with his free hand and set it on the table, then pulled her into a comforting bear hug. He sat quietly while she cried it out, occasionally patting her shoulder and rubbing his chin against the crown of her head. His warmth gradually penetrated, and when the tears finally abated and she was panting through her mouth because her nose was too stuffed up to breathe, he said, "That lousy shit," with the ready willingness to take her side that made him her best friend. "What'd he do—walk out again?"

"He said he *loved* me," she wailed.

"The bastard rat!" Then he went still. "Wait a minute. Isn't that a good thing?"

"Not when it's a dirty rotten lie!" She knuckled tears from her eyes and sniffed inelegantly, wiping her nose against his shirtfront. Then she pushed upright, sitting back on the couch to look him in the eye. "He doesn't know the meaning of the word, Reg. God, he is such a *liar*. He was all set to sell his photos to the tabloids!"

"Oh, shit." That drew Reggie's attention away from the mess she'd made on his shirt like nothing else could, because he knew better than most how it must have made her feel to discover it. "I'm sorry, kiddo. What a dog. I gotta ask, though: whose photos was he gonna sell?"

"Ones he took of—get this—J. Fitzgerald Douglass, of all people, getting it on with a young woman at a wedding."

"Get outta here! The man's a saint."

"According to Nick, the saint is on film doing the wild thing in glorious Technicolor with someone who's not his wife. Which led directly to Douglass siccing some pretty nasty characters on our boy Nick to retrieve said film. Which, of course, is where I came in."

"Wow. J. Fitzgerald Douglass. That's a tough one to swallow, but I guess if you say it's so, it's so." He reached out and patted the knee she'd pulled up on the cushion and said with a gentle smile, "You know, though, Daisy, there is a bright side to all this. At least Nick's not sleeping with a married woman."

"Yeah. I'm really comforted."

"I'm sorry, babe, I'm not trying to make light of your pain. I'm just trying to figure out how everything works. Like why did Coltrane choose now to sell to the tabloids?"

"Huh?"

"Given the kind of folks he photographs, he must have had ample opportunity to sell his stuff to them in the past. So why now?"

"He *says* it's because Mo was in trouble."

"That's his sister, right?"

"Yes." Daisy opened her mouth to say more, but a hard pounding on the front door made her jerk and she slapped her hand to her breast to contain the panicked thump of her heart.

Reggie pushed up off the couch. "Now, who the hell could that be? Hold that thought, Daise— I'd better deal with whoever it is before they break down the damn door." He yelled, "Hold your water—I'm coming already!" Then, his voice dropping back into its normal register, he said with a rueful smile, "And here I thought it was going to be a *boring* Friday night."

While he went to answer the door, Daisy clicked open the latches on her suitcase and pulled out a pair of jeans. She quickly shucked out of her evening slacks and donned them, then reached for the discarded slacks. She was pulling the inside holster from the waistband when Reggie opened the door.

"Is she here?" she heard Nick's voice demand, and she froze, her nerves zinging.

"She doesn't want to see you, Coltrane."

"Tough shit. She's just going to have to deal with me anyway."

He must have pushed his way past Reggie, because the next thing she knew he was in the living room doorway. Her heart tried to pound its way out of her chest and she tucked the

loaded holster inside the back of her jeans, then
shoved her hands in her front pockets for good
measure to keep from pointing the Glock at him.
She was through letting him force her into unprofessional acts.

Hands on his hips, Nick regarded her through
narrowed eyes. "Good, you're still packed. Let's
go—I've got a cab waiting."

She offered a creative suggestion as to what he
could do with the cab. "I'm sure as hell not going
anywhere with you."

Feigning nonchalance, she sat on the edge of
the cushion and pulled on a pair of socks. "How'd
you find me, anyhow?" She reached for a boot
that was poking up in the corner of the case.

"I called Benny at the Motherlode and asked
him where Reggie lived. When you weren't at
your place, I figured you'd come here. Listen, I
know I screwed up—"

"Fucking-A you screwed up," Reggie inter-
jected. "Do you have any idea how much she
hates the tabloids?"

Nick didn't take his eyes off Daisy. "Considering my dad was responsible for her mother being smeared across the front page of a number
of them, yeah, I think I have a pretty good idea."

"You don't know squat," Daisy said hotly.
"You don't have the first idea what it was like
to go back to the 'burbs where the neighbors
wouldn't even speak to her. Where for months
their kids catcalled every damn time she stepped
outside the door, calling her an uppity whore
and worse." God, she'd hated them for that, for
their small minds and their mean mouths.

Nick sank to his heels in front of her. "And how many of them did you take on for dissing your mama, Daisy? One? Two? The entire neighborhood?" He tried to take her hands, but his touch made her ache for things she didn't dare hope for and she shook him off.

Reggie, the traitor, answered for her. "Try every last one of them. That's how Daise and me met."

Nick looked up in surprise. "You were neighbors?"

"I lived a couple of blocks away. I came across her getting her butt kicked one day by three boys who thought beating up a girl—or a fag—made them big men, and I decided to even the score."

"We whipped their asses, too," Daisy said.

"Yeah." Reggie shrugged. "And the rest, as they say, is history. We've been best buds ever since."

"Then you can probably appreciate why I didn't tell her I was considering selling my stuff to the rags. She never would have agreed to take my case."

"So—and correct me if I'm wrong here—what you're saying is that you lied to her for her own good?"

"Hell no, I did it for *my* own good." He turned his full attention back on Daisy. "I needed you and I lied. So sue me. But don't shut me out, Blondie, because like I told you earlier, that was before I fell in love with you."

"And like I told you, you wouldn't know love if it came up and bit you on your solid gold butt." She placed a newly Doc Martened foot on his chest and straightened her leg with a gentle thrust. At least, she meant it to be gentle—she really did.

But somehow he flew backward and landed several feet away.

Pushing up on one elbow, he flipped his hair out of his eyes and said, "Fine. We can work on the relationship. But what about that professionalism you're so all-fired proud of? You just gonna leave me staked out for Douglass to destroy? He'd be more than happy to slit my throat, especially after tonight."

"Good. It'll save me the trouble."

"Jesus, Daisy. Did it ever occur to you that when I made the decision to sell to the tabloids, it was with the full knowledge that it would cost me my career? Betraying the discretion my clients have come to depend on would've destroyed what it's taken me years to build up—and, cupcake, that's not a prospect that thrilled me." She simply looked at him and he raked a hand through his hair in frustration. "Dammit, it was the last thing I wanted to do, I'm telling you, but Mo needed the money! What was I supposed to do, let her go to jail?"

Daisy straightened. "What do you mean, go to jail?"

Nick looked uncomfortable. Climbing to his feet, he busied himself brushing off his slacks. "Nothing. I shouldn't have said anything; it's Mo's story to tell."

Her spine stiffened; her chin raised. "Yes, of course. You wouldn't want a little nobody like me privy to the family's dirty laundry."

"Dammit, that's not what I meant! Just listen to m—"

"Go home, Coltrane." She was suddenly very tired. "I'm through listening. We have nothing left to say to each other."

"We have a *boat*load left to say to each other," he disagreed. He took a giant step toward her, but Reggie suddenly inserted himself between them. Nick looked at him and seemed to grow larger. Hostility radiated off him in waves and his chest rose and fell in rhythm to his heavy breathing. "Move."

"No. You heard her. She wants you to go home."

Nick's eyes flashed blue fire. "Get out of my way, Reggie, or I'll squash you like a bug."

"You can try. But do you honestly believe that will help your case?"

Nick looked at Daisy over Reggie's head. Her heart raced like a runaway train, and for one mad moment she wasn't sure just what she wanted—for him to do as she'd demanded, or to have him fight to make her see things his way. Then the aggression suddenly left him and he stepped back, stuffing his hands in his pockets. But he clearly wasn't happy. He looked down his nose at her with a snooty-cool expression she'd never seen on his face before.

"If you think I'm going to beg you to love me back, Blondie, you're crazy. And to hell with your professional services, too—who needs 'em? My shoulder's pretty much back up to speed now, so I can fight my own battles. But if you change your mind, little girl, you know where to find me. I'll welcome you back with open arms."

Then he turned on his heel and headed for the door. A second later, it clicked closed behind him.

No! Pure reflex sent her surging to her feet. *Don't leave me.* She stood rooted to the spot, her hands opening and closing at her sides. He was gone. Dully, she sat down again.

"Go after him, Daisy."

She looked up at Reggie, blinking to bring him into focus. "What?" Exhaustion sucked at every bone and muscle in her body.

"Go after him. I'd lay odds he loves you, and if you hurry, you can probably catch him."

"It's too late for us. We're so different anyway that it'd never work. But, you know . . . he was right about one thing." She jumped back to her feet with sudden resolve, stripping off her bustier. "I do still have a professional obligation to him."

"Yes, you do." Reggie fished a bra out of the suitcase and tossed it to her. "And that's not something you can just walk away from, or you'd never be able to hold your head up again around your peers."

"And besides, I've got his rental car. I mean, he was pretty upset with me when he left; he could call the cops and report it stolen. Then where would I be?"

"Up the creek, sister." He rummaged up a lightweight shell-pink sweater set and handed it over. "Here. Put these on and get going. Before you get busted for grand theft, auto."

"Right." She grabbed the car keys and scooped

up her suitcase and weapons case. Then, stopping to give Reggie a quick buss on the lips, she headed for the door. She paused there to look back at him. Hoping she didn't sound half as needy and uncertain as she felt, she asked softly, "Am I being the worst sort of fool, Reg, or do you truly think he was serious about loving me?"

"I think it's a distinct possibility, Daise. I really do."

"Which? That I'm being a fool?"

"No. That he loves you. I'd put money on it. Hell, girl, I'd put money on *you* any day."

"Thanks, Reg. I needed to hear that." She took a deep breath and blew it out. "Besides, I guess I'll never find out if I don't take a chance."

"Honey chile, you were born to take a chance. You just never knew it would be a risk of the heart."

She gave him a weak smile, but straightened her shoulders. "Yeah. Who knew that would be so much scarier than facing down pistol-toting maniacs?" Then she shrugged and headed out the door.

Nick had barely hit the street before he began to regret letting his ego get in the way of his objective. He should have checked it at the door, but instead he'd allowed it to muscle its way into his exchange with Daisy. *Way to go, champ.*

Damn.

Reaching the waiting cab, he opened the door but then paused, looking up at the bow-front window of Reggie's apartment. Maybe he should go back and try to do it right this time.

Then again, maybe not. He rolled his shoulders uneasily and climbed into the taxi, giving the driver his address. The problem was, he doubted he *would* do it right. He kept picturing Daisy looking at him with those big brown eyes so filled with hurt, clearly distrusting him right down to the ground because he'd lied to her. And he had a bad, bad feeling that one more face-to-face would send any attempt to do *right* clear out the window and him spinning into caveman mode.

And if he tried that, she'd probably stomp him flat.

Face it—he wasn't really the caveman type. But he had a nasty feeling he'd fail to remember that until after he'd already done something irretrievably stupid. She'd gotten his machismo all in an uproar, and he was feeling dangerously reckless.

And scared. Scared she'd remain too angry to ever come back. Scared she'd write him off and he would feel this awful for the rest of his life. He wasn't accustomed to being afraid of anything, and he didn't like it. He didn't like it one damn bit.

The taxi pulled up in front of the gate to his landlord's estate and he absentmindedly paid the cabbie and climbed out. The car pulled away from the curb as he punched in the numbers to the security code.

Hands thrust in his pockets, he rocked back on his heels while the gates made their slow sweep outward. Damn. How could he convince

Blondie that his feelings were real, and that the last thing he planned was to make a career out of lying to her?

Hands suddenly grabbed him and spun him around. Nick struggled to get his hands out of his pockets. "What the hell?"

A fist came out of nowhere and smashed into his chin, sending him flying. Sitting up on the sidewalk, he grasped his jaw and gingerly worked it side to side. Okay. It seemed to be intact. He looked into the face of the head honcho of Douglass' goon squad.

Blunt Face leaned down and offered him a hand, hauling him onto his feet. "Hey, there, asshole—long time, no see," he said. "Got a news flash for ya, bud: we're through playin' around with you. So you, me, and my friend here"—he indicated No-Neck, a refrigerator-sized shadow behind him—"are gonna take us a little ride."

24

DAISY turned the corner just in time to see the two bruisers manhandle Nick into a black Firebird. "Shit!" She smacked the steering wheel with the heel of her hand. "Shit, shit, *shit*!"

She stood on the brakes and the rental car rocked to a halt. Fortunately its abrupt stop didn't attract the thugs' attention. Hitting the lights to prevent the beams from acting like a spotlight, she slipped the gearshift into reverse and backed into a driveway where she'd be less conspicuous, yet still be able to see what was going on.

Dammit, this was all her fault. If she hadn't allowed her feelings to get in the way, Nick never would have been left vulnerable. Fear for him hit her hard. Her heart raced and sickness roiled in her stomach, and she took several deep breaths to get herself under control. Acting like a lovesick girlie-girl would benefit absolutely no one.

The Firebird headed down the block in the opposite direction, and she eased onto the street to follow in its wake. She kept the headlights off until they hit the main arterial.

She followed the Firebird down Divisadero, and turned left behind the Exploratorium and the Palace of Fine Arts until the street ran into Doyle Drive. They passed the Yacht Club on the right and the Presidio on the left, and the next thing she knew, she was several car lengths behind the black car on the Golden Gate Bridge, headed for Marin County.

Oh, man, where were they taking him? The wine country, maybe? She didn't like that idea at all. There were far too many miles of unpopulated countryside where anything could be done to him without a soul to bear witness . . . or where a body could easily be dumped.

Douglass would be more than happy to slit my throat, especially after tonight.

Oh, God, and she'd said, *Good.*

But instead of continuing along 101, the Firebird turned onto Highway 1 long before it came anywhere near the wine country. They drove along the coast, and a short while later the black car pulled off onto a tree-lined drive that led to an imposing mansion on a bluff overlooking the Pacific.

Daisy, who had dropped back to avoid detection, drove past the closing gate and slowed down to catch a glimpse. All she could see, however, was the red blink of taillights disappearing down the drive.

She found a spot to pull over and parked the car, then checked her Glock and strapped on her knives. She tucked the Beretta in her boot and, killing the interior lights, eased the door open and climbed out.

The stone wall that divided the estate from the road was merely ornamental and she scaled it easily. *Please, God, don't let there be dogs*, she prayed fervently as she slipped along the row of wind-shaped trees that lined the driveway. She'd had the unhappy experience of coming face-to-face with a vicious security dog once and had no desire to repeat it.

She encountered neither man nor beast, however, and a few moments later she crept up the set of shallow steps that lined the mansion's stone terrace. A light shone in a single window partway down the terrace, and she slipped to one side of it and eased her head around to peek into the room.

It was empty.

She whispered a mild curse and tried to think what to do next. The rest of the mansion was dark and Mrs. Douglass was probably asleep upstairs. That made the main floor her best bet, or the cellars, if there were any. Then she heard a muted crash come from around the back and, slipping from one shadow to the next, she ran lightly toward the sound.

Nick picked himself up off the floor, where he'd landed when the chair Blunt Face had thrown him into had careened over from the momentum of his landing. Above him, bottles clinked and clattered as the rack holding them resettled on the floor. He was damn lucky it hadn't toppled over on him, considering how

hard he'd struck it with his shoulder. Damn—
his barely healed shoulder. He resisted the urge
to feel for new injury, knowing the less weakness
he showed this crew, the better off he'd be.

Climbing to his feet, he brushed himself off,
pausing when his fingers encountered a separa-
tion in the shoulder seam of his tux. "My tailor
is not going to be happy," he said coolly as he
righted the chair. He swung it around and strad-
dled it, folding his arms nonchalantly across the
back.

His gaze flashed past his two captors to the
open door beyond them. They were in the mansion's wine cellar. Pristinely maintained bottles
reposed in rack after freestanding oak rack, and
he had a view straight down an aisle between
two of the racks to the wide-open doorway. He
could smell the salt air, and weak light from a
crescent moon illuminated a set of concrete steps
that beckoned the way to freedom.

A freedom that he very much desired . . . but
feared he wouldn't attain anytime soon.

"Listen up, asshole," Blunt Face said. "We can
do this the easy way or we can do it hard. It's
pretty much up to you."

Nick shrugged. "I choose easy."

"Good. Where're the photos?"

"In a nice, safe place."

The blow to his jaw snapped his head around,
but he maintained his seat.

Blunt Face slapped the leather sap he'd used
to hit him against the palm of his free hand. "I'm
not in the mood for cute, buddy boy. Where are
the fucking photos?"

"I've got them safely on ice. In a place where Douglass will never get his hands on them." He accepted the next blow stoically. Licking a trace of blood from his split lip, he stared up at Blunt Face. "What are you going to do, man, beat me to a pulp? Kill me? Over some frigging *photographs*?" If he truly believed that, he'd be a hell of a lot more apprehensive than he already was, but he didn't think it had come to that. Not yet, at any rate. "I can't stop you, obviously, so knock yourself out. But that won't get Douglass his photographs."

"Perhaps this will." J. Fitzgerald himself stepped out of the shadows. He had changed out of his formal wear into a pastel polo shirt and casual slacks. His silver hair was immaculately brushed and he looked like a wealthy magnate at his leisure.

A leisure he spent satisfying a passion for gardening, if the large pair of hedge clippers he held was any indication.

For the first time, No-Neck stirred from his position against one of the wine racks. "Like I told ya earlier," he said flatly, pushing upright and dropping arms that had been crossed over his massive chest, "I don't want no part of this shit."

"Then leave," Douglass replied. "But as I told you, if you want part of being paid, you won't get in my way."

Nick looked from the light reflecting off the blade of the clippers to the muscle-bound goon-for-hire. No-Neck returned his look, then shrugged. He turned on his heel and walked away, and as Nick watched him stalk down the alleyway and out the door, uneasiness coiled like a snake in his gut. The man didn't strike him as particularly squeamish . . . or even the kind of guy who would draw the line where most folks might.

Dammit, this was all Daisy's fault. If she'd been doing her job like she was supposed to, he wouldn't be about to have God-only-knew what done to him.

Remembrance of the look in her eyes when she'd discovered he'd been lying to her pulled him up short. No—the fault was his own. He'd made some really dumb-ass decisions this week, not the least of which was underestimating how far Douglass was prepared to go to get that ambassadorship. He should have set up precautionary measures to safeguard himself from this very situation.

"Hold his hands," J. Fitzgerald commanded Blunt Face.

No! No one was messing with his hands! His entrails turning to ice, Nick started to shove to his feet, only to have Blunt Face muscle him back down. Bracketing Nick in place with his body, the goon gripped him by the wrists and thrust his hands forward.

Nick clenched his fists.

"Open your hands," Douglass said.

Was he out of his fucking mind? "I don't think so. My hands are my livelihood." Not to mention how much pleasure he got out of using them on Daisy.

J. Fitzgerald smacked the gleaming, curved business end of the hedge clippers between the tendons of Nick's right hand, and the resultant scream of nerves caused his fingers to uncurl. "You should have thought of that before you started poking your camera where it didn't belong." He grasped Nick's index finger and straightened it. He then tried to maneuver what was intended to be a two-handed implement with his free hand. "Give me some help here, Autry."

"Are you *insane*?" Nick tried to pull free, but he was firmly pinned. Shit! Why hadn't he set up a plan that would've automatically sent Douglass' photos to the tabloids or to Uncle Greg if anything happened to him?

"Where are the photographs?" Douglass demanded. "Tell me right now, or I'll snip your finger off like a fucking twig."

Nick's mind spun as Blunt Face straightened his finger and held it steady, while J. Fitzgerald slid the bottom blade beneath it and grasped the uppermost handle to bring the top blade down. *Bluff, you fool! Start talking before it's too late.* He opened his mouth—

And heard Daisy yell, "Drop it, Douglass, or I'll drop you where you stand."

Nick looked down the aisle and saw her standing in a two-handed shooting stance, her gun aimed steadily at J. Fitzgerald. His very own avenging angel, blue combat boots, crazy-cut hairdo, and all. Love for her burst like champagne bubbles in his bloodstream; it exploded in his heart, suffusing him with warmth clear out to his endangered fingertips.

J. Fitzgerald let the hedge clippers drop to his side. Blunt Face released his hand.

Then Nick felt the thug's body shift against his back as Autry reached behind himself with his right hand. Assuming he was going for his gun, Nick yelled, "Blondie!"

She swung her Glock a few inches and Nick felt Blunt Face freeze. "Take your weapon out nice and slow," she advised the goon. "My trigger finger feels mighty itchy, so I'd advise you to keep your hands where I can see them. And you, Douglass, hand those clippers to Nick. You okay?" she asked him.

She barely spared him a glance, but that was fine with him—she had more important matters on her mind. He flashed her a huge grin as he relieved J. Fitzgerald of the hedge clippers and only winced a little at the pull to his abused lip. "I am now, doll face."

"You're making a big mistake, young woman," Douglass said with authority, and he took a step toward Daisy. The look she leveled on him halted him midstride.

"No, you're the one who's made the mistake, mister. I have a real low tolerance for hypocrites and liars, and you're about the worst of both I've ever had the misfortune to meet. And I'm acquainted with some damn proficient liars."

Nick winced at the reminder that he wasn't out of the woods with her yet. But right now, he just wanted to get them the hell out of here. He collected Blunt Face's gun.

"I'll tell you what's even more insulting," Blondie told Douglass, while gesturing for Blunt

Face to come stand where she could cover both of them without dividing her attention. "You're not even a particularly worthy opponent. I could at least respect intelligence. But you were too stupid to realize Nick would've destroyed the negatives if you'd just left him alone. And how on earth did you plan to explain his blood all over your cellar floor? You can't honestly believe you could disfigure him and *not* have him go to the police."

Douglass gave her a malevolent glare. "I don't like your tone or your attitude, young lady."

"Well, gee. How ever will I bear up under the strain?" Her dark eyes flashed fire. "You don't get it, do you, gramps? You aren't the final arbiter of acceptable behavior around here. And considering your recent behavior, what makes you think you would be?"

"Listen, you no-account little bitch, I'll have you know that I'm—"

"A criminal. You're nothing but a thug with a decent bank account and an inflated sense of his own importance. Which reminds me . . ." She tossed Nick her cell phone. "Call the cops. Let's get this clown behind bars where he belongs."

"I don't think so," rumbled a new voice from behind the wine racks, and No-Neck stepped into view. He had a gun in his hand and it was trained on Blondie.

Dammit! Daisy turned to face the new menace. Talk about inexcusably sloppy. She should have called the cops immediately instead of stopping to berate Douglass.

"Drop your gun, sweet thing." The man

grinned at her when she complied. "So, we meet again. Kick your weapon over here—there's a good girl. No, don't come any closer," he warned when she edged in his direction. "I remember your kung fu skills real well. You were pretty damn good."

"Yeah, I excelled in Goon-tossing 101."

"Funny girl. You sure got a mouth on you, don'tcha?"

She shrugged.

"You better watch what you say with it, or someone might take exception."

She almost said, *Wow, a three-syllable word*, but caught herself in time. No-Neck was so busy lording it over her, he wasn't totally on guard. No sense in putting him there by pissing him off.

"Wow," Nick said. "How about that? He knows a three-syllable word."

Daisy laughed and, scowling, No-Neck swung around to face Nick. "No one's talkin' to you, pretty boy, so if I were you, I'd mind my own fu—"

Daisy's kick hit his gun hand and the weapon went flying. She bent to draw her Beretta out of her boot, but No-Neck caught her shoulder with the toe of his shoe, sending her reeling. He grabbed her up in a bear hug while she was still midspin.

Dangling off the ground, facing away from No-Neck as his brawny arms squeezed the breath out of her, she saw Nick grab a wine bottle off a rack and bring it down across Blunt Face's wrist. It sent her Glock, which the goon had snatched from the floor, tumbling back down.

With dark spots beginning to crowd the edge of her vision, Daisy drew one of her knives and reached over shoulder and pressed it against No-Neck's jugular.

"I'll be darned, you do have a neck," she wheezed when he froze. His grip loosened and she drew in some much-needed air. She realized she had the blunt side of the knife pressed to his carotid and quickly reversed it before it dawned on him, too. "Now set me down nice and gentle and I won't have to slice your throat."

As he did as she bade him, Blunt Face dived for the gun Nick had knocked loose. Nick laid him out with one blow from the bottle of wine. He looked in amazement from the unconscious thug at his feet to the bottle in his hand.

"Good year," he murmured.

Daisy grinned and stepped away from No-Neck, whirling to face him, her expression once again menacingly serious as she brandished the knife.

He held his hands up in surrender, and she stepped back out of range of those long arms. From the corner of her eye she caught a glimpse of J. Fitzgerald, whom she'd momentarily forgotten. He had something black in his hand and was headed for the door. Thinking it was a gun, she was already bending for her Beretta when she heard him say excitedly, "Hello, *police*? Send someone quick. I've got burglars in my house and I think they're armed."

"Ah, sh—Nick!" She turned to tell him they

had to get the hell out of there, but he'd obviously heard for himself, for he was already loping toward her. She had one confused moment to notice he still held the bottle of wine in his hand, then she snatched up her Glock from the floor and they ran for the cellar door.

"The old goat's smarter than I thought," she said as Nick boosted her over the estate wall and vaulted it in her wake. "If the cops catch us they'll probably shoot first and ask questions later. By beating us to the punch, he pretty much guaranteed they'll never believe that you were brought here against your will." They skidded to a halt at the car and she slammed her hand down on its roof. "Damn! It just fries my bacon that he's going to get away with this." She shoved the key in the lock as clouds scudded across the slivered moon, turning Nick into an indistinct shadow across from her.

"He'll probably never go to jail," he agreed as they climbed in the car. "But he's not going to skate on this, either."

She turned over the engine and punched the accelerator and they sped down the coast highway. But she took her gaze off the road long enough to lift a skeptical eyebrow at him.

"I mean it, Daise," he said. "He'll probably send the goons to my place to intercept us, so pull into the first motel you see. We're going to get a few hours' sleep. Then I'm going to do what I should have done in the first place."

25

saturday

DAISY awoke to the sound of Nick's voice requesting a conversation with the senator. She squinted at the clock on the motel nightstand and saw that it was six-fifteen. Yawning, she slid her pillow against the headboard and eased upright to lean against it. The room was cool and she worked a hand out of the blankets to reach for the pink cardigan she'd discarded only a few short hours ago.

"Yes, I'm sure he's extremely busy," Nick said in his most reasonable, trained-at-the-best-schools-money-can-buy manner. "But tell him all the same that Nicholas Coltrane is calling and he says it's quite urgent, won't you?"

He sat on the edge of the bed with his back to her, dressed only in black silk boxers. The phone receiver tucked between his ear and one shoulder, he worked the opposite arm in slow rotations to get the kinks out of his abused shoulder.

Daisy leisurely tracked the bunch and flow of

the muscles bracketing the shallow groove of his spine. Against her will she remembered the way he'd felt when he'd ignored the extra bed last night and crawled into hers. He'd snuggled up behind her as if he had a perfect right, wrapped an arm around her waist, and pulled her close. Then, before she could even draw breath to demand what the heck he was doing, she'd felt him go lax against her in heavy, instantaneous sleep.

"Uncle Greg!" Dropping his arm to his side, Nick straightened. "I'm sorry to disturb you in D.C., sir, but I've gotten mixed up in a bit of trouble here at home, and I need your help straightening it out."

Daisy listened as he succinctly laid out the events of the past week. The only thing he left out was Mo's financial trouble and his jettisoned plan to sell J. Fitzgerald's photos to the tabloids in order to bail her out.

"Exactly!" he exclaimed. "Everybody does know that, sir, but he came after me hammer and tongs anyway, and frankly, destroying the negatives is no longer an option. After running afoul of his hedge clippers, I gotta tell you I find the side of himself he doesn't show the public downright scary, and I want that ambassadorship stopped in its tracks. It's a safe bet he's not going to back off while there's still a chance I can mess up his shot at it, and I'm damned if I'll spend the rest of my life looking over my shoulder. So if you'll see to quashing the appointment, this is what I plan do. . . ."

He hung up a few minutes later and climbed to his feet. Stretching his long body, he twisted his upper torso in first one direction, then the other. His rotation to the right brought her within his sights and, elbows up, he froze midtwist. Then a slow, warm smile curved his mouth, and he turned to face her fully. "Good mornin'. Did I wake you?"

She shook her head. "I heard you on the phone, but I was waking up anyhow." She had a sudden mad desire to explore his lower lip, which was slightly puffy from last night's adventure. Her fingers itched like crazy. When they began to spontaneously rise to touch his abused mouth, however, she sternly willed them back to her lap, entwining her fingers to ensure they behaved themselves. "How are you feeling?"

"Stiff."

"Yeah, I am a little, too."

His eyelids drooped. "Ah, but I doubt we're talking the same kinda stiff here, sweetpea."

She felt a clenching zing deep between her legs, and her gaze involuntarily flew to the fly of his silk shorts, which had some tremendous tenting action going on.

Then she could have kicked herself for falling for such a blatant setup. She met the much-too-pleased-with-himself glint in his eye with disdain. "You're just too funny for words, Coltrane."

"Hey, I take my hard-ons quite seriously."

She curled her lip at him. "It's a wonder you get any work done, then—considering they're pretty much your natural state. Now, if you'll excuse me," she said, throwing back the covers and climbing off the bed, "I'm going to go soak some of my boring old run-of-the-mill stiffness out in a hot bath."

Nick snagged her by the waist as she breezed past him. Sweeping her off her feet, he curved his chest against her back and buried his lips in that sensitive spot where her neck joined her shoulder. "Okay, my shoulder's a little stiff, too," he murmured. "But lighten up, Blondie. I have a feeling everything's going to work out just fine."

She jabbed back with her elbow, but although he grunted when it connected with his hard gut, she doubted it did any damage. It felt as if she'd connected with the wall.

But he did set her back on her feet.

She turned to face him. "You're deluding yourself if you think you can flash a little Coltrane charm and everything will be hunky-dory between us," she said. "I came after you last night for one reason only: because I'd signed a contract."

"Liar."

"I'm sure you'd like to think so." She went to her suitcase to collect fresh undies, but when she turned for the bathroom Nick stood in her way.

"Mo borrowed funds from one of her escrow accounts," he said, staring down at her with fierce-eyed intensity. "It was stupid and it was criminal, but she didn't do it for profit. I don't know all the reasons why she did it, but I can guarantee you she thought she was helping someone in trouble. I know how you feel about the tabloids, Blondie, but I'd do it again, because

I couldn't stand by and watch my sister go to jail."

She really didn't want it to, but the explanation made a difference. Feeling misused, she longed to be able to hang on to her grudge. But she nodded and stepped around him, clutching her clothing to her chest.

"You're gonna forgive me, you know," he said confidently.

Stopping at the bathroom door, she looked at him over her shoulder, thinking of all the ways in which he could break her heart. "Maybe."

"You will," he said with a cocky grin. "Because you love me, and I'm a funny guy, and you won't be able to help yourself."

"Pfft." But her traitorous heart wasn't so sure that he wasn't right. And, given everything that had ever gone between them, it scared the hell out of her.

"You do love me, cupcake," she heard him say as she closed the bathroom door and bent to turn on the bathtub faucet. "I'll make you admit it if it's the last thing I do."

As he drove them back to his place a short while later, Nick mulled over various ways to achieve that. He knew it could be done, because honesty was a big deal to Blondie and he was ninety-nine percent positive that she did love him. But he also knew better than to expect it to be easy—she was without a doubt the stubbornest wench God ever set on this good green earth. He smiled wryly, imagining her response to that description.

Luckily for him she wasn't a mind reader.

"Turn here," Daisy suddenly said when they were a block from the estate.

Nick didn't ask why; he simply made the turn. Neither did he argue when she instructed him to find a place to pull over and park the car. When it came to this cloak-and-dagger stuff, she was the boss.

He had second thoughts about that when he followed her over the back wall of the estate a few moments later. Between her and Douglass' thugs, his tux was never going to be the same— let alone his person. Ahead of him, Daisy dropped into the yard. She let go of the branch she'd been holding out of her way, and it whipped back to lash him. He rubbed at the welt it raised on his bare chest. Damn, that stung. If he'd known they'd be playing Tarzan and Jane, he probably would have done up all those damned shirt studs after all, instead of tossing them in his pocket.

But he forgot all that when he followed Daisy's stealthy lead up the staircase to his apartment and saw that the door was cracked open. She put a cautionary finger to her lips and pulled her gun out of the back of her jeans, then pointed into the apartment. He nodded and, accepting the Beretta she pulled from her boot, tried to accustom himself to its unfamiliar weight as he crept behind her down the hallway. They entered the living room to find Blunt Face and No-Neck tossing the joint.

Daisy leveled the Glock at the two thugs.

"Freeze!" she barked. "Don't even breathe deep."

"Ah, shit," No-Neck said in perfect synchronicity with Blunt Face's heartfelt, "Fuck!"

"Tell me about it," Daisy agreed. "Drop your guns to the floor and kick them over here. I'm getting real tired of this. And Mr. Coltrane here is probably even more fed up with the two of you making a mess of his place. Hand over the arsenal in your boots, too." When Blunt Face and No-Neck tried to look innocent, she gave them an impatient *c'mon-c'mon* curl of her fingers. "Don't try to kid a kidder—I know by now how many weapons you two carry." She spared a quick glance for Nick before turning her attention back to Douglass' hired muscle. "Call the police."

Nick did so and hanging up a couple of minutes later, he looked at the two goons sitting side by side on his couch where Daisy had ordered them. "I sure hope Douglass is paying you well," he said when they looked up at him with sullen eyes. "Because you're about to take a big fall for him. If I were you I'd save my own ass by shifting the blame squarely back where it belongs—on the man who hired you."

Blunt Face narrowed his eyes at him. "I don't know what the hell you're talkin' about."

He shrugged. "Hey, it's no skin off my knuckles if you wanna do the shower dance with the boys at the penitentiary." Then he wrapped his fingers around the back of Daisy's neck and give it a friendly squeeze. "Good work, Blondie. You're the queen of the security specialists."

The grin she flashed him gripped him by the heart and squeezed until he could barely breathe. He wanted to snatch her off her feet and kiss her silly, pull her into his arms for a bone-cracking hug, perform any number of acts that were inappropriate to the moment. "So"—he cleared his throat—"do you, uh, require any assistance here?"

"I'm the queen, remember? I've got it under control."

"In that case, I'll go change my clothes. I'll be out in a flash."

It didn't take him much longer than that, but by the time he came out of the bedroom still buttoning his shirt, the cops had arrived and were busy taking Daisy's statement. He watched as she showed them her gun permit and state license; then one of the cops broke away and came over to greet him.

"Mr. Coltrane?" At his nod the patrolwoman said, "Let's go down here where it's a little quieter. I just need to ask you a few questions."

They sat at the breakfast bar while he went over the break-in and established Blunt Face and No-Neck as the same two men who had broken into his garage earlier in the week and held Daisy at gunpoint. Eventually, all the cops' questions were answered and they took the two thugs away in handcuffs.

Daisy turned to him the minute his apartment emptied. "Why didn't you tell them about Douglass?"

"Once burned, twice shy, doll face. I tried telling the cop who came here Wednesday that

Douglass was behind the attack, but the idiot didn't believe a word I said. And it's not as if I can prove anything."

"You could have at least tried."

"Dammit, Daisy, I'm tired of knocking my head against that wall. But I can do what I told Uncle Greg I would." He rummaged through his desk and pulled out writing material. Sitting down, he drafted a letter. Three attempts later, he stood up, waved the finished product to dry the ink, and slid it into a manila envelope. He grabbed the tabloid bids and added them to the envelope, then looked over at Blondie. He caught her in a yawn.

Daisy belatedly covered her mouth. Nick was looking at her with a slight smile tilting up one corner of his mouth, and she braced herself for a smart-ass remark.

He was obviously feeling generous, however, for he merely said, "Grab your weapons, cupcake—you can catch up on your beauty sleep later." He gave her a big, feral grin that set her heart to pounding. "We might not be in a position to put Douglass in jail, but we can sure as hell do some damage control to get him off our backs."

Our backs. Not his back, theirs. She mulled that over as she followed him down to the garage, where he crossed over to the chest freezer in the corner. He lifted its top and leaned in, rearranging a few tubs of ice cream and several packages of wrapped meat to pull out a Rubbermaid container. Peeling off the lid, he tipped out a frozen chunk of indeterminate foodstuffs and reached into the bottom for a flat, plastic-wrapped rectangle. He wiped moisture from the heavy black plastic, then carefully peeled it open. Removing a small stack of photographs, he selected several, then rewrapped the rest, along with their negatives, and returned them to the container.

"Here," he said, thrusting the pictures into her hand and reaching for the frozen block to fit it back into the container. "You want to see what all the fuss was about?"

"I'm not sure I can stomach the sight of a naked J. Fitzgerald," she answered honestly. But the temptation to see what had caused so much strife proved too much and she slowly flipped through the photos.

There were only actually two separate shots—the rest were duplicates. She studied them, then handed them back. "You are so good." She made a face, wiggling uncomfortably. "A little too good in this instance. Yuk."

He grinned at her and added the pictures to his manila envelope. Then he reached for her hand. "Let's go, cupcake. I'll fill you in on the way how I want this handled."

Nick stopped the car in front of the gates to J. Fitzgerald's seaside estate a short while later. He looked over to see Daisy watching him, her eyebrows raised.

"What now?" she demanded. "Do we ring for admittance or storm the gates?"

"We ring the bell and—now, don't go all

postal on me—lie our heads off if that's what we have to do."

She looked at him down the length of her nose. "Postal. You are so amusing, Coltrane."

He grinned. He couldn't help it—she was just so damn appealing when she acted imperious. He wished he had the time to goad her a little further, but it would have to wait. He lowered the car window and reached out to push the button set in the gatepost.

A speaker crackled. "Yes?"

"Nicholas Coltrane to see Mr. Douglass."

"I'm sorry, but Mr. Douglass is not receiv— What?" The disembodied voice got fainter, as if its owner had turned away to speak to someone in the room. "It's a Mr. Nicholas Coltrane, sir. I say, Mr. Douglass, are you all right?" A low murmur too indistinct to comprehend replied, and the woman then said, "Yes, of course, sir." Her voice regained the volume it had lost. "You may come up to the house, Mr. Coltrane." The line went dead and the gates slowly swept open.

Daisy shifted to face him, drawing her knee up on the seat. "So," she said. "Just a shot in the dark here, but did you get the impression that he was a bit startled to have you land on his doorstep?"

"Sounds like."

A laugh, low and sweeter than honey to his ears, rumbled in her throat. "Good."

They were ushered into a study a few minutes later by a woman in a formal black uniform and white apron. J. Fitzgerald sat ensconced in solitary splendor behind a massive desk, his face pale. He remained seated at their entrance, and the moment the maid stepped out of the room and closed the door behind her, he demanded, "Where're Autry and Jacobsen, Coltrane?"

"Down at the jailhouse singing like canaries, I imagine."

Douglass whispered a curse and reached for the phone. "I'll get them the best lawyer money can buy," he said. He snatched up the receiver, but Nick leaned over the desk and broke the connection.

"Get your hand off my phone," Douglass said in an authoritative tone that was clearly accustomed to instant compliance.

Nick's temper reared up like a baited bear, but he sternly knocked it back on all fours. Reaching inside the manila envelope, he pulled out a photo and dropped it on the desk in front of J. Fitzgerald.

The older man snatched it up and stared at it. He grew even paler. But his chin raised defiantly and he ripped the photograph in two.

Nick shrugged and pulled two new ones from his jacket pocket and tossed them down on the desk to replace the one that had been destroyed. J. Fitzgerald snatched them up, gave them a frantic perusal, and then ripped them, too.

Daisy opened her purse and pulled out three new photographs. Without a word, she leaned forward and placed them side by side, face up, on the desk in front of Douglass. He gathered them together and, without even sparing them a glance, started to rip them also.

But he'd only torn them half an inch when he

stopped and set them back on the desk.

Nick nodded. "I see you're starting to get the message." He threw the stack of bids from the tabloids onto the desk.

As J. Fitzgerald read them, his color grew dangerously flushed. He glared up at Nick. "What do you want, Coltrane?"

"What I've wanted from the beginning: to be left the hell alone." He pulled the letter he'd written earlier out of the manila envelope and set it on top of the discarded photographs and tabloid bids. He waited until Douglass put on his reading glasses and read the missive detailing the events of the last week.

Then Nick planted his knuckles on the polished desktop, leaned his weight on them, and, towering over Douglass, said, "Several copies of that, along with copies of the photos I showed you, have been delivered in sealed envelopes to an influential friend. If he doesn't hear from me on the exact schedule we set up, he's instructed to turn one envelope over to the police and the rest to the rags—which, as you can see for yourself, are perfectly willing to bid sight-unseen for any damn thing I might care to give them."

He bent down farther, thrusting his face close to J. Fitzgerald's. "I want me and mine left alone. If anyone I love gets so much as a scratch on their *car*—never mind their person—I'm going to assume you're behind it. And I'll turn my copies over to the cops and the tabloids so fast you won't know what hit you, old man. I'm sick to death of this shit, and I give you fair warning: it would behoove you to see to it that nothing happens to anyone I care about." He straightened. "C'mon, Daise." Reaching for her hand, he headed for the door.

The telephone on the desk behind them rang and he heard J. Fitzgerald snatch it up. "I told you no interruptions, Ingrid," he snapped, but then there was a rustle and a sudden sense of expectation in the air, and Nick glanced over his shoulder to see Douglass snap erect. The magnate's hand adjusted his already immaculately knotted tie. "What? Senator Slater? Yes, yes, put him through!"

Nick and Daisy exchanged a brief glance, but neither said a word until they had walked out of the office and closed the door behind them.

"You think the senator is breaking the news?" she asked, and he'd bet big bucks the same smile that tilted up the corner of her soft mouth was reflected on his own.

"Yeah." His shoulder hitched. "Something tells me this is just not going to be Douglass' day."

peing to ignore I care about." He straightened. "Good, Daisy." Reaching for her hand, he headed for the door.

Her gaze remained on the spot behind them ... and it ... Thinking to catch up they ... the carriage door ... he stopped but then there was a roar and a sudden sw... splintering of the seat. She whirled ... the car as she caught a sight ... the w... taking out ... His ... by the Dough...

26
∽∾∽

DAISY didn't quite know what to do with herself once they got back to Nick's carriage house. The euphoria of neutralizing the threat Douglass had posed was fading, her job here was done, and she was scared to death to trust in Nick's declaration of love.

So she set about packing her stuff. She hadn't realized, until she began gathering her belongings, just how comfortable she'd gotten here. Her possessions were scattered throughout the apartment.

A shaft of sunlight broke through the late morning gloom outside. Refracted by the mullioned windows, it picked out the russet and bronze highlights in Nick's brown hair as he stood watching her, his hips propped against the windowsill, muscular arms crossed over his chest. "So, this is it, then?" he demanded when she made the mistake of meeting his gaze. "You're just going to run away?" His lip lifted in an expression of disdain that stabbed her right through the heart. "Funny, I never figured you for a chickenshit."

Her spine snapped erect. It was one thing to privately acknowledge her cowardice; *he* didn't get to throw it in her face. But damned if she'd make a liar out of herself by denying it.

"Hell, yes, I'm scared—I'd be a fool not to be! I still recall the last time I handed myself into your tender keeping, Coltrane. I gave you everything, and you told me you loved me then, too, remember? But it wasn't enough to make you stick around."

He opened his mouth to reply, but she roared right over him. "The minute you got yours, you sure as hell changed your story in a hurry. What was it you said—that people would say anthing in the heat of the moment and I oughtta grow up?"

"I was an idiot."

"No, *I* was the idiot for believing you in the first place."

"Where is this coming from, Daisy? I thought we'd worked our way past it."

"Well, that would certainly be convenient for you, wouldn't it?

"*Convenient?*" He was suddenly towering over her, eyes like blue flames, and the look that caused those flames made her feet back up nervously. He stalked her step for step, and the next thing she knew, her backside had hit the back of the couch. Gripping it to anchor herself, she thrust her chin up at him. He thrust his right back at her, and they were suddenly nose to nose. "Trust me on this, Blondie," he snarled through his teeth, "there's not a damn thing about loving you that's *convenient*. You're a hot-headed, armed-to-the-teeth smart-ass, and if I were the least bit intelligent, I'd run as far from you as I could get."

"Nobody could ever accuse you of being intelligent, though, could they, Coltrane, because here you are, getting all aggressive with me anyway." Dear God, where had that come from? It sounded almost . . . commendatory.

"That's the God's honest truth, Parker, so don't go thinking you can shake me now by giving me attitude." The aggression abruptly left his stance and he reached out to brush gentle fingertips down her cheek to the belligerent thrust of her chin. "I ran scared the night I took your virginity, Daise, but I'm not the terrified kid I was then. I've grown up; I'm no longer afraid of what I feel. I love you. I think we should get married."

"*What?*" Joy such as she'd never known exploded in her chest, and it scared the bejesus out of her. She pushed him back. "Are you *crazy*?"

"Crazy in love."

"No, just plain crazy! It would never work. Look at your dad; look at my mom."

"That's them. Where is it written that you and I have to make their mistakes? Everyone has choices to make, Blondie, and we can choose to do something entirely different. We could actually *fight* for our marriage and work things out when we hit a rough patch, instead of caving at the first sign of trouble."

"There's a concept." She straightened her spine. "But it wouldn't work."

"Yes, dammit, it would. If we put some real

effort into it." He bent his head and gave her a light kiss on the lips. "I love you, Daisy."

"We're too different."

He kissed her again, in a deeper, more leisurely manner. Raising his head, he said, "Not in the ways that matter, we aren't. I *love* you."

He bent his head to kiss her once again, and this time she couldn't stop herself from throwing her arms around his neck and kissing him back for all she was worth. Then, tearing her mouth free, she said, "You *lied* to me."

"And I swear to you I'll never do it again."

Looking into his eyes, she believed him. And yet . . . "Even so, we *are* different. In every way, Nick."

"Bullshit."

"It's not bull—it's a fact."

"Give me one for-instance."

"Okay. Say for just a minute that I actually said I'd marry you. I bet we couldn't even agree on what kind of wedding to have."

"What—do you think I'd insist on some hoop-de-do-dah society affair? Because if you want to get married by the justice of the peace, doll face, we'll do that—"

"*Ick!* I don't want some sterile, bureaucratic office wedding."

"What do you want?"

"I don't know—something intimate and warm. Where I could wear one of those really froufrou wedding gowns."

"No kidding?" The tenderness of his smile turned her knees to cream cheese. "That's the last thing I would have expected."

"Why? Just because I'm not a girlie-girl doesn't mean I haven't peeked at *Bride* magazine once or twice . . . or dreamed of wearing one of those gorgeous dresses." Then, terrified she was losing ground, she shot off the definitive volley. "And, of course, any wedding of mine wouldn't be complete without Reggie and the boys."

Nick narrowed his eyes at her. "I suppose Benny would insist on wearing a bridesmaid's dress."

"Yep." There went her wedding. She'd known bringing up the boys would scotch the deal—so where was the triumph in being right? Still, if he couldn't accept her for who she was—

"Works for me," he said. "But he buys new shoes, or the deal's off. Those heels he wears are a disgrace."

She felt her chin drop and closed her mouth with a snap. "Are you crazy? You'd lose half your business if San Francisco society found out you had a transvestite in your wedding!"

Nick shrugged. "Hey, as The Divine Miss M used to say before she went all mainstream, 'Fuck 'em if they can't take a joke.' " He grasped her by the hips and set her on the back of the couch, nudging her legs apart to step between them. "I'm not marrying you to advance my career—"

"No fooling!"

"—I'm marrying you because my life's had so much more color in it since we got together. I love you, cupcake. Do you love me?"

She longed to deny it, to protect herself against future pain. But she couldn't. "Yes."

His smile was blindingly white, and he kissed her, hard. "That's all that matters, then. Our wedding is our business and no one else's. You want Benny as an attendant, we'll have Benny."

"I'm really scared, Nick."

"Ah, no," he crooned and kissed her eyebrow, the bridge of her nose, her lips. Pulling back, he rearranged several spikes of hair into a pattern that seemed to please him. "Don't be scared. I want this so much, Blondie."

"It's such a huge step for two people with our family histories."

"Yeah, it is. But we're tough—we can make it through anything life throws at us. Besides, we've got a secret weapon."

"Oh, yeah? And what's that?"

"Your stubborn streak. Once you've made up your mind that something's gonna work, face it, Blondie, you're too damn stubborn to ever back down."

The grin that flashed across her face was a pale imitation of the pure happiness that bloomed in her breast. "Oh, God. That's true." She kissed him so hard they toppled over the back of the couch onto the cushions. "I love you, Nicholas Coltrane. Only you could take one of my worst character faults and turn it into a virtue."

He pulled the ribbon that fastened her pink cardigan between her breasts. "Is this a match made in heaven, or what?"

"Precisely. And I get to be the alpha angel." She wrestled with the buttons on his shirt.

He made a rude noise as he peeled her out of her sweaters. "Not on your life, Blondie." He unfastened her bra and murmured appreciation for the bounty he uncovered. Then he smiled into her eyes. "But I'm always happy to provide you with lots of opportunities to give it your best shot."

EPILOGUE
∽∾∾∽

NICK pressed Daisy up against the door and kissed her feverishly while he fumbled with the card key to the tenth-floor room at the Mark Hopkins. The door handle suddenly gave beneath his palm and they nearly fell into the room. Breaking apart, they looked at each other and laughed. Then Nick swept her up in a rustle of organza and lace and stepped over the threshold.

Setting her on her feet on the other side, he closed the door and leaned back against it. "Did I tell you what a spectacular bride you are, Mrs. Coltrane?"

"Yes, but tell me more." Standing proud and erect in front of him, she flashed a cocky grin and crooked her fingers at him in a gimme gesture. "I can take it."

"You're beautiful. Magnificent." And their wedding had turned out great. It had been small and intimate, just the way she'd wanted, and it had even ended up being fairly traditional since Benny had elected to wear a tux instead of a gown. Nick hated to admit it but he was kind of relieved, even though he'd been sincere when he'd told Daisy that Benny could wear any damn thing he wanted as long as she married him.

Her mom had been there, too, with her new husband, and she'd fussed and cried buckets to a degree he'd thought rather extreme. But Daisy had been tickled to see her, so who was he to complain about a few theatrics?

He smiled tenderly at his newly wedded wife, watching her take in their surroundings as he pushed away from the door.

She looked back at him, her eyebrows raised. "Am I having one of those déjà vu moments, or is this actually . . . ?"

He pulled her into his arms and kissed her, then raised his head. "I thought you might appreciate it if I got things right this time." Waltzing her into the same room they'd used nine years ago, he delivered them with a dramatic flourish to the room service cart, where he dipped her, brought her back upright, and yanked her flush with his body to give her another kiss. Then he set her free. Plucking a bottle of wine out of the silver bucket where it had been chilling, he turned it to present the label. "Madam."

"Oh, my God—this is too good." Staring at the bottle he'd used to coldcock Blunt Face that night in J. Fitzgerald's wine cellar, she laughed a deep, bawdy belly laugh. "This is just too perfect. That's what I like about you, Coltrane—you've got style."

"I thought we could drink one toast to Douglass, since he was responsible for getting us back together again. Then the old bastard's history for all time." He couldn't prevent a satisfied grin. "I was bluffing when I told him his goons were singing like canaries. Who knew I'd turn out to be a freaking prophet?"

No-Neck had had two prior convictions and no burning desire to spend ten-to-twenty in the state pen while Douglass lived free and high on the hog. Compared to what No-Neck faced, the older man's losing the ambassadorship hadn't seemed all that tragic to him, apparently. So he'd spilled his guts.

And the kicker was, it hadn't been the first time the "saint" of San Francisco had hired himself a little muscle to clean up after a mess he'd made. It turned out he'd had his fingers in more slippery situations, both business and personal, than you could shake a stick at.

"He wasn't very smart," Daisy said. "But he was clever enough that folks are still reeling."

Nick handed her a glass and clinked it with his own. "So here's to him. May he spend years and years in the slammer."

They took a sip. Then, wine flute held aloft once again, Daisy entwined their arms. "More importantly—here's to us. May our lives together and our love for each other prosper forever."

They drained their glasses.

And their lives *were* prospering. It turned out Nick had captured J. Fitzgerald's arrogance in the shot he'd taken the night of Douglass' bash, and it had become *the* photograph to accompany first the scandal, then the trial coverage, on the news and in the *Times*, *Chronicle*, and *Examiner*. When people remembered the way Nick had gotten physical with Douglass the night the photo was taken—coupled with the discovery of Daisy's occupation—they'd assumed he must have known more than he was telling all along. He kept his mouth shut and let the rumors run their course. But a side benefit was the sudden inundation of clients for Blondie.

Nick looked at his new bride—something he'd been doing a lot of, since exchanging the I-do's. Her cheeks were flushed and her dark eyes shone as she smiled back at him, and he reached out to trace her lower lip with his thumb. "I love you, Daisy Parker Coltrane."

Her face lit up even more. "I love you, too. Take off your pants."

His dick jumped to attention. "Oh, man, I love a forceful woman. You want me bad, huh?"

"Yeah, that, too. But the pants are my insurance policy. If you get a sudden urge to bolt this time, it's gonna be with the thinker there dangling out for all the world to see."

"Trust me, sweetheart, neither the Big Guy nor I are going anywhere." But he kicked out of his slacks and tossed them to her. Then he went to work on his shirt studs. "Love your gown, doll face, but you've got way too many clothes on."

She grinned and presented him with her back to undo the hidden zipper. As he slid it down, she looked at him over her shoulder. "That was pretty great news about Mo, huh?"

"Yeah, how about that? I'm going to be an uncle—that's pretty fresh."

"Reid sure is over the moon."

"No kidding. It's almost embarrassing, how much." Tossing his shirt aside, he looked up to find she'd beat him once again in the race to get naked. He tumbled them both onto the bed and rolled to his side to look down at her.

"If you ever get pregnant, I hope to hell I act cooler than that." He stroked her flat stomach as gently as if his child did rest within. Then he looked into her lambent chocolate-colored eyes and smiled wryly. "But when I stop and actually think about it?"

He shrugged. "I have to tell you, cupcake—I have my doubts."

DO YOU REMEMBER
THE FIRST TIME . . .

. . . you saw *him?* Perhaps your eyes met across a crowded room . . . and you knew he was the one destined to change your life. Or was the *last* person you thought you'd fall for . . . the one all your friends warned you about. Infuriating, fascinating, and ultimately irresistible . . . he's the man who can rouse your passions as no other.

Now, come meet six unforgettable men . . . cowboys and rakes, both honorable and scandalous (and some a bit of both!), as created by your favorite writers: Barbara Freethy, Cathy Maxwell, Christina Dodd, Lorraine Heath, Susan Andersen, and Kathleen Eagle.

Turn the page—you could be meeting the man you've been waiting for all your life. . . .

Katherine Whitfield thought she'd found herself a cowboy on the wrong side of the Mississippi. There she was, stranded on a Kentucky roadside, with no one to help her but lean, sexy Zach Tyler. Trouble is, Zach might be easy on the eyes, but he had the most annoying habit of telling her what to do. And although it soon became clear that he had a gentle hand with horses and a slow hand with women, Katherine sure didn't want him to get the upper hand with her!

ALMOST HOME
by Barbara Freethy

Coming in January 2000

KATHERINE shook her head, trying to figure out where she was and who was yelling at her. There was a man—a tall, dark-haired man with burning black eyes standing next to her car window. He was pulling on the door handle and yelling all sorts of absurdities that seemed to have less to do with her and more to do with a horse.

She roused herself enough to unlock the door. She pushed on it as the man pulled on it, sending her stumbling into his arms.

He caught her with a sureness, a strength that made her want to sink into his embrace and rest for a moment. She needed to catch her breath. She needed to feel safe.

"You could have killed my horse," he ground out angrily, his rough-edged voice right next to her ear. "Driving like a maniac. What were you thinking about?"

Katherine could barely keep up with his surge of angry words. "Let me go."

His grip eased slightly, but he didn't let go.

They stared at each other, their breaths coming in matching frightened gasps. Dressed in faded blue jeans and a white shirt with the sleeves rolled up to the forearms, the man towered over Katherine. His eyes were fierce and his thick dark hair looked like he'd run his fingers through it all day long. His face was too rugged to be handsome, but it was compelling, strong, stubborn, determined . . .

Good heavens—she had the distinct feeling she'd found herself a cowboy.

Forced to rusticate in the country to hide the disgraceful results of her elopement, Leah Carrollton is utterly dismayed to see Devon Marshall striding toward her across the English countryside. The beautiful debutante had fled the wagging tongues of London's *ton* and an arranged marriage to another, but could marrying Devon truly save her from scandal?

A SCANDALOUS MARRIAGE
by Cathy Maxwell

Coming in February 2000

LEAH had been standing a step apart from a group of other debutantes. They'd all worn pastels and smelled of rosewater. Their claim to conversation had been self-conscious giggles. She was one of them, and yet alone.

He instantly recognized a kindred soul. He understood. She wanted, no, *had* to be accepted by the group but exerted her own independence.

She sensed him staring at her. She turned, searching, and then looked straight at him.

In that moment, time halted. He even stopped breathing, knowing he still lived only because his heart pounded in his ears, its pulse abnormally fast. Cupid's famed arrow had found a mark.

For the first time in his adventurous life, he felt the sweaty palms and the singing in his blood of a man smitten beyond reason by the mere presence of a woman. The poets had been right!

Oh, she was lovely to look at. Petite, buxom, rounded. He could have spanned her waist with his two hands.

Her heavy black hair styled in a simple, elegant chignon held in place by gold pearl-tipped pins emphasized the slender grace of her neck. He imagined himself pulling those pins from her hair one by one. It would fall in a graceful, swinging curtain down to her waist. Her eyes were so dark and exotic they reminded him of full moons, Spanish dancers, and velvety nights.

But it wasn't her beauty that drew him. No, it was something deeper. Something he'd never felt before. He wasn't a fanciful man but he could swear he'd been waiting for her to walk into his life.

She smiled. The most charming dimple appeared at the corner of her mouth and his feet began moving of their own volition. He wasn't even conscious that he was walking until he stood in front of her.

"Dance with me." He held out his hand.

Carefully, as if she, too, understood the importance of her actions, she placed her hand in his. It was a magic moment. He felt changed in some indefinable way.

Lady Ruskin had a twinge of guilt in hiring Charlotte, Lady Dalrumple, also known as Miss Civility to the members of the *ton.* Though Charlotte was well-connected and highly recommended, she was working as a governess, of all things. But it wasn't Lady Ruskin's grandchildren who needed lessons in manners. No, it was her handsome, incorrigible son, leaving the fearful mama to dread the moment the two would meet and Charlotte would give her real lessons in . . .

RULES OF SURRENDER
by Christina Dodd

Coming in March 2000

ADORNA, Lady Ruskin, could scarcely contain her fascination. She knew the current marquess of Avon, and he had both children and wealth. Why his niece was working as a governess, Adorna could not imagine. Nor, because of the restrictions of refinement, could she inquire. "Sit down, Lady Dalrumple. Let us have tea."

Lady Dalrumple sat, but with such rigidity Adorna would have sworn her spine never touched the back of the chair.

Adorna picked up her tea and confessed the least of her problems. "My grandchildren have lived abroad all their lives."

"Abroad?" Lady Dalrumple arched her brows.

Adorna ignored the delicate inquiry as to the place. "They are, I'm afraid, savages."

"Of course they must be," Lady Dalrumple said. "The lack of a stabilizing English influence must have worked against them. As the eldest, I suppose the son is the worst."

"Actually, no." Words failed her.

Lady Dalrumple set down her cup. "So let me understand you, Lady Ruskin. If I train your grandchildren to behave like civilized English people in three months, your plan is to keep me on as their governess until the youngest makes her bow ten years from now?"

"This first three months will irrevocably try your patience."

Lady Dalrumple allowed the slightest of a patronizing smile to touch her lips. "With all due respect, Lady Ruskin, I believe I am capable of handling two small children."

Lady Ruskin knew as a decent matron, a respectable grandmother, she ought to tell the rest. She ought to. But really, this attractive young woman would find out soon enough.

But in order to salve her guilty conscience, she did offer a magnificent salary. "And you guarantee your complete discretion?"

"Absolutely."

Lady Ruskin rose. "Send a bill to my town house. I will instruct that it be paid at once. Lady Dalrumple, how much time do you need to prepare for a trip to my country house?"

"I can be ready tomorrow morning. There is no time to waste."

"I will send a carriage for you at eleven." Adorna pulled on her gloves with a sense of accomplishment and looked around the room again. What would this young woman do when she discovered the real savage that needed taming was not one of her grandchildren, but her son.

Saucy Jessye Kane knew from the get-go that Harrison Bainbridge, the second son to an English earl, didn't belong in a sun-baked place like Fortune, Texas. He was a mysterious scoundrel, an aristocrat who managed to keep her riled up whenever he came near. Jessye told herself that she wished he would sail on the first ship home . . . but she knew she was just lying to herself . . .

NEVER LOVE A COWBOY
by Lorraine Heath

Coming in April 2000

JESSYE saw the pale lamplight spill out of a window—Harry's window. The intense heat swirled through her like flames bursting to life. She didn't want to think about what Harry might be doing—but she seemed unable to stop herself.

He'd take off those fancy clothes he wore, clothes that would make any other man look like a dandy—but they only provided Harry with the appearance of sophistication.

Whenever she joined him at a table, she felt like a sow's ear sitting next to a silk purse. Sauntering through the cotton fields had bronzed his skin. When he shuffled those cards, his deft fingers mesmerized her.

She enjoyed their verbal sparring, was challenged by his ability to always win with the hand he was dealt. Out of deference to her suspicions, he played with his sleeves rolled up so she knew he wasn't cheating. He swore he never cheated when he played her, but she knew that was an outright lie—otherwise, she'd occasionally win a hand. She wasn't that poor of a poker player.

Now he needed her—or more accurately, he needed her money. She might have given it to him with no strings attached if he didn't always call her "Jessye-love." She trusted the endearment as much as she trusted the man. She knew he didn't love her, and using the word made a mockery of an emotion that could wound unmercifully and heal unconditionally.

The light from his window faded into darkness, and she realized he'd gone to bed. She dared not contemplate what he might *not* wear while he slept. Every time she changed the sheets on his bed, she wondered if they'd known the touch of his bare back . . . stomach . . . buttocks . . .

Squeezing her eyes shut, she spun around. She'd sworn never again to become involved with a man until she was a woman of independence, although Harrison had a disconcerting way of making her regret that vow . . .

Daisy Parker had never forgotten Nick Coltrane. She'd been sixteen, he'd been twenty-two . . . and he'd driven her crazy! Nine blissful, Nick-less years had passed since then, when suddenly he was back in her life as gorgeous and self-assured as ever . . . and he still had the nerve to call her by that awful nickname "Blondie." But if she really thought Nick was so awful, why did she feel so curiously wonderful whenever he came near?

BABY, DON'T GO
by Susan Andersen

Coming in May 2000

DAISY Parker glared at her secretary. "For crying out loud, Reg. I may not be wearing dress-for-success pinstripes, but my clothes are eminently suitable for guarding this guy's butt. Why should he care what I wear, anyway? Is he the crown Prince of England?"

"Close," said a cool voice from the doorway behind her.

No. Oh, dear God, please, no. Her heart pounding an erratic tattoo, Daisy slowly pivoted, hoping against hope that her ears had played a trick on her.

They hadn't. It was exactly who she'd feared

it would be: Nick Coltrane. The last man in the world she wanted to see.

He was as gorgeous as ever, too; damn his blue eyes. That tall, beautifully formed body looked as hard and fit as she remembered, even covered by an old pair of jeans and a V-neck sweater. Nick had always looked like he was born in tennis whites. He had an air of casual sophistication, of *belonging*, that was as natural to him as breathing.

But then, why shouldn't he? He did belong; he always had. It was she who had been the outsider.

Nick gave her a thorough perusal. "How are you, Blondie? You're looking good."

"*Don't*"—she took an incensed step forward before she caught herself—"call me Blondie," she finished with a mildness that burned her gullet. The nickname was a hot button and he damn well knew it, which was undoubtedly why he'd pushed it. She'd been sixteen years old to his twenty-two when he'd first started calling her that, and fish that she was, she never quit rising to the bait. Feeling heat radiating in her cheeks, she drew in a deep breath and held it a moment before easing it out again, perilously close to losing her composure.

She would eat *worms* before she gave him that satisfaction. And certainly before she'd allow him to see that when he looked at her with those cool, casually amused eyes, she felt the ache of rejection all over again.

"I take it you two know each other," Reggie said when the silence had stretched thin.

"My father was married to her mother for a while," Nick said.

Daisy froze. *That's* what he saw as their strongest connection? It shouldn't hurt—not after all the other ways he'd managed to hurt her. But damned if she'd let him see he still had the power to get to her.

"Yeah?" Reg demanded, giving her a distraction to focus on. "Which marriage was that?"

"Her third," she said.

"It was my dad's fifth," Nick offered.

"So, what's it been, Coltrane, six, seven years since we last saw each other?" Daisy asked coolly. As if she didn't know to the minute.

"Nine."

"That long? My, time really flies when you're not being annoyed. What brings you slumming in my neck of the woods?"

"Uh, he's our two o'clock appointment, Daise."

Slowly, she turned to look at her secretary. "He's what?"

Reggie held his palms up in surrender. "When I made the appointment I had no idea he was your step—"

"I am *not* her brother," Nick cut in peremptorily, his voice flat.

Daisy turned her attention back to him. "No," she said, "you certainly never wanted that role, did you?"

He met her angry gaze head-on. "No, I didn't. And if you haven't figured out why by now, you're not half as bright as I always thought you were."